S0-ATR-587

Praise for Gena Showalter

"I love this world and these alpha males—this is
Gena Showalter at her best!"

—J.R. Ward,
#1 *New York Times* bestselling author, on *Shadow and Ice*

"One of the premier authors of paranormal romance.
Gena Showalter delivers an utterly spellbinding story!"

—Kresley Cole,
#1 *New York Times* bestselling author

"Gena Showalter never fails to dazzle."

—Jeaniene Frost,
New York Times bestselling author

"Showalter…rocks me every time!"

—Sylvia Day,
#1 *New York Times* bestselling author

"Showalter writes fun, sexy characters you fall in love
with!"

—Lori Foster,
New York Times bestselling author

"Showalter makes romance sizzle on every page!"

—Jill Shalvis,
New York Times bestselling author

"A fascinating premise, a sexy hero and non-stop
action, *The Darkest Night* is Showalter at her finest."

—Karen Marie Moning,
New York Times bestselling author

"Sexy paranormal romance at its hottest!"

—Christine Feehan,
#1 *New York Times* bestselling author

Also available by Gena Showalter

Look for Gena Showalter's next
all-new paranormal romance
The Warlord
coming soon in hardcover from HQN!

For additional books by Gena Showalter,
visit her website, genashowalter.com.

GENA SHOWALTER

The Darkest
KING

HQN

If you purchased this book without a cover you should be aware that this book is stolen property. It was reported as "unsold and destroyed" to the publisher, and neither the author nor the publisher has received any payment for this "stripped book."

HQN

ISBN-13: 978-1-335-40000-0

The Darkest King

Recycling programs
for this product may
not exist in your area.

First published in 2020. This edition published in 2020.

Copyright © 2020 by Gena Showalter

All rights reserved. No part of this book may be used or reproduced in any manner whatsoever without written permission except in the case of brief quotations embodied in critical articles and reviews.

This is a work of fiction. Names, characters, places and incidents are either the product of the author's imagination or are used fictitiously. Any resemblance to actual persons, living or dead, businesses, companies, events or locales is entirely coincidental.

This edition published by arrangement with Harlequin Books S.A.

For questions and comments about the quality of this book, please contact us at CustomerService@Harlequin.com.

HQN
22 Adelaide St. West, 40th Floor
Toronto, Ontario M5H 4E3, Canada
www.Harlequin.com

Printed in Spain

To my own personal William—Max. You always brighten my day. You feed me, love my menagerie of dogs and cats, and make me feel like the most beautiful woman in the world, even when I look like butt. Well, that one time I looked like butt. I mean, that one time I thought I looked like butt but didn't, because I can't. Wait. Am I saying the word butt too much? (Trick question—you can't say the word *butt* too much. Naomi at French 'n' Bookish doesn't call me the magnificent Buttwalter for nothing!) I love you, babe!

Speaking of Naomi, the best social media manager in the world, I concede. Book William is yours! You are an amazing woman and I'm blessed to know you.

And to my work spouse, the incredibly beautiful and talented Jill Monroe, one of the most amazing people on the planet! You pick me up when I'm down. You've spent countless hours plotting, critiquing and helping me torture or save my characters (depending on the day). Bottom line (I almost typed "butt line" lol)— you make my world a better place!

The Darkest
KING

Prologue

Part One
The Realm of Lleh
Many millennia ago

A BRUTAL PUNCH broke the boy's jaw. He wheeled to the rocky, soot-covered ground, spitting blood and teeth. Searing pain snatched the air from his lungs as stars flashed before his eyes and acid filled his stomach. He healed faster than most, his bones quickly fusing back together, but the pain continued to radiate.

Claw, the male responsible for his current torment, kicked him in the ribs. "When we give you food, you eat it." Kick, kick. The overgrown brute had horns, tusks and muscle stacked upon muscle. Like everyone else in the realm, he wore a stained loincloth for "easy access," shin guards and boots made of stone. "Do you understand?"

Between wheezing breaths, the boy sneered, "Oh, I understand." Even as blood trickled from his ears and mouth, he remained aware of his surroundings. A hilly wasteland completely devoid of vegetation, overcrowded with immortal cannibals, rapists and murderers who'd been exiled from their homeworlds. Night had fallen, the camp illuminated by firepits...where prisoners roasted on a spit, their melting flesh dripping into the hissing flames.

Acrid wind blustered, stinging Scum's wounds, and whisking his mind back to Claw. "By *food* you mean *another captive's thigh*. You can take your food and—"

Kick. "Months ago, you fell from the sky and we welcomed you with open arms. You had no name, so we gave you one. You had no home, so we took you in. Your mind was a blank slate, so we gave you memories. *This* is how you repay our kindnesses?"

Kindnesses? He gave a bitter laugh, only to choke on blood as—he assumed—a broken piece of rib punctured and deflated his lung. "You call me Scum. And your precious shelter? A too-small mud hut bursting with captives, all chained."

As for his memories, he shuddered. The terrible acts these awful males had committed against him and others... Part of him would do *anything* to scour his mind. The other part preferred horrors to near blankness. How sad was that? He just... He wanted to know his truths.

Who am I? How did I get here? Why *am I here? Do I have a family desperate to save me?*

A pang of longing nearly rent Scum in two. *There are so many people here, yet I feel as if I'm alone, always alone.*

"You dare complain?" Claw kicked the back of Scum's head.

Tears stung his eyes, and panic set in. The moment you revealed a weakness, you taught your enemy how to defeat you. As quickly as possible, he blinked those tears away. If anyone spotted a glistening drop—

"Tears?" Claw laughed with glee. The growing crowd of onlookers laughed, too, and Scum ducked his head, ashamed.

Hoping to distract Claw, Scum said, "You were wrong. I wasn't memory-less." Anytime he closed his eyes, he saw a single moment on repeat. An echo of a life before this one.

"Tell me you remember your mother, and I'll go get her for you." Another brutal punch, this one to the temple.

A rush of dizziness, of agony, and the laughter reignited.

Vision blurring, Scum reached out a hand, praying someone, anyone, would help him. Someone stomped on his wrist, breaking the bones. The pain! More than any one person could bear, surely. Yet, the beating still did not compare to his sense of isolation.

Punch, punch. His brain rattled against his skull, his body going blessedly numb. Punch, punch. His eyes swelled shut. The beating faded from his awareness, the memory overtaking him.

I stand beside a boy I do not know. I'm not sure why we're together, or how we ended up in the clouds. I only know his nearness comforts me.

A beautiful woman with curly black hair and flawless black skin descends from a haze of fog. She wears a flowing ivory gown, her white-and-gold wings gliding up and down. Up and down. I am awed by her. Is she an angel or Sent One? Maybe a Harpy or bird-shifter? The possibilities are endless, for every myth and legend is steeped in truth.

I feel a connection to her. What if she is...my mother?

My heart leaps at the idea, but I'm not sure I'm joyous or fearful. She lands, tears glinting in her baby blue eyes. She's definitely not a Harpy, then. Not a shifter, either. Somehow, I know those species believe as I do: tears are a weakness, and weaknesses must be eliminated.

With a sniffle, she crouches before us. The other boy has bronze skin, black hair and those same baby blues. He also has white-and-gold wings. Are the two related? Are we all related? What do I look like?

"I love you both so much," she says. "This wasn't supposed to happen. You were supposed to save us, not—" A sob escapes. "If there were any other way...we just... We never should have birthed you. He found out, and now he wants you dead."

My stomach turns over. How can she love us, but also wish we were never born? Who is "he," and why does he want us dead?

Trembling, she places a clammy hand on me, and one on the winged boy. "I'll do everything I can to keep you safe but—"

A man cloaked in shadows appears behind her. He is tall—a giant—and has the biggest muscles I've ever seen. An agonized gasp leaves her as the tip of his onyx spear sinks into her back and comes out of her chest. The color drains from her cheeks as blood rushes from the wound, soaking her robe. Crimson streams gurgle from the corners of her mouth.

I know I should be frightened, furious or both, but I feel nothing. I look beyond the female once again, curious about the male who stabbed her. Shadows distort his visage, hiding his identity.

The other boy grabs my hand and drags me backward, pulling me toward a wall of portals—doorways to other worlds, realms and dimensions. Fear contorts his features. He opens his mouth to speak and—

The memory ended as it always had: abruptly and unfinished.

A lump grew in Scum's throat, silencing his scream of

denial. Why couldn't he recall anything more about the boy, the woman or the one who'd murdered her? *Must find out!*

His chest tightened. *Why should I never have been birthed?*

With Claw's next punch, reality overshadowed fantasy, that blessed numbness wearing off. Punch. His lungs emptied, deflating again. Punch. His nerve endings wailed in protest. Kick. He vomited blood and bile as the crowd cheered.

Do not scream. Ignore the pain.

Claw kicked the backs of his thighs, bellowing, "Meat is better when it's tenderized, yeah?"

Scum fought to draw in air as snickers and shouts of agreement rang out. *Breathe. Just need to breathe. No, no. Need to stand. Need to slay!*

The urge surged through him. He felt as if he was born to murder these males. As if he lived for no other purpose. *I will chop off Claw's hands and feet, so he cannot fight back or run. Then I'll yank out his teeth one by one, rip off his cock and shove the tiny appendage down his throat. Finally...*

I'll kill the rest of them. Slowly.

A slow smile bloomed. Hatred singed his veins. Bitterness iced his thoughts. Vengeance lived and breathed in Scum.

Claw scowled. "You find this funny?"

"I do." The words emerged slurred, as insubstantial as mist, but he didn't care. "Dead man kicking."

Growling, Claw kicked him between the legs.

As the crowd went wild, Scum vomited more blood. Black dots wove through his vision, but he forced himself to laugh. "That the best...you can do?"

Claw's eyes widened, the unexpected taunt shredding

his pride. He dove down, pinned Scum's shoulders with his knees and whaled, punching, punching, punching.

Blistering pain. For one beat, two, Scum's heart stilled. He didn't…he couldn't…

"Beg me for mercy, Scum, and this will stop."

Never! *I would rather die than break. And I refuse to die!* He would…

He must have blacked out. The next thing he knew, Claw was on his feet, his bloody arms raised as he stalked around Scum. The crowd shouted praises.

Scum's drive to kill—gone. Hopelessness engulfed him, an insidious force more devastating than any physical pain. He tried to crawl away, to lose himself in the crowd, but someone clubbed his calves, stopping him. He threw back his head and screamed; there was no stopping it.

The crowd jeered and tightened the circle around him.

Someone else pressed a cattle prod against his skull, volts of electricity charging through every inch of him. His skin pulled taut, and his muscles knotted, his blood boiling in an instant. Scum could only pant, sweat and blink, willing himself to survive, whatever the cost.

You can't kill your enemies if you're dead. Hold on, just hold on. The beating would end soon enough—Scum was too valuable to kill. In spite of his youth, he could regrow limbs and organs. Meaning, he was the only never-ending buffet.

Claw pushed the mob back, then shackled chains around Scum's wrists. "Tonight, you'll be our dessert in every sense of the word."

New cheers abounded, and he bit his tongue to silence a second scream. Maybe…maybe he *would* beg for mercy. To be their sustenance, then their plaything…

Tears welled once again, a whimper escaping. *They've done it? They've broken me?*

Suddenly Claw straightened, frowned. "Be silent! Something strange approaches."

The others obeyed, going quiet. Aggression charged the atmosphere.

Scum's ears twitched, different sounds registering. A whoosh. A whistle. A husky chuckle. Though he struggled, nearly vomiting twice, he managed to sit up. A whirlwind of jet-black smoke approached the camp.

Every instinct shouted, *Danger! Run. Run now!*

Fear drove Scum to his hands and knees. But his weakened body shook, unhealed bones and muscle throbbing, and he remained immobile.

Warriors readied their weapons: swords, crossbows and machetes. Too little, too late. The tornado picked up speed, soon swallowing one…two…three of the brutes.

As the tornado moved on, it spat out headless bodies.

Other brutes cursed and ran, but they, too, soon got swallowed up and ejected, minus a head.

Excitement bloomed, eclipsing the fear as the brutes continued to drop. If this kept up, they'd be slaughtered in a matter of minutes. Scum, too. His grin returned. With the brutes dead, he could die happy, his suffering over, done.

More screams erupted, each one shriller than the last. More and more barbarians crumpled. *Thud, thud, thud. Like music to my ears.* A decapitated head tumbled past Scum's feet, followed by another and another. He inhaled as deeply as his mutilated lungs allowed, satisfaction fizzing in his veins.

Finally, Scum was the last male standing. And yet, the smoke did not strike at him. No, it circled him. Taking his measure? He crouched and raised his chin. He *wanted* this. What did he have to live for?

The smoke thinned, and a tall, muscular man appeared. He held a scythe and looked like Death, with tanned skin, black hair and blacker eyes. A never-ending abyss. He wore leather pants, but no shirt, displaying an array of piercings and tattoos on his bare chest. Blood splattered his face and torso, and dripped from his weapon.

Beside him stood an equally blood-splattered teenager with golden skin, a mop of pale curls and blue eyes. His son?

Death raised the scythe, preparing to deliver the final blow. Yes. Yes! But their gazes met and held, and Death paused, his expression a tapestry of emotion: determination, fury, dismay, regret, even guilt.

"You have his eyes," Death stated baldly, his voice rumbly and rough.

"His?" The barest flicker of hope sparked in Scum's chest. Was he to learn about his family mere seconds before he died? "You know my father?"

"I do…and I do not."

"What does that mean?" he snapped, out of patience.

"Exactly what I said. No one truly knows your father." Death continued to raise the scythe…only to lower it, without striking.

What? No, no, no. "Go on. Do it!"

With a tone as harsh as Claw's beating, Death said, "You dare to command me?"

"Yes! So kill me already."

Those dark abyss eyes narrowed. "Do you know who I am, child?"

"You are Death." Why deny it? "You are as evil as the ones you killed."

"I am nothing like them. I'm worse." He leaned forward, as if he had a secret to impart. "However, Death *is* one of my designations."

Designations?

"You may call me Hades," the male continued. "I am the underworld king of kings, and I've searched the worlds for you."

Scum tapped his bruised chest, the chains rattling. "Me? Why?" Had they met before? What did he know about Hades?

To his shock, details sprang from the deepest recesses of his mind. One of twelve kings of the underworld. Known for his coldness and cruelty. He killed without hesitation or mercy, and dealt ruthlessly with anyone who broke his only rule—obey him at all times, in all ways. He possessed no moral compass, and had no concerns with right and wrong.

"My reasons are my own and always subject to change," Hades replied. "This is my adopted son, Prince Lucifer." He patted the top of the teenager's head, his many rings glittering in the firelight. "Do you know who *you* are?"

The boy did not like the pat. The corners of his eyes twitched, the beginning of a scowl. But, in a blink, his expression blanked.

"I do...not," Scum admitted, glancing between father and son. Jealousy flared. Oh, to have a family. Someone who would love him unconditionally, adore and protect him.

"Your name is William. It means *determined protector*," Hades said, a note of relish in his tone. "I have decided to make you my son, just as I did with Lucifer. You will be my protector. My hand of vengeance."

William... A real name, and a purpose. Both resonated with him, sparking... What *was* that? His first taste of happiness?

The king added, "You will learn the intricacies of magic, and how to fight to win, no matter the odds stacked against you. I will ensure you become your own rescuer."

Yes, yes. He wanted those things. But… "Why do you wish to make *me* your son? Sons are prized." According to Claw, Scum—William—had no worth outside of his regeneration.

Hades crouched a few inches away, the sweet fragrance of roses emanating from him. "Do you know *what* you are, William?"

He gave his head another shake, his too-long, dirt-clumped hair slapping his cheeks. "I only know I'm not human." Sometimes, when rage overtook him, ambrosia-scented smoke wafted from his back, and flashes of lightning streaked below the surface of his skin.

Smoke… His heart raced. Could *Hades* be his true father?

"You are right," Hades said. "You are not human. You are so much better, so much stronger. And one day, all the worlds will quake before you."

Prologue

Part Two
The Realm of Maradelle
Sixteen years later

BEAMS OF GOLDEN light spilled from a blazing firepit, chasing away night's shadows. Tendrils of sandalwood-scented smoke curled up, up, creating a dreamlike haze as witches wearing see-through scarves danced around the flames, tempting and luring the audience. Warlocks pounded on drums, creating a sensual beat.

The entire village considered the sons of Hades gods of the underworld. And they weren't wrong. Though a more accurate title for William might be "god *killer*" and "goddess seducer." Over the years, he'd become Hades's go-to assassin and spy.

The bulk of William's targets were Wrathlings, a horde of different species working together to rid the worlds of demons, dragons-shifters, vampires and witches. The supposedly *evil* races.

"Which one do you want? Her, her or her?" Lucifer nudged William's shoulder with his own. They sat with the husbands of the dancers, forming a circle around the firepit. "Or do you want to bed them one after the other, assembly line–style?"

The same way they liked to kill their enemies.

William pursed his lips. Anytime they visited, they had their pick of females. Anyone they'd like. Married or single, it mattered not.

"You take half, and I'll take half," Lucifer added.

"Tsk-tsk. Shouldn't you abstain?" Tomorrow Lucifer would be wedding their princess, Evelina Maradelle. The only child of a dragon-shifter empress and the warlock lord who ruled this realm.

From birth, Evelina had been kept under lock and key. Not even Lucifer had seen her. Only her parents had the honor. And Hades, of course, who had arranged the union, claiming the girl was beautiful beyond imagining, kind despite a violent temper and incomparably powerful.

Lucifer tried to pull off a scowl, but a snicker got the better of him. William snickered, too. The marriage would change nothing. Why should it? Most people treated their vows as a suggestion.

Most? Try all. He'd never met anyone willing to remain true to their spouse.

If a married woman doesn't wish to honor her union, why should I?

"The princess won't affect my life," Lucifer said. "Nothing will. Nothing *should*."

"Agreed. Why mess with perfection?" And life as a twentysomething-year-old immortal prince *was* perfect.

William had a father he loved more than life, and a brother he appreciated. Each morning, he trained with the pair, as well as survivalists, honing his combat skills and learning to overcome the worst situations. At night, he indulged his every carnal desire, pleasure at his disposal.

So his birth family hadn't wanted him. So they thought the world would be better off without him. So what? He ignored the tightening in his chest. His new family enjoyed his company, and his lovers couldn't get enough of him. They plied him with affection and acceptance. The true gifts of life.

Who am I kidding? I'm a true gift of life. What? It wasn't bragging if it was true. He had wealth, beauty and an array of memories no one could ever take from him. He wielded magic more powerful than any warlock here and possessed supernatural powers others envied. He could flash or portal anywhere in any world, control demons and spark fear and loathing in enemies and allies alike. When enraged, he produced wings of smoke. Soon, he would rule his own principality—a kingdom within Hades's territory—just like Lucifer. What more did he need? What could be better?

So why am I still unhappy? Why couldn't he let go of a past he couldn't remember, or forget the past he despised?

Only twice had he questioned Hades about the boy from his first memory. Both times, he'd received the same response. *Trust me. You're better off not knowing.*

Though he craved answers the same way a drowning man craved air, he couldn't bring himself to push for more. Not after everything Hades had done for him.

Lucifer passed him a carafe of ambrosia-laced whiskey, saying, "The blonde can't take her eyes off you, brother."

"No need to ask which blonde." William took a swig. "I'm guessing it's the one rocking her hips as she slinks closer." She lifted her arms overhead and arched her back to better display her breasts. Her nipples puckered.

Mmm. Nipples were his favorite bull's-eye.

"You going to accept her offer?" Lucifer asked.

"I will—" He forced his gaze to lift to her face. "Not." Lilith of Lleh, Evelina's half sister, and the wife of the army's commander. A witch as well as an oracle. She was short and curvy, with skin as white as snow, eyes as green as emeralds and lips as red as rubies.

William never cared about size or color. Beauty came in different packages, and he appreciated them all. His only requirements? Soft, warm and temporary. If the female happened to have the heart of a saint and fuck like a demon, even better. Meek and biddable were bonuses.

While the witch met two out of three—soft and warm— she lacked the most important one. Temporary. They'd slept together weeks ago. Afterward, she'd clung.

He shuddered. Even if she were the one woman destined to complete him, he would reject her tonight. Clingers like Lilith expected monogamy without reciprocation, and often erupted into fits of jealousy. No, thanks. He preferred variety, the spice of life.

Only when he won a new female did he experience true satisfaction. For a moment. The barest taste. Of course, the moment always passed, making him eager—desperate—for another. Still, he wouldn't trade those moments for anything; they were proof that he—the boy no one had wanted—was desired, even admired.

"I'll take her off your hands." Lucifer studied the witch over the carafe of whiskey. "I'll make her think she's bedding you."

"No!" William roared, earning several stares. His breath quickened, and sweat beaded on the back of his neck. Lucifer was known as the Great Deceiver for a reason; he could shift into anyone, anytime, and did. Often. It was their biggest source of discontent. "No," he repeated in a calmer tone. "That's rape." There were few lines he refused to cross, but sexual violation topped the list.

"You're wrong. That is the opposite of rape. I would be giving her exactly what she wants. But," Lucifer tacked on with a brittle smile, holding up his palms in a gesture of innocence, "you are my cherished brother. I will honor your wishes."

Another reason Lucifer had earned his designation? He constantly lied.

Did I receive the truth or another falsehood? William bit his tongue, tasting blood. He wanted to love Lucifer. Hell, he wanted to *like* Lucifer. But…

He secretly struggled with both. But, they were a family, the most precious gift to mankind. He would not abandon the male.

With a beguiling lick of her lips, Lilith crooked her finger at him. "Come to me, William. I'll be everything you want, do anything you crave."

As gently as possible, he told her, "I'm sorry, but I want someone—" *anyone* "—else."

"I can change your mind." She dropped to her knees and crawled closer, a strange, hypnotic light glimmering in her eyes. "I've foreseen it."

Hardly. Using a harder, harsher tone, he told her, "The answer remains no."

Expression dark with anger, she flattened her hands on his thighs, piercing his leather pants with dagger-sharp nails. "Please, William. I want you more than I've ever wanted anyone."

"Ahhh. Desperation," Lucifer sang, offering his customary smirk. "The greatest aphrodisiac."

The witch hissed at the male.

All right. Being direct had worked as well as being gentle. Now, he'd go with cruel. "Spend the night with your husband. He wants you. I do not."

She flinched. "I love you, and I know we can be happy together. Forever."

By the fires of Hell, what would it take to discourage this woman? "Love is a myth, and monogamy isn't sustainable. I will *never* desire a long-term relationship."

Again, she flinched. "I'll be good to you, William. Just give me a chance. Run away with me."

"You don't even know me, princess." Few did. She only saw the man he pretended to be. The playboy prince and merciless assassin. No one knew the man inside, not even William.

"You're wrong. I've learned so much about you." She straddled his waist and trailed her fingers up his chest. "Weeks ago, you chose me. Afterward, I dreamed of you. Of us and our future. I realized that, as twisted as you are, you need someone like me to experience true satisfaction."

Wonderful. A premiere delusionist. "If a black heart and skewed sense of right and wrong does it for you, you'll have a better time with my brother." He hiked his thumb in Lucifer's direction. "He even volunteered to don my face, if you'd like."

"Fair warning, my sweet." Lucifer slurred his words and swayed back and forth, and yet he displayed no other signs of intoxication. "One night with me, and no other male will compare."

The witch ignored him, her frantic gaze remaining on William. "I've seen into your heart, and I know how hopelessly you want a family of your own."

He went still, not even daring to breathe. What if she

had—or could—see into his heart…into the past he couldn't remember? "What else do you know, witch? Tell me!"

Triumphant, thinking she'd won him over, she grinned. "Take me to my hut, and I will."

"Tell me here, and I swear I will take you to my hut after." Or not. Yes, definitely not.

She stared into his eyes for a long while, silent. Finally, she spoke. "I know you have no recollection of your childhood. I know someone cast a spell to bury your memories. I know you and Lucifer will war, and only one of you will survive. I know you will grow to despise your father, for a time, and love your brother."

He listened, every "I know" like a punch of shock to the gut. Despise Hades? Never! Kill Hades's son? No again. But a memory-burying spell…made a lot of sense. "You contradict yourself, witch. How can I war with Lucifer, survive, then fall in love with Lucifer, who died?" Unless…

Did she reference the winged boy?

William looked more like him than their maybe/maybe-not mother had. They possessed the same bronzed skin, black hair and blue eyes.

What had happened to the boy? Where was he now?

The muscles in his chest clenched and unclenched, squeezing so tightly he lost his breath.

"Why am I the one who dies?" Lucifer demanded of the witch. Suddenly steady, he set the whiskey aside and palmed a dagger. "No, it doesn't matter. You lie about a coming war, hoping to sow discord between us. Unfortunately for you, I love killing liars. After I've had a little fun."

Lips pursed, William patted his brother's hand, a put-the-dagger-away gesture. "She's unworthy of our time. Let her find someone else to love. That is a true punishment."

Lilith glanced between them, eyes narrowing. "You think love is a punishment? Very well. I will teach you its value." She plucked her nails from his thighs and spread her arms wide, a violent wind gusted around them.

Pale locks danced around her face as she intoned, "I curse you, William of the Dark. I curse you to a life of misery and war with those you care about. A life devoid of genuine companionship. But. If ever you *do* fall in love… if ever the object of your affection falls in love with you in return… I curse her to lose her mind along with her heart. She will attack you, again and again, and she will not stop until you are dead."

William snorted. "You mean I'll never settle down and bed the same woman over and over while raising our brood of squalling brats? Oh, no. Not that. Anything but that." He rolled his eyes.

Lilith motored on, her tone sharper. "Allow me to prove myself. I curse you, William of the Dark, to lose both of your hands before the rise of the sun."

Again, he rolled his eyes. "I'll regrow the hands in a matter of days."

"Yes, but as those dark days pass, your thoughts will be consumed with me, and you will be unable to touch a lover."

A growl rumbled low in his chest, and she laughed.

"But, I'm not a monster," she said. "I'll offer a blessing, as well. A chance to save yourself from your ladylove." She waved her hand, and a book materialized in his lap. A thick, leather-bound tome with a large sapphire affixed to the cover. "Inside those pages, you'll find a magical code. Find someone to break the code, and you'll break the curse."

Unease pricked his nape. Done with her and her threats, he stood. The book thudded to the ground. He turned on a booted heel, intending to return to the underworld.

"Leave your only shot at redemption here, if you wish," she called, smug. "Let your enemies use it against you."

William paused to glance over his shoulder. With a dry tone, he said, "And I doubted your love? What a fool I am." Still. She made a good point. He held out a hand, and the book flew into his grip.

He blew the witch a kiss and strode away.

Lucifer chased after him and slung an arm over William's shoulders. "I will never war against you, brother."

"This, I know." They might have their differences, but they would never disrespect Hades in such a way.

"Allow me to prove it. I'll guard the book on your behalf. My armies are double the size of yours, my magic's stronger. I'll ensure the code cannot be used against you."

Once again, unease pricked his nape. "I appreciate the offer, but I think I'll keep it. I could use a laugh." Magic could do many amazing, impossible things, but crafting true love wasn't one of them. And there was no way he would lose his hands by sunrise. Someone would have the skill to sneak up on him and knock him out. *Good luck.*

Lucifer portaled to his own Hell territory, while William portaled to his principality. He holed up in his bedroom and set traps for anyone foolish enough to enter.

As one hour bled into another, he fought to remain awake. Eventually he drifted off...

He awoke to indescribably pain and blood, so much blood. It wet his sheets, his body—and still spurted from his wrists.

His hands were missing, his traps undisturbed.

Abject fear joined the deluge of agony. The second part of Lilith's curse had come true. Why wouldn't the first?

Shit. *Shit!* What was he going to do?

1

"Forget a cloak of invisibility. I prefer to wear a cloak of hot as hell-ness."

—William the Ever Randy

Third level of the heavens
The Downfall, a nightclub for immortals
Present day

WILLIAM STALKED THROUGH the overcrowded nightclub, shoving an assortment of vampires, shifters and Fae out of his path. Bodies slammed together, protests rising then dying as the patrons glimpsed his expression—homicidal rage.

"Make a move against me," he grated. "Dare you."

The crowd thinned in seconds, ninety percent of the immortals racing away, their footsteps shaking the building.

Over the centuries, both enemies and friends had likened William to a grenade without a pin. He could blow at any moment and torch the entire world.

Two females remained at the bar, peering at him with

interest. "I heard he moved back to Hell to war with Lucifer," one whispered to the other, his sensitive ears picking up every word.

"Poor Lucifer," the other said, sounding gleeful rather than pitying. "*I* heard the Ever Randy is even more powerful in Hell."

Well. The beauties weren't wrong. William did war with Lucifer, just as Lilith predicted, and he did grow more powerful in Hell, his supernatural abilities turning sinister.

The first female smiled and blew him a kiss before telling the other, "I wonder what he's doing here."

"Ask him," the other suggested. "Go on, Helen. Do it!"

"No way, Wendy. You heard his voice, right? He's like a siren, able to seduce with a single word. Unfortunately for him, I've decided to save myself for Strider Lord. He'll get tired of Kaia any day. Maybe. Probably."

William heaved a sigh. His presence here served one purpose: obtaining freedom from Lilith's curse. Finally!

Yesterday, a powerful seer delivered astounding news. Soon, he would find the answer to his every problem: the only person in existence with the necessary skills to decipher his magic codebook, breaking Lilith's curse at long last. He or she had signed up to attend a conference for cryptanalysts. Location: Manhattan.

Was the codebreaker human or immortal? Young or old? Fragile or strong?

Doesn't matter. I will find who I'm looking for or die trying.

A female vampire stepped inside his path. A beautiful brunette in a crop top and micro-miniskirt, the club's uniform. She smiled sweetly. Too sweetly. "You're driving away our customers and therefore our tips." All sensual grace and coy charm, she traced a fingertip between his pectorals. "I'm real close to having the bouncers throw you out."

They could try. Anyone foolish enough to put hands on him died horribly, always. A necessity. If you failed to punish those who harmed you, others would think they could harm you, too.

He cast his gaze throughout the club, easily picking out the bouncers: a mix of Berserkers and Phoenix warriors. He heaved another sigh. As much as he'd enjoy making them beg for mercy he didn't have, he had precious little time.

"I'll pay you double what you make in a week," he told her, his wealth incalculable. "Just get rid of the stragglers."

"And I'm getting rid of the stragglers," she sang, pumping her fist toward the ceiling. "Everyone out. Now! Go, go, go, before I start cutting off appendages." She unveiled a wicked smile. "Or maybe I'll tell Bjorn you guys made me cry."

In the mad dash to leave, chairs were overturned. Ah, retreat. Good call. Bjorn the Last True Dread was one of three owners of the Downfall, half Sent One—or winged demon assassin with more firepower than angels—and half Dread. One of the most violent species ever to walk the Earth. He possessed a temper as dark and legendary as William's own, but only erupted when "the weaker sex" cried.

Hi. The 1950s called, and they'd like their misogyny back. Women, the *weaker* sex? William snorted. Three females had impacted his past and present and one would affect his future in ways no male ever had. One had told him that he never should have been birthed, and he'd carried the stigma of it ever since. Another had cursed him, affecting every relationship he'd ever had. A third had offered hope in a hopeless situation, something even Hades, his idol, hadn't done. The last would try to kill him if ever he fell in love with her.

William inhaled a deep breath, shook his head to dislodge the hated musings and motored on. Different scents layered the air: candle wax, hormones, clashing perfumes and sweat. The moment he spotted the final patron—the reason for his visit—boiling rage became a simmer of annoyance.

Keeleycael, aka the Red Queen, was powerful beyond imagining, and annoying as hell. As old as time, and as far into the future as she could see, memories tended to tangle up in her mind. Sometimes she struggled to distinguish present, past and future. More often, she lacked focus, unable to complete a task as simple as dressing. Like today. Her clothes were inside out and backward, a sock clinging to her jeans. Around her neck, a necklace made of candy.

"William! Willy! Will!" she called, waving. A vision of loveliness with pale pink hair, golden skin and green eyes, she occupied a table in back. "I know I saw you yesterday, but I've missed you terribly. Or maybe I saw you ten…twenty years ago? Or maybe I'm thinking of fifteen years from now?"

Wonderful. The crazy had already started. He quickened his pace. Once upon a time, this mad hatter had been Hades's fiancée and William's almost stepmother. Though the couple had split, he'd never stopped caring about her. Recently, she'd ended up wedding a demon-possessed male named Torin, one of William's closest friends.

As soon as he reached her, he kicked out a chair and plopped down. "Hello, Keeley."

She smiled a sweet smile in welcome, rousing a wave of affection inside him. "So nice of you to join me for this meeting we never planned."

Careful. No conversation had ever been so important to him. He needed her lucid; the wrong question might push her over the edge. "Do you know the name of my decoder?"

"Why? Because everything Lilith promised you has come true? An ongoing war with Lucifer—check. A miserable past and present, devoid of genuine, romantic companionship—check. A bleak future—checkmate."

"Yes," he said, his teeth gritted. With the curse hanging over his head, he refused to spend more than a night or two with a woman, something he'd like to change.

Not because he hoped to settle down. He didn't. After everything he'd suffered, he *deserved* a happily-ever-after with as many women as he desired.

Had his views on monogamy changed? Yes. For others. His friends had mates, and they were perfect examples of love and loyalty. But, William still preferred variety. A single partner would never fully meet his needs.

To him, women were like spices. Some days you wanted sweet, some days you wanted spicy. Or salty. No reason to stick with the same flavor.

"Well," he prompted. "Do you know the name or not?"

"I do," she exclaimed. "Duh. Why else would I invite you to this name-and-gender-reveal party?"

He pinched the bridge of his nose.

"Surprise," she said, spreading her arms wide. "The codebreaker is a girl…and your lifemate."

What? Shock and horror inundated him, a thousand problems forming at once, with only one solution.

"I know you assumed you'd found your mate not too long ago," she continued, "but you were wrong."

His chest tightened, squeezing his lungs. He'd met a (once) human female named Gillian Shaw, who'd suffered a childhood more tragic than his own. Not wanting to activate the curse, he'd ruthlessly combated any softer emotions for her, constantly playing the "what if" game with himself.

What if he committed to her, and Gillian did, in fact, try to kill him?

What if he harmed her irrevocably while guarding himself against her attack?

What if he inadvertently killed her? Could he ever forgive himself?

In the end, she'd fallen for a beastly POS who—William shuddered—*needed* her. In other words, a fool! Needing another only ever ended in heartbreak.

"I will not give my future murderer access to the object of my salvation," he bit out. "I would rather kill her straightaway and void the curse before it ever activates." But...could he truly slay his one and only lifemate, ending her life simply because she'd one day try to slay him?

Keeley gaped at him. "You would give up your one chance at eternal contentment?"

"Yes," he hissed, the muscles in his shoulders knotting. How could he miss what he'd never had?

She flicked her tongue over an incisor. "What if you cannot defeat Lucifer without her?"

He went still. "Can I not?"

She ignored his question, saying, "Do you remember when I told you that Scarlet and Gideon's baby would aid you in the breaking of your curse?"

"I do," he replied, cautious. Scarlet and Gideon were part of a select group of friends. Demon-possessed men and women and their assortment of mates known as the Lords of the Underworld. The same group as Torin and Keeley. "As much as I love them, I doubt their baby will have the power to help a prince of the underworld."

"Well, you're right. I misspoke. Their baby won't aid

you at all. Their baby will aid *your daughters*. Daughters you won't have without your lifemate."

What! Daughters, plural? Girls who would grow into beautiful women and fall in love with shit-ass males he'd have to murder? No! "Another reason to kill the code-breaker. I won't be having any more children."

"Oh, you'll be having kids, all right. Enough to create a base...foot...sports team." As if she hadn't just dropped a bomb, she leaned closer and said, "There's no way you'll fall in love with your lifemate in two weeks, right? So, you'll let her live and work on the code for fourteen days. Vow it, or I'll keep the list of names to myself."

"Very well." No need to ponder it. When you lived for-ever, two weeks was nothing. But what had she meant, list of names? There should be only one. "If she behaves, I vow I will not harm her for fourteen days." Never would he make a vow without a caveat.

"Excellent! Now, before I reveal the nineteen names on my list—"

"Nineteen?" he roared.

"—you're going to tell me why you grow more power-ful in Hell. And don't say no. In our world, you have to give to get."

So she'd heard the girls at the bar, too. He sighed. "I don't know the reason." Nor did he know why it mattered. "I only know I produce wings of smoke up here. Down there, that smoke is laced with *sopor*, a pain toxin. Here, I grow claws. There, those claws leak *poena*, a death venom. Here, I have no fangs. There, I can grow sabers, if I wish."

Canting her head to the side, she asked, "Is that why you moved to the mortal realm so soon after your dad and I called it quits?"

He gave a clipped nod. Had he stayed, he feared he would have become as vile as Lucifer.

"How interesting." Keeley stroked her chin all villain-like, the wheels in her brain obviously spinning. "Definitely take your lifemate slash codebreaker to Hell." Finally, she extended an arm, revealing an array of ink smudges that began at the inside of her elbow and ended at her palm. "Ta-da! The names, as promised."

With only a glance, he memorized every word. Then he arched a brow. "There's a codebreaker named spaghetti and meatless balls?"

"Oh, my bad." She licked her thumb and rubbed the culinary disaster off her arm. "That was my dinner."

"Your name is also on the list."

Her eyes hooded. A dreamy smile curled her mouth as she twirled a lock of hair around her finger. "I was *Torin's* dinner."

May I never be as whipped as my friends. "Which name belongs to my codebreaker?"

The waitress appeared, handed a bottle of champagne to Keeley and muttered, "On the house. Don't kill me!" then raced away.

As the Red Queen tasted the beverage—straight from the bottle—he stroked the dagger sheathed at his waist, waiting.

"Keeley," he prompted. "I asked you a question."

"Oh, yes. I remember. You wanted to know where you could find a crown of Hell."

Again, he went still. Long ago, eleven crowns were made by the Most High, the leader of the Sent Ones. Own a single crown, and you would transform into a powerful king, whoever—or whatever—you were. Lose the crown, and you would lose everything.

After failing to usurp the Most High, young Lucifer managed to steal ten of those crowns, or so the story went, and presented them to Hades, who selected others to rule at his side, saving the tenth crown for Lucifer. Only, Hades and the other kings stole it back after Lucifer's coronation.

Now, Hades claimed the tenth crown was lost. William planned to find it, becoming the tenth Hell king, undermining and humiliating his ex-brother.

Fighting to maintain his composure while his nerve endings buzzed, he grated, "Do you know where the tenth Hell crown is?"

"No. Why would I?"

I won't kill her. I won't. "Do you remember the name of my mate, then?"

"No, but I remember what she looks like." Her sweet, sweet smile made another appearance. "You're getting your most fevered dream...and your worst nightmare. Enjoy! And good luck."

2

"You want a piece of me? Your girlfriend certainly does."

Sipping sugar water from a wineglass all classy-like, Sunday "Sunny" Lane meandered through a shadowy hotel bar teeming with youngish and oldish codebreakers, hackers and hobbyists. Most were humans who'd flown into New York City early that morning to network and party before the world's premiere cryptanalyst conference kicked off tomorrow. Her longtime friend…er, acquaintance Sable remained at her side. The six-foot black beauty came from the same realm and ancient village as Sunny.

They'd come to set honeytraps for any immortals who hunted their kind.

A waiter approached with a bottle of white. "May I refill your drink, ma'am?"

Ma'am? The worst insult known to womankind.

Able to read auras, she easily distinguished immortals from humans. The waiter was human. "No, thanks," she said. "As a self-appointed superhero and proud vigilante, I prefer to stay sober and scumbag-aware." *Asterhole.*

Sunny was born with an innate magic that prevented her from cursing, changing obscenities into flowers. *Daisy* replaced *damn. Argh! D-a-m-n. Hellebore* replaced *h-e-l-l. Sage* replaced *s-h-i-t. Bluebell* replaced *b-a-s-t-a-r-d* and *b-i-t-c-h. Aster* replaced *a-s-s*, and *freesia* replaced *f-u-c-k.*

The waiter offered her an unsure smile before rushing off.

"Here's hoping the duality serves us well tonight." Sable clinked her glass of sugar water against Sunny's.

Oh, yes. The duality. Half their nature longed to hunt and kill baddies, whether immortal or human. That part of her—Horror Show Sunny—worked as an assassin. A girl needed a purpose, right? The other half demanded they spread love, joy and peace. She'd dubbed that part Roses and Rainbows Sunny, and worked as a decoder.

The two sides were forever locked in a brutal tug-of-war.

"I posted online to let the world know I'd be here," Sunny said, fingering the medallion that hung at her neck. Her most prized possession, capable of feats few could imagine.

As an extremely rare "mythical" creature, they had to remain armed at all times. Poachers hunted them for sport, and collectors hunted them for pleasure. Little wonder Sunny trusted no one, not even Sable, and never stayed in one location more than a couple weeks. She constantly looked over her shoulder and rarely slept.

"If anyone attacks," Sable began.

"They die screaming."

Crackling with excitement, Sable gulped back the rest of her water and set her glass aside. "Once we've eliminated the poachers and collectors, we won't have to worry about being ambushed every second of every day. We can turn our sights to the underworld royals."

"All nine kings, and every last prince of darkness." Two princes of darkness in particular topped her list. Lucifer the Destroyer, and William the Ever Randy. Even their names filled her with blistering rage. The terrible things Lucifer had done to her people…things he'd done while shouting, "For William!"

The two might be at war now, but they'd been inseparable back then.

Focus up. You're here for a purpose, remember? Right. Sunny scanned the sea of faces. Some attendees ambled from group to group. Some remained in place, talking, laughing and generally clogging the pathways. Others stayed at their tables, nursing drinks. Many were relaxed and at ease. Oh, to be so uninvolved, unconcerned and untouched by the world's evil, as oblivious to the surrounding danger as everyone else. Sunny couldn't recall a time she'd ever felt safe.

Somewhere in the bar, glass shattered. Both Sunny and Sable jolted.

Deep breath in, out. Good, that's good.

"I'm so ready to stop running and live without fear," she muttered. She'd buy a house and plant a garden. Adopt a dog and a cat. The oldest, crankiest, ugliest mutt and tom at the pound. She'd go on a date for the first time in years…decades…probably centuries; she just had to find the right guy. Someone willing to put in the work to earn her trust. Then, she'd never again have to suffer through mating season alone. A time of clawing, gnawing, uncontrollable sexual arousal.

The next one kicked off in only two weeks.

"Me, too," Sable said. "I'm ready to stop chaining myself in a locked room so that I won't jump unsuspecting or unwilling males."

"Yes!"

"One day, I'm going to melt those chains and make them into a butt plug. I'll gift it to Lucifer before I kill him."

Sunny snickered. "I like the way your mind works."

The deeper they ventured into the bar, the more perfumes clashed. Flickering lights illuminated a sea of unfamiliar faces. Human. Human. Human. Vampire. Witch. Human. Human. Human. Werewolf. Though no one seemed to pay them any undue attention, Sunny kept a wary eye on the immortal trio.

Until husky male laughter snagged her attention.

Warm shivers raced down her spine, and she frowned. What a strange reaction to something so ordinary. Yes, his voice was sexy hot, but she'd heard hotter. Surely!

Sunny scanned the bar—there! Him. Though she couldn't see his face, she knew he was the one. He had thick black hair, broad shoulders and a unique aura. One she couldn't read.

He threw back his head, laughing again, and a new tide of shivers raced down her spine.

"Daisy," she muttered.

The woman on his left leaned in to whisper in his ear. The woman on his right ran a hand all over his back.

He was the meat in a flesh sandwich.

Finally he shifted, presenting Sunny with his profile. She sucked in a ragged breath.

A woman never forgot a face like his. *Hello, William the Ever Randy, brother to Lucifer.* The bluebell.

He looked tailor-made, as if every feature had been chosen from a catalog. *I'll take that face, that hair and those eyes. Oh, and don't forget those muscles.* He had flawless bronzed skin, jet-black hair and eyes like a sapphire-diamond hybrid framed by long, spiky lashes. Broad cheekbones tapered to a strong jaw shadowed with dark stubble. Perfect nose, perfect lips, perfect everything—to everyone in the worlds *but* her.

"What? What's wrong?" Sage asked, already reaching for the dagger hidden beneath her sleeveless jacket.

Rage sparked, quickly catching fire. "Look." She motioned to William.

Had he heard about their vendetta against his family and come to stop them? Why else would he be here? And why not sneak up on them?

"Speak of the devil," Sable ground out, "and he appears."

Sunny had done her research. She knew William was an infamous mercenary and legendary womanizer who disdained the sanctity of marriage. A few years ago, he'd helped slay a god king. More recently, he'd gotten drunk at a nightclub and shouted, "I consider myself a pleasuretarian. I only eat organic pussy." *Cat.* Only, he hadn't used the word *cat*, like she had to do to bypass the stupid, magical filter.

"If rumors are true," she said, "he sleeps with a new woman every night, possesses a fiery temper, sometimes injures his friends for laughs and enjoys killing his enemies as painfully as possible." So much to admire. So much to disdain.

"In that case, I think we should rearrange our list of hits, and take out the royal first, while we've got the chance."

"Agreed. One way or another, William the Ever Randy will die today." *Vengeance will be mine!* "Problem. I can't read his aura. Can you?"

"I…can't," Sable said, and frowned.

Daisy! "Despite tons of research, I failed to learn his true origins or species, so I don't know what strengths to guard against or what weaknesses to exploit."

"Well, no matter. We'll find out." Sable chewed on her bottom lip. "He's beautiful, though, isn't he?"

"He is." *Beautiful beyond imagining.* And oh, the admission grated. Sunny did her best to ignore the flutter in her belly. "He looks like an incubus, ready to lure unsuspecting women into his bed." *Was* he an incubus?

Arrogance and sensuality clung to him like a second skin.

Heart thudding, she dragged her gaze over the rest of him. Mmm, mmm, mmm. Had she ever seen such a perfect example of raw, rugged sex appeal? Such a deliciously large muscle mass? A black shirt molded to his bulging biceps, and black leathers clung to powerful thighs. On his feet, combat boots.

When he shifted a little more, she saw the writing on his shirt. It read Check Out the Cipher in My Pants. When he draped an arm around each woman, she spotted the metal cuffs on his wrists and the spiked rings on his fingers. Or rather, the weapons on his fingers. But so what? She had a weapon-ring, too: a tiny gun with brass pinfire rounds.

He threw back his head and laughed a third time. The fires of rage grew into an inferno. "After the terrible things he and his brother did to our people, *innocent* people, he deserves misery."

"Agreed."

With movements as sexy as hellebore, he lifted a glass of whiskey to his lips.

Swallowing a moan, Sunny switched her attention to the females at his table. There were three, and they hung on his every word. She recognized two of them. Their screen names were Jaybird and Cash, and they were cryptanalysts, like her.

Jaybird touched her lips to draw his gaze there. Cash leaned forward, putting her wealth of cleavage on display.

"Dude. They have the art of the flirt nailed, and I kind of want their autographs." Both Horror Show Sunny and Roses and Rainbows Sunny sucked at flirting.

She set her glass on a table and led Sable into a shadowy spot beside a potted plant, so they could plan their attack.

"—yeah, man, it's true," the man near the table was saying to a group of his friends. "I kicked the sage—" Pause. "Sage." He frowned. "Why can't I say *sage*?"

His companions guffawed, as if he were teasing. One even elbowed him in the sternum.

Oops. Sunny and Sable's magic filters prevented *anyone* from cursing in their presence. On the flip side, their magic stopped people from speaking lies, as well.

Gotta take the bad with the good.

"How should we play this?" Sunny tossed a flower petal into her mouth and—oh, hellebore! She'd been eating leaves and petals this entire time, the potted plant almost bare. Bad Sunny! This wasn't snack time. She dropped the remaining foliage and dusted the dirt from her fingers. *Anyway.*

"I think we should go in hot. A real ambush. He won't see it coming, because he doesn't know who or what we are. At least, I doubt he knows. If he did, Hades would be here, too. Last I heard, the king hoped to recruit creatures like us to use our magic against Lucifer."

"You're right. Besides, how would he have learned of our determination to slay him? Everyone we interrogate about the royal families of the underworld, we kill, ensuring word about us and our mission never spreads."

Sable chewed her bottom lip again. "I guess the only question now—how do we ambush him?"

Should they wait around and hope William approached them? What if he didn't? Should they lure him over with a come-hither smile? He might not go for it. His current dates wore fancy dresses; as usual, Sunny and Sable wore unadorned T-shirts and jeans, the perfect blend-in and forget-we-were-ever-here outfit.

Should one of them close the distance and make a move? Like hit on him, letting him believe he was going to score, then lead him to their hotel room?

Yeah. That. It guaranteed contact.

As she explained the idea to Sable, her heart sprinted.

"Perfect. Let's draw straws," Sable said. "Girl with the shorter one has to approach him. The lucky girl waits in the room and shoots him as soon as he enters."

Sunny snorted. "No need to draw. I'll do the grunt work. I can't flirt, but I can turn a man's mind to soup with my personality alone." Anticipation fizzed in her veins. "Just... don't kill him when he gets to the room. Let's interrogate him first. We can finally discover the coordinates to Lucifer's territory."

"Done! Before you go over there and do your mind-soup trick, your appearance needs a little tweak. By the way, I'm gonna need you to teach me how you do that. I'm foaming at the mouth with jealousy." Sable unwound Sunny's braid and combed her fingers through the long waves.

Oh, what Sunny wouldn't give for a trim. But even if she shaved her head, the thick azure mass would grow back in a matter of hours.

Sable nodded, satisfied. "All right, you're ready. Irresistible, and all that crap. Just remember. Your biggest weakness is your expressive face. You have trouble hiding your true emotions."

"Ten-four." Sunny jutted her chin and squared her shoulders. "Here goes nothing."

"You got this." Sable patted her butt before heading for the lobby. Like all of their kind, she walked silently, her footsteps inaudible.

I do. I've got this. Sunny stepped from the shadows... and got hit with a wave of nervousness as people looked her way. What if she didn't have this? Perspiration wet her palms.

No, no. I can do anything.

"—like a computer," a guy sitting at one of the tables was saying. He had a familiar voice. "I'm serious. She can break a code with only a glance. Any code. It's shocking to witness. She's—no way! She's right there!" The speaker pointed at her and waved. "Sunny! Sunny Lane. Hi. I'm Harry. Harry Shorts. Can I buy you a drink?"

More people looked her way. Including William. Their gazes met. Suddenly, she felt as if she'd been smacked with a crowbar. She lost her breath and stutter-stepped.

He studied her face, his attention lingering on each individual feature. *His* features darkened with heat.

The heat of attraction? She licked her lips, the nervousness gaining new ground, beading sweat on her nape.

She scowled. Finding a target sexy? Fine. Whatever. Being fluttered and maybe even kinda sorta aroused by one? No! Unacceptable. Either he exuded some kind of lust dust—*yes, yes, all his fault*—or mating season had screwed with her hormones early. Or both!

Then he turned away, dismissing her, and Sunny skidded to a halt halfway to his table. Sage! He *didn't* want her? She ran her tongue over her teeth. Irritation overshadowed the nervousness. Her heart calmed and her blood cooled, the synapses in her brain firing again.

The prick is going down. Determined, she glided forward once again. When she reached his table, she stopped, expecting him to notice her arrival. He didn't.

She worked her jaw and—her eyes widened. Oh, wow. He wielded magic, too. A *lot* of magic. Ancient, dark and powerful. The air around him vibrated with it, making her skin tingle.

The women ignored her as well, too wrapped up in William to care about anyone else.

Eventually, William stiffened ever so slightly, and she had to fight a smile. Breaking news! His awareness of her hadn't dulled in the slightest; he just didn't want her to know it.

Too bad, so sad. Deep breath in, out. Mistake! His scent… She closed her eyes and savored, her mouth watering. He smelled like angel food cake laced with crack.

Calm. Steady. No need to act like an uncouth wolf-shifter.

"—my best thinking naked," he was saying to Jaybird and Cash, pretending Sunny wasn't there. "You?"

Enough! "Hi. Hello. Hey," Sunny said, rapping her knuckles against the table. *Blowing this already.*

At first, only the women acknowledged her presence. But William continued talking and sipping his whiskey, and they forgot all about her.

She rapped the table again.

Finally, he canted his head in her direction, all languid grace self-assurance. He made a real event of it, too, as if premiering a blockbuster movie. Why bother going to so much trou—*ohhh. That's why.* Up close and personal, his eyes were even more of a showstopper, sparkling with arousal, glinting with a sheen of icy rage and glittering with steely determination.

Electrical currents zapped her nerve endings, and she almost yelped. *Ignore the hint of pleasure. Forge ahead.*

She pasted on her best come-hither smile and waved. *A wave? Seriously? Get it together, Sun. Remember what his family did to yours.*

As she balled her hands into fists, he looked her over slowly, starting at the bottom and working his way up—

singeing her. When he reached the apex of her thighs, shivers and heat consumed her.

No, no. I will not react. He—and mating season—will not affect me.

His gaze continued moving up, singeing hotter...

He reached her pasted-on smile and unveiled a smirking grin. But...but...why?

"How may I service you, pet?" he asked, slow and deliberate.

She felt the words like a caress. Wait. Pet? Pet! Such an insult to her kind! "In ways you never imagined, handsome," she replied, careful to moderate her tone. She glanced at Jaybird, then Cash. They had to go. Letting her savage, violent side glaze her eyes, she snapped, "Get lost."

William's smirking grin made another appearance.

Jaybird stared at him, exasperated. "Are you going to send her away?"

"No," he said simply.

"Fine. She's all yours. We'll go." With a huff, she stood. Paused. Waiting for him to stop her? When he remained quiet, she flounced off. Cash and the other female followed.

Here's hoping Willy-boy is just as easy to manipulate. "Hello." Ugh. Not this again. "I'm Sunny. My turn-ons include kindness and responsibility. I look twenty-one, but I'm older. Promise!" Nearly ten thousand years old.

A flash of intrigue, there and gone. "I'm William. Lovers call me the Panty Melter. Everyone else calls me the Ever Randy. My turn-ons are living and breathing. I'm older than twenty-one, as well."

Mmm. His voice...like audible sex. If women were "sex kittens," this man was a "sex panther." Meow.

What are you doing, admiring him? She reminded herself of his many crimes. Long ago, Lucifer and his horde of demons had ridden into her village. They'd raped, pillaged and utterly slaughtered her people. Men, women and children. Her family. Her friends.

Sometimes, when she closed her eyes, she still heard their screams.

The only home she'd ever known had been razed, and the entire scope of her life changed.

There'd been six survivors, Sunny included. No one remembered seeing William, only Lucifer, but Willy must have been involved. Why else would Lucifer have cried, "For William"?

Perhaps the Ever Randy had planned the raid. Perhaps he'd hidden behind a mask. Either way, Sunny had lost *everything*. Even the other survivors. To better the odds of hiding their origins, they decided to split up and reach out only when necessary.

She and Sable were together now only because Sunny had requested assistance.

Fingers snapped in front of her face, yanking her back to the present.

Realization: she'd gotten lost inside her head. Did she *want* to die? Sunny repasted the smile on her face. "Ever Randy, hmm? Does anyone call you ER for short?"

"Only if they wish to die," he replied, his tone dry. Despite the dryness, he thrummed with tension. Did her nearness rattle him?

"So he's cute *and* ferocious. Good job, Sunny." She patted herself on the shoulder, playing her role. "I picked the best slab of beef in the deli."

He winged up one brow. "So I'm a piece of meat to you?"

"Yes, pork chop. Yes. But in my defense, I only think it because I'm right." She leaned over and patted his cheek, the urge to slap him almost impossible to ignore. "You should come with a warning label. Or eyeball condoms."

"Why? Do you plan to stuff your eyes inside my sockets?"

"Maybe?"

"Sorry, but I think I'll pass." He crossed his arms, his shirt pulling taut over deliciously flexed muscles. "No, you know what? I'm feeling daring today. Let's go for it. Gotta try everything once, right?"

A laugh slipped from her. What the hellebore! A prince of darkness would *not* amuse her. "Sorry not sorry I sent your companions away. When I want something, I go for it." Truth!

He moved his gaze over her once again. "And you decided you want me?"

His tone...she thought she detected a hint of certainty *and* uncertainty. How odd. "I spent a whole five minutes planning your seduction. That's six minutes longer than usual."

"That means you're only twenty-four hours behind me," he replied, ignoring her screwed-up math.

Did he make a joke...or a statement of fact? Did he just admit to attending the conference to find her?

So. *There's a chance I was wrong.* A chance he knew or suspected who she was, and he'd come to stop her—forever.

Rage flared anew. Soon, it would be appeased...

For now, she forced another smile. The jerk had yet to invite her to join him, or express a desire to leave with her. *Playing hard to get?* Time to take their banter to the next level to give him an excuse to act. "If you were a pizza topping, you'd be hamburger and jalapeno, because you're grade-A beef and hot. I'd be ham and pineapple because

I'm salty and sweet." *No. No way I just openly compared us to pizza toppings, as if we're taking a Facebook quiz.*

Okay, so she didn't just suck at flirting. She sucked, period. But wait! He smiled a genuine smile, not one of those smirking grins, as if she'd truly amused him. The sight made her belly quiver.

Only a second later, he jerked as if she'd punched him, his smile vanishing. He tossed back the remains of his drink, his movements powerful, aggressive and seductive. The quivering worsened. *What is he doing to me?*

As he slammed down the glass, a blank mask covered his features. "You may go." He'd blanked his tone, too. "We'll chat later, when it's your turn."

Her turn for what? Interrogation? Maybe he suspected every female codebreaker of being the one hunting his family. And leave him? Hardly. Now that she'd breathed in his magnificent scent, experienced the caress of his voice and the lethal seduction of his gaze, she wanted him dead sooner rather than later. *More dangerous than I realized.*

There had to be a way to override his desire to wait. Oh! Oh! "Your loss, baby. I'm *super* horny." Horny to end his life! "I'm probably dying and only an orgasm will save me. I'd planned to invite you to my room for a couple hours of…you know…thought and reflection." She traced a finger between her breasts and purred, "I heard you say you do your best thinking naked."

His pupils enlarged, spilling over all that pale blue. A sign of sexual yearning. But he didn't null and void his demand.

Daisy! She had one last ace to play. If he still turned her down, she'd hide out, then follow him to his hotel room. "Fine, I'll go. Thankfully, you aren't the only slice of beefcake on the menu. Enjoy the rest of your evening. I know I will." She blew him a kiss and pivoted, revealing her best feature: a rounded aster. Argh! A rounded ass-ter. Freesia! Stupid magic filter. She had a freaking rounded butt, okay?

He sucked in a breath. "Or stay for a few minutes," he croaked.

Relief washed over her, cool and soothing. As hoped, her butt had succeeded where her wit had failed. *One step closer.*

Tremors plagued Sunny as she eased into the chair across from him. He watched her, intent and intense, absentmindedly tracing a finger over the rim of his glass.

Ignore the tingle of awareness. Ignore the crackle of need. Ignore the sizzle of want.

Without looking away from her, he raised an arm and snapped his fingers. A waitress came running, offering him a fresh glass of whiskey. One he polished off in seconds.

Sunny planted her elbows on the table. "So. What should we—"

He slammed the glass onto the table, silencing her. Then he stood and extended a helping hand. "I've already selected the night's entertainment, and I never rearrange my plans. On the other hand, I'm a giver, incredibly generous, and your life hangs in the balance. So, I will do this for you. I will give you an orgasm." He waved his fingers at her. "Come. Let's go to my room."

"No. Let's go to *my* room," she insisted, smiling a real smile this time. She'd done it! She'd won him over!

He jerked again, but he also gave a stiff nod. "Very well. We'll go to your room, and I'll ensure you survive the night."

3

"Go ahead. Call me Sexy. Everyone does."

WILLIAM USHERED HIS "super horny" temptress through the hotel lobby, her sweet, earthy scent keeping him at the razor's edge of desire. *Like a bouquet of freshly cut flowers dipped in vanilla and sprinkled with lust.*

Outwardly, he exuded casual confidence, with zero cares. Inwardly, he frothed with irritation as much as arousal. Until five minutes ago, Sunday "Sunny" Lane had occupied the second to last spot on his list of potential codebreakers/lifemates. The moment he'd spotted her, his entire body had reacted, muscles knotting and blood warming. He'd moved her to the number two. On paper, there was another woman with more experience with complicated codes. Then, Sunny had smiled at him, *genuinely* smiled, and he'd move her to number one. No one else had roused any kind of physical reaction.

If his codebreaker did, in fact, double as his lifemate, his body would *continue* to react to her. To Sunny.

Is *she my mate?* She had beauty, brains, a wry sense of humor and a jaded air that challenged him in a thousand different ways. William loved a good challenge.

But, he didn't think she desired him in turn. Women came on to him all the time, sure, but the little temptress had only projected a bit of desire. Mostly, she'd radiated pure, undiluted rage. Why? Had he slept with her and forgotten?

Whatever the reason, there was no way she planned to have sex with him tonight. Which meant…what? She intended to attack him?

Survival instincts screamed, *Destroy a threat, any threat.* Even one with such exquisite packaging. Common sense shouted, *Do nothing…yet.* If she *was* his codebreaker and lifemate, he would find out, one way or another.

He had fourteen days before he could act. Fourteen days. Two weeks. A blip of time, there and gone.

Then, if she was the one, she died.

The thought stopped him in his tracks. Could he do it?

"Is something wrong?" she asked, probably trying to hide her annoyance and failing.

Hoping to soothe the hottest flames of her fury, he brought out the big guns: charm. As they moved forward once again, he asked, "Have you ever considered changing the spelling of your name from *S-U-N-D-A-Y* to *S-U-N-D-A-E*?"

Her head whipped to the side, her gaze zooming to his and narrowing, her rage blazing at full force. At the moment, he couldn't make himself care. The way she moved, all grace and eroticism. *Sex on legs. Lovely beyond com-*

pare. When she recalled her role of femme fatale, however, she pasted on a cheery smile, and he had to swallow a laugh.

"How do you know the spelling of my name?" she asked, batting her lashes in what she must assume was a flirty manner. "How do you know my name at all? I only told you my nickname."

"Maybe I came here to meet you." He flicked a fingertip over the name tag glued to her shirt. "Or maybe I read this."

"Oh. Right." The eyelash batting stopped as she huffed out a breath. "Do you want to call me 'sundae' because you're interested in licking me up like an ice-cream cone?"

Her voice flowed over him, as warm and rich as fresh honey. Although, fresh honey had never reminded him of unadulterated sex.

Sex, with Sunny. His muscles knotted with more force, and his shaft hardened in seconds. "I'll tell you everything I want to do to you as soon as we get to your room."

Shivers—shudders?—brushed her body against his, sparking a heat wave in his veins. Sweat beaded on his upper lip. A first. Irritated, he swiped a hand over his mouth and yanked his attention straight ahead. To his consternation, his mind refused to think of anything else and immediately conjured her image.

She was on the short side—to him—no more than five-eight. A total pocket rocket with lickable brown skin, vibrant amber eyes and a waterfall of azure waves. Her features possessed a doll-like delicacy he found enthralling. A smattering of freckles dotted her nose. Freckles. A new must-have for him. And her body…shit! *The body on this woman.* Fine-boned yet gloriously curvy, with plump breasts and widish hips.

Want her. Want her now.
Resist!

As they entered the lobby, brighter light chased away the bar's shadows, she pushed her fall of bangs to the side, and he noticed faded scar tissue that formed a quarter-size ring in the center of her forehead.

He frowned. First, when had he looked at her again? And second, what had caused such a perfectly rounded wound? Third, why did faint, half-moon bruises mar the flesh beneath bloodshot eyes? Signs of fatigue, perhaps?

"You're staring," she snapped, then pasted on another fake-happy smile. "Please continue."

He bit his tongue to silence a laugh. "I'd planned on it, pet, but thanks for permission." To be honest, he hadn't noticed her beauty at first glance. Or second. Or even third. But something about her had repeatedly drawn his gaze, each new glance captivating him further. In less than a minute, she'd gone from plain, to pretty, to exquisite, to utterly mesmerizing. A truly remarkable feat. A *magical* feat? Maybe she wore a type of glamour?

No, she wasn't a witch. They had a different energy. He thought she might be a shifter of some sort. But which kind? Wolf, the best known? Or one of the rarer breeds, like dragons, selkies or sirens? No, she didn't smell like a sea creature or fire-breather.

Enough! Only one detail mattered: *Is she my code-breaker?*

If not, he might seduce her out of those clothes. *Could* he seduce her, despite her rage?

Anticipation went straight to his head, intoxicating him. *Challenge accepted.*

When they reached the bank of elevators, he guided Sunny to a stop behind a family of four. Two dads, and two young daughters. Lest Sunny change her mind and decide to bolt, he looped an arm around her waist, resting his hand on her hip.

To his delight, she melted against him. *Such a perfect fit.* Questioning her would be as easy as—

Nope. Celebrated too soon. She stiffened and straightened, tension pulsing from her.

The young girls noticed Sunny and gaped.

"Your hair is so pretty," the older sister said, her eyes as wide as saucers.

"The most beautifulest I've ever seen!" the younger one piped up.

"Thank you." Beaming, Sunny gave her hair a fluff. "Want to feel how soft it is?"

In unison, they cried, "Yes, yes, yes!"

As Sunny bent down to let the girls sift their fingers through her azure locks, the fathers donned indulgent grins.

William's chest tightened. He didn't think this was part of her act.

He'd created a mental file for every woman that graced his list; he added a new detail to Sunny's. ~~Plain. Pretty. Beautiful. Gorgeous.~~ Exquisite. Turned-on but fighting it. Witty. Confident. A bit immature. Kind to children.

What did she think about him? That he was exquisite, too, no doubt. And also witty and confident. Probably stunningly mature-ish. Definitely indifferent to other people's kids. Well, most people's. His friends Maddox and Ashlyn had twins—Urban and Ever—and William loved the little shits more than life.

Oh, you'll be having kids, all right. Enough to create a base...foot...sports team.

He scowled and shook his head, doing his best to dislodge Keeley's prediction. He would be choosing a different life path, thank you very much.

Ding. The elevator doors opened, the family of four striding inside. William gave Sunny a gentle nudge, urging her to the back of the car.

The little girls stood at the panel of numbers, eager to push a button.

"Seventeenth floor, please," she told them.

Oh, oh, oh. What was *that*? Had he detected a hint of nervousness in her voice?

The car jostled as it began to ascend. William maintained complete awareness of every occupant, lest anyone launch a sneak attack. Some immortals had the power to shape-shift into anyone or anything, including children.

On the third floor, the girls exited, waving goodbye. The doors closed, sealing William and Sunny inside. Alone. Her incredible scent saturated the air, making his head swim. All that sweetness melded with earthiness... His skin pulled tight, his blood a river of molten lava.

He turned and faced her, unable to stop himself. He needed...wanted... Damn it, he didn't know!

Why the hell didn't he know?

He gnashed his molars. She'd broken his brain, so she *must* be his lifemate. Yes? If so, she was his codebreaker, and the next victim to fall by his sword.

I shouldn't bed a woman I plan to murder...right?

Nah. It's fine. A moral compass wasn't something William liked to carry; they got in the way. And he might be wrong about Sunny. She might not be the one he sought.

So why is a primal urge to protect her welling?

He had to remind himself of an important fact. *I can protect her and endanger myself, or endanger her and protect myself.*

I choose me. Always.

With ragged growls rumbling deep inside him, he told

her, "If you're wearing perfume, never stop." Damn it! He'd meant to tell her to toss the bottle.

She turned toward *him*, her cheeks a lovely shade of rose. Passion-fever? The growls grew louder.

"I'm not wearing perfume," she croaked.

Oh, yes. Passion-fever. The air around them thickened as they breathed harder, faster. Neither of them looked away.

He took a step closer.

She took a step closer, too.

With her next inhalation, her nipples rubbed against his shirt. Delicious friction. He fought to contain a groan, his shaft *throbbing*.

Do not lose focus with a potential threat.

Right. He would kiss her, distracting her enough to wipe her mind of fury and remove the bullets from her gun-ring, all while remaining detached. Then, he would question her. If he liked her answers, they could spend a few hours in bed. If not...

They could still spend a few hours in bed.

Excellent plan. No flaws.

Now he backed her against the wall. Her breath hitched, but she offered no protests. He pinned her arms overhead. Still no protests. Emboldened, he shoved a leg between hers, keeping them spread.

There was no stopping his next groan.

Flecks of green, blue and pink appeared in her eyes as she asked, "Am I about to experience elevator foreplay?"

"You are. It's my specialty." What *was* she, damn it? Holding her gaze, he ground his erection into her core...

"You're very good at humblebrags."

"No, I'm not. I'm *great* at them."

To his delight, she whipped her hips forward, meeting him. Oh, shit! Pleasure seized him. He began to pant.

Inner shake. Concentrate! What had he planned to do? Oh, yes. As stealthily as possible, he removed the bullets from her gun-ring.

"The other girls must have really primed your pump," she said, breathless.

"What other girls?" he asked with a wink.

The corners of her mouth twitched with genuine amusement. "Oh, you're very, very good at this."

"This?"

"Flirting."

William dropped his gaze to her breasts, watching as her nipples pearled for him. A mistake. He couldn't stop himself from grinding against her again. Again. "Soon, I'm going to lavish your little nipples with kisses. How they must ache."

With a groan, she curled her fingers around his hand, the one binding her wrists. She dug her nails into his flesh, and he jolted with a realization. *I'm getting to her, and I haven't even kissed her yet.*

Masculine pride threw kindling on the fires of his lust.

What the hell are you doing? Forgetting your purpose? He shook his head—a negation for her as well as himself. "You're wrong, sundae."

Eyes glazed, seemingly entranced, she breathed, "Wrong?"

"About me and flirting. I'm not good at it. I'm *amazing*."

She peered at his lips. Stared, really. "I should warn you. I'm really bad in bed. Like, ice your blue balls for a week bad."

An indulgent grin bloomed, the one that usually sent a woman's pulse on an around-the-world trip. "There's no such thing as bad in bed, sweetness. Not with me."

The roses faded from her cheeks and the sparkles died in her eyes, her fury returning in a flash. "You've bedded enough women to know beyond a doubt?" she asked with a deceptively sweet tone. "How many have there been, then? Go ahead. Ballpark it."

Honest to a fault, when he wanted to be, William said, "The number is incalculable." He'd had more lovers than any immortal he knew. A fact that did not guilt or shame him. Nor did it make him proud. It was what it was, and he'd done what he'd done.

In the back of his mind, he'd been keeping track of the floors they passed. In a matter of seconds, they would reach sixteen. A few seconds after that, seventeen. *Need more time.*

Without moving away from Sunny, he reached out to press sixteen, ensuring they would stop once before reaching their destination, buying him a minute or so.

The elevator stopped, and the doors opened. No one waited there.

He dipped his head, letting his lips hover over Sunny's. "Shall I add one more to the tally?"

Awaiting her answer…breathing her in…*already addicted to her scent?*

A stronger shiver rocked her. "Yes," she finally whispered.

He wasted no time, pressing his lips against hers once, twice, then for good, slipping his tongue into her mouth. *Fuck!* Sweeter than ambrosia. She tasted like power and tranquility, his two favorite things.

Addicted? Yes. No question now, and zero regrets. *Want more. Need it.*

Will have it. With a desperate moan, he deepened the kiss.

No, no, no. There would be no deepening. Not with her,

not yet. *Must remain detached until I know who and what I'm dealing with.*

Here and now I'll give a little to get a lot.

But…she hadn't lied or exaggerated. She was a bad kisser. The worst. She sucked his tongue too hard, banged her teeth against his and bit tender spots, drawing blood.

Somewhat shell-shocked, he lifted his head to peer down at her. He expected to see a return of the sensual flush. Or a smile to indicate she'd played a joke on him. He saw nothing. No hint of emotion. Not even her previous rage.

Am I losing my touch?

"Why'd you stop?" she asked, *not* out of breath. "You're as bad at this as I am, so we're kind of perfect for each other."

He…what? "I am *not* bad at this, and I'll prove it," he bellowed. Back down he went.

William kissed her with every bit of skill he'd acquired in his multimillennia-long life of he-whoring, feeding her passion straight from the tap. Again, she kissed him back, but she remained stiff and wooden, as if distracted.

Even still, he felt… No, impossible. But maybe? Lightning flashed in his veins, something he'd only ever experienced when enraged. Here, now, his temper remained at bay. So, what had caused it? Sunny? Because she *was* his lifemate?

Icy fingers of dread crept down his spine.

Then a miracle occurred. She softened against him, easing the suction on his tongue. She stopped biting and started laving. In seconds, sharp desire pummeled him. He felt as if he'd craved her forever, and it only magnified his dread.

Ding. The elevator doors opened on the seventeenth floor.

Damn it! Things had just started to get good. The fact

that he had to stop… *Now* his temper flared, a new growl rumbling in his chest. He jerked his head up, grating, "Which room?" They would finish what they'd started, then return to their conversation.

"Last one on the right," she told him, more breathless than before.

William twined their fingers, ushered her into the hallway, and maintained a brisk pace to their destination. She keyed into the room, entering first with an excited spring in her step.

Either she wanted him, or she wanted him to experience whatever waited beyond the door. Prepared for anything, he entered on her heels, doing a quick visual sweep. Small room. Beige walls. Generic artwork. King-size bed, plush white comforter. No weapons. Except for the temperature. She'd set the thermostat to Hotter than Hell.

Sweat beaded on his brow, his insides quickly boiling. Wonderful. A nice William stew.

Behind him, the exit closed with a soft *snick*.

Sunny spun, her mouth opening and closing. "But I… She… I don't understand."

"What don't you understand?"

"She's not here. Why isn't she here?"

"She?" Would Sunny reveal her true purpose now or wait until—

She whirled around, her arm raised, her hand fisted, the gun-ring aimed at his face. *Okay. "Now," it is.* "Very well," she said. "I'll do this myself."

Never, in all the centuries of his life, had a woman pulled a gun on him post-kissing. After screwing him, yes. It'd happened once or maybe a dozen times. He'd lost count, all right? Apparently, he had a terrible bedside manner. Many females had suggested he seek help. And he would, just as soon as he started caring about what other people thought of him.

"I know who you are," Sunny snapped. "William of the Dark, also known as the Ever Randy and the Panty Melter. The son of Hades and brother of Lucifer. You're scum! How many villages did you and your brother pillage over the centuries, hmm? Tell me! And don't lie. I'll know."

He flinched at "scum." *The little bitch.* But, no matter. With her outburst, she'd appeased his pride, explaining her resistance to his charms, her rage and her insults. She'd waged mental war, attempting to undermine his confidence and make him second-guess himself, all to punish him for something she believed he'd done in the past.

Unfortunately for her, William excelled at mental warfare. He won, always. "How many villages have I pillaged? Again, the number is incalculable." He leaned to the side, resting his shoulder against the wall. A relaxed pose. "Why? Did I pillage yours?"

"Yes! No! Argh! Maybe. I lived in the Realm of Mythstica."

Finally. Information. "I've never visited the Realm of Mythstica." Where many creatures of myth and legend hailed, like dragons, minotaurs and the mighty Pegasus.

"Did you ever help your brother plan an attack on a village in Mythstica?" she demanded.

"No." Had he helped Lucifer plan other attacks? Yes. Many times. Afterward, he'd regretted them all.

"But…but… You're lying to me. You must be lying. I don't know how, but there's no other explanation. So tell me why you did it—the truth this time!—or I'm going to shoot you in your pretty face."

He patted his stubble-dusted cheeks. "You think I'm pretty?" When she screeched, he decided to move on.

"What are you going to shoot me with, hmm?" Trying not to smirk, and failing, he fished the bullets out of his pocket.

She shocked him. A grin lit her features, making his chest tighten all over again. "You think I'm freesia-ed," she said, her smirk a rival for his. "But I clocked your every move during our pathetic excuse for a kiss, and I knew the second you removed the bullets. Too bad for you I've already reloaded."

"Freesia-ed?" William was reluctantly impressed with her bravado, but also furious. She'd dared to threaten *him*, a prince of darkness? She would learn better. "Shoot me, then." Bullets only served as an annoyance. Like flies. "Or do you find me too attractive to damage?" How far would she take this?

If she was, in fact, the one he sought, he needed to know.

"I'm sure there are *some* women who find you passable," she sneered, making it clear she considered those women idiots.

The insult hit its mark, little snarling sounds leaving him. Guess he cared more about the opinion of others than he'd realized.

"Ohhhh. That one stung, huh?" Shaking her fist in his direction, she commanded, "Stop acting tough and start talking. What did my people ever do to you and your family?"

Would she actually pull the trigger? One second he thought, *No way*; the next he thought, *Hell, yes*. "Who are your people? *What* are your people?"

Ignoring his questions, she snapped, "Why did you pillage *any* village?"

That one had an easy answer. "In the past, if someone threatened me, I killed them as well as their entire family and collection of friends, all to prevent others from avenging their deaths." He offered the admission without shame. Fine! With a hint of shame.

"We never threatened you. We spent our days helping anyone in need."

"For the last time, I did not plan or participate in the destruction of any village in Mythstica." But Lucifer might have, while wearing William's face. Son of a bitch! His ex-bro had enjoyed blaming others for his worst deeds. "Did you see me there?"

"Well. I…" She bowed up. "No," she grated. "I didn't. They didn't."

Confusion muddied his thoughts, his brows drawing together. "So why assume I'm lying? Why assume I'm responsible?"

"Your brother's war cry. *For William!*"

Electrified coils of rage unfurled inside him. *I'll kill him.* "He framed me for many things. I never asked him to murder for me. I've always taken care of my own killings."

"Then why haven't you killed *him*?"

I'm trying! Rather than voice his failure, he hooded his eyelids. *Look at me…relax your guard…* "If you're going to shoot my—what did you call it? Oh, yes. My pretty face. If you're going to shoot regardless of what I say, I have no incentive to share information with you."

She smiled the wickedest, evilest smile he'd ever beheld, somehow seeming to shock his deadened heart back to life. "You want incentive?" she purred. "Here it is. Tell me what I want to know, and I'll kill you quick and painless. Don't, and I'll make it hurt in ways you've never experienced."

Another threat. Unlike others, he did not fear pain. What truly terrified him? Whatever she'd done to his now-pounding heart. "What is it you want to know exactly? Lucifer's location?"

She gave a clipped nod. "Yes. But first, we'll start with the reason you came to the conference. To kill someone, yes, as your dark nature demands?"

As a matter of fact… "I'm here to find a codebreaker who can work with magical codes. If you're the one, I'll kill to *protect* you. For two weeks. So. I'll show you a photo, and you'll tell me if you can translate the symbols into words."

A crease formed above the bridge of her nose. "Why such a specific timeline?" Then she shook her head and stomped her foot. "No! You're lying again. Somehow. The photo is probably laced with poison."

Another item to add to her file. Nope, two items. Bad kisser, and suspicious as hell. Two reasons to hard pass. So why was he *more* attracted to her by the second?

Lifemate…

No, no. Can't be sure.

"All right. New plan," he grated. "I'll give you an orgasm or twelve. Sated, you'll relax. Relaxed, you'll think clearly. Then you'll admit I'm the best lover you've ever had, and we'll hash out this village pillaging business like semiadults." He'd never failed to make a woman climax, and he wouldn't start today.

"Let me think about your offer…thinking…nah. I'm not interested in faking it."

"Faking? Faking!" He fisted his hands. "I've already soaked your thong, guaranteed."

Her smirk returned, and oh, it looked as good on her as the evil grin. "Thong? Please. I'm proud to say I wear granny panties exclusively. I'm not putting a piece of cloth up my butt for anyone, and lace itches. I like cotton, and I like coverage."

How the hell is she working me into a lather with this

granny panty nonsense? "Today's your lucky day. I'm going to give you a crash course in William 101. You'll get to know me, and realize I always tell the truth, because I don't care what anyone thinks about me." Somehow, he would get through to this woman…and make her desperate for his touch in the process. Because priorities. "I love games of every kind. Video. Wits. Board. Bedroom. I've stabbed as many friends as enemies, just for grins and giggles, and I never leave an enemy alive."

"Enough!" Again, she shook the gun-ring. This time, the circular scar on her forehead glowed with soft white light. *Mesmerizing.* He'd thought he'd seen that light once before, long, long ago. But where? And what did it mean? *Think!* "You assume these details will make me less inclined to shoot you, because I'll view you as a living being versus a target. But, I'll *never* see you as anything more than scum."

He flinched again. "Shoot me, then," he repeated. "Do it!" *If she is my lifemate, I am hers.* She wouldn't be able to harm her man. Few immortals could. *I am the exception, of course.*

"I will do it. Don't think I won't." The evil smile returned, and she lowered the gun to his shaft. "Still eager to be shot?"

He rolled his eyes while secretly applauding her spirit. "Like I haven't been shot in my man-junk before." Hoping to fluster her, he said, "Ah. I understand the switch. You're a bad shot, so you need a bigger target. No wonder you selected my cock."

"Good point," she said, returning the barrel to his face. "There's nothing bigger than your ego."

He took a step closer, unafraid. "My time is valuable, and you're wasting it. Fucking shoot me already, or put the gun away."

The F-bomb made her gasp with...wonder? "You can use obscenities in my presence. Obscenities and lies."

"Baby, I know all the dirty words." Should he disarm her now or continue to wait? Dismissing normal sounds—the air vent, a dripping facet, stomping footsteps above—he listened to her heartbeat. Pounding so hard, so fast. Not the heartbeat of a cold-blooded killer.

Wait.

The decision solidified as her intoxicating scent rendered him light-headed. He would kiss her instead, teaching her how to kiss him back properly, and she would lower the weapon on her own. Then, he would make her beg for a climax. A climax he might—might!—be inclined to grant, *after* she'd apologized for her hostility.

Excitement sparked. *I will have this woman.*

"You have nothing else to say to me?" she asked, the words clipped.

"Take off your clothes, and I'll tell you anything you want to know."

A strange calm descended over her, her aim steadying. Voice flat, she told him, "I warned you and I gave you a chance to talk. Now, you die."

Shocked, he stumbled back a step. This woman would shoot *anyone*...and he liked it. He liked her.

Want her? No. He needed. Desire clawed at him, and there was no ignoring it, no shoving it aside to deal with later. He hungered. *Ravenous.*

Get her into bed. Sort the rest out later. Yes! Another flawless plan.

He unveiled his most indulgent smile, ready to seduce. Then. That very second. The signature of her magic changed, too, from sweet and innocent to dark and menacing.

He'd misread this female from the start, hadn't he?

"Sunny," he began.

"Goodbye, William." *Boom!*

Pain exploded in his beautiful face and quickly spread through the rest of him. His world went black. His knees buckled, and he collapsed, crash-landing with a heavy thud.

As he lay there, shock reverberated inside his bones. She'd done it; the sexy little bitch had actually pulled the trigger.

She couldn't be his lifemate, which meant she wasn't his codebreaker. Which meant he could do whatever he wished to her. But...

He wanted to know what *she* would do next.

William set aside his fury with her—for the moment—and played dead. At least everything made sense now. Her weird shifter magic. Her sometimes sweet, sometimes evil personality. Her drugging voice. Her sweet, earthy scent. Her propensity for eating leaves. Yeah, he'd caught her munching on foliage in the bar. Her attempt to turn the word *freesia* into an obscenity. The ability to sift truth from lie. The small round light on her forehead.

William had just found a unicorn-shifter.

This was not a good turn. The unicorns of myth: *Watch as I spread happiness across the land.* The unicorns of reality: *I'mma kill you and dance in your blood.*

She had the power to slay gods.

She might be my lifemate, after all. She just didn't want him as much as he wanted her.

Shit. Shit! *What am I going to do now?*

4

"Be my baby tonight. Tomorrow, be absent."

SUNNY FOUGHT TO retain her cold, calm bravado, but panic and hysteria fought back. So many things had gone wrong. First, desire had stirred when she kissed William. Genuine desire. Uncontrollable and wild. Their bodies had fit perfectly, like two lost puzzle pieces finally found. His taste drugged, while his ambrosial scent warmed and his wicked touch thrilled. But, though a fire had blazed in her veins for the first time in memory, her thoughts had acted like a bucket of ice water. *Prince of darkness. Destroyer of families.*

Her thoughts *always* doused the flames of her desires, no matter the situation or the male. Her dual nature was simply too strong, her trust issues too deeply ingrained, causing a constant tug-of-war inside her. Over the years, she'd learned to expect an ambush at every turn, which had broken her ability to relax. Yet, for that one brief moment, she'd lost herself in William.

Then she'd entered an empty hotel room and found no sign of Sable. Had the other unicorn misled Sunny? Or, had a poacher or collector captured her? Fear had taken hold.

Then Sunny had entertained doubts about William's involvement in the slaughter of her village. He'd seemed so surprised by her accusation, and legit angry with his brother.

In the end, she'd erred on the side of caution and plugged a magic bullet in his face. A bullet designed to slay gods. Now blood and brain matter splattered the walls and the floor, and a metallic scent of death tainted the air.

Realization set in. She'd just killed William the Ever Randy. Horror Show Sunny rejoiced in a job well done. Roses and Rainbows Sunny grieved. She'd taken a life. What if William had told the truth? What if she'd killed an innocent man?

Half laugh, half sob bubbled from her. A common reaction to murder, and a testament to her dual nature.

Buck up, buttercup. Lucifer slayed your family, and you slayed a member of his. You did the right thing. Still, tears singed her eyes and blurred her vision.

Okay, maybe she wouldn't buck up just yet.

"Why'd you have to prick my temper?" she whispered at William. With a sniffle, she trudged to the bathroom, where she collected the supplies she and Sable had brought: plastic tarps, towels and blankets. To start. She also had a bucket filled with air fresheners, bleach and other cleaning products. Crouching beside the body and trying not to sob again, she fit the towels around him to soak up the blood. Then she draped the plastic over him. Finally, the blankets.

Though she needed to dispose of the body, clean the room and find Sable, she lingered next to William. "You left me with more questions than answers. What were you, species-wise? How were you able to belt out an obscenity, evincing no reaction to my magic? Only one species can bypass the supernatural filter. The Fae. But there's no way you're Fae." Every Fae possessed an aura tied to the four elements. "And why do you have a magically coded book?"

Since he was dead and all, she decided to share a secret. "I have a coded book, too. A diary of lists. I kept track of everyone who's ever wronged me, everyone I've ever killed, sexual fantasies, all the things I hope to do before I die and life hacks for living my best life."

Wait. Had his chest lifted ever so slightly?

Heart racing—with hope? Dread? Both?—she pressed two fingers against his throat, feeling for a pulse. Nope. Nothing. Her shoulders rolled in.

Focus. She'd brought several insulated, waterproof bags, planning to stuff her victims inside and wheel them to her car at the appropriate time. But body dismemberment was a two-person job. The very reason she'd reached out to Sable about the conference in the first place.

No way around it; she had to find Sable before she worked on William.

Halfway expecting cops to be congregating in the hall-way, questioning guests about the source of the gunshot, Sunny trembled as she opened the door. Shocker! Not one person stood nearby. Of course, the gun-ring wasn't as loud as, say, a .44, so anyone within earshot might have assumed the pop came from a TV show.

Head high, expression (hopefully) serene despite her churning stomach, she anchored the Do Not Disturb sign on the knob and exited. After double-checking the lock, she meandered down the hallway. *I'm just a normal girl, not a shifter who murdered the most carnally sensual male on earth.*

As she entered an empty elevator, a sense of isolation engulfed her. Of course, she felt isolated every second of every day, even when surrounded by hundreds of people. Except...

Standing here, she thought she detected a lingering hint of William's scent, causing the memory of his kiss to surface, eclipsing the sense of isolation. Her tremors started up again. The man had focused every bit of his intense masculinity on her. When he'd thrust his thigh between her legs, taking her on one hellebore of a carnival ride, his blue, blue eyes had lit with sizzling arousal.

Her blood heated and her belly quivered, just as before.

What are you doing? Stop! Why torture herself with feelings she could never explore? Not with William, not with anyone. Her trust issues wouldn't let her. Too many beings hoped to steal her horn, a conduit and siphon for mystical power. Aka a magic wand.

The elevators doors closed, and she realized she hadn't pressed a button. Thinking to start her search at the bottom and work her way up, she selected the first-floor.

A jostle. A ride. Then a *ding*. The elevator doors opened, and Sunny rushed out as fast as her feet could carry her, eager to escape the site of her undoing. She hurried through the lobby, the bar, her gaze constantly darting. Before coming to the convention, she'd studied a map of the hotel and memorized every exit and possible escape route. She'd check each one. If Sable had been chased, she would have left a warning for Sunny. Surely!

In the distance, a man shouted her name. He sprinted over, and she moaned. Harry, the one who'd requested a demonstration of her abilities earlier.

Lest he draw more attention her way, she stopped in her tracks, awaiting him. He halted a few feet away, his lips pulled back in a toothy, goofy grin. Close to her age—

appearance-wise—he was handsome, with dark brown hair, darker eyes and tan skin.

"Hi," he said, only to add, "I'm not creepy or anything, I promise."

The words pinged her inner lie detector, a vibration speeding along her spine. Okay, yeah, he absolutely considered himself a creep. Since she hadn't reloaded the gun-ring, she slid her hand in her pocket to grip the hilt of the dagger hidden there.

He continued, saying, "I'm Anomaly. No, sorry. That's my screen name. I don't know if you remember, but I'm Harry Shorts. I just, I know you're Sunny Lane, and I'm totally starstruck right now. You're, like, my hero, and I'd love to buy you a drink."

"No, thank you." She tried to go around him, but he moved with her, blocking her path. "I'm busy."

"Just one drink." He pushed his palms together, creating a steeple. "Pretty please. I'll make sure you have a good time."

He was too eager. Could *he* be a poacher? He was human, yes, and he wasn't on her list of suspects, but the longer they stood together, the more reddish gray his aura became, tendrils of evil spilled from his heart.

He was a bad man, who liked to do bad things.

Self-preservation instincts demanded she take him out now, now, now. Sunny resisted—for the moment. Tomorrow, she would shadow him and maybe he'd incriminate himself. But here, now? Precious time ticked away.

"Have you seen my friend?" she asked, watching his face for any hint of his emotions. "Female. Six feet tall. Black. Gorgeous."

"No, sorry. So about that drink…"

No change in his emotions or aura. He *hadn't* seen Sable.

"No, thank you," she repeated, then faked left and spun right, darting away.

Harry got the hint and didn't bother chasing after her, saving his life.

Guard up, she scanned the area. No sign of Sable.

No sign of Sable on the first eight...ten...seventeen floors, either.

Dread coiled around her throat and squeezed. By the time she reached her room, perspiration dampened her skin. Still, no policemen, thank goodness.

Shaking now, she keyed inside and kicked the door shut. The scent of roses greeted her. Roses? Had Sable returned with flowers, maybe? She inhaled deeply, just to be sure she'd scented what she'd scented. Yep. Roses. Curious, she tripped forward and—

No flowers. And no body. Her heart and stomach traded places, her head spinning. William and the pool of blood were gone. He—or whoever had carried him away and cleaned the room—had left a note on the mirror. In still-dripping blood.

What. The. Hellebore? Her tremors amplified as she read, *You were wrong. If I were a pizza topping, I'd be a double order of smoked sausage. I'll see you soon, duna. Very soon...*

Duna, meaning "little dark one"? Eyes wide, she tore through the room, but found no trace of William. If he were alive...

No, no. He was dead. Had to be. No one could survive the magic bullet. But...

If he *wasn't* dead, he would return for vengeance.

She gulped. She needed to be ready.

5

"Fate is a bitch, but she favors the bold. If ever she closes a door, kick it down."

THE NEXT MORNING, William stood outside a hotel ballroom. One of his sons stood at his left, and Hades's newest adoptee stood at his right. The pair remained impassive, while William vibrated with a tantalizing mix of fury, satisfaction and anticipation.

Sunny had entered the ballroom ten minutes and twenty-nine...thirty...thirty-one seconds ago to attend a workshop called "The Voynich Manuscript: Too Difficult to Crack, or a Hoax?" Now only a set of double doors separated him from his prey.

Funny how fate worked. Of all the codes in all the worlds, William considered the Voynich manuscript most like his book. Two hundred and forty-six calfskin pages, written in an unknown script. The author had used a twenty-eight-character alphabet, with zero punctuation. As the workshop name suggested, the code had yet to be solved.

Popping the bones in his neck, he asked his companions, "You remember your job?"

"Yep. Thanks to Hades, I've now done dozens of these. Got the process memorized." Pandora rubbed her hands together, a bit gleeful. "This is a basic snatch and go. So, enough chitchat, yeah? Let's get it done."

So impatient, his new sister. A dark-haired, pale-skinned beauty, and, yes, the woman behind the infamous legend. The one Zeus, former king of the Greeks, had once commanded to guard a mysterious box. According to legend, curiosity had driven her to open it, unleashing all the world's evil, or demons.

Truth was, fourteen others had been jealous of her military success. Thirteen men, and one woman. Hoping to prove Pandora unworthy of her special assignment, *they* stole and opened the box. As punishment, they were each forced to house one of the demons—inside their bodies.

Within minutes of their possession, one newly possessed warrior had murdered Pandora. Then, last year, Hades brought her back from the dead—resurrection was a specialty of his.

Those fourteen soldiers had gone on to become William's closest friends. They were irreverent assholes, sure, but they were his irreverent assholes. He trusted them with his life.

Green, William's son, happened to be a horseman of the apocalypse. One of one set of four, anyway. Green was an ambassador of Death. He possessed dark hair, dark skin and eyes like an abyss; he loved poker, cigars and women, in that order. Loyal only to his brothers and William, Green had little tolerance for anyone else.

Red and Black, William's only other sons, were the same. At the moment, they were out spying for him. White, his only daughter, had been murdered a few years back, her loss a thorn in his heart and a white-hot poker in his soul.

He curled his hands into fists. *One day, I'll have her back.* Not through traditional means. No, oh, no. His children had no mother. William had made them all on his own. Well, not on his own exactly. Magic had helped.

The first magic he'd ever absorbed had mated with the vengeance, greed, envy and wickedness in his soul. He hadn't known until months later, when black mist had seeped from his pores, four adults standing in its midst.

"And you?" he demanded of Green. "What aren't you to do?"

His son rolled his eyes. "I'm not to kill the attendees, even if they try to kill us."

"And?" William prompted.

Pandora heaved a sigh. "We do not touch the blue-haired one. She's yours, only yours, and if we dare make a move on her, you'll shove a metal hook down our throats, and fish out our organs."

"Exactly right." After Sunny had bolted, he'd cleaned the hotel room with magic, written her a message in blood and opened a portal to his home in Hell. He'd had to use magic to see, too, his eyes decimated by the bullet, along with his nose, mouth and parts of his brain. Good times. Payback would be fun—for him.

Eager and impatient to get started, he waved, placing a magical barrier around the room, ensuring no one outside it would hear what happened inside.

"Let's go," he said. "Let's get this done."

Instinct whispered, *If she leaves this room without you, you will never see her again.* Impatience welled.

"Now," he insisted when his companions failed to act.

Pandora flipped him off. "I need a minute. I'm pondering why a man known as the Ever Randy is going batshit crazy over a woman who pureed his face."

Green cracked a grin; no doubt he enjoyed seeing his unflappable father so...flapped. Over a female no less.

"Ponder on your own time," William snapped. Ready to see Sunny, he kicked open the double doors and prowled into the ballroom. His companions flanked his sides.

The speakers sat atop a makeshift dais; in the middle of a speech, they went quiet. Clothes rustled, and chairs skidded, every set of eyes sliding his way. Gasps resounded. What a fearsome sight they must make, the amazingly fierce warlord and his mediocre assistants.

In one hand, William held an ordinary knife. In the other, a special dagger with a curved blade and the barrel of a gun fused against it.

"M-may we help you?" one of the speakers asked. William had met her last night. Her name was Cash, and before his encounter with Sunny, she'd been number one on his list.

"Someone can help, yes," he said. "The rest of you are collateral damage. For now, anyway. Do what I say, when I say, and you'll walk away...at some point. Or roll the dice and disobey me. See what happens." Sunny, Sunny, where was Sunny? He dragged his gaze over the sea of faces... There she was, the prize at the bottom of his cereal box.

His heart pumped harder as their eyes met. Surprise, surprise. Lust punched him, his breath heaving. Every muscle in his body tense, his blood heating to a boil. The woman looked good enough to eat.

Go ahead. Take a bite. Earn a jaw-cracking yawn in response.

No! Unacceptable. He was a god among men. He could make anyone come, at any time, even the seemingly arousal-less Sunny Lane. And he would—

Not. He absolutely would not touch her again. That primal urge to protect her had just resurged, only stronger. A major inconvenience requiring eradication, not encouragement.

But, he couldn't force his gaze away from her. Today, a faint but noticeable sheen of glitter illuminated her skin. Anyone else would assume it came from a bottle. Not William. He knew better now. Unicorn-shifters glittered with strong emotion. A type of camouflage. Who would suspect a walking glitter bomb of being one of the most powerful and devious species in *any* world?

A thick azure braid hung over one delicate shoulder. A braid that hung over her breast, and the pink handmade cashmere sweater molded there. Sloppy threadwork provided a glimpse of the plain tank top beneath.

She'd knitted the garment herself, hadn't she?

Damn it! He refused—utterly refused!—to desire a granny panty–wearing knitter who dabbled in murder. *And yet, I would give anything to rip away that sweater, drag those panties off with my teeth and feast on the curves underneath.*

Her only makeup? A smear of gloss over her cupid's-bow lips. Lips he wanted wrapped around his cock. What? Truth was truth. He craved raw, filthy sex. The kind he hadn't gotten to have last night, thanks to a bullet to the face.

He waited for a fresh dose of fury…

Still waiting…

Mostly he felt excruciating awareness of the one woman he shouldn't want and couldn't let himself have.

"You truly survived," she gasped out.

"Disappointed, duna?"

"Yes!" Color drained from her cheeks as she jumped to her feet. "You survived. You survived and you're breathing," she babbled. "You're alive."

The action bounced her breasts, which accelerated his breathing. He scoured a hand over his mouth, then looked the rest of her over. A mistake. Had she grown curvier overnight? Skinny jeans hugged her toned legs and dog-shaped house slippers adorned her feet. *Sexy and adorable.*

Voice filled with mocking indulgence, he asked, "Dressing for the job you want? Good news. You're hired! I'm certain you'll make a wonderful house pet."

"House pet? Please!" She wagged a finger in his direction. "You're here to pick up where we left off, and we both know it."

"So what if I am? We both know your granny panties are already soaked." Know...dream. Semantics.

Her eyes narrowed to tiny slits. "Accept the fact that your match doesn't light my wick, and move on before I put another bullet in your face."

"Oh, my match will light your wick, all right." *It will?* "I'm not a quitter. By the time I'm finished with you, you'll be begging me for more." He hurled the words like daggers, his decision to remain hands-off in shreds.

Two weeks. They had two weeks together. Like Keeley had said, he wouldn't be falling for his lifemate in such a limited time. Therefore, he *could* afford to indulge her sexually, as long as he rid himself of the urge to protect her. And he *should* indulge her, he realized now. He should treat her like every other woman he'd ever desired: seduced and forgotten.

Sex meant nothing. An itch to be scratched.

As for sleeping with a female he planned to kill...he

would not feel guilty, since *she* had tried to kill *him*. But. He would admit the truth before he ever touched her. That way, the ultimate decision—to welcome him into her bed despite his plans—would be hers.

She'll say yes. No one resists for long.

"There's only one thing I'll beg for, and that's your absence!" she bellowed.

Or not.

How nice of her shrewy side to come out to play again. "Shall I prove to you, to everyone, I've *already* lit your wick, duna?" Had he? Could he do it again?

More color drained from her cheeks, leaving her pale and waxen, a sight those primal instincts found disturbing. She opened her mouth, closed it. Opened, closed. Only choking sounds emerged.

Yeah, that's what I thought.

"Go ahead," Sunny said, calling his bluff. "Try. I could use a good laugh."

As Pandora climbed the dais to stand behind the speakers, she smashed her hands over her mouth, smothering a grin. Green hung back to guard the door, a pillar of muscle; he let *his* grin loose.

How had William forgotten his audience? The codebreakers had begun to freak out, muttering among themselves, eyeing the doors.

He called, "Attention, ladies and genitalmen. I'm abducting everyone in this room. If you resist…don't resist."

Protests sounded, one after the other. A man stood and ran for the door.

Staring at his unicorn once more, William lifted the dagger-gun and aimed at the male. A tap of the trigger. A bit of a recoil. A slight *pop*. The observers whimpered. The victim grunted; with a brand-new hole between his eyes—this season's top fashion accessory—he dropped.

A savage action on William's part, yes. Merciless. Heinous. Yes, those, too. All necessary.

Someone screamed. Several someones, actually, everyone but Sunny peering at him with horror. She regarded the dead body with satisfaction. Another shock.

Though he'd seen everything the world had to offer, good and bad, she continued to surprise him.

"Quiet," he shouted, and the screaming ceased. Excellent. "I have a book written in code. One of you will break the code, or all of you will die." The only way to truly pinpoint his lifemate? The book.

An-n-nd the screams were replaced by whimpers.

Why had he planned to kill his codebreaker? What if she managed to break the curse within the two-week time frame? His great problem would be solved, and he'd have no reason to kill her. He could then have the unicorn as much or as little as he desired, thereby ridding himself of this attraction.

Yes! Want her so bad my balls ache. Need her.

No! I need no one. But the want…

Oh, the wicked things I'll do to her.

Excitement lashed his control, until anger usurped the excitement. *Manage your expectations. She might fail.*

He figured they had fifty-fifty odds. *Hope for the best, plan for the worst.*

"In the meantime," he continued, "you'll be my prisoners. The rules are simple. Try to escape, and you'll be punished. Resist my demands, and I'll do to your loved ones what I did to your friend. Cause harm to another prisoner, and I'll cause even worse harm to you. I'll cross any line to get my way. Understand?"

A chorus of protests, sobs and shrieks assailed his ears, every face evincing extreme terror—Sunny remained the exception. His luscious unicorn displayed more of that fury.

Am I about to receive another visit from Killer Unicorn Barbie?

From the corner of his eye, he noticed one of the speakers slipping to the floor and attempting to crawl to the back door. Pandora noticed, too, and performed a badass tackle, knocking the woman out with a single punch.

Fear turned humans into idiots. William spread his arms, the last sane man in the universe. "Anyone else want to ignore my warning? No? Excellent." Now, to open a portal. A process as easy as breathing, thanks to the runes Hades had branded into his flesh—swirling golden designs set in a Fibonacci sequence, as subtly raised as scars. Those runes turned his body into a mystical conduit.

Most unnatural magic wielders burned through whatever they absorbed. They had to kill someone with magic to acquire more. What William took, he kept...until he took too much and expelled it, making horsemen.

With a wave, he utilized enough magic to torch a hole in the center of the room. Sparks crackled in the air, growing and spreading, creating a seven-by-seven-foot doorway that led to William's palace. More specifically, a doorless, soundproof bunkroom underneath the palace.

At the creation of the portal, the crowd nearly rioted.

Pandora hefted the unconscious bolter over her shoulder and said, "Ladies first." With a salute to William, she carted the human through the portal, into the bunkroom, where she stayed.

"Be quiet, line up and walk through," William commanded the others. Most cried and shook, but all obeyed.

Yet again, Sunny was an exception. She stood her ground, radiating challenge.

Her unwillingness to back down, even for a moment, threatened to put him in a lather. She deserved praise. And a spanking.

When his son approached her, intending to…what? William shook his head, saying, "What's the golden rule, Greenie?" His son despised the nickname, so of course he used it as frequently as possible.

Green took a page from Panda's book and flipped him off. "You sure you don't need help with her?" He hiked a thumb in Sunny's direction. "She seems feral."

"She *is* feral." William strode over and shoved his son through the portal, fixated on his unicorn, the sole remaining occupant in the ballroom. *So lovely. So powerful.*

I prefer meek, biddable females, remember? Then why was steam rising from his boiling blood, fogging his mind?

Inner shake. "Desirous of another kiss, duna? Why else would you disobey a direct order?"

She smirked. "How fitting. You deem your kisses a punishment, too."

Her come-hither voice swept over him, and he decided his must-haves were due for a change. Forget meek and biddable. *Snarky* and *voice of a porn star* now topped the list. Then her words registered, and he scowled, his ego taking another hit. *Little witch.*

"I'll go as your guest," she said, "not your prisoner."

"As if you have a choice."

"Are you sure this is the hill you want to die upon? As a guest, I reward. As a captive, I punish."

Tone wry, he said, "I'll risk it."

"Very well." How did excitement *and* rage coat her words? "What does *duna* mean to you, anyway?"

"Abyss of darkness." The nickname served as a reminder for William. His friends might consider their women beacons of light, but he could not do the same. If Sunny proved to be the one, she would destroy him *if* he let her. "Would you prefer 'My Little Horned Pony'?"

"Horned—" Fluttering a hand over her heart, she stumbled back. "You know what I am."

"I do. Just as you know what I am. A ruthless killer with an agenda."

Now terror darkened her features. The sight threw him, an unexpected pang ripping through his gut. At least he didn't have to wonder why she'd reacted so strongly. Last night he'd done his homework. Since the dawn of time, unicorns had been hunted. Poachers removed their horns to grind up and snort, to use as a magic wand or to sell. Collectors either killed and stuffed the unicorns for display, or kept them alive and caged.

Most immortal species feared the magical beasts, since you never knew which side of their nature you'd get. The loving saint, or the hated sinner. Sometimes unicorns spread joy, other times fear. Sometimes they aided, sometimes they killed without remorse. Damn if William wasn't intrigued by both.

"You have no reason to fear me, Sunny." Yet. "For fourteen days, I will be your protector. Poachers and collectors will be murdered on sight. I'll put a sign on my door and everything."

Adopting a defensive stance, she said, "Why such a short time frame? What happens on day fifteen?"

Perceptive female. "We'll discuss it later." *After I've decided which path to walk with you, but before we have sex.*

Sex is now a forgone conclusion, then? He'd changed his mind too many times.

"I don't know how you survived my magic bullet," she said, menace pulsing from her. "Unless you're a cockroach-shifter?"

He ran his tongue over his teeth. Did she hope to spur an attack, so she'd have an excuse to strike at him, or did she believe insulting him would sending him fleeing?

"If you mean *cock-shifter*, then yes. That is what I am." As casually as possible, he asked, "So you'll offer no apology for your actions last night?" Not even the pretense of one?

"I probably *should* apologize," she grumbled. "I mean, immortals usually regenerate exact replicas of lost body parts, but you…your face… My bad." She exaggerated a wince.

I'm hot as fire, damn it.

"People apologize for accidents or regrets," she said. "I *meant* to shoot you, so I'm not remorseful." She pointed at the dead codebreaker. "Do you plan to apologize to Harry?"

He offered a negligent shrug. "Professor Willy needed to teach an unforgettable lesson to his class. Harry volunteered."

"And when did you speak with Harry?"

"After I recovered from my face swap with the floor." He'd returned to the hotel, intending to sneak into Sunny's room and teach her a lesson. Never mess with William King. But, he'd spotted this Harry guy in the bar, spiking a woman's drink. Rape was a crime he avenged swiftly and without exception, so, he'd rushed to intervene, stealing the woman away and locking her in her room, alone. Not killing Harry then and there had been the true challenge. But, William ultimately decided to punish Harry in front of the other codebreakers, proving he wasn't some closeted white knight they could manage. "His T-shirt offended me."

"You mean the T-shirt covered in smiley faces?"

"You hate it, too?" All right, enough banter. *Ticktock.* William prowled closer, saying, "Don't worry, duna. Your punishment is an all-night tongue-lashing."

Intrigue lit those amber eyes, and he did a double take. She *liked* the idea?

He shot harder than stone. Shit! He liked it, too.

Before she had a chance to respond, making his desire worse, he grated, "I have a message for you. Are you listening?"

Sunny pasted on a brittle smile and gave a royal wave. "Today's your lucky day. I remembered to wear my listening ears. Do continue."

Smart-ass. The closer he came, the faster she breathed, her breasts rising and falling. *She wants me; she just doesn't want to want me.* Satisfaction stirred in the marrow of his bones.

Finally, he stood a whisper away. He inhaled her maddeningly sweet scent and drank in those sparkling eyes, so like liquid gold. Awe nearly dropped him to his knees.

"Well," she prompted, a little irritated and a lot anticipatory. "Let's hear the message."

Yes. Let's. Voice low and smoky, he said, "You tried to kill me. Therefore, you owe me a life-debt, and I *will* collect. From now on, you are my property. Every breath you take is my gift to you. Meaning, yes. I *own* you, body and soul."

As she sputtered, William's darkest instincts went to war with his lightest. *Punish. Possess. Protect.*

He would. Nothing would stop him. Oh, the things he would do to this woman…

6

"My humbleness is one of my greatest attributes."

A THOUSAND THOUGHTS jumbled together, creating a quagmire of confusion in Sunny's mind. Only one remained untangled and crystal clear. William King did, in fact, light her wick. Her body craved his, hunger gnawing at her.

Had he aided Lucifer all those centuries ago? She didn't know anymore.

Did he truly own a coded book and require a translator? Yes. That, she believed. At the start of the workshop, Jaybird and Cash had droned on and on about William, a "hot piece of beefcake with photos of a unique code." But why protect the codebreakers for only two weeks?

The exact same time frame as mating season.

Her instincts pinged. *Something's fishy here.* If he desperately needed the book decoded, why not give her the time she needed to succeed?

For that question and a thousand other reasons, she

would not be trusting William with her life, even for two short weeks. Why should she? The man considered her a dark abyss. He defied her magic and wielded his own. And let's not forget his propensity for murdering people sporting novelty tees.

"I'm not going with you, William," she said. "My acquaint—friend is still missing. I'd hoped she'd be here. Alas." She pressed her lips into a thin line, going quiet. Her chin trembled. *I am near tears?*

No, never. And there was no reason to share her secrets with a man, any man, especially one who tied her insides into knots…and turned her into lust on legs.

Already Sunny burned and quaked, her body starved for pleasure. And cuddles! Oh, what she wouldn't give for the after-sex cuddles so many people took for granted. When you had no one and nothing, the smallest bit of affection made the biggest difference to your mind-set. But she couldn't enjoy a man unless she felt safe. So. Yeah. She'd never enjoyed a man. But she wanted to. Badly.

"I'll send my best tracker to find her," William promised.

So he could bag and tag another unicorn? "No, thanks." *Sable can take care of herself. No doubt she got spooked, ran and plans to hole up until the coast is clear.*

Besides, Sable had lived thousands of years without Sunny. She could survive a couple weeks more, yes?

Daisy! Sunny didn't know. She *could* use William's help. William…who'd dressed as a living lollipop today. His pink T-shirt read Save the Boobies and stretched taut across his chest and biceps. Black leather pants molded to powerful legs. With his dark hair in disarray and a night's worth of beard scruff on his jaw, he sent her heart into overdrive.

"Lookit. Part of me *is* sorry I caused you pain," she said, and she meant it. "The other part of me will *never* be sorry." Yep. She meant that, too. Dual natured and all that jazz. "You provoked me, and also, I have a legit beef with your family."

He did that annoying brow lift thing and slowly circled her, his stride graceful but predatory. "Are you saying I asked for it?"

"No. I'm saying you *begged* for it. *Shoot me, then,*" she mocked, following his movements. She peered into his electric blues as his wicked scent filled her nose, and his delicious heat enveloped her. Her defenses began to crumple.

All night she'd tossed and turned, worried about Sable and hyperfocused on William, glad he'd survived the gunshot and shockingly eager for his return. Even though he'd basically vowed revenge.

She'd wondered how she would react to the sight of him. Now she knew. *Breathless. Racing heart. Puckered nipples. Aching core.*

How did he react to the sight of her?

Sunny dragged her gaze down his broad chest and gasped. A massive erection strained his fly. A rush of feminine power flooded her, leaving her dazed and light-headed. He might consider her a dark abyss, but he craved her, too.

"Sunny." He snapped his fingers in front of her face. "My cock is a work of art, I know, but you must combat your fascination and concentrate on the matter at hand."

A flush warmed her cheeks. "If you don't want people mentally measuring your cockscomb—" the use of a flower in this particular situation, with this particular male, made the flush a thousand degrees hotter "—don't put it on display."

"Cockscomb?" He belted out a sensual laugh, amusement transforming his features from darkly sardonic to sinfully angelic. "I haven't put anything on display...yet."

Sunny's heart raced faster. She didn't give jack-sage about that "yet." Only here and now mattered.

"With its immense length and gargantuan girth," he said, "my cockscomb cannot be hidden at full salute."

Her panties all but disintegrated. "Men! You're all obsessed with your genitals."

"Women! You're all obsessed with my genitals."

Argh! He had a comeback for everything, didn't he? She scowled. "News flash. A penis doesn't make you special."

"Counterpoint. *This* penis makes me *very* special."

If she shifted into a unicorn and stabbed him with her horn, no one would blame her.

"Just out of curiosity," he said, canting his head to the side, "if you were a car, what kind would you be?"

Daisy! Why did he have to remind her of their first meeting, when she'd asked about pizza? It made him seem nice and normal, and she didn't have the strength to resist. "I'd be a food truck, because I serve what you order. And you? Wait. I'll guess. You'd be a Viper, because you're a snake."

"Wrong. I'd be a tank, because I mow down any obstacles in my way."

Why, why, why did she find his answer so sexy?

Inhale, exhale. She glanced at the portal. A glittery veil of dappled air. The muscly bald man stood front and center, watching her. Ready to act if Sunny struck at William? The hard-core brunette corralled the freaked-out codebreakers.

Not yet ready to decide whether to go or fight to stay, she stalled, asking, "Who are your friends?"

"My sister, Pandora, and my son Green." The ease of his admission surprised her.

So did the connection. William had a son? The two looked nothing alike. Although, they *did* possess a similar blurry aura. Difference was, Green's aura had specks of emerald and black, a strange mix of life and death.

"I've always wanted a sibling," she admitted. A ready-made friend who *had* to love her. Someone who would listen to her complain about her problems and offer advice. Right now, Sunny had Sable. But. Before the conference, she hadn't seen the unicorn in over one hundred and seventy-five years. Before *that*, she hadn't seen her for three centuries.

The lack of companionship bothered her. Unicorns were pack-minded creatures, far stronger together than apart. The bigger the pack, the easier it was to control their dark sides.

"Sunny," William said, then sighed with impatience. Gah! She'd gotten lost in her head again. A dangerous habit to indulge. "This is your last chance to enter the portal of your own volition."

Or what? He'd throw her over his shoulder fireman-style? *Shiver*.

She looked at the portal…then William. The portal. William. To escape or not to escape? Maybe, by helping William with his book, she'd have opportunities to learn more about his family, discover their greatest weaknesses, hideouts and fears, and finally execute Lucifer. But, again, she'd be a prisoner.

And what about Sable? Was the other unicorn truly okay? "You know what I am," Sunny said, lifting her chin. "What if you decide to steal my horn?" *I'll stop him.* Yes, but what if he locked her up, forever? *I'll escape.* If she had to fight her way free, she would. He'd never be able to stop her.

"Keep your horn to yourself, and we won't have any problems," he said, his derisive tone a real teeth-grinder.

"Come to my palace, decode my book, and I'll escort you to Lucifer's home. You wish to kill him, yes?"

She sucked in a breath. Her greatest desire! But had William spoken a truth or a lie? With him, she couldn't tell. "If you truly are at war with your brother, I'll be doing you two favors. Decoding your book and killing your brother. How is that fair to me?"

"Ex-brother. If you break the curse in the two-week time frame, I'll give you anything you want. Absolutely anything."

Her heart leaped. "What about the other codebreakers? Will you let them go unharmed if I can decode your book?"

"I will, yes." He gave the assurance with zero hesitation and one hundred percent confidence, as if he'd just made a blood oath, and she thought, hoped, he'd meant it.

"All right. Show me a photo of the book."

He went still, his intent expression bordering on psychotic. Then he held out a hand. Did she detect a slight tremor? A second later, a photograph appeared over his palm.

She lifted and studied the image. An open book, with two yellowed pages visible. They were frayed at the edges and littered with odd symbols she'd never before seen. But…the code remained unbroken.

Truly a first for Sunny, and she frowned. No matter the complexity of a code, cipher or encryption, her magic always unlocked the truth. Why not now?

Maybe she *wasn't* the one William needed. And that was fine. Whatever. *So why do I want to beat the one who is?* "I got nothing. Either I'm not the one you seek, or I need to see the original pages."

His mood changed in an instant, a toxic mix of dis-

appointment, frustration and fury crackling in his irises.
"You'll work with photographs or nothing."

"Oh. Okay. In that case, I'll go with nothing."

"You'll go with whatever I tell you," he bellowed. As
his voice echoed from the walls, he blanched. He inhaled
sharply, exhaled slowly. More calmly, he asked, "Do you
have the skill to decipher it or not?"

Realization: the code, whatever it was, didn't mean a
great deal to him—it meant *everything* to him. "Maybe.
Probably," she admitted, stuffing the photo into her pocket.
"Without the original pages, it'll take more time." A lot
more.

"My offer hasn't changed. Two weeks, in exchange for
a trip to Lucifer's home. Succeed, and you can name your
prize." He waved to the portal, somehow making the action more menacing than his gun.

"My offer hasn't changed, either. Despite our agreed-
upon give-and-take, I'll still be a prisoner, so, I *will* punish you."

He shrugged. Shrugged! *He does not fear my wrath...yet.*
But he would.

Decision made. Head high and palms sweating, she
walked through the glittery air of her own volition. Magic
tickled her skin, the strongest magic she'd ever encountered.

One second she stood in a hotel ballroom, the next she
stood in a bunkroom, aka military barracks. A row of bunk-
beds lined each plain white wall. A couch and table occupied the center of the enclosure, creating a common meeting
space. In back, there was a small kitchenette complete with
a sink, stove and locked refrigerator. There were no decorations, no colors. No doors, either. Not that she could see.

The other codebreakers huddled in a far corner, most
crying, the rest whispering words of comfort.

William entered behind Sunny. Exuding complete satisfaction, he moved to Sunny's side. "Has everyone been disarmed?" he asked his sibling.

"Yep," his sister replied. Her brow wrinkled with distaste. "I confiscated a handful of nail files and tweezers."

"I could kill everyone here with a nail file or a pair of tweezers." As he spoke, he pivoted into Sunny, just as he'd done in the elevator. His warm breath fanned her face, his hard, muscular chest pressing against her breasts. Eyes magnetic and hypnotic, he leaned down, putting his mouth at her ear. "Time for *your* weapons check, duna."

Her heart rate picked up speed, her nerve endings tingling. Sage! How did he affect her so strongly?

How else? He was the epitome of seduction and temptation, and she had no defenses.

"Go ahead," she said, hating the quiver in her voice. "Get your mauling and pawing over with."

"Mauling and pawing?" A muscle jumped underneath his eye. He hooked one hand around her waist and yanked her closer. Every point of contact sparked a current of electricity, and she trembled.

His gaze never left hers as he unwound her braid and pulled out the pens. Her scalp tingled. Next, he ran his big, calloused hands over her shoulders, down her arms and her sides, then along her legs. Every weapon he encountered, he dropped. Three daggers, the gun-ring and a locket filled with poison. The medallion—the most powerful weapon—he studied but left alone. Fool! All the while, she floundered between total vulnerability, abject helplessness and wild arousal.

In the end, the arousal won. Sweet freesia! *His hands on me...feel so good.* Trust issues, smush issues. Sunny couldn't remember the last time she'd enjoyed a touch, or anticipated *more*.

Maybe, just maybe, she could keep her mind in the game if he kissed her again...

Nope. As soon as she got into it, enjoying herself, paranoia set in, and she stiffened. *A single moment of distraction can cost you* everything. "Hurry up," she demanded.

"Why? Do you enjoy my touch too much?" He squeezed her waist. "You do, don't you? Don't try to deny it. Your pupils are blown."

Something she'd learned as a child. When you needed to get your point across without admitting the truth, shout. "Deny!"

Unfortunately, he wasn't buying it. And why would he? She'd started to pant. "Tsk-tsk. If you truly wish me to stop, you have to say, *William, darling, I want you to remove your magnificent hands from my aching body.*"

She *couldn't* say those words, so she pressed her lips together instead, acting stubborn.

"Very well." He waved a hand, unleashing a stream of magic. A blurry veil appeared around them, shielding them from the others.

Her breath caught. What did he have planned?

"Must check the rest of you." With a sinfully delicious glint in his baby blues, he moved behind her, pressing his chest flush against her back.

Tremors whipped through her as he reached around to cup her aching breasts. *Tell him to stop. Do it!* But...once again, her mouth refused to obey. *I want more.*

"Be honest," he whispered. "My duna craves passion. *Needs* it. She wants to be ridden."

His duna? *Do not tremble again. Don't you dare.*

"Wrong," she whispered back. "She wants to be ridden *well*."

"And I bring you no pleasure. Say it. Get the insults over with, and I'll move on."

"You spoke…t-true? You're so unskilled?" The words emerged as questions rather than statements, and her cheeks blazed. Oh, how she longed to lie.

"So why haven't you told me to stop?" he rasped, then bit her earlobe. When her nipples stiffened against his palms, he uttered a husky chuckle. "We both know why. Parts of you love these *unskilled* hands."

Mmm. Yes. It was a miracle and an inconvenience. A surprise and a puzzle. Of all the men in all the worlds, why him? Sunny hadn't even desired her husband this intently. Actually, she hadn't desired Blaze, period. He'd been chosen for her.

Her mind drifted to the past…to the day of her sixteenth birthday, when she'd wed Prince Blaze Lane, the king's eldest son. Blaze and Sunny had grown up together, yet they'd never really gotten along. He'd been selfish, and had lacked a backbone and self-control. Neither side of her had respected him. Still, her parents had agreed to the match, so she'd done her duty. If she'd refused, she would have been banished, along with everyone in her line. Mostly, though, she'd said yes because she'd felt fated to rule, had strongly believed Princess Sunny would one day become Queen Sunny.

Alas, Lucifer attacked only a few years later. Her hopes for becoming queen, dashed. Her status as princess, done. Her husband, dead.

At the time of the attack, Sunny had been trapped in a pit, only able to listen to a cacophony of noises. Agonized screams. Gleeful laughter. Unheeded pleas for mercy.

The whoosh of different weapons. Metal clanging against metal. The pop of breaking bones. The gurgle of blood. The wheeze of death. And, of course, Lucifer's war cry, "For William!"

Earlier that week, the king had sentenced her to two weeks of solitary confinement. Her crime? Embarrassing her husband in public.

"—paying attention to me?" William snapped, his irritation clanging like a bell.

"No, I'm not," she admitted, blinking into focus. Gross. She'd gotten lost in her head again. That wasn't good. Wasn't good at all. Attentiveness was often the difference between life and death. "If you must know, I was thinking of another man."

A low growl rumbled deep in his chest. The same growl she'd heard in the elevator, just before he'd kissed her. This time, he dropped his arms, severing contact, and stepped back.

Had she gained the upper hand? That had to bother him. Why not make it worse? "Shouldn't you do a body cavity search? I could be packing daggers in my panties."

Menace palpable, he released an angry huff and waved his hand, erasing the veil that separated them from the others. "I'll return in an hour to meet with each of you privately. You will show me the extent of your decoding talents. Be ready." Without casting a glance her way, he opened a new portal.

After his sister and son had walked through, he followed on their heels. Why this fit of pique? Unless... Had the thought of her with someone else roused jealousy?

No. No way. She shifted from one slipper to the other. But hopefully? She'd promised him punishment, after all. What better way to start?

"You sure you want to go?" Sunny called, fighting a grin. "No telling what I'll do, or who I'll do it with, while you're gone."

The muscles in his back knotted, bulging, and he faced her once again. Rage simmered in his eyes. "Do whatever you wish, with whomever you wish."

Bluebell! *His dismissal doesn't matter. Actually,* he *doesn't matter.*

"Where are you going?" she grumbled. "Why do you need an hour?" Before, he'd frothed at the mouth, eager to get his book decoded. Now he couldn't wait to abandon ship? Why?

"Perhaps there's a beautiful woman waiting in my bed, ready for my return. Someone who doesn't think of others while she's with me."

Her temper took the wheel, and she snipped, "Good! You could use the practice." No doubt this nameless, faceless woman would be screaming his name in a matter of minutes. Sunny balled her hands. *Hold up. Now* I'm *jealous?*

Maybe. Probably. But he was for sure jealous, too. No doubt about it now. In this, they were equals.

And now I want to grin? Well, yeah. No one had ever been jealous over her before.

Another growl rumbled from William. Behind him, both Green and Pandora gave her a pitying glance.

"What?" she snapped at them.

The newest portal closed before they had a chance to respond. Silence reigned in the bunkroom, thick and oppressive.

Then everyone spoke at once.

"What are we going to do?"

"That man killed Harry. Shot him dead."

"How well do you know our captors, Sunny?"

"I don't," she admitted. She needed to pick a bed and set traps, ensuring no one approached her while she slept. *If* she slept.

If there'd been a narrator for her life, they would have said: "She won't."

Lots of scrambling ensued. Some people beat at the walls, searching for a hidden doorway. Others attempted to create one.

She selected a bottom bunk and plopped onto the mattress, her thoughts whirling. What if she used William for more than a mystical Uber to Lucifer? He said he'd grant any boon if she decoded the book, so, why not make him hunt and kill the immortals on her list, all those poachers and collectors? That'd mean no more running. No more hiding. Not for her, and not for the other unicorns.

For the short term, William could be an incredible ally.

Excitement skyrocketed, only to crash. She'd have to trust him with the names—men and women he could then portal straight to her door, encouraging an ambush.

Despite everything, she kinda sorta *wanted* to trust him. In this, and only this. However, wanting to do something didn't always mean you *should*.

So. Should she?

And what about the approach of mating season? Shivers of dread and eagerness trekked down her spine. When extreme lust set in, and it would, her trust issues would cease to matter. She would crave sex, sex and more sex. With anyone nearby. What if she used her boon to request William's services?

She'd never experienced mating season with a lover, not even Blaze. They hadn't wanted to risk a pregnancy, so she'd chained herself...while Blaze slept with another.

William could maybe, possibly use magic to prevent a pregnancy.

Was he in bed with another woman right this second?

A ripping sound yanked her from her musings, and Sunny blinked into focus. Her claws were bared and buried in the bedsheet, the linen shredded in spots. Well, no help for it now. The damage was done.

She let her thoughts return to William. She'd meant what she'd said. She would help him with his book *and* tormenting him. Unicorn torture involved little things guaranteed to make him as uncomfortable as possible. Like baking his least favorite food and guilting him into eating it. Or shrinking his favorite sweater in the wash. To start. The punishments grew increasingly hard-core.

But. She had two weeks. She'd need to get to the hard-core punishments sooner rather than later. How else would William learn not to mess with a unicorn?

As long as he kept her locked up, he would get no relief.

Her lips curved into a grin. *This is going to be fun—for me!* If he set her free, then and only then would she stop the punishments. If he refused to let her go at the end of their two weeks, as promised, the punishments would stop. Because she would kill him dead.

Sunny shuddered, the grin fading. At least she knew just what to do to make him miserable...

7

"I once gave Death a near-William experience."

HE'D DONE IT. William had successfully imprisoned every codebreaker on his list, plus a few extras to use as leverage. He'd interrogated everyone but Sunny, and every single codebreaker had told him, "You should talk to Sunny Lane. She can do things no one else can." Which meant...

She's the one.

Had she decoded the page of his book and lied about it? Did it matter? If she was his codebreaker, she was also his lifemate, and she had to die in two weeks. *If* she failed to break the curse. Exactly as planned.

It's her or it's me. Choose.

Me.

Yet, lust for her continued to blaze in his veins. Only lust. He kept replaying the moments he'd held her in his arms. The lush softness of her breasts, with their hardened peaks. How he'd almost fallen to his knees like a lovesick fool.

Damn it, he'd never reacted to a woman this quickly or this intensely, obsessing about her, and possessive of her. Not even Gillian. He'd wanted her, but he hadn't needed her. He hadn't craved her while they were apart.

I don't need Sunny, either, damn it. He pounded a fist into his desk, a crack spreading from one side to the other. But, just as swiftly as the crack appeared, it vanished, repaired by magic.

When Sunny admitted she'd thought about another man as William patted her down, he'd wanted to shove a dagger in the bastard's gut. He'd even warned other men away from a woman like some human with low self-esteem and zero confidence. A first. He'd told them, *Touch her, and I will eat the marrow from your bones.*

Would *she* touch *them*?

Wham, wham. He punched the desk twice more. The woman teased and tormented William the way he'd teased and tormented so many of his lovers, driving him half-mad.

Face it, Panty Melter. Sunny is *the one.*

With a groan, he flopped back in his seat. He might have found his lifemate, but he couldn't wrap his mind around a long-term relationship. Would he ever be able to relinquish his dreams of kingship and variety to settle down with one woman, playing house and raising brats? What if he missed out on something better?

His heart raced. He fought to breathe, just as he'd done as a child, the walls seeming to close in around him.

"You look constipated. Thinking about your Sunshine?"

Green stood in the doorway of his office, his voice wrenching William from the first stirring of panic. He sucked in a much-needed breath. Then again. And again. Finally, his heart rate slowed.

"I'm thinking about lifemates," he replied, choosing to be somewhat vague. "And her name is Sunny. Sunday."

His son shuddered. "Lifemates? How sensitive of you. Are you on your period or something?"

William deadpanned, "Yes, but I'm out of tampons. Have an extra in your purse?"

Green snickered at him. "Sorry, but the only thing I'm packing are these guns." He flexed his biceps.

William rolled his eyes. His attention snagged on a framed photograph of a beautiful brunette. He traced a finger over her sweet face. At the age of fifteen, Gillian had run away from home to escape years of sexual abuse. But she'd fared no better on the streets. Physically, mentally and emotionally battered, she'd been desperate for a protector.

At sixteen, she'd moved in with the Lords. Back then, she'd been a quiet little mouse with shattered eyes. One look at her and William had relived his own abuse; he'd longed to give Gillian a better life. And, over the next two years, he had, teasing smiles and laughter out of her. Some nights, they'd played video games till dawn. Mostly, he'd safeguarded her present and future, building an investment portfolio to ensure she'd never need anyone for anything.

As her eighteenth birthday had neared, William had truly believed he loved her romantically, that they would be together for a time and leave their pasts behind. At the same time, he'd continued to sleep with other women, anyone who caught his fancy, never really committing to Gillian. Soon, she'd decided to commit to another male, a beastly king possessed by the demon of Indifference. Puck of Amaranthia adored her and desired no others. A circumstance William had once lamented but now celebrated.

Truth was, he'd seen himself in her. He'd wanted to love her, just as he'd once wanted someone to love *him*.

"Wonderful. You're lost in your head again." Again, Green snickered at him. "You might want to pep up. Grandpa is here to see you."

Grandpa? William laughed. "I'm confident Hades prefers Pop Pop. He'll rage if you call him anything else." He cast his gaze over the spacious office. Nothing out of place. Excellent. Above the fireplace hung a portrait of William wearing a whipped cream bikini, holding a sparkler in one hand and a banana in the other. A real classy piece, and a gift from Anya, the minor goddess of Anarchy as well as his oldest friend. In fact, she was engaged to Lucien, the keeper of Death and a coleader of the Lords.

Bookshelves graced every wall, displaying part of his collection of skulls—men, women and creatures he'd killed. Or, in Claw's case, the skull of a man who'd been killed on his behalf. He kept Gillian's entire family in his bedroom: the stepfather, both stepbrothers and even the mother, who'd accused her of lying about the abuse. His crowning glory, however? Lilith's. Satisfaction stirred deep in his chest every time he glimpsed it.

He told his son, "Send him in."

"Why don't I send myself in?" Hades strode past Green, his lips curved in a sardonic smile. "Also, the first one to call me Pop Pop gets a boot to the short and curlies."

William barked a laugh. Damn, he loved this complicated, mysterious man. Hades had raised him with an iron fist, tolerating zero disrespect. He'd helped William shed his "Scum" identity, snuff out and destroy his greatest weaknesses, and ensured he had the skill to survive anywhere, anytime, no matter the hardships. In the king's care,

William had flourished; he'd been safe, content and adored, a tri-miracle few experienced in their lifetime.

"Careful," Green said to Hades. "Daddy Dearest is in a *mood*. He's contemplating lifemates."

Hades stiffened, no doubt assuming the mate in question was Gillian. He'd never liked the girl, not for William. *And now I understand why.*

"I'll risk it," the king responded, his tone dry. Smoothing the lines of his pin-striped suit, he eased into the seat across from the desk.

I recognize this suit. Hades changed his appearance on the reg. To him, clothing doubled as a weapon. William had seen him wear everything from a tux, to black leather, to crocheted underwear and decorative beard beads. Just depended on his audience. He only wore the suit when he wanted to look like a partner in a law firm and swindle someone.

When Hades dismissed Green with a tilt of his chin, Green looked to William, one brow arched. He nodded, and his son left, shutting the door behind him.

Am I to be the swindled? If Hades had heard about the unicorn and hoped to use her as a weapon...

William curled his fingers around the arms of his chair, his claws cutting into the leather. "What's going on?" He loved and admired Hades, yes, but he also recognized the male's faults. Hades was power hungry, zealous in his determination and blinded to anything outside his endgame—whatever his endgame happened to be. He rarely shared his goals with anyone.

"I'm here to discuss war business." Hades leaned back, getting more comfortable. "Counting us, we have nine kings of the underworld, two princes, a princess, three horsemen, thirteen Lords, a minor goddess, the keeper of nightmares, a hellhound trainer, the son of a gorgon and dragon-shifter, not to mention the Harpies, the queen of Titans, the queen of Fae, a seer who peers into heaven and hell, and a Sent One. We even have the Red Queen. We should be unstoppable, and yet we have failed to neutralize Lucifer, a piece of shit with only legions of demons at his disposal." He scoured a hand over his weary face. "If we lose this war, we do not deserve to live."

Agreed. Harpies were as bloodthirsty and strong as unicorn-shifters. Sent Ones commanded armies of angels and assassinated demons. Everyone else had powers and abilities beyond imagining. They *should* have this in the bag.

"His demons outnumber us ten to one," William pointed out.

"Doesn't matter. We should have defeated him already."

Hades wasn't wrong. "If we want different results, we'll have to do something different."

"Exactly. I have a plan to reduce his numbers, giving us a bigger advantage."

"I'm in." The bastard had grown into the world's most prolific rapist. Gender, age and species never factored into it. He tortured and murdered with abandon, leaving no one safe. Rumors suggested he liked to sneak his minions of disease out of Hell just to infect humans. "What do you need me to do?"

"We'll get to that. But first." Hades flashed a scowl, there and gone. "Earlier today, I consulted my mirror about your list of decoders."

The mirror. A magic glass with Siobhan, the Goddess of Many Futures trapped inside it.

"Are you sure we can trust her to aid us?" William asked. She blamed Hades for her captivity.

Same as Sunny blames me for hers.

What had the unicorn said? *As a guest, I reward. As a captive, I punish.*

How did she expect to punish him?

"Yes and no," Hades said. "Either way, you need to know what Siobhan showed me."

"Which is?"

"A blue-haired woman holding a vial of poison. According to Pandora, you have a blue-haired woman among your captives."

His brow furrowed. "Poison means what exactly?" That Sunny would poison him? Good luck. He'd already confiscated her locket. That their current path was toxic? Too bad. There would be no turning back. That he was destined to die by her hand? Okay, yeah, that one raised concerns, considering the curse.

Voice as hard as steel, Hades said, "I want the blue-haired woman killed, William. Today. *Before* she has a chance to poison you."

A denial rushed across his tongue...a denial he brutally murdered before it escaped. One, a denial would only rally Hades's determination, and two, Hades might decide to take the matter into his own hands. When it came to his few loved ones, "murder the threat" was his go-to answer.

There was only one proclamation that would make the king back down. "Keeley says Sunny is not to be harmed for two weeks, because the girl is...my lifemate."

Hades valued Keeley's insight. Interest gleamed in his eyes as he sat up straighter. "Keeley told *me* your lifemate has the power to destroy us all."

No wonder the king had wanted Gillian murdered, too.

And wasn't this more evidence of Sunny's connection to him, and another reason to kill her quick? A muscle ticked in William's jaw. "If she has the power to destroy us, she has the power to destroy Lucifer as well, aiding us."

"But why risk it?" Hades white-knuckled the arms of his chair. He was *that* concerned for William's safety? "Keep your vow. Let *me* kill the girl...and burn your book. Mates are overrated, anyway."

"No!" William bellowed. Cheeks heating, he repeated more calmly, "No. For the next two weeks, no one, and I do mean no one, is to touch, harm or even yell at her."

Hades slitted his gaze. "So you hold out hope this Sunny will break your curse and what? The two of you will live happily ever after?"

No. Yes. Maybe? Minus "ever after," of course. But what kind of (temporary) future could he build with the woman who derived little pleasure from his kiss, trusted no one and insulted him regularly?

Wild and crazy? Problematic? Fulfilling?
You won't know until you try.

"Help me help you, son," Hades said. "Do not be the fool who romantically pursues the woman predicted to end his life. Do burn your book. I know curses, and I've never sensed one in you."

"We've talked about this. You can't sense the curse, because it hasn't activated. First, I must fall in love." He lifted a pen and repeatedly whacked the edge of the desk. "Forget the girl and the book." For now. "Tell me why you rescued me as a boy." The only topic guaranteed to shut down any conversation, anywhere, anytime.

He'd made the request before, but he'd only ever received a nonanswer: *I wanted to, so I did.* Fact was, Hades did nothing without an ulterior motive. A fact William greatly admired. Why give if you weren't going to get?

Glowering now, Hades rubbed his fingers over his beard

stubble. "We've talked about this," he said, mimicking William. "I won't discuss this topic. Explaining my reasons might result in a *genuine* curse and lead to your death."

But how? Why? William dropped the pen, leaned back in his chair and locked his fingers behind his head. "All right. Tell me why you made me vow to avoid the Sent One named Axel." *The one I suspect is my brother.*

"You know why," the king snapped. "The day you meet Axel, a part of you will die."

So confusing! "What part of me? Why?"

Silence reigned. Hades's lips pressed into a thin line.

Frustration stormed through William. Sometimes, the desire to know his brother all but choked him, their separation making him feel as if a part of him were *already* dead.

He longed to talk with the Sent One. Were they similar? Or opposites? The warrior longed to talk with William, too; he'd been searching for William for over a year, had even questioned the Lords about his whereabouts. But, he owed his life to Hades. He owed *everything* to Hades, and loved the man unconditionally. If he had to eschew his past to keep his father happy, he would eschew his past. Plain and simple.

Tone guarded, Hades said, "Axel still searches for you."

"And I still avoid him," he grated.

"Good boy." The king stood and adjusted the lines of his jacket. "Before I go, we have a final piece of business."

Great. Wonderful. He performed a royal wave. "Let's hear it."

"I requested a meeting with Lucifer to discuss a truce. Tomorrow morning, eight sharp. You will attend."

"A truce?" he roared, jumping to his feet. The chair skidded behind him, slamming into the wall.

"Don't worry, my son. He'll show up, but he won't accept. Exactly as I hope."

Though William had too much on his plate already, he unveiled his coldest smile. "I'll attend. For a price. Just like you taught me. Do nothing without requiring something in return."

To his surprise, Hades smiled. "I know just what to offer." A large, jagged crystal appeared on the desk, a rainbow of color trapped inside. "That is a Sphere of Knowledge."

"I know what it is." He'd seen pictures. There were four in existence, each one specializing in a different type of knowledge. "I just didn't know you'd acquired one."

Pride smoldered in Hades's dark eyes. "A recent purchase. This one reveals cold, hard facts about anyone or thing. Like, say, a lifemate. But I caution you to choose your questions wisely. You are only allotted ten."

William grinned. He could learn a lot with ten questions. "How do I operate it?"

"Easily. Simply ask it a question, and it will respond." With a wink, Hades flashed away, moving from one location to another with only a thought.

William glanced at the crystal, trembled like a puss and decided to pour himself two…three…four fingers of whiskey first. By the time he'd polished off the glass, he'd steadied. He made a list of his questions, then refocused on the sphere.

Gripping the arms of his chair, he asked the first. "Why did Lucifer slaughter the unicorn-shifters?"

Light shot from the tip of the crystal, an image taking shape inside it. A tiny pixie with white hair, gold skin and translucent, glittery wings. She hovered there, devoid of emotion. "A powerful oracle told Lucifer a unicorn would aid you in his defeat. Desperate to negate the prediction, he led legions of demons to the Realm of Mythstica, intending to slay every unicorn in existence. Only, he failed in his endeavors. There were six survivors."

William licked his suddenly dry lips. So much to unpack. A prediction about Lucifer's defeat. But only with Sunny's help?

A cool tide of relief washed over him. *I can't* kill her.

One question down, nine to go. "Where was Sunday Lane during the attack?"

"She was trapped at the bottom of a pit." A new image superseded the pixie, one of war and pain. As screams of fear and pain echoed, an emaciated woman with tangled red hair lay in a puddle of mud and filth, trying to dig her way out with hands tipped by bloody, broken nails.

When she shifted, he caught sight of her face and—

"Fuck!" William exploded from his chair. Once again, his heart pounded, and he heaved his breaths. The redhead was Sunny.

When he'd calmed—slightly—he plopped back into the chair. More information. Now.

Two questions down, eight remaining.

Teeth clenched, he asked, "Are unicorns capable of loyalty?" *Is Sunny?* With her dual nature, the woman wasn't a single spice—she was the entire spice rack.

The pixie returned, telling him, "Oh, yes. But they are only loyal to those in their pack."

Three down. He tossed his list, other questions already forming. "Are outsiders ever accepted into a pack?"

"At times, yes."

He waited for the pixie to say more. She didn't, and he ground his molars. Four down, and only six to go. "What are a unicorn's most dominant personality traits?"

"When unicorns feel safe, they are playful. When fearful, they are violent. Always they are highly territorial and private. To protect their horns, they refuse to shift outside ceremonies and war. To defend their loved ones and homes, they will fight to the death. During mating season, they are highly sexual and desperate for a partner."

Mating season? Two words, and yet he hardened in seconds. "When is mating season?"

"Starts in two weeks, and ends two weeks later."

Two weeks. The exact time frame Keeley had given him. He bellowed another curse. Sunny was close to being "highly sexual and desperate for a partner" and he'd left her in a bunkroom with sixteen males who would no doubt kill to kiss those soft lips, knead those lush breasts and delve their fingers, tongues and cocks into that sweet little body.

For the thousandth time that day, fury scorched William's veins. With every breath, air sliced at his lungs. If Sunny failed to decipher his book in the very short—too short—timeline, she would require a lover.

Who would she choose?

He grabbed the crystal and nearly hurled it into a wall, just to watch the pieces scatter. Instead, he asked his seventh question.

Harkening back to the pixie's statement about unicorns and playfulness, and eager to see Sunny in such a state, he asked, "How can I make a unicorn feel safe?"

"Never lie. Never imprison. Never harm."

Never imprison? Too late. How could he make her feel safe *while* imprisoned?

He wouldn't ask. Only three questions remained. "How is Sunday Lane able to decode at a glance?"

"Magic," the pixie told him. "Magic makes unicorns natural lie detectors—they see truth."

Fascinating.

Only two questions left. *Make them count.* "Why does Sunny's magic not affect me?"

The light dimmed, the pixie fading. He frowned. Did the crystal not know? Or were questions about William forbidden?

He frowned. "Am I truly cursed?" Nothing. "Do you know *anything* about Lilith's curse?" Nothing. "What do you know about a Sent One named Axel?" Again, nothing. Now he scowled. "What else do you know about unicorn-shifters and Sunday Lane in particular?"

A new flare of light, the pixie reappearing. "Get past Princess Sunday's defenses, and you will have a friend for eternity."

His brows shot into his hairline. Princess Sunny? A royal?

When the pixie offered no more, he pursed his lips. "That's it? That's all you'll tell me about her or all you know?"

She grinned slowly, a little wickedly, as adorable as the bride of Chucky. "No. I know more. And, yes, that is all I'll tell you. And now your ten questions have been answered. I bid you farewell, William of the Dark."

What! "I didn't mean—" He pinched the bridge of his nose. Why argue with a beam of light that contained all knowledge of the universe? Manipulation on the other hand... "Go, then. Leave me unsatisfied with your response to my ninth question."

She canted her head to the side. "Hades requested a report of everything you asked, and how I responded. Do you truly wish to learn more, knowing this?"

Should have known. Annoyance scraped at his insides. Still, he nodded. "Tell me." The damage was already done.

"Princess Sunday is a vegetarian, flower petals her favorite meal…snack…and dessert. She can see auras. To her, to all unicorns, color—rainbows—equals life. With her dual nature, she is able to laugh one minute and savagely kill the next. She is stubborn and inquisitive, and she will not be easily seduced."

William absorbed every tidbit, a sense of challenge growing. Not easily seduced? *I'm ready to play the game, coach.*

"That," the pixie said, "is all I know." As the light faded once again, she vanished for good, and he wondered what his distrustful, mulish and curious unicorn was doing right this second. *Must know.*

He jabbed at his computer keyboard, pulling up video feed of the bunkroom. Everyone but Sunny huddled around a single bed, whispering escape strategies. Where…where… there! But what the hell was she doing?

Zooming in. She sat at the edge of a bottom bunk, her head bent as she tore strips of cloth from the comforter to braid together.

There are no windows, yet she makes a rope?

Realization punched him in the throat. *No, she's making a noose.*

Was she feeling frightened and violent, then? *Because of me?* Airways constricting, William picked up his cell phone and dialed Pandora, saying, "Bring me Sunny. And have Green deliver a bouquet of roses. And a sandwich. And chips. And other side dishes." Neither he nor the unicorn had eaten, so they might as well do it together while they had their chat.

One way or another, he and Sunny would come to an understanding. Today.

8

"Take what you want, when you want. I do."

"Yo. Sunny Lane. You're up."

As Sunny's bunkmates fell silent, she studied the speaker. Pandora stood inside a new portal. Behind her was a spacious living room with antique settees and side tables, a crystal chandelier and a finely detailed mural featuring naked females lounging on shells.

How perfectly William. Add some men to the mural, and you'd have Sunny's decorative style, too.

The other codebreakers turned to stare at her, all but pointing.

She rolled her eyes. Throughout the day, Pandora had come and gone, escorting people to William one at a time. Everyone but Sunny. Whatever he'd done and said had filled her fellow prisoners with dread. Even Jaybird and Cash referred to him as a monster now.

Sunny had used the time to start an arsenal. Using pieces

of wood she'd pulled from the bed frames, she'd already made a couple of shivs. At the moment, she crafted a trip wire with a noose at the end. If anyone approached her bed at any point during the night, they would hang for it.

"Is it my turn to speak with William?" A Q and A with the sexiest man alive sounded both terrible and wonderful, and she'd never anticipated and dreaded an activity more.

"It is."

Nerves buzzing, Sunny stuffed her makeshift rope under a pillow, leaped from the bed and stalked over.

Pandora remained on the other side of the portal. "You look like hellebore." She blinked. "Hell...bore. Hellebore. Sage! Freesia! Argh! Why can't I cuss?"

So, the magic censor worked with William's sibling, but not William himself. Why?

Unable to lie, Sunny did her best "who? what? me?" impression and shrugged, then walked through the portal. Huh. No tingles this time. Again, she had to wonder why.

As the doorway whooshed closed behind her, she breathed deep. Notes of ambrosia, whiskey, candle wax and...vegetables? Her stomach rumbled. Yesterday she'd eaten a handful of petals and leaves. Today? Nothing.

"You can gawk at the palace later. Right now, Willy's in a major snit, and I have orders to hand deliver you fast." Pandora wasted no time, striding down a wide hallway.

Sunny followed, stutter-stepping when she noticed the many portraits that decorated the walls. In one, William wore an apron and a smile, nothing else. In another, he had a feather boa wrapped around his penis.

Oh, sweet heat. Was the image true to size, or scaled? Because sage! In a third painting, he reclined on a plush leather chair, naked, reading a copy of *The Darkest Kiss*.

Other books were piled around him, all with *darkest* in the title.

People must look at these images, severely underestimate the darkness of William's nature and relax their guard. His purpose, no doubt. *Wily warrior.* Impressive, too. But the poor bastard had no idea what she planned to do for his first punishment.

Sunny fought a grin. Her plan? Force him to commit to a fake relationship in order to gain her cooperation. Not that he'd know it was fake. *Ah, it's the little things.*

Pandora noticed her preoccupation with the artwork and asked, "Are you a connoisseur of paintings, or William?"

Yeah, no way in hellebore she'd answer that. She changed the subject instead. "Does William prefer to date a certain type of female?" The more she knew, the better she could tailor the torture to his needs and wants, hopes and dreams.

"William connoisseur, then," Pandora said, a teasing twinkle in her dark eyes. "And, yeah, he has a type. It's called breathing. He's a total he-ho. He gets tired of a woman as soon as he nuts."

Nuts? Ohhhh. A term for shooting his load. Got it. They turned a corner. "Has he ever committed to someone?"

"He considered it once," Pandora said. "There was a girl. Gillian. He thought he loved her but they split, so…" Shrug.

Sunny curled her hands into fists, a common reaction whenever William dominated a conversation. A prince of darkness deserved no happiness. "*Thought* he loved?"

"Lookit. I'm not going to give you the gory details. It's not my story to tell. But it's clear you're interested in him, and I get it. You have eyes. So I'll give it to you straight. He used to sleep with married women exclusively, because they never sought a commitment. And even though he thought he loved Gillian, he *still* slept around. Honestly, I doubt he'll ever let himself fall in love and do the whole family thing because of—argh! I've shared too much. I *never* share too much. Why would I do that? You'll get no more out of me."

Perhaps Pandora wished for a girlfriend as desperately as Sunny? "No worries. I've heard enough." She squeezed her fists tighter, bothered by William's former propensity for bedding married women. Like Blaze, he had no respect for the sanctity of marriage. No loyalty or consideration for the people he hurt.

Another reason to punish him, administering unicorn justice...

Switching the direction of the conversation, she said, "So you and William are siblings, huh?"

"Yes and no. We were both adopted by Hades."

Sunny stiffened. Hades, one of nine kings of the underworld. A commander of demons. Death incarnate. Adopted father of Lucifer, too. *Deep breath in, out.* "If demons are black holes of evil, with no hint of goodness, and they are, so are the ones who lead them."

"You are so right," Pandora said with a nod. "But you shouldn't compliment the Hell royals in such a way. It'll only go to their heads."

Funny. "I've done a little research on William, and I know he left the underworld at some point, giving up his territory and his armies."

"Your info is dated. William recently moved back to Hell. I mean, where do we think you are right now?"

Sunny tripped over her own foot. William had taken her to Hell? That...that...bluebell!

Pandora led her into a small office with a massive desk, a metal filing cabinet and a water cooler filled with what looked to be whiskey. No sign of William.

"Hang on. Gotta let him know you're here." Pandora

plopped into the chair behind the desk and picked up the landline. Holding the phone to her ear, she said, "Stuff your man meat back into your pants, sir. We're about to enter." As she listened to his response, her features twisted into a sneer. "I will not tell her I'm joking. For all I know, you *are* beating off in there. You never summoned a quick lay like you—yeah, yeah, yeah. Screw you, too." She slammed the phone down, grinned and pointed to the door. "He's through there. Enjoy. Or not. Yeah, probably not. I mentioned his mood, right?"

He hadn't summoned a 'quick lay'? *Why do I want to sing and dance like a Disney princess?* Easy. A horny William was a more manageable William. She *needed* a manageable William.

In a matter of seconds, round three of their private war would begin. And so would his punishment.

Heart racing, Sunny walked forward. With each step closer, her anticipation sharpened. By the time she opened the door and crossed the threshold, entering a second, more spacious office, she trembled wildly.

William sat behind the desk, tension thrumming from him. When his incredible scent hit her—the essence of sex, masculinity and carnal indulgence—her cells blazed with sudden desire. She swallowed a moan, her breasts aching anew, the apex of her thighs throbbing.

See! Lust dust and a pre-mating-season haze *sucked*.

Needing a moment to compose herself, she looked about the room. Wood floor, draped by a plush rug with a tree of life pattern. Hand-carved furnishings. A wet bar and a desk, with one chair in front, two chairs behind and a side table between them. Two doors, both closed. Possible escape routes, or traps? A window with shaded glass, hiding the view outside. A bare-chested mermaid bracketed each side of the marble fireplace. Bookshelves lined every wall, the shelves filled with goodies: a stuffed squirrel wearing a doll dress, an assortment of skulls and framed photos of a lovely dark-haired girl and a gorgeous blonde. More members of his family? Former ladyloves?

Do not unpack that thought; you'll only welcome another surge of ridiculous jealousy. Forge ahead. "After I kill Lucifer, I will display his skull on *my* mantel." Finally, she turned her attention to the portrait hanging on the walls, interspersed between axes, swords and daggers. In this one, William was fully nude.

Oh, my. The guy had width, length and heft. The trifecta. A true battering ram, and her neglected body ached for it. Not his specifically. Just any one like it. Surely!

Voice blissfully gravel-like, he said, "Why stare at a painting when you're in the company of the real thing?"

Her heart raced faster. Embarrassed heat flushed her cheeks…her breasts. Yes. Embarrassed. Not turned-on. Nope. Time to embarrass *him* in turn. "I'll look your way," she said, hating how breathless she sounded, "if you'll whip out your… What did Pandora call it? Oh, yes. Your man meat, and prove your girth. Get it? *Girth* rhymes with *worth*." Or she'd look his way when she'd mounted a defense against his appeal.

"You poor, sweet darling." His husky chuckle was more sexual than a striptease. "You've got to *earn* a viewing."

Shiver. No, shudder. Definitely a shudder. "That's not the word on the street," she said, still staring at the portrait.

"Panda ran her mouth about my private affairs, I presume. No matter. I've changed my mind. Come closer, little sundae, and I'll give you a private showing free of charge."

Dang him! He'd caved too easily. It wasn't a punishment

if he'd enjoy it. "No, thanks. You'll probably maul and paw me afterward. We both know you like to seize any excuse."

She thought she heard him grind his teeth, and she had to curb another grin.

"I wouldn't touch you with my ten-inch rod," he grated.

Liar, liar. "I think you mean *ten-foot pole*."

"I said what I said. But we can measure it to be sure."

An-n-nd her cheeks heated another thousand degrees. So far, the man had run verbal circles around her. *Gonna have to take things up a notch.* "Want to know what I just heard you say?" Mimicking him, she said, "If I can't touch you, darling Sunny, I'll plot ways to make *you* touch *me*."

No reaction. "Maybe. Although you're as bad a kisser as you claimed, so I might be better off without you."

There was no reason to take offense. Truth was truth, after all. But...offense! "I sucked, yes, but you sucked worse. Think about it. A chain is only as strong as its weakest link."

He concealed a look of uncertainty—a hint of vulnerability—but not before she snuck a peek at him. How astonishing. Maybe he had insecurities like the rest of the world? Maybe—

No! She couldn't soften. *Prince of darkness. Royal of Hell. Leader of demons.* She needed to dig this particular knife a little deeper. "One day, I'm going to pick a gaggle of men for my reverse harem. *Good* men. I'll practice my...kissing."

She snuck another peek at him. His eyes were flashing. Oh, oh, oh. What was this? Another bout of jealousy? Then the first portion of his torment had begun. Slowly, ensuring he watched her every move, she reached toward the portrait.

Had his breath just hitched?

She let her fingers hover over his calf...his knee... Did

he wonder which body part she intended to caress? When she reached the area above his penis, she paused. He went still, as if enraptured.

Pretending to forget her purpose, Sunny dropped her arm to her side, never making contact. "You're probably wondering why I decided to drop by," she said breezily.

He pouted for a moment. *Do not laugh.* "You mean you didn't drop by because your master summoned you?"

"It's because I have two lists for you," she continued as though he hadn't spoken. "A list of demands, and a list of poachers and collectors you're going to find and decapitate on my behalf."

He glowered, jumping up. When he realized what he'd done, he smoothed the sleeves of his shirt and eased back down. With a voice all gravelly again, he told her, "You aren't in a good enough position to make demands, duna."

From duna to sundae, then back to duna. A testament of his darkening mood? "You're right. I'm in the *best* position to make demands. You need me—"

"Me? Need you?" He scoffed. "You have yet to prove your decoding skills."

"—and I need toiletries, clothes and laptops loaded with games. For everyone. Don't be cheap, either. Get e-readers loaded with an assortment of books, too. I prefer romance. The sexy ones. Knitting needles and yarn would be appreciated. So would snacks. If I get hangry or bored, bad things will happen. Finally, I require private quarters. I will not be staying in the bunkhouse."

Crackling silence.

Thanks to excellent periphery vision, she knew William stared at her with an impassive expression. Talk about false advertising. He rested his elbows on the edge of the desk, his fingers linked and white-knuckled. Impassive? Hardly.

When he finally unlocked his fingers, he scrubbed a trembling hand over his mouth. "I will provide you with a room of your own. I will buy you the things you need, and I will take care of the poachers and collectors. Anything else?"

How sweet. Too sweet? Yes! Why cave mere seconds after he'd claimed she had no bargaining power? Unless... "What price do you expect me to pay?" she asked, her tone drier than desert sands. "My new room will be next to yours, right? For convenient booty-calling?"

More silence. She waited, on edge, and...hopeful?

He grated, "You have only to decode my book in the two-week time frame."

At last, she cobbled together a defense and pivoted in his direction. Did she look directly at him? Not yet. The urge was *too* strong. She focused on the desk, the surface crammed with a smorgasbord of food. Oh! A bowl overflowed with different-colored rose petals. Her mouth watered, and her stomach rumbled at a much higher volume.

None of the other codebreakers mentioned a snack, much less an entire meal. Which meant he'd gone to a lot of trouble for Sunny, and Sunny alone.

"Is this our first date?" she asked, curious about how he'd react to the idea.

His fingers jerked. "I do not date."

Not exactly a denial... "Ever?"

"Ever," he confirmed.

But you kind of want to date me, *Ever Randy?* The idea wasn't unpleasant. In fact, it caused a sultry fog to envelope her mind. Finally she lifted her gaze, because she couldn't resist the urge a moment longer. Daisy! Undiluted lust flared inside those electric blues. She began to pant.

Somehow, he was *more* handsome than she remembered.

No, not somehow. Science. The more time you spent with someone, the more you got to know them. The more you got to know them, the more or less attractive they became to you, their personality as much a feature as their eyes and nose. William, providing her favorite food...straight-up sexy.

Her tremors returned and redoubled as she cataloged his differences. His dark hair now stuck out in spikes, as if he or a lover had fisted the strands. He had—

Son of a swine-shifter! "Pandora lied," Sunny snarled. "You actually did it. You slept with someone."

"Many times," he said, a wicked grin blooming.

She would tear the office apart piece by piece! He had no right to enjoy himself while a powerful unicorn languished in captivity.

"Just not today," he added, calming her temper.

Wait. I think he *torments* me. Still. Feeling magnanimous all of a sudden, she eased into the chair across from him and eyed the bowl of rose petals. Sweet, sweet petals.

"Eat." He pushed the bowl in her direction.

Suspicions roused, she reared back. "Why? Are they poisoned?"

"Because I don't have the balls to stab you?"

He'd sounded offended. And...did she perceive a gleam of sadness in his irises?

Oh, yes. Definitely sadness. His called to hers, attempting to raze her sense of calm. But, why would a warlord as confident and successful as William ever feel sad?

"If you do not want the petals," he said, reaching for the bowl.

She snatched it before he ever made contact. At first, she ate slowly. Properly. The way she'd been trained. Since her parents had betrothed her to Blaze at birth, she'd been raised as a royal, etiquette lessons drilled into her head as soon as she could walk. But all too soon, ravenous hunger pulled her strings, and she shoveled in the remaining petals at lightning speed.

Far from sated, she exchanged the empty bowl for one filled with fruit. "By the way," she said between bites of oranges, strawberries and pineapple. "I'm newly furious with you. You brought me to Hell. I hate demons, and this is their hub."

Darkly magnetic, he arched a brow. "If you think I would allow demons to harm someone under my care, you're a fool."

"If you think you can control pure evil, you're an even bigger fool." She gave him a pitying glance. "How many unicorns have you interacted with over the years?"

"You are the first."

She nodded. "It shows." But... "How'd you know what I was?"

"Hades collects rare weapons, artifacts and, yes, even beings. I stay up-to-date on his must-haves. For centuries, a unicorn has topped the list."

Her stomach twisted. "Does he hope to study or kill us?" In other words, how awful did she need to make his death?

William's features softened, a true shock. "He hopes to adopt or recruit."

Gross. "Pass!" She toyed with a lock of hair, asking, "Are you one of his collectables?"

He flicked his tongue against an incisor, raw challenge blazing in his eyes, singeing her. Color tinged his cheek, making her wonder how hot his skin burned, and a muscle jumped in his chiseled jawline. "I am his son."

A tad bit defensive, eh? "And you can't be both?" she asked, that raw challenge making different parts of her tingle. For a moment, she yearned to leap into his lap, wrap her arms around him, and…do things. Wanton, wild things. "What kind of—"

"Don't do it," he interjected, his tone stern. "Don't ask what kind of being I am."

"Why? What kind of being are you?"

He scowled, the picture of annoyed male.

Why so secretive? "Unless…" She gasped. "You don't know, do you?"

The pen he held? He snapped it in two. "You're here to decode my book. Let's get to work."

A pang ripped through her. He *didn't* know his own origins. How awful. Did he ever feel as if he didn't belong? *I know the feeling.* "I'm still on my lunch break," she said, voice soft. Knowledge was power, and she wasn't done learning about him. "I'd rather talk about you."

The corners of his mouth quirked up. Why? Had she maybe, perchance…pleased him? "Since I'm a benevolent captor, and you've been such a pleasant captive, I'll grant you a boon. Five minutes to finish your food and ask me anything you'd like, and I'll answer."

Ask him to strip. Ask him to strip!

Sage! Mating season made her stupid. "Why is the book of codes so important to you?" she asked.

A terse pause before he admitted, "Centuries ago, I rejected a bitch of a witch, and she cursed me in the worst possible way." Another pause, the wheels clearly rolling in his mind as he decided what to confess and what to omit. "The day I fall in love is the day the object of my affections kills—attempts to kill—me."

Interesting. Tapping a finger against her bottom lip, she replayed Pandora's earlier revelation. *I don't think he'll ever let himself fall in love, because when he does—*so. The curse centered around his affections. "Are you sure you're cursed? You've obviously fallen in love with *yourself*, yet you haven't committed suicide."

"I'm sure?" No doubt he'd meant the words as a statement. Now he scowled. "According to the witch, I can break the curse by deciphering the code."

"And you're sure she told the truth? Vengeful beings, no matter their species, do not create a magical loophole without a nefarious reason. What if *breaking the curse—*" she used air quotes "*—causes* you more harm than good?"

He shifted in his seat. "And what if she expected me to fear breaking the curse so much, I wallow in misery, doing nothing, while holding the key to my happiness?"

Yeah. Fair point. "Is the witch still alive?" Maybe, if Sunny pressed a razor-sharp horn against her carotid, she'd null and void her curse. Simple, easy.

"If Lilith lived, she'd be chained to my side so I could torture her every minute of every day." Relish fizzed in each word, giving her a glimpse of the diabolical underworld prince who lurked beneath the pretty face...and her dark side loved it. "I cut off her head." With Lucifer's help.

Lucifer. *Hate him!*

Sunny bit into another strawberry, and William snapped a second pen in two. Her pulse leaped. Why had he—his gaze had dipped to her mouth, she realized. Clearly he'd lost track of the conversation.

Could she distract him even more?

Infused with feminine power, she traced the strawberry around her lips. He watched, his pupils expanding, causing warmth to dance over her skin. She told herself she licked the juice away to torment him, but she also tormented herself. So sweet! She imagined dripping the juice over his body and laving away every droplet. He'd never have reason to feel sad again.

Another groan left him, shattering her musings. Good! She did not need to concern herself with his emotions.

"Your five minutes are up," he announced.

Pulse fluttering, she rasped, "Do us both a favor, and reset the countdown clock. I have more questions…and more strawberries."

"I will not reset—"

"Do it, and I'll kiss you," she blurted out, the words leaving her unbidden. A flush heated her cheeks. If he rejected her…

He jolted upright in his chair, saying, "Resetting the countdown clock *now*."

9

"Willy's life hack #69. Always use an ax. They hack up a life better than anything."

SHE CRAVES MY KISS. Might even ache *for it.* William nearly pounded his chest in a beastly display of masculine satisfaction.

Ever since she'd entered the office, lust had *seethed* inside him, demanding its due. A naked Sunny splayed across his desk, long legs spread. He would feast, and she would come with a scream. Twice.

Pride demanded he turn fantasy into reality. Pride, only pride.

He should have done as claimed and used someone else to slake his desires. One-night stands were his go-to form of stress relief, after all. He just… The thought of being with anyone else left him cold right now.

The power of a lifemate. He pressed his tongue to the roof of his mouth.

He'd always believed he craved variety in order to make as many memories as possible. But he'd forgotten the women as soon as he'd come. Therefore, his rationale made no sense.

What if he didn't need variety to be satisfied?

What if he just needed...her?

Why not kiss her and find out? With her death off the table, thanks to the prediction about Lucifer's defeat, William had nothing to explain to her first.

If their second kiss was as bad as their first? What, then? And what if she got better, and he fell for her?

Better to tell her no. And he would. No. Nay. Nyet. Any second now, he'd say the word...

She perched in the chair across from his desk, her amber eyes bright pools of arousal, her chest rising and falling in quick succession, her breasts straining her T-shirt.

She pants with arousal—for me? She must. His keen senses picked up the harried speed of her heartbeat. And her nipples...still sweet little peaks. *How the beauties must ache.*

Tell her no? Not in this lifetime. Why fight the inevitable?

Desire drove him to his feet, the chair rolling behind him. Head high, he rounded the desk. Rather than approaching her directly, he stopped just in front of her and leaned against the desk's edge. Let her explain her unexpected urge for a kiss before he made a move. For all he knew, she'd only hoped to tie him in knots. Hadn't she promised to punish him for keeping her in captivity?

Well, mission accomplished, beauty.

He crossed his arms, and she clocked the movement with a heavy-lidded gaze. Her scent changed from deliciously sweet to... *What the hell is that?* She smelled like the incarnation of sex and pleasure, turning his every inhalation into an internal caress.

He hardened in an instant, his blood heating. His hands trembled, his gut clenched and he ached…everywhere.

What did Sunny experience?

"You claim to find no pleasure in my kisses," he reminded her, his ego taking another hit. "Why ask for a repeat?" Did she want something from him, perhaps?

A calculated gleam lit her eyes, and he had to silence a groan. *About to deal with her dark side again.*

"You're hot and strong, with all the right equipment—" she leered at his erection and wiggled her brows "—and there's a good chance I'm a shallow, hard-up size queen."

"Are you, then?" He massaged the back of his neck. To keep her guessing, he said, "I've been with shallow, hard-up size queens before. I think I'll pass."

Her nails grew into claws, a good sign. "Fine. Mating season approaches, and I'm losing control. In other words… I'm horny. Anyone will do."

A laugh lived and died at the back of his throat. Sunny, consumed by sexual desires… He quaked with riotous need. Then the rest of her words registered. *Anyone will do.*

Between gritted teeth, he rasped, "Have you ever had an orgasm, duna?"

"Oh, yes. When I'm flying solo, I'm an incredible lover. The best I've ever had."

He white-knuckled the edge of his desk to stop from reaching for her. "Have you ever had an orgasm with another person?"

"I…yes…no…maybe?"

He went motionless, not even daring to breathe. "Let me clear up your confusion, sundae. No, you haven't." *But I will introduce you to shared pleasure. I will teach you to love it. Me, and no other.* "Tell me how you felt when we kissed?"

After a moment of hesitation, she admitted, "I felt distracted, stressed and unsafe. Granted, I feel unsafe every minute of every day."

"That's it?" No hint of arousal?

She didn't answer, which was answer enough.

He grinned, and she sputtered, her innate fragrance intensifying, drugging him. But the grin didn't last long. To pleasure this girl, he'd have to first earn her trust. The only way to do that? Time. Time he didn't have.

Sunny ran her bottom lip between her teeth, leaving a sheen of moisture behind. A sheen he wanted to lap up. Her skin flushed, and he wondered how hot it burned.

Maybe he *could* pleasure her without earning her trust. He just had to turn her focus to something other than fear. If he whipped her into a furious lather, he could smuggle passion past her defenses. In theory.

Worth a shot. "We're going to try this again," he told her. "I'm your master, after all, and you must learn to respond to me appropriately."

Her eyes narrowed. A promising start.

"My darling sundae," he continued on. "This is the part where you say *thank you*."

Narrowing further... "I have no master, you pompous douchebag."

Ding, ding, ding. Fury. Time for a little passion smuggling.

Her tirade intensified. "There's no way in hellebore I'll say thank—"

William shot out his arm, cupped her nape and yanked her against the hard line of his body. Her lips parted on a surprised gasp, and he swooped down, claiming her mouth with his own, thrusting his tongue past her teeth.

At first, she accepted his kiss as passively as before. Then she gripped the hem of his shirt, holding on for dear life, and actively participated, chasing his tongue with her own.

His pulse quickened. He rewarded her with a suck and a nip. Plaintive moans spilled from her. So sweet. Those plump, irresistible lips…so perfect. Every inch of her… *so mine*.

"Wrap your arms around my shoulders," he commanded. She obeyed, zero hesitation, and he shoved a hand into her hair, then used the other to grip her ass and grind his erection against her core.

The bliss! Had he ever experienced something, anything so good? *Want more.* He spun her around and lifted her onto the desk, then spread her legs farther apart with his hips. When he pressed his erection against her core yet again, a ragged moan left her. A siren's song he couldn't resist.

She makes me crazed.

No, no. Focus. Must ensure her *pleasure.* He licked, sucked and nibbled, tilted his head this way, tilted his head that way, exactly how most females loved but… Sunny returned to passive acceptance.

Damn it! What the hell had even happened? What had he done wrong this time?

He lifted his head, ending the kiss, and pressed his forehead against hers. His pulse did not slow.

"Why'd you stop?" she asked, and he was pleased to note she panted ever so slightly. "You were doing slightly better than before."

Slightly? Slightly! He worked his jaw. *She baits me, nothing more.* "You enjoyed the kiss. For a bit. What changed?"

"Honestly? *You* changed."

He pinched her chin, forcing her gaze to lift to his. Uncertainty and sadness blazed in her eyes, the gleam of calculation gone. Her defenses had toppled, giving him a glimpse of the real Sunny. It affected him on a level so deep, he couldn't analyze it.

Finally he told her, "I don't understand."

"At first, you were like a live wire. But the more we kissed, the more detached you became, as if you were a robot programmed to kiss everyone the exact same way. I could have been anyone, and you wouldn't have cared, which meant you weren't invested. Which meant you didn't care about my pleasure, or even your own, only the outcome. Which meant your reasons for kissing me had nothing to do with genuine desire. Which meant you could go from my bed to another's in a blink. Which meant—"

"Enough," he snapped. "I get your point." And what a sharp point it was, his ego already in tatters.

Somehow, William found the strength to pry his hands from her silken hair and off her perfect ass, and take a step back. As many women as he'd bedded, Sunny was the first to complain, and the only one he'd hoped to impress.

Not good enough. Never good enough.

He rubbed the spot just over his heart. What prince of darkness couldn't satisfy his woman?

"Why do you sleep with so many women?" she asked, soft, so soft.

"Why else?" he quipped, going for a light tone, as if he hadn't a care. Needing contact, any contact, with the woman who maddened him as no other, he pinched a lock of her hair between his fingers. "Pleasure."

"I don't think so." She shook her head, pulling the lock free of his fingers. "I think there's more to it than that."

"There isn't," he said, his tone flat. "As a young prince of the underworld, I had a startling epiphany. If being wanted by one woman thrilled me, how much more amazing would it feel to be wanted by *many* women?"

"Or you were searching for…your mate."

"I wasn't." *Maybe I was?* Mates were supposed to complete you, something he'd always longed to feel. What if he *had* searched for his, but he'd been too afraid to admit it, even to himself?

The mere possibility… *Reeling…*

He needed to talk this through with someone. Shockingly enough, he wanted that someone to be Sunny. She'd proven quick and bright, her insights astoundingly accurate. But as he peered at her, his gaze rapt, the calculated gleam returned to her eyes, and he knew. *The only thing I'll get from her now—trouble.*

Did he kick her out? No.

She jutted her chin and glided closer, closer still. When she stood a whisper away, she reached out to touch his face.

He caught her wrist, stopping her. Then he had to mask a tremor of excitement with a cough. What did she have planned for him?

A sweet smile bloomed. Too sweet. She batted her lashes at him. "Don't beat yourself up, baby doll. So you're not as sexually suave as you assumed. So what. We'll keep practicing. Together. Just you and me."

He knew she played some kind of game, but still he thought, *Practice, yes. You and me.*

Scowling, he released her and stalked behind the desk, where he plopped into the plush leather chair. He would hand her a stack of photographs and send her on her way.

Any second now.

He had things to do. Like craft a game plan of his own.

Something to help him resist her allure. He could want her, yes. Fall for her, no.

Any. Second.

"Yesterday, you mentioned you keep track of your sexual fantasies. Tell me about them." Damn it! Not even close to what he'd planned to say. Did he take back the question, though? Hell, no.

Still batting those lashes, she said, "I'll tell you, happily, if you'll tell me how often you beat off and what you think about when you do it. Use the lotion, get the potion, yeah?"

Hoping to embarrass him? Soon she'd learn. *Nothing* embarrassed him. "I prefer the expression *whack the meat, spring a leak*. And if you average the last eight thousand years or so, including a decade of abstinence, I'd guess twice a day."

Her eyes flashed. "Seriously? An entire *decade* without a little nooky hooky? But you're just so…you."

Shrug. "I was in my early hundreds, still just a lad, when Lucifer and I were brand-new enemies. Hades told me abstinence would increase my strength, helping me win the feud. A decade later, when I was out of my mind with lust, he admitted he'd punked me." Fun times. William waved his hand, telling her, "Your turn. Let's hear a sexual fantasy."

She thought for a moment. Eyes going dreamy, setting off all kinds of warning bells inside his head, she said, "I picture a strong, gorgeous man. He's dressed, but not for long. He strips. I watch."

William's mouth went dry. The warning bells? Forgotten. "And then?"

She purred with pure, sexual carnality, nearly unmanning him. "He strips me, too, and…does a load of laundry, washing our dirty clothes. Oh, yeah. Oh, baby."

William snickered, genuinely amused by her wit. Which

irritated him! She'd successfully avoided his question, while getting an answer from him, and it was sexy as hell.

Definitely need a game plan. He handed her a stack of photographs. "Go over these. If you discover any kind of message, contact me immediately."

"Sure. But contact you how?"

Since his cell phones tended to get destroyed by bullets, daggers and fire, he purchased or stole prepaid burners all the time. Wanting some kind of 24/7 link with Sunny, he dug through his top desk drawer to find the phone he'd already bespelled to work in any realm. Tossing it her way, he said, "You'll find my number in the address book. The passcode is—"

"Let me guess. Sixty-nine sixty-nine?"

"Please. I am not so childish as that. The passcode is *e-m-k-c-u-f*, no spaces. In case you forget, that's *fuck me* backward."

Amusement crinkled the corners of her incredible eyes as she shifted from one foot to the other. "How are you able to speak profanity in front of me? No one else can."

"My age and experience, perhaps." He hiked a shoulder. "I've killed gods. I've gained and lost powers most people can't even fathom."

"Or...your species?"

He gave a stiff nod. He had no clue about his lineage. Was he a fallen Sent One, like Axel? Maybe a hybrid of some sort?

Did Axel remember their parents?

Longing squeezed William's chest. *Ignore it.* He'd had to make a choice. Speak with Axel or believe Hades's prediction—some part of him would die, if ever he met his brother. He'd chosen to believe Hades, and he would live with the consequences. No matter how bad it hurt.

"You have really long eyelashes," Sunny blurted out.

Interesting segue. But he could roll. He leaned back, crossing his ankles, saying, "My eyes sparkle like sapphires. I'm built like a tank and hung like a stallion."

Now she wrinkled her brow, clearly confused. "I don't understand what you're doing."

That makes two of us. "You started a list of all the things you like about me, yes? I contributed."

A tinkling laugh left her, the sound of it melodious. He closed his eyes briefly and savored the audible caress. "I do keep lists in my diary."

His shaft jerked beneath his fly. "I remember. You keep a list of sexual fantasies." And damn it, he needed stronger defenses against her allure, before he morphed into a lovesick puppy who followed her around, yapping at her heels. He needed...magic.

He sucked in a breath, a game plan taking shape. Of course, the more magic he possessed, the more it would interact with his emotions, increasing the likelihood of "birthing" another "child." The most excruciating experience of his life. Couldn't be helped, though. He would do anything to combat his growing fascination with the unicorn.

To acquire more magic, he had only to kill demons. His runes would do the rest, absorbing their immortality and converting it to magic. Much like trees converted carbon dioxide to oxygen.

Snap, snap, snap. He blinked.

Sunny braced her weight on a single palm and she leaned his way, snapping her fingers in front of his face.

He snarled a curse. He'd gotten lost in his head—again. *Do I want to die?*

"What thoughts keep dragging you from my spectacular presence?" she asked, the calculated gleam brightening.

Wary, he told her, "Doesn't matter. You are my decoder." *And lifemate.* "Not my therapist."

"Ohhh. Now there's a fantasy to add to my list." Once again, she batted her lashes. "Sex therapist and patient. I just have to pick the right partner."

The calculated gleam…those batting lashes… He understood now. She *wanted* to irritate him. This was, indeed, part of his punishment.

Her mistake.

In the land of sexual torment, he was king. *My turf, my rules.* "In this scenario, what do *I* do?" he asked, using his huskiest tone. "Do I watch or take notes?"

She gulped, goose bumps spreading over her arms. "Take notes? As if! You don't do any—"

"You're right," he interjected. "How can I take notes when my face is buried between your legs?"

At first, she blinked at him. Then she dropped her jaw. Then she laughed outright, awakening something hot, dark and possessive inside him. He barely refrained from grabbing her and hauling her fine ass into his chair.

Unaware of the insatiable beast she provoked, she clutched the photos to her chest and said, "I know you're ready for me to leave. And I will. Just as soon as you tell me three facts about you. And don't refuse. For all you know, I'm deciding whether or not to bail on you and mount an escape."

He admired her spirit. "You think you have a choice?"

"You think you can force me?"

Nix that. He *lamented* her spirit. "Very well. Three facts in exchange for zero escape attempts. One—"

"You're a bad kisser. I know. I meant, tell me things I *haven't* yet learned."

Still punishing me. Noted. "I'm not a bad kisser, damn

it." He pinched the bridge of his nose and prayed for patience. His phone buzzed, signaling a text had come in. In desperate need of a reprieve, he hurriedly reached for the device.

"Is that your dad? I bet it's your dad. Do you think I'm the kind of girl he's always dreamed of for his precious little boy? Are you going to tell him you're falling in lust with me, a paranoid unicorn who has the paranormal version of a multiple personality disorder? If I were you, I maybe wouldn't lead with that. We want him to be super excited when you bring me home to show me off."

William ground his teeth. "Fact one. I did not receive a text from my father, my friend." He read the screen.

Lucien, Anya's Boy Toy: Code red. The Sent Ones want Fox dead. Granted, they have reason. She killed 10 innocent Warriors. (Galen is on a rampage about it, making HIMSELF a target for elimination.) Anything you can do to help?

Galen was a Lord, just like Lucien, only Galen carried *two* demons. Jealousy and False Hope. Fox, Galen's right-hand woman, hailed from a species known as Gatekeepers, able to portal anywhere, anytime. On top of that, she carried the demon of Distrust. Both were allies. Hades hoped to exploit them both, Fox especially. But first, William would have to save her life, it seemed.

Besides, an ally was an ally, and Sent Ones needed a reminder of that. Mess with William's people, and suffer.

He texted back: I'll take care of it.

Then he texted Zacharel, the only Sent One he dealt with. One of their most powerful.

"Who's Lucien?" Sunny asked. "Who's Anya, Fox, Galen and Zacharel?"

"Doesn't matter." He stifled a spark of anger—at himself. Because he wanted to tell her, wanted her advice. "How did you read the screen? Unicorn magic?"

"Maybe. Or maybe the mirror behind you."

Well. He set his phone aside. *Where was I?* Oh, yes. Facts about himself. "Two, I survived torture and imprisonment more times than you can count. And three, I kill everyone who betrays me, always, without exception. I value loyalty far more than pleasure."

She half smiled at him. "Wily prince. You used your facts to warn me."

Perceptive female. And now he absolutely needed to make that game plan. He reached out to jab the call button on the landline, only to discover Pandora had been listening the entire time. He pinched the bride of his nose. Sisters sucked. "Panties—yes, that's your new nickname. Deal with it. Do me a solid and escort Sunny to her new quarters. When you get there, she's going to write a list of supplies." He tossed the unicorn a notebook and pen. "Buy her whatever she wants."

"Without complaint," Sunny piped up.

"Without complaint," he added, wanting to smile. No, frown. Definitely frown.

"And where will she be staying, hmm?" Pandora asked, her voice spilling from the speaker.

Where else? "The stable."

10

"For me, there's a time and place for lust. Always, and
everywhere."

SUNNY PROWLED THROUGH her new home, breathing in the
musty, dusty scent of a forgotten space. Bigger than the
bunkroom, with an open floor plan, it had a tiered ceiling,
three windows and a row of stalls, all empty. In back were
the living quarters, complete with a bedroom, bathroom,
laundry and kitchenette. Unless she counted dust bunnies,
no animals lived here.

She had some cleaning to do, though. And traps to make.
She'd set them around the perimeter, ensuring no one entered without permission. But… *I think I'll like it here.* For
so long, too long, she'd been on the run, moving from one
run-down motel to another. Now she could roost.

Pandora stood in a portal, a vision of strength and beauty
with her angular features, bedroom eyes and toned body.
Her arsenal of weapons only added to her appeal. Two

short swords were strapped to her back, and two semiau-
tomatics were holstered to her waist. She had a dagger anchored to each thigh, and also stuffed into the sides of her
combat boots.

To steal one or not to steal one?

Nah. There was no need. Sunny wore the world's best
weapon around her neck. The medallion.

"Just so you know," Pandora said, "William is my family now. Something I lacked for a very long time. If you
harm him, I'll harm you back, only worse."

Oh, to have someone so loyal in her corner. Envy
bloomed. "William survived a magic death-bullet to the
face. I assure you, he can take whatever I dish." But what
would it take to actually kill him? Best she find out ASAP.
Not because she wanted to kill him. She didn't. Not at this
moment. But because he was a prince of darkness who
might turn on her. She needed to be ready.

Sunny placed the notebook, pen and stack of photos
at the edge of the bed, then stuffed the cell phone in her
pocket. She would so not be surprised if William had pre-
loaded a couple dickpix in the camera roll.

Would he use *your* instead of *you're* when—if—he
texted? Or maybe *their* instead of *there*? Dude. He did,
and she would take sex off the table because priorities!

Sex…with William… *From adamantly opposed, to eagerly for?* Well, earlier she'd thought to tease him with a
kiss—and ended up teasing *herself*. Pleasure had burned
hot, torching her trust issues. For a moment.

A moment she would forever replay.

Then he'd done his robot thing, ruining it. Still, she
wanted to kiss him again, wanted to bask in the softness
of his lips, the decadence of his taste and the undeniable
strength in his every touch. Afterward, she wanted to talk

with him. The man might be coarse and crude, but his sense of humor was unparalleled. And...and...she wanted everything and nothing, solitude and companionship.

"You think physical survival is all that matters?" Pandora tsk-tsked. "That's sad."

Yeah. It kinda was. Her shoulders rolled in. But, in her defense, William's mental and emotional health shouldn't matter to her. Captor/prisoner, remember?

So why can't I forget the sadness I glimpsed in his eyes?

"I heard your conversation with him," Pandora admitted. "I know what you are, and I'm impressed. Just don't go thinking you're special to William. He'll never settle down."

"Whoa. Who says *I* want to settle down?" *Me! Me! I do!* While a prince of the underworld would never be boyfriend material for Sunny, he might be great...boy-toy material?

She no longer believed William had aided Lucifer in the destruction of her village. And the way he looked at her...

As if they were already in bed, naked, their limbs intertwined. Her pulse spiked, her thoughts growing muddled.

Pandora sighed. "I know that look. You've just sprung yourself a lady boner."

I have, haven't I?

"Come on," the other woman said, waving her over. "Forget William, and give me your list."

Forget William? *I don't think I can.*

Sunny returned to the bed and drafted the shopping list, adding everything she'd mentioned to William, plus clothes with sizes, comfortable lingerie—no thongs!—toiletries, games and a few other necessities. Lastly, she added a no-exceptions must-have: everything she'd left in the hotel room, including *her* book. The one with her lists.

Her new cell phone beeped just as she finished. A little eager and a lot anticipatory, she rushed to read the screen.

Master W: Does my little tuna miss me?

A second message arrived a split second later.

Master W: Duna. Stupid autocorrect.

Master W? A grin teased her lips. This man...oh, this man. Part of her *did* miss him.

No more mooning over kisses and sex. Start decoding. Only thirteen days until William's protection ends and mating season starts. Her stomach churned.

Why the time limit, though? She still didn't know.

Before she had a chance to type a reply, Pandora clapped her hands and barked, "Chop, chop."

She tossed the phone on the bed, planning to respond later, in private, then crossed the distance to hand over the list. "Before you comment about the number of items or the expense incurred, don't. William acquired a thoroughbred, and as you can guess, my upkeep is expensive." She snickered at her own joke. Unicorn humor never got old.

"The lingerie is meant to seduce William, yes?" Pandora asked, glancing from the list to Sunny.

She shrugged. Actually, the lingerie was meant to *torment* William. She had not and would not cease making him uncomfortable, not until she became a guest rather than a prisoner.

"Well, I approve." The dark-haired female winked and stepped backward. As the portal closed, she said, "I'll return shortly."

Wait. Had anyone thought to lock the stable door?

Marveling at the possibility, Sunny checked the knob. No resistance. She didn't... She couldn't... With a single push, the entrance swung open. Shocked stupid but grinning, she stepped beyond the threshold. Overwarm air enveloped her, but she didn't care. If she wished, she could escape.

Her grinned widened. Another step and another. Should she or shouldn't—

Sunny slammed into some kind of invisible barrier and bounced back. She tripped over nothing and crash-landed on her butt, air bursting from her lungs and stars flashing before her eyes.

She pounded a fist into the dirt. *I will double his torment!*

Huffing and puffing, she lumbered to her feet and marched forward, arms outstretched. When she reached the barrier, she hit it with magic...but it remained in place.

Disappointed, she cast her gaze over the landscape. An array of hills and valleys greeted her, with random fires raging throughout. Wind howled, ash falling like wisps of snow. There were a handful of trees, but all were spindly with huge black thorns dripping...motor oil?

Demons wandered about. Some had horns. Others had scales, wings or tails. All had weapons.

Enemy! Her violent side bowed up, ready to fight and slay superhero-style. Could the fiends enter the stable? *Would* they? If they were part of William's army, she wouldn't harm—no. Not true. Loyal to William or not, demons had to die. Evil was evil, and the fiends could not be trusted. She would set traps, not to dissuade unwanted visitors, as she'd planned before—to kill.

At the moment, the entire horde hyperfocused on... Sunny sucked in a breath. Swinging two short swords with masterful skill, William worked his way through their ranks. Golden runes branched over his muscular arms, lightning flashing just under the surface of his skin.

As he struck down one demon after another, he was absolutely, utterly vicious. Brutal. *Magnificent.* Such beautiful temptation. *So deadly, and yet he handled me with such care.*

Her body reacted as it always did in his presence. Heating and dampening, preparing for rough, vigorous sex. Then she remembered the barrier surrounding the stable.

Scowling, she called, "Don't mind me, Willy. Pretend I'm not here, thinking about rubbing one out while I watch you."

He spun so fast he'd have whiplash, his electric blues glittering with excitement. The distraction cost him, just as she'd hoped. He failed to track the demon sneaking up behind him, which meant he failed to brace for a blow to the back of the head.

Ouch! "That's what you get!"

He righted quickly and—*Oh. My. Wow.* Massive jet-black smoke-wings exploded from his back. Her jaw went slack. The lightning under his skin spread to his wings, a storm raging within each appendage. *Amazing.*

Around him, demons toppled. Were they dead or unconscious? Either way, they lost their heads the moment William moved within striking distance.

"Enjoy your concussion, warden. In the coming days, it'll be your fondest memory," Sunny whispered, backtracking into the stable and kicking the double doors shut.

She paced, her mind whirling. In the ballroom, she'd considered him no match for unicorn strength. Now? *I might have met my match.*

If ever he decided to make a play for her horn... *Who*

am I kidding? He would. Every non-unicorn who'd ever discovered her origins had coveted it.

Cold spread through Sunny's limbs. If he did manage to steal her horn, she would lose *everything*. Without the horn, she had no magic. No strength. No way to shift forms. She wouldn't be able to read auras and wouldn't know ordinary citizens from garbage humans, mortals from immortals or truth from lie.

She would work on his book, as promised, while continuing his punishments, enjoying his shelter and provision, spending his money, and using his battlefield skill to pare down the number of collectors and poachers on her trail. Still, she needed to get that escort to Lucifer's door. But. With this new development, she also needed to win his trust and gain possession of his book. She'd have to be careful and take measures to ensure *he* didn't somehow win *her* trust, ruining everything. She'd never be able to torment, betray and evade someone she trusted.

In two weeks, she would use the book as collateral if necessary. *Set me free or watch the precious burn.*

11

"Try to stop me. Dare you."

WONDERING IF SUNNY still watched him, William exaggerated his movements as he stabbed and beheaded demon after demon. He wanted her to note his skill, to know he could and would protect what belonged to him. So she'd feel safe. Of course.

Black smoke rose from the bodies, absorbing into his glowing runes. Strength flooded him, plumping his muscles, doubling their size.

He fought methodically, mercilessly. For months the demons had skulked around the house—once Hades's country estate, now William's headquarters. They spied for Lucifer, continually painted penises on the walls, vandalized the stable and peed on any foliage that managed to grow.

I'll kill them all.

A demon clawed William's side; skin split, blood poured and pain flared. With a growl, he reached into the culprit's throat. Teeth and fangs chomped on him as grabbed the male's larynx and ripped it out, along with pieces of lung.

A faint whistle caught his attention. A sound he recognized. Someone had tossed a sword at him. With a dark oath, William ducked. The weapon flew overhead, and he threw himself back into the fray.

By the time he took down his final opponent, his yard was a sea of dead bodies and body parts. The stable doors?

His gaze whipped to the right. Closed. They were closed, Sunny sealed inside. Another oath left him. He'd hoped to speak to her…and maybe perhaps he'd hoped she would fawn all over him and patch up his wounds. What? He deserved a little fawning.

At least he didn't have to worry she'd escape and he'd lose her. The first time she and the other codebreakers had stepped through the portal, he'd tagged them all with a mystical tracker. From now on, he could find his unicorn with only a thought.

He returned to the house, stomping on corpses along the way. Under his boots, bones crunched and blood splashed. The front doors opened automatically, the home bespelled to do what he wanted, when he wanted. The scent of sulfur, brimstone and death faded, the blistering wind dying down.

Pandora was out shopping for Sunny and the other prisoners, and Green had rejoined his brothers to complete a mission to find Evelina, Lucifer's absentee bride. She'd run away soon after the wedding, never to be heard from again.

So, William should be alone, yet someone stood in his foyer.

He ground to a halt, his bloody hands fisting. A dark-haired Sent One faced the far wall, his back to William. Had to be Zacharel, here to discuss Fox. He wore a white robe with purple trim, with golden wings tucked into his sides. Solid gold wings = one of seven Elite soldiers.

"Hello, Zacharel. To what do I owe this...pleasure?" Lies tasted foul to the Sent Ones. So, every now and then—or always—William told the male a falsehood just for grins and giggles.

Z didn't react to William's voice in any way. Meaning he'd known the moment William entered. Slowly he turned...

Dread punched William. An uppercut followed by a backhand of shock. A jab of wonder. A kick of elation. An elbow of foreboding. A pat of joy. A punch of sadness. Another punch. Horror. Punch. Hope. His guest wasn't Zacharel, after all...but Axel.

"We meet at last, William of the Dark."

Their gazes locked, every emotion sharpening. Soon William felt as if he were hemorrhaging inside. He didn't know what to say, didn't know what to do.

Hades's warning played inside his head at full blast. *The day you meet Axel, a part of you will die.*

Air wheezed from between clenched teeth. What part of him was supposed to die this day?

He should send Axel away. Or leave. Yes. Leave. Just walk off without looking back. Now, now, now, damn it. For Hades. Yes. Hades would expect it, and rightfully so. William had vowed to avoid Axel at every possible turn. But...

The damage was already done, his feet rooted in place. No part of him wished to abandon his...brother. The moisture in his mouth dried, and he swallowed the lump growing in his throat. How many nights had he dreamed of this moment? How many times had he wondered about what could have been?

"Uncanny right?" Axel patted his stubble-darkened jaw.

"Anyone ever tell you that you're the most beautiful man ever to live, or is it just me?"

Their resemblance truly was extraordinary. They had the same dark hair, same electric blues and perfect nose. Same...everything. Heart racing, he asked, "Why are you here, Axel?"

"Why do you *think* I'm here? Or did I get the beauty *and* the brains?"

Okay. A halfway decent burn. But damn it! He didn't want to admire this man. He'd only want to spend more time with him, something he absolutely could not do, not if he wanted to appease the only father he'd ever known.

"Obviously we've heard the same rumors. We look alike, and we might be brothers. You wanted to meet me. So. What do you think?" William extended his arms and performed a spin, crimson bubbles popping beneath his boots. A piece of demon liver fell out of his hair and plopped to the floor. "Am I everything you hoped or more?"

Axel hid his emotions behind a bland expression. "You assume I cared enough to wonder about the brother who never sought me out?"

A much better burn. One with bite. "Let me try this again. Are you here because of Fox?"

"I am, yes." Pretending to wipe dust off a side table, Axel added, "As you may or may not know, I recently received a promotion to Elite."

Soon, I will receive a promotion, as well. King William. No better name. "Why remind me? Trying to impress me?"

Axel's cheeks reddened. *I'll take that as a yes.* "I acted as one of the judges for Fox's case. She is to be executed right away."

William ran his tongue over his teeth. "Ah. I see. You

went with retaliation, the demon way, versus forgiveness, the Sent One way."

Now Axel scowled.

If the Sent Ones captured Fox, she would die screaming. No one unleashed wrath quite like Axel's crew. William might have avoided Axel all these years, not even allowing himself to think about the male most days, but he'd also collected stories about his exploits. "Who did you appoint as her executioner?"

"Bjorn the Last True Dread."

Not good. Not good at all. Bjorn wasn't exactly right in the head, his mind filled with land mines ready to explode at any moment. Long ago, demons had captured, imprisoned and tortured him, along with his two closest friends. Centuries later, some kind of shadow queen had forced a mystical bond with him, draining his life force bit by bit. He would be difficult to manage.

"You should know Fox's execution will be a declaration of war." While William couldn't afford to fight a second war right now, he *really* couldn't ignore a slight against an ally. To do so would invite incursion by countless enemies.

Axel offered a cold smile. "I'm sure Bjorn will tremble— with laughter." He waved a hand, dismissing the subject. "As for my second order of business. Armies of Sent Ones will be moving to Hell. We've decided to join your war against Lucifer. Now you can actually win."

Fighting beside Axel…having him close…planning and scheming together…

William should protest. His world had just turned upside down and inside out. Worse, Hades would be upset. But, what if he could have Hades *and* Axel in his life?

Hope and worry collided. *The day you meet Axel, a part of you will die.*

What part, damn it? And why?

"Axel," he began.

"No," Axel snapped. "Whatever you're going to say, don't. I delivered my news. We're done." A second later, he vanished, flashing away. A surprise. Most Sent Ones didn't possess the ability to flash.

William expelled a breath and rubbed the center of his chest. Had he ever felt so raw? So confused and unsure? So needy, but also defensive? Inside, William still carried pieces of the broken little boy he'd been.

He wondered if this was how his dual-natured unicorn felt all the time. Pulled in two different directions.

She deserves better.

His hand—a hand that had remained steady during countless battles and wars—trembled as he palmed his cell phone and typed a message to Hades. Better to confess as quickly as possible to mitigate any damage.

I met Axel. It was an accident, but it happened. You'll be happy to know all parts of me survived.

All the while his inner little boy cried, *Don't be mad. Don't stop loving me.*

Hades's response arrived a second later, the cell vibrating. Daddy Dearest: Then it has already begun.

His tremors worsened. And what is "it" exactly?

Daddy Dearest: The death of our relationship.

12

"I don't do temptation. I am temptation."

WILLIAM PUSHED OPEN the stable doors. As he stalked inside, morning sunlight framed his big body, creating a halo effect. Sunny's heart kicked into a wild rhythm. With his head high and his shoulders back, he was the master of all he surveyed. Powerful. Beautiful. And pure temptation...

Blood wet his three-piece suit. Why so dressed up? And had he run into one of her traps? Using magic, she'd created invisible stakes along the outer walls of the stable.

"Where's my sweet little tuna?" he bellowed. "You never texted me back."

She lay on the bed, poring over the photos of his book for the bazillionth time, the code still a total and complete mystery. A first for her. She'd tossed and turned all night long, going over the swirls and points again and again, doing her best to ignore an increasingly intense sexual ache. *One day closer to mating season.*

"So we're starting the new day with a complaint? How wonderful," she grumbled, climbing to her feet. Knowing he would turn up sooner or later, she'd showered and dressed in a half shirt that revealed serious under-boob and a sexy, non-granny pair of panties. From shoulders to ankles she had incredibly detailed tattoos of thorny vines, dew-dotted leaves and blooming roses.

Let his next round of torment begin. *You can look but you can't touch...*

William spotted her and stopped in his tracks. He raked his gaze over her, his irises catching fire. His shaft hardened in seconds, stretching the fly of his slacks, and she tried not to grin.

She twirled a lock of hair around her finger, asking, "Something wrong, sweet prince?"

He jolted as if she'd punched him, then scrubbed a hand over his mouth. "Yes, something's wrong. You lied to me."

What! "I never lied to you or anyone. I *can't*."

"Oh, really? I was promised geriatric chic, and I got stay-at-home-mom cozy."

A husky laugh spilled from her. Would she ever be able to predict this man's reactions? He was a mystery she couldn't solve, and an aphrodisiac she shouldn't want. But want him she did. He made her ache, turned her internal thermostat to white-hot, and caused flutters to tantalize her core.

Remember your purpose. Right. Sobering up in a hurry, she told him, "I have a list for you. The names of poachers and collectors on my trail. You said you'd kill them if they came after me, but why wait? I want their heads *now*."

"Let's see the list."

She dropped the photos and lifted the appropriate page, but she didn't close the distance—yet. *Deep breath in, out. Good, that's good.* The aching, heating and throbbing eased.

She stood and strolled over. As his gaze tracked her every move, she rolled her hips with carnal indulgence. She might lack proper flirting skills, but she excelled at kinetic energy. She handed over the paper.

A muscle jumped beneath his eye. "Consider everyone on the list dead."

"I'll consider them dead when you bring me their heads."

Features softening, he said, "Are you worried because of mating season?"

She went still. "How do you know about mating season?"

An-n-nd the muscle started jumping again. "Doesn't matter. I will—" He pressed his lips together. "You will—" Again, he pressed his lips into a thin line. "We'll discuss it later," he repeated.

Red dotted her vision. *What does he hide from me?* "*Later* is what you told me last time, too. Now *is* later."

Scanning the stable, he said, "You've redecorated, I see."

A change of subject. One she allowed, the sight of her acquisitions calming her. "I have, yes." Pandora had gotten everything on her list, and then some. Christmas lights twinkled from the ceiling, creating an illusion of stars. Potted plants and fruit trees abounded, the once-musty space now fragrant with florals and fruits, everything from lemons to peaches.

Her diary rested on the desk, opened to a passage of sexual positions she hoped to try. Another torment. All he had to do was glance over… "FYI, you're welcome to enter the stable anytime you wish, but I can't promise I'll be dressed. Or that I won't be masturbating." Soon, the urges would be undeniable…

He blinked with surprise. Then he scowled. "I have a

meeting with Lucifer later this morning. But first, I wish to check on your progress with the book."

Hearing the name of her greatest enemy raised her hackles. "Take me with you."

"No. And do not dare ask again," he added when she opened her mouth to do just that.

Fine! She'd see and kill the bluebell in two weeks. "If you don't come back covered in his blood, I'll be hugely disappointed."

William blinked faster. "What makes you think I plan to fight him?"

Easy. "I've met you."

A moment passed without a reaction from him. Then a full-fledged smile spread, lighting his entire face, and all the aching, heating and throbbing started up again. Only worse. Her nipples drew tight, and her thighs shook, desire wetting her panties.

"Your book," she grated, more ready to ruin his good mood now. "I've been unable to translate a single word."

As expected, his smile vanished in a hurry. "Why am I giving you preferential treatment, then?"

"Because I'm the only one who *can* translate it. But I must see the actual book to do it," she explained. "I want to touch it, and feel its magic."

"No." Anger and frustration pulsed from him in great, sweeping waves. "That will *never* happen. Work with the photographs, or don't work at all."

He'd gone total alpha. He'd decided, and he expected Sunny to fall into line. What he failed to realize? She was an alpha, too. "No problem. Let's say our goodbyes, and part ways, since I can't be of use to you."

"We do *not* part," he snarled.

Four words. Individually, they meant nothing. Together, uttered by William the Ever Randy, they rocked her world.

"You are a decoder," he snarled next. "Do your job."

Oh, the gall! "I'm so sorry you got saddled with a smoking hot decoder who's doing you two huge favors, but the failure isn't my fault. It's yours. Do as I ask, and you'll get what you want."

He huffed and puffed, tension radiated from him. Finally he grumbled, "I'll think about it. *If* I can. When we're together, it's difficult to ponder anything other than sex."

Though his last words soothed her temper, she knew she had to continue his punishments. With a sugar-sweet voice, she said, "Why don't I do the thinking for both of us, then?"

That little remark pushed him over the edge. "You presume too much, woman!" Lightning flashed under the surface of his skin and smoke curled up, up over his shoulders.

Had any man ever exuded such ferocious aggression?

Far from cowed, she quipped, "Or maybe I don't presume enough? Why don't you flash or portal me to a sealed room and remain at my side as I study your book?" *Look how accommodating I can be, warrior.* "If I attempt to damage it, you can stab me."

His eyes went wide. "You are the most paranoid person in all the worlds, yet you'd trust me enough to let me hold a blade against your vulnerable throat?"

No. She would *never* trust him. But desperate times and all that. Exceptions had to be made. Unable to lie, she simply said, "I will let you do it, yes."

Judging by his slow release of breath, her admission pleased him. "I will trust you with my book...if you will trust me with your unicorn form."

What! What kind of brilliant manipulation was *this*? *He uses my own tricks against me, the dirty bluebell.* "Not just no, but hellebore, no." She shook her head for emphasis. To reveal her unicorn form, something more private and personal than her naked body... "No," she repeated.

"Then I won't show you the book," he said, his tone firm and unwavering. "When my meeting concludes, I'll return. Until then, you are to remain in the stable. Understand? A mystical border ensures demons and other beings cannot enter. Your invisible spikes help, too," he added dryly, while pressing a hand against his side. Oh, yes. He'd tangled with her traps. "A poacher *did* follow you here. I got nailed by a spike when I fought him. His head now rests atop a pole in my front yard. If you escape my blocks and exit, demons and other poachers will give chase." He pivoted on a booted heel and stalked to the doors. "Text me if there's an emergency."

Hate to see him leave, love to watch his aster—argh! Butt. Love to watch his butt. "Oh, William, darling," she called, deciding to take his torture to the next level. "Before you go, we have two more pieces of business to discuss."

He stopped and stiffened, but he didn't glance her way. A good sign. Well, the fact that he'd stopped at all was a good sign. She let the moment drag out in silence, until the muscles in his shoulder bulging with tension.

"I'm listening," he prompted.

The first bit of business was easy enough. "If other poachers come—"

"They won't. I will be sending my best soldiers to track down each and every one. If they aren't dead by the end of the day, I'll be shocked."

Excellent. Now, for the second bit of business, which packed more of a punch. His torment was about to reach new heights. "I've decided we're together now. You and me. We're boyfriend and girlfriend. Fully committed. We're going to be the underworld's 'it' couple, and that's that. If you want your book decoded, I mean."

Now he swung around, his eyes were wide, his pupils blown. A flush brightened his cheeks. "You've decided?"

"Yep. It's a done deal."

"Let me see if I understand you correctly," he said, pushing the words through clenched teeth. *Do not laugh.* "You plan to endure my unskilled lovemaking for eternity, as my one and only girlfriend?"

"Yes, and you aren't to practice with others. Cheating is unacceptable."

"I... You... I haven't agreed to a relationship, much less an exclusive one!" he bellowed. "We are not a couple, Sunny."

Do. Not. Laugh. "But, darling. I'm the smart one in this relationship, remember?" She faked a wince, as if embarrassed for him. "*Of course* I realized we'd make a great couple first. That doesn't mean your poor, sweet brain won't get there eventually. Just don't be too hard on yourself, okay? From now on, that's *my* job."

His lips pulled back from his teeth, his expression pure menace. "You aren't the first female to want more than I'm willing to give. I prefer to remain single."

She blew him a kiss. "Be honest. Would you prefer roses or orchids at our wedding?"

He bowed up, all he-man-like, and the laughter that brewed at the back of her throat nearly escaped. "You cannot tell a man he's yours and expect him to comply. He must agree."

"Are you sure? Because that sounds dumb."

"I'm sure," he huffed, glaring at her.

"But...you're mine," she insisted.

The longer he glared, the more his gaze sizzled with possessiveness, making it harder for Sunny to breathe. Pressure built inside her, her skin pulling too tight over her bones. Need and want collided, wrecking her calm.

"W-William," she rasped.

His aura grew darker by the second, reminding her of molten lava. Then he looked past her and frowned. Why the—

She sensed another presence and whipped around. A ginormous man with red skin, dark hair and extra-large muscles appeared. He was handsome in a monstrous kind of way.

"Sunny, cover yourself," William demanded. "Rathbone, turn around."

The guy—Rathbone—never turned around. Sunny remained in place, too. How would William react if she let the other man look his fill?

Play with fire, and you'll get burned.

Good! She wanted to burn. She'd scar, and she'd remember: never crave a prince of darkness.

Muttering under his breath about stubborn females and irreverent kings, William stalked to the closet, grabbed a robe, then returned to Sunny. He draped the cloth over her shoulders, effectively hiding her curves, and she wasn't sure how she felt about it. Fine! She knew how she felt—delighted—and hated herself.

William snapped, "What are you doing here, Rathbone?"

"I came with a message from your father." Rathbone perused Sunny from head to toe. Slowly. With mating season so close, she expected shivers and heat, bu-u-ut daisy! She felt nothing. Only William affected her.

Why, why, why?

"The message," William said, and sighed.

"You are two minutes late. Get to the club. Oh, and he

requests your presence for dinner tonight." Rathbone's dark gaze returned to Sunny. "Feel free to bring a guest."

Judging by the male's tone, *requests* meant *commands*.

"Hello." Sunny waved. "I'm Sunny. William's girlfriend. We're committed, aren't we, cuddles?"

The newcomer shook his head as if he'd misheard and zoomed his attention back to William. "Girlfriend?"

She expected another denial. Instead, he grated, "Committed," then finished making introductions, leaving her flummoxed. "Sunny, this is Rathbone. He's one of nine Hell kings."

"I've heard of you," she said, suddenly awed. "You're the original shape-shifter, able to morph into anything. I was your biggest fan until you became an underworld king." She'd heard he ruled with an iron fist, executed any and all who betrayed him, never offering a second chance, and had once skinned his own brother alive. Rumors his black-as-night aura supported, but even still he didn't ping her "must destroy evil" instincts. "Then you went and totally redeemed yourself, helping to downgrade Lucifer from king to prince."

Every underworld king owned a crown with special powers. Without it, they lost their spot at the royal table. From her researching, she knew Rathbone had used his ability to shape-shift to help Hades steal back the crown.

"Would it be terribly forward of me to ask you to transform—" Between one blink and the next, Rathbone morphed into William. She laughed and clapped. "Do it again, do it again!"

William blew the male a kiss with his middle finger. "You better change back, bones. I've never been so attracted to someone in my life, and I'm about to jump you."

With a wink, Rathbone returned to his original visage. "I'll tell Hades you're on your way to the meeting, and you're happy to join him for dinner. Should I mention you're in the middle of planning your wedding or not?" He grinned and vanished.

William unleashed an unholy snarl, and Sunny slapped a hand over her mouth to stop her giggle.

He wagged a finger at her, opened and closed his mouth without saying a word, then turned on his heel and marched out of the stable, never looking back.

She released her laughter at long last, though it quickly ended in a groan, mating season never letting her forget her attraction to William for long.

What to do next, what to do next?

13

"I've killed thousands—a number that does not compare with the carnage to come."

YOU'RE MINE.

Sunny's words continued to reverberate inside William's head, her image seared into his memory. That waterfall of blue waves...the half shirt, leaving the bottom swell of her breasts visible...those rock-hard nipples...that slender build and flawless brown skin with a wealth of rose tattoos he'd longed to trace with his tongue...that tiny scrap of fabric pretending to be panties...those perfect legs.

The woman's body was incredible, a masterpiece of femininity and sparkly unicorn goodness. One look at her, and blood had rushed straight to his groin. Where it had stayed ever since.

In her presence, everything heightened. He needed to keep his distance, but she drew him like a magnet drew metal.

The magic he'd taken from the demons? Hadn't helped.
He craved Sunny with every ounce of his being. And she
craved him. The most exquisite creature in any world saw
him as boyfriend material. Him. A male with no memory
of his childhood and too many memories of rape and torture. A prince of Hell without a true kingdom of his own.
A cursed warlord who'd never known true, genuine love.

Hold up. Am I questioning my worth? He scowled. Because yes. Yes, he was. Would his past disgust Sunny? It
certainly disgusted William.

Won't tell her. Ever. If she failed to decode his book in
two weeks, there'd be no need. Mating season would take
over, and she'd want him, regardless.

"Damn it!" He punched a wall. Skin split, and bone
cracked. Pain shot through his knuckles, pooling in his
wrist. He didn't want her to want him because of hormones
or pheromones, or whatever mating season did to her body.
He wanted her to want him because of the man he'd become.

*Most fevered dream and worst nightmare, Keeley? You
nailed it.*

Sunny made him feel alive. Sometimes she even reminded him of…himself. *Oh, shit.* She did. She was his
female counterpart. A feminine William. The best of the
best. She was confident but vulnerable, solitary but social.
Sometimes finicky and always irreverent. Determined and
witty. Smart and gorgeous. A wild creature in need of a
wild ride. A challenge. Exuberant. She demanded what she
wanted and took nothing less.

William admired her greatly and wanted her desperately, madly. Making her come was becoming an obsession.
How would she react when he succeeded? How would *he*?

The urge to return to the stable hit, and hit hard. *I won't race back to Sunny. I won't.* Not now, not later. After the meeting, he would be ensuring the poachers and collectors were dead, as expected.

With a huff, William flashed to a nightclub known as the Downfall. The club's owners—Bjorn, Thane and Xerxes—had closed to patrons for the day, allowing Hades to rent the entire building for the meeting with Lucifer.

Menace crackled in the air, buzzing against the back of his neck. Black velvet covered the walls, the perfect frame for a gallery of portraits featuring different mythological creatures performing different depraved sexual acts. There were hundreds of small round tables with four chairs. Elaborate chandeliers cast muted beams of golden light.

Bjorn stood on the other side of the room. He met William's gaze and nodded, acknowledging his arrival without saying a word. He had brown hair, eyes the color of a rainbow and mother-of-pearl skin that sometimes looked dark, sometimes looked light. His wings were solid gold.

Like Axel, Bjorn and his partners had recently received a promotion. They'd gone from Warriors to part of the Elite 7, when most of the former Elite had died in a heavenly explosion.

Thane looked like an angel with curly blond hair, flawless tanned skin and wicked blue eyes, while Xerxes looked like a devil with white hair, scarred white skin and neon red eyes.

Hades was there, along with Pandora, Lucien—coruler of the Lords of the Underworld—and Anya. In the far corner stood another Sent One. Axel.

In an instant, longing threatened to choke William. *Close the distance. Hear his voice. Breathe his scent.* Why had Hades allowed Axel to stay? Or had he tried to force the male to go, but Axel refused?

Knowing both males…yeah. That.

As he stared at his brother, longing darkened Axel's features, too—until he reshaped his expression into his customary smirk. *Know that smirk well. I've donned it every time I've wanted something I couldn't have.*

William looked to Hades. Shit! His father watched him through slitted lids, no doubt expecting him to defect to the Sent Ones, ditching the male who raised him in order to be with a blood relative.

I want…both in my life. For now, he moved toward Hades.

Axel stiffened, obviously offended.

Damn it! William paused. He felt like a frayed rope in a violent game of tug-of-war.

Before Axel had ambushed him at home, William had believed he could keep his brother out of his life, no problem. As he'd told Keeley, you couldn't miss what you'd never had. But he'd since had a taste of what could be, and he only wanted more. So much more.

However, he wouldn't dismiss the concerns of the man who'd taught him to protect himself and those he loved. Not until they'd had a chance to speak in private. So, William gave Axel another nod, then trekked the rest of the way to the tables and sat between Hades and Anya.

Hades remained quiet and unmoving while his brother fisted his hands. William's chest tightened. *Can't aid one without hurting the other.* Had he made a mistake? Should he have shown Axel support instead, helping repair an already damaged relationship?

"So. Where are your brats, huh?" A grinning Anya bumped his shoulder. One of the loveliest females in existence, she had a wealth of pale hair, perfect golden skin and sparkling blue eyes. "I hoped I'd get to see the Rainbow Brigade."

"They're on a mission for me." They'd heard a rumor about a possible hideout for Evelina.

William couldn't wait to use her to ruin Lucifer's life.

"Beer?" a female vampire called. "Wine? Me?"

Ah. One of three waitresses shlepping drinks. The vampire approached to take William's order, eyeing him like the last slab of ribs at an all-you-can-eat buffet.

Not even tempted.

Damn that Sunny Lane! What has she done to me? William sent the woman on her way.

"So, what's this I hear about a female codebreaker living in your stable?" Anya asked, offering the perfect distraction.

"I have *many* codebreakers in a *bunkroom*, some female, some male." *Reveal nothing about Sunny.* Anya would insist on meeting her. Together, they'd destroy what little sanity he'd maintained.

"So, you've got yourself a Panty Melter harem. Sweet!"

He rolled his eyes, saying, "Shut it and concentrate on the meeting to come."

"Ohhh. Is that what you tell your concubines just before you introduce your penis to their vaginas?"

Leaning back, he shifted his gaze to the man on her other side, Lucien, who had black hair, darkish skin and a face disfigured with self-inflicted scars. He also had bicolored eyes—one blue, one brown. The blue one saw into the spirit world, while the brown one saw into the natural world.

"Do me a solid and handle your woman," William said. "No more talk of penises and vaginas." *Or I might have to rush back to Sunny.*

No more thinking about her, either!

Anya wiggled her brows. "He handled me just before we got here."

Lucien looked to be fighting a grin as he gazed adoringly at the mate who'd fought hard to win his once-battered heart. The fact that a by-the-book male had ended up engaged to the minor goddess of Anarchy blew William's mind. Anya followed no rules but her own, and even those she broke whenever she pleased.

What had initially drawn the two together? The same elusive connection that drew William to Sunny?

What kind of men had Sunny dated in the past?

The muscles in his shoulders flexed, the urge to strike at someone, anyone, strong. *Not thinking about the unicorn, remember?*

Projecting relish, Lucien said, "I will handle her again as soon as we get home. You have my word."

"So how long do we plan to wait for Lucifer to arrive?" Pandora demanded from the other side of the table. She popped her knuckles. "There's only one reason I agreed to come. I was promised murder and mayhem, not sit and await 'em."

"You'll have murder and mayhem later," Hades said, his tone indulgent. "We all gave our word. Today we will chat, nothing more. While Lucifer doesn't possess honor, we're going to pretend we do."

Honor shmoner. William believed you had to strike when opportunity arose. Anything for victory. Some attacks could be won using words, the most dangerous weapon in the world. The tongue could create...and destroy. In a battle of wits, William wielded his with expert precision. But so did Lucifer.

Hate him with every fiber of my being. There was no one more selfish or greedier. No one more repulsive.

Once Lucifer had been the most beloved and powerful angel in the heavens. As a young lad, he'd adored the Most High, his creator…until a desire to rule the heavens consumed him. When he made a play against his king, he lost, and he fell. Hades took him in. Now Lucifer hungered for more power. He was repeating his mistakes, hoping to take his adoptive father's place in the underworld, so he could lead every demon into the heavens, and fight to dethrone the Most High yet again.

May I never be so foolish.

Roughly fifty feet away, a crackling ember sparked from nothing. That ember grew, burning through the atmosphere, a portal forming.

Lucifer had arrived.

William's hate magnified, engulfing him. A type of armor. Red dots infiltrated his line of sight.

Chairs skidded back, everyone but the Ever Randy standing. Hatred and anticipation tinged the air, a malignant combination.

The portal opened the rest of the way, and Lucifer stepped through, entering the nightclub.

Nothing about the bastard had changed. He had the same curly blond hair, golden skin and sky blue eyes, and wore the same angel's robe made of soft white feathers.

Lucifer offered an easy grin that pricked William's temper. "Hello, ladies. I apologize for my tardiness, but I'm positively giddy you were willing to wait for me."

William downed someone's shot of ambrosia-laced whiskey before standing. He popped the bones in his neck and pasted on an irreverent smile before facing the male.

Lucifer didn't notice. He was too busy watching Hades, gauging his reaction.

When Hades took a step forward, William gripped his shoulder, stopping him. *I've got this.*

The strongest king in the underworld wasn't someone who obeyed the commands of others, not even his son's. Even still, he gave William a barely perceptible nod.

William crossed the distance, and Lucifer did the same. They met in the middle, surrounded by a sea of tables and chairs. What William noticed first? An unmistakable flicker of envy in his brother's eyes. He fought a smile. The interaction between father and son must have bothered the black sheep.

Using his easiest tone, he said, "Your apology is accepted. Anytime I get to spend with my adoring father, I savor." See? Words were weapons, and he'd just plunged a knife into Lucifer's heart.

His ex-brother scowled before hurrying to erase all emotion from his features. A skill he and William learned from Hades. "I'm so glad," Lucifer replied, his voice a silk-covered dagger. "I'd be careful, though. With the whopper of a secret he's keeping from you, he owes you more than his time."

And he'd just taken a dagger to the gut himself. *No reaction. He lies to upset you.*

William studied Lucifer more intently, a volatile mix of affection and remorse razing his nerve endings. Maybe even regret?

The trio of emotion had been buried underneath centuries of hatred. Since the hatred had surfaced, so had everything else.

As if reading his thoughts—a skill Lucifer did *not* possess—his brother said, "Why do you hate me so, hmm?"

"Oh, let me count the reasons." Known as the Great Deceiver and the Destroyer, Lucifer was evil personified. He damaged everything he touched, and he could not be redeemed. The horrors his victims had suffered...

Rage simmered in his every cell. *Reveal nothing. Act calm...for now.*

"Only a few short years after Lilith issued her curse, a pain awoke me from a deep sleep," William said with an easy tone. "I opened my eyes to find you at the side of his bed, a bloody dagger in hand, about to deliver a *second* blow."

When Hades had learned of their battle, he'd sided with William. Lucifer had felt slighted and moved out. The beginning of the end for the king and his first adopted son.

Lucifer dismissed his claim with a wave. "Some people walk and talk in their sleep. I commit acts of murder. Not my fault."

Ah, revisionist history. A very human way of comforting one's self for deeds done. "You know," William said, still using that easy tone. "If you wanted to see me, you didn't have to arrange some elaborate meeting. Your desperation is showing."

A tinge of red suffused Lucifer's cheeks, his precious pride nicked. William—2. Lucifer—1. "I gave *you* an excuse to see *me*." He scowled and added, "I didn't come here to argue with you."

"That, I know. You came to threaten us, the only play in your *How to Be a Supervillain* guidebook. By the way, I'll be posting my review online." William took a page from *Sunny's* guidebook and faked a wince. "One star."

"The same score I gave *your* book. Speaking of, I hear you've found a cryptanalyst to break your curse." Lucifer all but bubbled over with glee.

No reaction. *Calm. Steady.* "What I have is hope, something you would be a fool to feel." For years, he'd kept his long-term goals a secret, waiting for the perfect moment to confess. *That perfect moment is* now. "I'm going to find your crown and claim your kingdom, Lucy. I will rule your armies, free everyone you've kept as a sexual captive and strip you of your most prized possession—your pride. In the years to come, your name will be a joke, cautionary tale and curse, all rolled into one."

Lucifer bared a set of razor-sharp fangs. "We should be on the same side, fighting against Hades's tyranny."

"As if I would ever work with you. You steal, kill and destroy anything anyone else loves."

"Perhaps I'm a changed man. Either way, this is your first and last chance to join the winning team. Mine," Lucifer said, his smug grin returning. He truly believed he would win. *Deceives himself as much as others.* "Together, we can strip *Hades* of his kingdom and pride."

"Afraid you can't do it alone?"

The grin fell. Another nick to his inflated pride.

Slow and measured, Lucifer walked a circle around William, the hem of his robe brushing against the ashy ground. William let him do it, not bothering to turn with him. By remaining still, he conveyed a crystal clear message: Lucifer wasn't enough of a threat to bother.

Yet another nick. Maybe the bastard would bleed out by the end of the conversation.

"You are content to be under Hades's thumb?" Lucifer asked. "To be his hand of vengeance rather than your own man? Poor William. I do what I want, when I want. And soon, I'll want to steal the crown from every king in Hell, so I will. No one can stop me. No one can defeat me."

As Lucifer had already proven, reacting to barbs merely revealed a weakness. Ignoring the jabs, he said, "Go ahead.

Keep underestimating me." *I have an ace up my sleeve. A unicorn predicted to aid my cause.* Although…

Did he want Sunny going head-to-head with Lucifer?

The red haze returned to his eyes. "Until now," he grated, "I've treated our battles as a form of foreplay. But the time has come to seriously fuck you up. Enjoy it. Or not. The choice is yours."

Now, to do the thing his ex-brother hated most—walk away. In essence: *You mean nothing to me.*

William blew Lucifer a kiss, turned and rejoined the others.

Lucifer maintained a neutral expression, but failed to release his fists. So telling. "You continue to provoke me when I have something you want very, very badly. You see, I went back to the Realm of Lleh soon after the witch cursed you. I took her and locked her away. If I couldn't have your book, I'd have the next best thing."

With a laugh, William slung an arm around Hades's shoulders. "Is that so? And what of my memories of removing her head?"

"I was at your side, and you saw only what I wanted you to see." In a blink, Lucifer's image changed. From tall and stacked with muscle to the willowy Lilith. "An illusion, nothing more. You killed an innocent, and keep an innocent's skull in your collection."

William swallowed, doubts surging. No, no. The Deceiver was doing what he did best. Lying.

Lucifer returned to his original shape, and William wondered, *What if he's…not?*

His heart sped up, and his mind churned. Did the witch live? Could she negate her curse, or make it worse?

Grinning, Lucifer walked backward. He slipped through the still-open portal. As he moved his gaze over the rest of the group, the grin turned brittle. Because they had what he didn't? Friends.

"One last thing before you go," Hades said with a slow grin of his own. "I know you and every play in your war-book. I borrowed the one you just demonstrated."

Confusion abounded.

"Oh?" Lucifer faked a yawn. "Do tell."

Hades's grin grew wider. "The moment you left your principality, King Rathbone assumed your visage. By now, I'm sure he's decimated half of your army. He's good like that."

William patted the male on the back. *That's my father.*

Lucifer paled. "He can kill as many demons as he likes. He'll never stop me." He returned his attention to William. "You won't, either. Lilith is helping me with a present for you and Axel. Expect it soon—and tears." The portal closed, the bastard disappearing from view.

Hades stalked to the front of the group. "Underworld wars tend to last centuries, but often lag. A strike here, a strike there, interspersed with periods of seeming peace. Judging by the look of murderous rage that fell over Lucifer's face, the strikes are about to start up again. Be ready."

Oh, I'm ready, all right.

Ding, ding, ding. Let the next battle begin.

14

"I have two loves: my dagger and my dick. One slays hard and fast, and the other is my dagger."

A MOAN PARTED Sunny's lips as she writhed on the bed. *Inhale. Exhale.* Good, that was good. *Innnn...ouuuut. In-out.* Mating season hadn't started, not officially, but the preseason practice rounds certainly had. Sudden bouts of sexual arousal, sated only with a male's release. Trying to get herself off only made it worse. The fact that she hadn't slept in forever made it unbearable.

Fatigued, she became irritable. Irritable, she lamented Sable's disappearance. Thoughts about Sable's disappearance made her crave a distraction. Craving a distraction made her want William. Wanting William made her want to get off, but she couldn't. See! Worse.

She *needed* his kisses and his touch. His naked body pressed against hers. Her legs wrapped around his waist, or draped over his back. His ginormous shaft pounding in and out of her.

Another moan escaped, this one ragged.

Eventually, blessedly, she calmed. Feeling like she'd just survived a seven-car pileup, she trekked to the desk. Angry with William, she opened her diary of lists. Specifically, the list of sexual positions. She added a name to each position—Rathbone, Green, Galen, Rathbone again, Lucien and Fox. Something guaranteed to hit William where it hurt. Let him think she desired his friends.

She left the diary open on the desk. Soon, he would return for their dinner with Hades...

Tingling with anticipation, she showered, moisturized her skin and painted her nails black. Leaving her hair loose and free-flowing, she donned sexy-ish lingerie and a frilly blue dress, then applied shimmery lip gloss. Today's torture? Teasing William with what he could not have. Her outfit had nothing to do with impressing him. Nope. Nothing.

Bonus: her loveliness might distract him from the fact that she'd only managed to decode a single symbol in his book, *despite* staring at the photos all morning and afternoon. She'd seen a vial of poison, and she *still* didn't know what it meant.

Oh, she could guess. The method William's ladylove would use to slay him, perhaps? But how was anyone supposed to poison an immortal like William? A Venus flytrap vagina?

Sunny preferred to slay with a horn. Either hers, or ones she'd taken from fallen unicorns. Few immortals had the strength to recover from a horn wound. Would William?

As if her thoughts had summoned him *Beetlejuice*-style, he pushed open the stable doors and strode inside. Just as before, he was all swagger and ferocity, the master of all he surveyed. His eyes blazed with...what *was* that? Sexual frustration?

Must be. One look at him, and she burned with passion-fever all over again. Sweat beaded on her brow, her heart attempting to hurdle-jump her ribs.

Never had she reacted to a male like this. The fact that it kept happening with her captor...

She had two options. Keep fighting it, or finally give in, trusting him just enough to sleep with him.

The different sides of her went to war.

Fight it!

Sleep with him!

Fight!

Sleep!

Argh! *Despise my dual nature.*

She couldn't blame Roses and Rainbows Sunny for being a hussy, though. William had ditched the suit and changed into a black T-shirt and matching leathers. He looked good. Really good. Mouthwateringly good. There was a wildness to him now, a sharp edge and intensity she found irresist-ible, but also kind of disturbing. Had something bad hap-pened during the meeting?

"You tried to kill me when you thought I'd aided Lucifer in the destruction of your village," he began, scanning the stable for her, "and you traded your freedom for an escort to his door. Which leads me to believe you are one of the assassins who has killed his allies over the years."

She didn't try to deny it. "Yeah. So?"

"So, I want to know who you took out, and I want to know everything you learned. Spare no detail. And don't say no. You owe me. Ninety-five percent of the poachers and collec-tors on your list are now dead. The rest are soon to follow."

Ninety-five percent? So swiftly? Amazing! *He* was amazing. *Admiring your captor again? Stop. You've got a punishment to oversee.* "Shouldn't you compliment me first?" *Look at me, William...desire me...*

Spotting her, he skidded to a halt and scoured a hand through his hair. His shirt hiked up a bit, revealing a patch of bare skin, and she all but drooled. "Do us both a favor and stop getting more beautiful every time I see you."

He'd just complimented her, offering praise without expecting anything in return, and she jolted with surprise. Maybe she would cease the day's torment. "So you like?"

"I like." His raspy voice sent shivers coursing down her spine. "I *crave*."

Her cheeks warmed. "I'll tell you all about my experience with Lucifer's allies, promise, but first I'd like to show you what I did."

"Show me—" He sucked air between his teeth. "You broke the code?" His long stride ate up the distance. He stopped directly in front of her, his masculine musk filling her nose and fogging her head.

Nerve endings sensitized, and pulse points fluttered, Sunny bit her tongue to silence a groan. "I decoded a single symbol, but I'm not sure what it means." Exaggerating the roll of her hips, because why not, she sauntered to the bed, where she'd left the photos, and lifted a certain page.

He followed, looked at her drawing, then Sunny herself. The drawing. Sunny. Appearing shell-shocked, he said, "It *is* you. There's no doubt now."

"Me?" Her brows knitted together as she looked left, then right, and pointed to her chest. "It's me, what? Your decoder?"

"Yes," he hissed, then shook his head, as if dislodging a painful thought. "You saw a vial of poison."

His awe had deepened along with his shock, yet she still didn't understand. "Do you know what the poison signifies, then? Besides the obvious, I mean."

"Not yet, but I will." Determination hardened his muscles. "But, let's forget the poison for a moment. I need that info on Lucifer. Everything you've learned."

"What's the rush?"

"He claims he's imprisoned the witch who cursed me." He rested his hands on the hilts of his daggers, rage pulsing from him. "I want to know if it's true, if any of his allies have mentioned Queen Lilith of Lleh. I want to know if they mentioned *any* prisoners."

Wait. "If Lilith lives, whose skull decorates your shelf?"

"I don't know," he snapped. "Maybe hers, maybe not. Lucifer is a known liar, so I can't be sure until I'm sure." He popped his knuckles, no doubt imagining all the ways he could break his brother's face. "Before coming here, I spoke with my children. Two are searching for the truth even now."

Two? She'd known he had a son, singular. She hadn't known there were others. "How many kids do you have?"

"Three boys. I had a daughter as well, but a phoenix shifter removed her head." Now his fingers curled around those dagger hilts. "The boys spy and kill for me, as I once spied and killed for Hades."

Astonishment knocked her back a few steps. "Do they have different mothers?"

A faint pink tint spread over his cheeks, confusing her. William was embarrassed by the female(s)? But why? This was a man who had nude portraits of himself hanging throughout his home.

"There's no mother in the picture," he muttered. "That's all you need to know."

Had the woman abandoned the boys or died? So badly Sunny wanted to push for answers, and she would. Later. Right now, she grabbed her laptop and diary, then led William to the small table in the kitchen. "I kept detailed notes about every enemy I ever interrogated."

He pulled out a chair for her, but she shook her head and motioned for him to sit. He frowned, but he did it. Hoping to avoid his scent, she perched directly across from him. Nope. No better. Every time she inhaled, her hormones turned feral and she only wanted to jump him. Didn't help that he was being so chivalrous to her.

"I've nabbed three generals, over three hundred soldiers, eight of his best assassins and four of his mistresses," she began as she typed, her fingers flying over the laptop's keyboard. Once she found the correct files, she slid the laptop William's way. "Here's everything they admitted."

As he scrolled through the pages at a clipped pace, his nails lengthened into ebony claws, and a vein bulged in his forehead.

Voice rough with irritation, he snapped, "No mention of Lilith." He slammed his fist into the table, the wood cracking.

She canted her head to the side. "Why did you and Lucifer break up?"

He ran his tongue over his pearly whites. "To answer that question, you need backstory."

"Perfect. I love a good backstory."

He puffed a breath. "We met the day he helped Hades rescue me from…a hellish realm. I was lonely, traumatized and desperate. Lucifer was older, stronger and, for a while, kind. But every day I heard new rumors about secret black-magic rituals, rapes and animal sacrifices." Bitterness dripped from every word. "Still, I chose to believe his claims of innocence."

Why the pause after "rescue me from"? What had he

planned to say originally? And how had he been traumatized? What horrors had little William been forced to endure?

Sympathy welled. "Go on."

"Later, he attempted to sacrifice me—while I slept. It was a betrayal I could not forgive."

"I'm sorry, William. You must have been devastated."

He pulled at his collar, clearly uncomfortable, and returned the conversation to the interrogations. "In your notes, you mention an artifact Lucifer wanted. A medallion. Do you know what it does?"

Oh, yes. No way she'd spill the best and worst of the details, though. Instead, she'd stick with the basics. Things Lucifer and his crew had known. "It's round and flat, about the size of a half-dollar, and roughly two inches thick. It's a weapon." It required effort, but she stopped herself from reaching up to stroke the medallion hidden under her shirt. It wasn't the one Lucifer had hunted, but it was similar. Of course, she owned the other one, too. Anything the bluebell had wanted, she'd acquired. "A spear grows from the center."

"There must be more to it than that." William reached for the book, intending to read her handwritten notes, but she jerked it out of range, pretending she didn't want him seeing her lists.

"You're right. It isn't a normal spear. The shallowest incision can paralyze your opponent for several seconds, giving you just enough time to remove their head." *Among other things.* "Details about the spear are not in my diary."

"Only your lists."

"Exactly. So, you understand why the book is off-limits to you, I'm sure."

His interest was palpable, and she shivered.

Lids going heavy and sinking to half-mast, he asked, "What have you written about me?"

The perfect response rolled from her tongue. "Absolutely nothing." Truth! In the list of sexual positions she hoped to try, she'd mentioned his friends, but never William himself.

"Nothing?" he roared, glaring at the diary as if he imagined burning it.

"That's right." When she closed the book with a flick of her wrist, he growled. Growled! *Do not laugh.* Dismissing the diary, she said, "If you want to return the favor and tell me everything *you* know about Lucifer, I wouldn't be opposed."

Though he continued to glare at the book, he told her, "He's a shape-shifter able to morph into anyone he's seen in person or photos. In fact, we should use a code word from now on, to prove our identities to each other."

"No need. I see auras, so I can pick a shape-shifter out of a crowd of thousands."

"What happens if Lucifer acquires a person's aura when he shifts?"

Good point. It wasn't impossible. "You're right. We need a code word. How about *Your penis is cute!*"

For a long while, William peered at her, silent. Then he hooked his foot underneath her chair and dragged her closer. "Since you cannot lie, it's safe to assume you do, in fact, think my penis is cute."

Again, she caught a whiff of his delicious scent. The heat his body radiated…the startling intensity of his gaze… New shivers rocked her. *Stronger* shivers.

He seemed to be waiting for her to say something else. When she remained quiet, too busy praying he would lean over and kiss her, he added, "Do you know where the medallion is?"

"I do." *Tell him.* No doubt he'd want the weapon for himself. Who wouldn't? Would he demand she give it to him? Probably. Then, she could resist him, no problem. "I kind of…own it."

He stopped breathing. "I want it." Excitement flushed his skin. "Name your price."

What! No demands? He'd rather bargain?

Oh, she was tempted. Over the centuries, she'd found six medallions. She wore one, and had hidden the others. That way, she had backups, just in case. For the right incentive, she might, maybe, possibly part with one.

"I'll give you anything," he rushed to add. "Within reason."

Can't believe I'm about to do this. Her heart hammered against her ribs. *Inhale, exhale.* "I'll give you the medallion if you release the other codebreakers."

He thought for a moment, then nodded stiffly. "Done."

"*And* me. Set me free, William." She would stick around to break the curse and get that escort to Lucifer's door, willingly rather than forced.

"No!" he roared.

With that one word, shouted so loudly, her temper threatened to redline.

"I'll release the others," he offered at a more reasonable volume, "but not you."

Forget his earlier compliment. He'd earned another torment. "Then you will release them *and* move into the stable with me. You'll put your clothes in the closet, your toiletries in the bathroom and your body in the bed. Every. Single. Night. Think *Real Househusbands of the Underworld.*"

A tinge of panic infiltrated his expression, but he quickly wiped his features clean of emotion. He even schooled his body language. "Why do you want this?"

"Maybe I hope to steal your sperm while you're sleeping, artificially inseminate myself and use a baby to trap

you into a long-term relationship. Who's to say? Unless…
You're rich, right? I'd like my baby daddy to be rich."

He stared at her as if she'd sprouted horns. "I am rich,
yes," he finally said, still masking his emotions. "Is that the
only reason you'd want me to father your child?"

"Well, you're hot, too. The most handsome contender."

"Who are the other contenders?" A vein pulsed in his
forehead. *"They. Will. Die."*

His jealousy helped sooth her temper. "How cute are
you. Look at me," she said, doing her best impersonation
of him. "I'll kill anyone who looks at my woman."

Steam curled from his nostrils. "I'm not—never mind."
Gentling his tone, he told her, "If I move in with you, sundae, you'll fall in love with me. And I…" He shook his
head. "You'll cling."

"Me, cling to *you*?" And her temper redlined again. *He's
going to pay for that comment. I'm going to plant a verbal
dagger in his heart. But…what if he's right and I do cling
to him?* No. No! He'd never been more wrong. "If you're
secretly hoping I'll *start* clinging, I suggest you watch a
few how-to-kiss videos on YouTube first."

"I know how to kiss!" He huffed and puffed like a big,
bad wolf. "But you've given me my marching orders, and
I—"

"Hold up. I'm not done." *Gotta twist the knife.* "Since
we're committed and all, you must remain monogamous
or I'm out of here."

Inhalations ragged, he slapped his hands on the arms
of her chair and leaned close…closer…getting in her face.
"Very well," he said, shocking her. "You have a deal, sundae, but I don't think you'll be happy about it when all is
said and done."

15

"If I have a sword, and you have a sword, then I have two swords."

WILLIAM RESETTLED AGAINST the desk, struggling to maintain a stern, even angry, expression. Sunny thought she'd gained the upper hand. Instead, she'd done exactly as he'd hoped. After killing the poacher early this morning, he'd *wanted* to move in. The closer he was to Sunny, the better he could protect her if anyone managed to make it past the traps outside. Like, say, a certain witch.

Lucifer is a liar. Lilith is dead. Surely.

So why did foreboding sting his nape?

A mystery for later. When he wasn't verbally warring with his unicorn. During their "negotiation," Sunny had revealed more than she'd concealed, and he'd realized she'd pushed his move-in as another punishment, not because she'd wanted a roommate. That *had* angered him.

I want her to want *me to move in? Who am I?*

Why did he look forward to her *next* punishment? And what the hell had she written in that diary? He would be reading those fantasies of hers just as soon as he moved in. His house, his rules.

"Now that I've agreed to your terms, sacrificing my desires to fulfill yours," he intoned, "you will tell me where the medallion is located."

She chewed on her bottom lip, as if nervous about the conditions of their bargain. Too late. No take backs.

In the end, she whispered the coordinates to a realm tucked and hidden inside the mortal world. *Her* realm. Mythstica.

Intrigued, he stood, took her hand and drew her to her feet. He didn't release her right away. She was so close, so soft, and she could give him more pleasure than anyone else.

Sunny Lane *was* his lifemate. No longer could he doubt it.

She'd translated a small section of his book, proving herself to be his one and only codebreaker, and his one and only lifemate. William still reeled.

He remembered how blithely he'd told Keeley he would kill his lifemate. How he'd later balked at the idea. How he now *seethed* at the thought. No one harmed Sunday Lane. No one. Not now, not ever. Not even William.

Shit. Shit! Trembling but trying to hide it, he waved, unleashing a stream of magic. Embers sparked and spread, burning a seven-by-seven-foot hole in the atmosphere. Through it, he glimpsed a mossy, rocky cliff teeming with different-colored flowers, white trees and countless rainbows.

Just in case Sunny decide to bolt, he tightened his hold. "You will stay in the stable," he told her.

She sputtered, "How are you going to find the medallion without me? For that matter, *you* might want to stay here. Rainbows burn demons the same way sunlight burns vampires, so it'll probably burn a prince of darkness worse."

"Or," he continued, as if she hadn't spoken, "you can vow to remain by my side." As for the rainbows, parts of William *would* burn, yes. Other parts would not. Most likely he had a demon in his lineage. Perhaps the reason Hades had gone searching for him as a boy? When he returned home, he would ask Axel how *he* reacted to rainbows.

William went still. *That's right.* Axel had moved into the underworld. They'd met; they'd interacted. Hades's prediction was null and void. No part of William had died; no part of him *would* die. His love for the male was as strong as ever.

Now that he thought about it…who had made the death prediction in the first place?

"I vow to stay by your side," Sunny snarled. "Okay? Happy now?"

Yes. Very. "Do you miss this realm?" he asked. The scent of orchids, earth and rain wafted into the stable— Sunny's scent, only jacked up a thousand degrees. Instant hard-on. Again.

Was he ever *not* hard around her?

"I do." She peered at the rainbows, her eyes soft with longing. "My pack ran faster than the wind and loved to frolic in the meadows. We helped people in need and even granted wishes."

Longing coated each of her words, too, causing unease and guilt to hammer at William. Once, she'd warned him unicorns and captivity did not work. As if it worked for anyone. Now, though, he thought he understood better. To unicorns, freedom was life. But...

Can't let her go. Just...can't. Not yet. He couldn't risk losing his codebreaker or his lifemate—the one destined to murder him.

He *needed* Sunny to break the curse. Then he could take her in every possible way, as many times as he wished. He could talk to her without reservation, fearing he would reveal too much and aid her crusade, if ever she turned on him. And damn, did he enjoy talking to her. He loved her wit, and thrilled every time she surprised him.

The woman *constantly* surprised him.

Does she *thrill every time she talks to* me, *her captor?*

She continued, "I was married here and planned to rule over—"

"Married?" William bellowed. Aggression seared his limbs. Once, he'd preferred married women. *Wham, bam, go back to your hubby, ma'am.* But no longer. The thought of Sunny bound to some piece of shit male... Fuck!

With a snarl, he released Sunny, grabbed a chair and tossed it across the stable. It hit the wall and shattered upon impact.

Tonight, Sunny becomes a widow. His codebreaker, lifemate and temporary, live-in girlfriend would *not* have divided loyalties. *By the Hell kings, I will be her one and only.*

"Shall I fetch another chair, or are you done with your tantrum?" she asked.

"Fetch. Another. Chair."

She rolled her eyes. "I was married, yes, but I'm not now. Blaze was the son of the unicorn king, killed in the battle with Lucifer."

A heavy breath escaped William. Okay. All right. The urge to commit murder faded. Now he only wanted to dig up the bastard's grave and spit on his corpse. "Do you miss *him*?"

"Not even a little. We never liked each other and only wed for duty."

Appeased, William took her hand once again and tugged her through the portal. He wanted that medallion.

They emerged onto a cliff situated between two rainbows. Gusts of floral-scented wind nearly flung him over the ledge, as if the realm itself wanted him gone ASAP. Tree limbs clapped together, and leaves glittered in beams of sunlight. He sensed life, but didn't know if that life was animal, insect or unicorn.

"Mmm." Azure hair whipped around Sunny's face as she closed her eyes and breathed deep. "Home. There's nothing better."

He observed her, entranced.

When she opened her eyes, she said, "I gave you coordinates to the medallion, not just the realm." She leaned over to reach *inside* a rainbow, then withdrew a small golden disc, exactly as she'd described.

Exactly like the one she wore around her neck, he realized now. What did this—

His mind short-circuited. Her hair. Her hair had changed. She had touched the rainbow, and the blue locks had become neon pink. Her eyes had changed, too. Once amber, now a pale but vivid green. Her skin acquired more glitter.

Glorious female. "How? Why?"

"Unicorns absorb the essence of the rainbow."

The Sphere of Knowledge had failed to mention this, a trait he found fascinating. Sunny looked more delicate, even dainty. Fragile. No one would suspect her of being a hard-core demon slayer.

When she held out her hand, offering the medallion, he

accepted, trembling with desire. *I want to watch this pink-haired, green-eyed vixen shatter.*

Focus! As he studied his new weapon, a mix of light and dark magic prickled his skin. Powerful. Ancient. No wonder Lucifer had hunted it. *And now I have it.* William grinned. He would safeguard it with his life.

Instinct flared. *I'm fated to wield this medallion.*

An instinct he didn't understand, but would. "Now we have his and her matching medallions," he said with a wry tone.

Her cheeks pinkened. "So you noticed mine."

"I did." He'd noted every detail about her. *My new addiction.* "I just didn't know what it could do."

"Well, yours is different than mine," she said, shifting from one foot to the other, "but, uh, still the same. If that makes sense."

It did, and it didn't. But why the sudden bout of nerves? Hoping to make her smile, he asked, "Do you wish to explore the realm before we go home?"

First, she brightened. Then she wilted. "No. The longer I stay, the harder it'll be to leave."

That, he understood. In the back of his mind, he scheduled a return trip. Once his curse was broken and Lucifer was dead, they could stay for weeks. Months even. Or as long as they were together.

Still think you'll come to want another?

Unsure what he wanted from a woman for the first time in his existence, William led Sunny through the portal. He closed it and strode to the desk, where he plopped into the chair.

When she headed his way, he said, "I need to study, and you are too much of a distraction. Give me space."

She stopped and blew him a kiss with her middle finger, but she made no protests. Instead, she busied herself with the photos of his book. Another surprise. Did she not want to spend time with him, her brand-spanking-new *boyfriend*?

Inner shake. What did it matter? He flipped on the desk lamp and bent his head over the medallion but…he failed to block Sunny from his thoughts. His awareness of her sharpened, and he spent the next half hour pretending to study his prize while covertly watching *her*, wishing she would ignore his request.

The more she concentrated on the photos, the more the crease between her brows deepened. A crease he longed to trace with his fingertip.

Patience eroded, he slammed a fist against the desk. "I've learned nothing new, and I've run out of time. I must go."

"If the big, strong he-man had asked the sweet little woman," she said, sauntering over to claim his medallion, "she would have shown him how to use it. Watch." She pressed the medallion against her palm and curled her fingers into specific grooves.

A hard, black protrusion grew from the center. A spear, just as she'd claimed. When she pried her fingers free, the protrusion retracted. Fascinating.

"Where are you going?" she asked.

"I must pack a bag so I can move in. I'll return sometime before midnight." Thereby meeting the parameters of her request.

"What about our dinner with Hades?" She performed a twirl, her skirt flaring just above her knees. Those silken pink waves hung free, and he would give anything to fist the strands, angle her face and take her mouth. Holding out her arms, she asked, "Are my clothes appropriate or should I change?"

The ice-blue cloth molded to her curves, turning her into

a fantasy made flesh with peekaboo slits. Desire *seethed* inside him.

"I go alone," he told her. One, he had no idea what Hades wished to discuss. And two, she was a distraction he could ill afford.

"Oh." Her shoulders rolled in. "I see."

So forlorn. A pang ripped through him. "What exactly do you *see*, duna?"

She flinched as if he'd punched her. Why, damn it? Then she smiled without a speck of amusement, and *he* flinched. "Doesn't matter." She shooed him off. "Go. Have fun without me."

What thoughts rolled through that cunning mind of hers? The temptation to stay and question her proved strong. Nearly too strong to resist.

In the end, William opened a portal to his bedroom. He would change his clothes, then head to Hades's. He would *not* spend the evening agonizing over Sunny's reaction.

He walked through the doorway. Without a backward glance—*don't you fucking do it*—he waved, sealing the exit. Guilt attempted to devour him whole.

I won't think about Sunny. I—

What would she think about my bedroom? He used one entire wall as a television screen. Video games and controllers littered the floor. The wet bar offered an assortment of ambrosia-laced whiskeys. Instead of a nightstand, he had a minifridge stocked with all his favorites—anything loaded with high-fructose corn syrup. Yeah, he had the sophisticated palette of a frat boy. So what? The bed was a masterpiece of craftsmanship, bigger than a king, but surprise, surprise Pandora lay in the center of it, flipping through a magazine.

A wave of affection washed over him, a side effect of

Hades's adoption. He strode to the closet, asking, "What are you doing here?"

She didn't bother to glance up. "You sent me a message and told me to meet you here. So nice of you to remember."

He'd never sent a message. "In other words, Hades expects you to act as my chaperone and ensure I'm a good boy who attends the family dinner."

Page-flip. "If you knew the answer, why'd you ask?"

Two hellhound pups poked their heads out from under the bed.

William jolted back, already reaching for a dagger. Hellhounds could rip an immortal to shreds in a matter of seconds. And once a hellhound locked onto a target, nothing but the target's death dissuaded it from a hunt. "Panda?"

"Oh, yeah," she said, flipping another page. "Baden dropped off a couple hellhounds. They're a gift from Hades."

Baden, another of Hades's adopted sons, as well as a Lord of the Underworld formerly possessed by the demon of Distrust. A male of honor who meant what he said and said what he meant. His wife, Katarina, trained packs of hellhounds for Hades.

My own hellhounds. William grinned as the pair ducked back under the bed. The first pup was a little cutie with white-and-black fur, two heads, two sets of red eyes and a single forked tail. The second was a larger female with dirt-caked fur of indeterminate color, one head, three black eyes and a wealth of scars.

How did Sunny feel about pets?

His cell phone vibrated in his pocket. He rushed to check the screen, just in case she had need of him.

Gilly Gumdrop: Liam, I'm so thrilled for you! I hear you

found your decoder. Now you're one step closer to being curse-less :) :) :)

He grinned as he typed, That I am. How about a celebration video game marathon? Torin created a Lords of the Underworld demon slaying game. As you probably guessed, the Slick Willy character is undefeatable.

Gilly Gumdrop: Puck and I would love to destroy Slick Willy! We're currently locked in negotiations with Sent Ones. They've still got his brother locked away, and we want him back. As soon as we're done, we'll come for a visit.

William couldn't wait to see her. She always brightened his life.

What would she think of Sunny?

As for Puck's brother, Sin, they'd never get him back. Possessed by the demons of Paranoia and Indifference—the worst of the worst combination—he was the one who'd bombed the heavens, killing hundreds of Sent Ones. He wasn't just imprisoned; he was being tortured.

William might have to get involved.

He sighed, pocketed the phone and began packing an overnight bag to stay in the stable. "Have you ever spent an entire night with a lover?" he asked Pandora.

"No. Gross. I get what I want, and I get out."

Exactly! To sleep with a woman, actually sleep, he'd have to trust her with his life. He'd never trusted *anyone* with his life, not even Gillian, whom he'd treasured. He'd seen too many friends fall victim to "bait." Males and females who seduced in order to kill.

Sunny wasn't bait, but she *was* destined to kill him.

Won't leave her alone, unprotected. Can't resist her charms.

Perhaps he'd use the nighttime hours to scheme ways to kill Lucifer and acquire Lilith. If she truly lived.

Or he'd just have sex 24/7 to prepare for mating season. Because yes, he would be taking care of Sunny.

At the thought, desire scorched him, inside and out, and he hissed a pained breath. *I want her. I want her* now. He'd been celibate since they'd met…what? Two days ago? That was two days longer than usual. And damn if it didn't seem like he'd known her two years.

Was that how matehood worked? A day seemed like a year, and a year seemed like a day?

"Why'd you ask about the lover thing?" Pandora asked. "No, you know what? Never mind. Let's just change the subject before I start barfing. So. You know Lucifer better than any of us." While rocking her legs back and forth, her ankles crossed, she flipped another page. "Could he really keep the witch locked up for centuries and resist the urge to kill her?"

"I don't know him anymore. I *never* knew him." William stuffed a few shirts and an entire box of condoms in his bag, saying, "He's always been a deceiver, changing personalities the way other people change clothes. But I'll learn the truth one way or another."

A straight-up invasion of Lucifer's palace would be foolish. Lucifer was a master at rigging traps so that the one who broke in inadvertently murdered the one they hoped to save.

Panda nodded her agreement. "Where are your boys?"

"Two are chasing rumors about Lilith, and one is hunting for Evelina Maradelle, Lucifer's absentee wife." The few things William remembered about her: a witchy dragon-shifter with a kind heart who spoke with a stutter. She'd run off soon after the wedding, sending Lucifer into an unstoppable rage.

William couldn't wait to taunt his ex-brother. *I have your wife. Want her back? Too bad, so sad.*

He snickered as he shoved a favorite video game system, games and a deep conditioning—totally manly—hair treatment into the bag.

The little hellhounds decided to emerge, prowl over and sniff his leg.

Teasing them, he said, "Put your noses in my ass, and we will have problems."

"As if! I would never put—" Pandora glanced up from the magazine at last, noticed the hounds and muttered, "Never mind."

William bent down to pet the pups. The one caked in dirt flinched, as if expecting a hit, and a sharp pang of sympathy tore through him. Had Baden and Katarina found her in the wilds of hell? The other hound nipped his fingers. As blood welled in the pad of his thumb, the pair backed away. Afraid of him?

"You remind me of an acquaintance," he told the two-headed baby. "Only, she uses bullets instead of teeth. Her name is Sunny, so let's keep the sky theme going and call you Dawn. And you…" He gave the dirty one his kindest smile. "We'll call you Aurora. You're as pretty as the northern lights, sweetheart."

Aurora understood him; she must. She softened, even rubbed against him.

Pandora tossed the magazine. "I was hoping you'd bring Sunny to dinner. Can you imagine Rathbone using *freesia* as an expletive? Talk about hilarious!"

A faint pitter-patter of claws on wood caught William's attention, and he frowned. Sounded like an entire pack of hellhounds. Then the scent of sulfur, brimstone and malice tainted the air, stinging his nostrils, and he palmed two daggers.

Demons. A horde. They hadn't come for a chat; they'd come for blood.

Pandora sensed the threat, too, and reached under a pillow, pulling out a minicrossbow and a mythical dagger with the power to incinerate its victims.

His daggers weren't going to do shit. *Use the medallion?* No. He wouldn't wield an untried weapon against an enemy.

Within the borders of Hell, otherwise intangible demons had the ability to materialize and dematerialize on command. Since one spirit could be fought only by another spirit—like called to like—William would have to dematerialize at times, too. Both a blessing and a curse. He would land blows, but he would also burn through energy faster. Too fast.

Dawn's neon red eyes glowed with fear. Aurora kept her head bowed as her body shook. Usually, hellhounds exhibited massive amounts of aggression. That these two feared... Something awful must have happened to them. Katarina must have thought they'd do like every other woman, and melt for him.

Every other woman but Sunny.

"Back under the bed, girls." He strode over to hold up the bed skirt. The pups rushed to obey. "I will do everything in my power to keep you safe, I swear it."

He dropped his daggers, raced back to his closet and grabbed two sickles.

An enemy has invaded my father's home. Rage transformed his blood into fuel, the barest hint of smoke already seeping from his pores. *Careful.* They were in Hell; the smoke could hurt Pandora just as easily as the demons.

"This must be payback for Hades's attack against Lucifer," Pandora said, darting to William's side. They would fight back-to-back, ensuring no one snuck up behind them.

"Then they want blood. Ours." The pitter-patter grew louder...louder...soon becoming a stampede. "Should arrive in three...two..."

The horde ghosted through the walls in droves, flooding the room with a cloud of dark smoke.

William coughed, blood leaking from his eyes and nose. No time to clean up. The demons swarmed him, ready to kill.

16

"If you allow an enemy to live today, expect to die by his hand tomorrow."

PANDORA REMAINED AT William's back as he dematerialized to slash at one demon and rematerialized to slash at another. Sweat poured from him, a crazy intense surge of adrenaline turning his torso into a furnace. He sliced and diced limbs, genitals, wings and tails. He removed eyes and severed spines. Heads thudded to the floor and rolled away, sizzling black blood spraying in every direction. Bodies collapsed, piling up around him, filling the room with the pungent scent of old pennies and emptied bowels.

A cacophony of noise assaulted his ears. Grunts and groans. The gurgle and swish of liquids—blood, bile and piss. The pop of breaking bones. The raggedness of panting breaths.

One of the fiends managed to claw William's neck. The pain! The demon must have injected him with some kind of venom; the gashes heated, soon boiling.

Venom…akin to a vial of poison?

Shit! The heat singed a path to his brain. In seconds, he felt as if his head had been dropped into a vat of boiling oil, agony overtaking him.

Do not slow. He drew back his elbow, about to remove his opponent's head. Then he paused, horrified. The demon was no longer a demon, but Gillian, wearing a bloody tank top and shorts.

William had almost murdered the girl he treasured above all—most—others.

Panic fragmented his thoughts. How had she… She couldn't… This…? "You shouldn't have come. Go!" Why weren't the demons attacking her? "You have to go *now*." She'd grown into a fierce warrior, yes, but she wasn't ready for a battle like this.

"I'm not leaving you," Pandora snarled, her body jerking against his.

Gleeful snickers. He'd amused the demons?

"Not you." Did his sister not see his friend?

Gillian smiled and strutted closer, oblivious to the danger. The moment she stood within striking distance, he latched on to her forearm, intending to yank her between him and Pandora. *Will protect her with my life!* Only, her skin wasn't soft and supple but dry and patchy like scales. A green tail uncoiled between her legs, slithering out from behind her. The spiked tip resembled the head of a demonic snake.

What the hell?

Oh, shit. The demons, they belonged to the Hallucina horde, Lucifer's favorite pets. They leaked venom that screwed with the minds of their victims, causing them to see vivid hallucinations.

Before William could strike, fake Gillian cracked her

tail across his cheek. Skin split, and his head whipped to the side. A new flare of heat and pain.

Sunny appeared a few feet away, and his heart nearly stopped. Sunny, with her pink hair, emerald eyes and untapped sensuality. Logically, he knew she was a hallucination created by his mind. Still, he panicked all over again. What if she'd flashed, following him here? *Could* she flash? *Think!*

Did the answer really matter? He couldn't risk her life.

"Stay where you are," he bellowed at her. "Do not move." He would remain out of striking distance, just in case, but he would allow no others to near her.

Readjusting his grip on the sickles, William freed a hand. With a roar, he bent down, grabbed one of the daggers he'd dropped earlier and tossed it, nailing the demon next to Sunny.

Arms remaining in a constant flow of motion, he cut through another demon, then another. Swinging. Slashing. Jabbing.

Every time he sliced the curved edge of a sickle into a demon's body, he twisted the blade for maximum damage. Drops of black blood splattered over his skin, blisters welling.

"Help me," Sunny pleaded. She wrapped her arms around her middle, as if terrified, and attempted to edge closer to him.

Though sharp pangs tore through him, he jumped back—and inadvertently collided with a demon. More pain and heat. The sharp edge of a wing ripped through cotton and flesh, a stream of crimson trickling down his abdomen.

Whoosh. An arrow embedded in the space between Sunny's eyes. Her knees buckled, and she collapsed.

"No!" He dove to catch her before she hit the floor. More pain and heat, but he didn't care. Dead. She was dead.

Vision blurring, he cradled her beautiful face against his chest. A war cry lodged in his throat.

This isn't her. Can't be her.

Please, please, don't let this be my Sunny.

Another demon launched at him. Contorting, William kicked out his leg. Impact. The demon collided with his steel-toed boot and stumbled backward.

"Hades?" Pandora gasped out. She stilled, her crossbow lifted but shaking.

Hades had come? Struggling to control his breathing, William chanced a look over his shoulder. No sign of his father but... No! *Every* demon wore Sunny's face.

Terror rattled him to his core, his vitals icing over. In that moment, he felt as if he'd lost the battle, one hundred percent. What if the demons had hidden the real Sunny in their midst?

Could William risk the murder of his codebreaker?

My woman. Mine! I'll protect her with my life. But he had to do something fast, or he would die in this room.

Die? No! Not today, not ever. Determination hardened his heart into stone. Today, he killed. Them. All. No mercy. "The venom," he bellowed for Pandora's benefit. She'd lived in the underworld for a very short period, and she had yet to learn about the different demon breeds. "It causes hallucinations. Feel the skin. If it's rough, deliver a death blow, no matter who it is."

Something came up, but I'll return to the stable in an hour. Be ready.

BE READY FOR WHAT? Sunny had received William's text message three hours ago. That "an hour" had come and gone without another word from him.

I'm not good enough to meet my fake boyfriend's beloved father or *get an explanation for his tardiness.*

Hurt pricked her, but so did worry. Where was he? What if something bad had happened?

She sent a message, asking for an update but...another minute passed. Then five. Ten. Thirty. No response.

Hellebore! Daisy! Sage! Freesia! Something bad *must* have happened. But there was nothing she could do about, trapped in a stable.

She paced, her emotions running the gamut. Everything from paralyzing fear to righteous anger. She wanted him here with her *now*. She wanted to hug him and patch him up if he were injured. And then she wanted to throat punch him for making her worry.

Desperate for a distraction, she opened her diary and ripped out the list of sexual positions. Magic supplied a brand-new page, only blank.

She wrote a new list titled All the Ways to Punish William for His Poor Treatment of Me.

—*Staked to a wall naked.*

—*Orgasm denial.*

—*Chained to bed and whipped.*

"I'm sensing a theme," she muttered. She created a second list of made-up sexual positions. Things he couldn't possibly have heard of, since she'd just invented them. Fingers crossed he would feel totally inadequate. *Read 'em and weep, big boy.*

Another half hour passed, but still no word from William.

Why was she still sitting here, doing nothing? She was a freaking killer unicorn, not some lame-aster princess in distress. If her prince charming needed aid, Sunny would provide aid. If he needed a reminder that he'd acquired a vengeful superhero vigilante of a girlfriend, she would provide a reminder.

She strapped on a pair of daggers she'd lifted from William during his last visit, then stuffed his photos into a backpack. With the pack anchored to her shoulders and the daggers in hand, she kicked open the barn doors. There had to be a way around the invisible block. And if not around, over. If not over, under.

Nobody locks me in a glorified barn!

Despite the legions of demons William had killed, more fiends already congregated in the area. They stopped what they were doing, turned and faced her. As countless red eyes looked her over, rage coursed through her veins, hot and hungry. *Hate demons! Evil must be eradicated.*

One of the first lessons taught by her battle instructors: *Never leave an evil being behind. They'll only slither away and return with friends at a later date.*

Her heart thudded as she took a step forward. *Let's do this.* She'd take out every fiend and—

A calloused hand snagged her bicep, squeezing tight, yanking her backward and spinning her around. William! Silent, he removed and dropped her backpack, then kicked the doors shut.

Eyes narrowed, still silent, he stalked forward, backing her against the wood and flattening his palms at her temples to cage her in. Her heart thudded harder and faster, snatching the air from her lungs. He looked like a man possessed, dark and sinister, with streaks of black all over his body. Dried demon blood. She'd worn her fair share, too. His raven locks stuck out in spikes, framing a beautiful face littered with gashes and bruises. His clothes were ripped, the scent of sulfur and death emanating from him.

But hidden beneath the stink were hints of his innate fragrance. *Mouthwatering.*

Finally he said, "Safe word. Tell me. Now."

Uh, what the what? "Your penis is cute?"

Relief softened his harsher edges. Within seconds, however, fury eclipsed the relief, and he snarled, "Where the hell were you going?"

Ooookay. Splatters of red, green and rusty yellow glowed in his blurry aura. His emotions were as interchangeable and turbulent as hers. But his eyes...his eyes became two open wounds, bleeding pain.

"Tell me," he croaked.

The thought of her absence upset him that much? "I planned to find a way past your barrier, kill the demons, then find and save you," she admitted softly.

He did that surprised-blink thing.

"You messaged to say you'd be here in an hour," she reminded him. "That hour passed almost five hours ago without another word from you. So, you had better be mortally wounded or something." She searched him for an outside sign of injury, but found none. All right, then. Her rage returned and redoubled. "What in hellebore happened to you? Why didn't you respond to my text?"

Another blink of surprise. "I was ambushed." He popped his jaw. "Lucifer sent a horde of Hallucina demons. Their fangs and claws produce a hallucinogenic venom, and I only just recovered."

Now her rage switched targets. *I'll slay them. Slay them all!* "Take me to them. Now."

"Can't. They're dead. Killed by my hand."

Okay. Fine. *But now he's even sexier!*

William ran his tongue over his perfect white teeth. "No

questions about my state of being? No fawning over my wounds?"

"Why? Do you have hidden owies in need of tending?"

"Yes," he hissed.

Finally, she had a legit excuse to run her greedy hands over every inch of his sculpted body. Maybe, just maybe, she could turn off her paranoia, if only for a bit, and have fun. Had she *ever* had fun? Other than killing demons, of course.

No. Now wasn't the time for fun. As a child, the king had loved telling her that her duty came before everything. And right now, Sunny had a duty to perform. A lesson to teach. William might have a good reason for failing to update her, but he'd still caused her unnecessary worry. For that, he would pay.

Let's get started.

17

"Love without might is misery."

SUNNY DELIVERED A quick jab to William's throat. "That's for making me worry." As he gasped for breath he couldn't catch, she slammed her fist into his nose. Cartilage snapped, and blood trickled from his nostrils. "That's for being too embarrassed to introduce me to your dad."

Her knuckles pulsated. He had a freakishly hard head.

With a growl, he got in her face. The tip of his nose brushed hers, and he blinked. Between panting breaths, he grated, "I'm not embarrassed of you, sundae. I just don't want my father trying to recruit you. I'd have to decline on your behalf, and our relationship is already strained."

Really? He'd been protecting her? Softening, she flattened her hands on his chest. To her surprise and delight, his heart raced against a palm.

He heaved a heavy breath. "I'm sorry I hurt you."

See! A little punishment, and he'd learned. So had she. *Never assume I understand his motives. Always ask.*

"Why don't you hop in the shower?" she said, feeling magnanimous now. "Afterward, I'll—" A dog barked, and she yelped, jumping up. A peek beyond William. The cutest two-headed, red-eyed dog in all of creation raced through the still-open portal.

Sunny went soft and liquid against him, peering up at him with what had to be the dreamiest eyes ever. "You brought me a puppy?" That was, hands down, the sweetest, kindest thing anyone had ever—

"Her name is Dawn. I saved her from the demons, and now she follows my every move. Typical female," he grumbled. "There was a second one, but I don't know where she—"

Dawn barked louder and shot through the portal, reentering what looked to be a bedroom. The little sweetie turned to face them and barked again.

"I think she's trying to tell us something." Sunny darted through the portal before William had a chance to stop her. "Show me, girl. What's wrong?"

Dawn moved to the closet and barked again. Sunny crouched beside her. Movement underneath a rumpled coat. She pushed the material out of the way...and gasped. The second dog. This one flicked in and out of view, blood spurting from her head. The poor, sweet darling had been mutilated. Her throat had been slashed, and her lungs wheezed every time she tried to breathe. The death wheeze.

Too far gone to heal with magic. "Oh, baby. I'm so sorry for your pain." As she gathered the wee darling close, tears welled in Sunny's eyes.

William flashed to her side, the color in his cheeks dulling. He attempted to take the dog.

Sunny shook her head. "I've got her."

"Her name is Aurora," he said, his voice cracking.

"Aurora." Tears spilling over, Sunny carried the precious bundle to the stable and laid her on the bed, then stretched out beside her. So the sheets would get bloody. So what. "C-can you heal her, William? Please! I'll pay any price. Heal her, and you don't even have to move in!"

"I'm sorry, sundae," he croaked, "but there's no magic strong enough."

A sob bubbled up, but she swallowed it back. To the dog, she whispered, "You are not alone, baby girl. I'm here, and I'm staying by your side. May you have the sweetest dreams, my darling." Then, she waved her hand over Aurora's face, using magic to put the dog into a deep sleep. That way, when her organs failed, she would simply drift off forever, pain-free.

To his credit, William stayed by her side, too. And the other dog, Dawn, watched from a corner, her red eyes projecting misery and fear. Together, their trio cooed to the sleeping Aurora until her little heart stopped.

Sunny's tears fell in earnest then. Still, she and William remained in place. She hadn't known the dog, but one look, and she'd fallen in love. That was her way with all animals, and the reason she would be a vegetarian for the rest of eternity.

"Who is responsible for this?" she demanded softly.

"Who else?"

"Lucifer." She spat his name like the vile curse it was.

William reached out and linked his fingers with Sunny's. "He will pay. I swear it."

Trembling now, she glided her free hand through the hound's biggest wound, collecting blood on her fingertips—

blood she smeared under her eyes. "The demons outside belong to your ex-brother?"

William sat up, nodded.

"Then they die. Today. By my hand." William had never seen her fight. He didn't know her skill level. If he attempted to stop her—

"Very well," he said, releasing her. He stood. "We will do this together."

Though surprised, she marched to the door. Centuries had passed since she'd gone to battle with a partner. How would they work together?

William flashed to her side. "Are you s—"

"Do *not* ask me if I'm sure I want to do this. I'm sure. I'm ready."

He nodded, as if impressed, then kicked open the door. Sunlight flooded into the stable and—

"Daisy!"

The demons were gone. Not a single creature dotted the landscape.

Unable to contain her rage, she screeched, turned and punched the wall. Her knuckles broke, and her skin split, but the pain barely registered.

William ushered her into the bathroom, where he tended to her wounds gently, tenderly. To her shock, he kissed the bandage when he finished.

Without saying a word, he gathered Aurora and carried the slain hellhound outside. During his absence, Sunny changed the sheets, showered off the blood and petted Dawn, fighting to shed a heavy weight of sadness.

William returned. Alone. Dirt streaked his face and caked his hands. He'd buried her, hadn't he?

What a sweet thing to do. Sunny sniff-sniffed and plopped into the chair at the desk.

He flashed in front of her, crouched down and clasped her chin, tilting her head up. Their eyes met, and a frisson of heat whisked through her. He looked so earnest.

"I've decided to take you to the book, sundae."

His words registered, and her eyes widened. "Really? You aren't afraid I'll destroy your precious to punish you?"

"Part of me is, but I'm desperate enough to trust you. Don't make me regret it, sundae."

"I won't," she whispered, and daisy, she meant it. If he stayed sweet like this, she'd never be able to use his book against him, would she?

"Do not leave the stable," he called to Dawn. He opened a portal and, after a slight hesitation, escorted Sunny into a small windowless room with white walls, an old wooden table and a plush recliner.

In the center of the table rested a display case with a leather-bound tome tucked inside.

The hound did not stay put. She followed them into the room. William scowled at her, and Sunny grinned.

"Are you sure you're irresistible to women?" she teased. "We continue to defy you."

The look he gave her…scorching hot, dark and sardonic. "Laugh it up, chuckles. One day soon, I'll have you screaming my name to the rafters."

She gulped. Embers of lust sparked and caught fire, a fever spreading through her body.

Hoping to cool down, she drew in a deep breath. *Wait.* Another deep breath. *Huh.* The air contained zero odors; she couldn't even smell William's ambrosial scent. A true travesty.

"What is this place?" she asked. Dawn explored, sniffing here and there, clearly annoyed by the lack, too.

"A pocket dimension in Hell I created with my magic.

Scents are filtered out, preventing others from tracking the book. My friend Anya likes to joke about…"

Sunny tried to listen, she really did—magic, scents, Anya, joke—but the room reminded her of the unicorn punishment pit. Small and isolated, with no way out. Horrible memories rose from the mire of her mind. The loneliness. The screams. The taste and feel of blood-soaked mud.

Calm. Steady.

"What is this? Panic?" William asked, confused. Again, he pinched her chin and angled her head, forcing her to meet his gaze. "Why?"

Don't do it. Don't tell him. Never reveal a vulnerability.

Except, that was how single Sunny thought. If she wanted William, and she did, she had to let herself be vulnerable with him.

Isn't the relationship fake?

Yes. No. Argh! She didn't know anymore. If she'd never detected his deep, abiding sadness, if he'd never been so kind to the dog…but he had, and now, here they were. "It's not panic," she told him. "It's unease."

"The woman who planned to combat a legion of demons fears…a room?"

"Have you ever been buried alive, William?" Her voice cracked. "I have. It was the unicorn king's favorite punishment. When Lucifer and his demons invaded our camp, I couldn't fight them because I was trapped in a dark, damp hole." Her chin trembled. "They slaughtered everyone as I listened, helpless. The screams…so many screams. Blood poured into the pit in rivers of crimson while demons laughed. Then there was silence, and it was so much worse."

He cupped her nape and pulled her close, then settled his palm on her lower back. "I'm sorry, sundae."

Smashed up against him like this, she only wanted to

burrow. With her face resting in the hollow of his neck, she sank her fingers into his silken hair, absorbing his heat.

This. So many people craved a significant other, and now she knew why. The right person comforted you, accepted you and built you up, never tearing you down.

But. William hated clingers, and Sunny hated being one. She pried her fingers free, straightened and stepped back, severing contact. Regret hit her in an instant. No heat. No comfort. Only cold and loneliness, exactly what she'd had pre-William.

Maybe clinging wasn't so bad.

With yearning in his eyes, he advanced on her, *forcing* her back into his embrace. A gentle embrace, despite his ferocity.

Marveling, she peered up at him. He *clings to* me? Who was this man?

He finger-combed her hair before grazing his knuckles along her jawline, every touch a revelation of tenderness, as if he...cherished her. "Why were you punished, sundae?"

For the first time, she had no voice in her head telling her to keep her past to herself. Maybe because William wasn't her captor right now; he was her friend. "I wanted to divorce Blaze, but he refused, even though he wanted to be with someone else and we were miserable together." She tried for a casual tone, but pain seeped into her words. "I made a public scene, hoping to change his mind, but I only managed to injure his pride and infuriate his father, the king."

William tensed, but he also kissed her temple. "I'm sorry."

The unexpected smooch shocked her to the core. A simple but profound gesture she thought she would replay for the rest of her days. Okay, she really, really needed out of his arms, before she asked about his day, fetched his favorite whiskey and sat at his feet while he read a paper.

Once again, she stepped back. He glared, until he noticed a smear of blood on her shirt. Concerned, he traced a finger over the stain, collecting a droplet.

"It's you," she whispered. "You're bleeding."

He yanked his shirt overhead, revealing claw marks on his sternum. "I healed this wound earlier, which means the demons used *infirmədē*, too. A venom that cause the wound to come back again and again, until you've taken the antidote." With a wave of his hand, the wounds wove back together. "Or neutralized it with magic."

She wanted to engage with him conversationally but… those pecs…that eight-pack, each row of strength hotter than the last…tattoos galore…his adorable navel…the black goodie trail that led to the waist of his leathers.

Breathless, she twirled a finger. "Turn around." She wanted, needed, to see him. All of him.

He looked ready to grin, his eyes flashing. "Should I remove the rest of my clothing first?"

"Yes!"

He laughed but he did turn around, without removing his pants. His back… Wow! He had a treasure map tattooed there, and she had a sudden urge to lick every inch of it.

Lick. Yes. Shivers traipsed down her spine, and champagne spilled through her veins. *No. Focus!* "Let's, uh, get to work." She turned away, one of the most difficult things she'd ever done, and removed the lid from the display case, surprised to discover her unease had been eradicated.

Magic tingled over her skin, dark and insidious, and she shuddered. But even still… *Must touch…*

She eased into the chair. When she reached for the book,

William flashed to her side and latched on to her wrist once again, stopping her just before contact.

"I'm not going to rip the pages," she promised, unable to look away from the object of her fascination. So powerful.

"I'm trusting you in a way I've never trusted another. Do not betray me, Sunny."

"As long as you're my captor, betrayal is a strong possibility," she confessed. When would he let her go? She *needed* her hand on the paper.

He pursed his lips and mumbled, "You don't see me as a bloodthirsty warlord, do you?"

"Of course I do." With her free hand, she reached up to blindly pat his stubble-roughened cheek. "The bloodthirstiest. Now, about the book. A girl's gotta work."

A pause. She felt the heat of his gaze searching her face. Then he sighed. "I deserve this, I really do."

"Don't worry, baby doll," she intoned. "You don't deserve me—yet—but keep tweaking your personality flaws, and you will." Book! Book! Book! She tugged on her hand.

At last, he released her. Giddy, she did it; she glided her fingertips over the outer edge of a page and moaned with delight. The magical tingles had intensified.

"Well?" he croaked.

She studied the symbols but...nothing translated. Hmm. She traced a swirling design, then another, but again, no part of the code revealed itself. "I'm sorry. I can feel the magic, I can. It's oddly entrancing but also disinterested in opening itself to me."

A moment passed in terse silence. "I told you I'd give you anything you desire if you decode this, and I meant it. Wealth. Another list of people killed. Enough orgasms to put you in a coma of bliss. I'll move heaven and earth to get the job done, sundae."

Just then, she wanted all of that and more. "Can I be brutally honest with you?" she asked as Dawn settled under the table, lying down at her feet.

He stared at Sunny, incredulous. "You mean you've been gentle with me until now?"

Yes! "First, you'll be giving me orgasms, anyway. We're going to have sex, and we both know it. Second, by letting you give me orgasms, I'm doing you *another* favor. Which means you'll owe me big-time. But don't worry. I will decode this. The magic might be playing hard to get but it wants me to win." She chewed on her bottom lip, knowing her next suggestion would be met with ire. "Maybe we should take the book back to the stable, so I can have more time with it." Those symbols…so hypnotic. Mesmerizing. Nothing would stop her from figuring out this mystery. Nothing! "Pretty please."

Strain carved fine lines around his eyes as he grated, "It stays here."

"You aren't worried about keeping your prized unicorn in the stable," she pointed out, "so why worry about the book? Let me study it in the comfort of my own prison-home."

"*My* home."

"Our home," she corrected, neither side of her nature trying to punish him. "I can free you from your curse, William, *if* you'll trust me and let me study. Granted, I'll have to take a bunch of breaks to pleasure myself. And you'll have to watch me. How else will you learn?" As frequently as sexual urges were overtaking her now, she needed to store as much satisfaction as possible before the official kickoff of mating season.

He went still, a thousand emotions flashing in his eyes, there and gone. She wondered how many thoughts he'd entertained in that split second. "Very well," he said, perhaps harsher than he'd intended. "We'll take the book back to the stable. But the same stipulation applies. You will do the book no harm. And, sundae? If you have needs while we're together, you'll tell me, and *I* will tend to you—since we both know we're going to be having sex and all. I'm trusting you with my future. You're going to trust me with your present."

"But—"

"That is my deal. Take it or leave it." He hooked a lock of hair behind her ear, his knuckles grazing her cheek-bone, reminding her of his former caress. His kindness. "And don't cry foul," he added. "A man's gotta do what a man's gotta do when his woman is a stubborn, paranoid unicorn who wouldn't know an orgasm if it bit her on the ass. Which it just might do."

I'm his woman? For real?

The thought…pleased her. *He* pleased her. She'd trusted him with certain information, and he'd rewarded her, trust-ing her with his precious. Now they were making plans to trust *each other* with their bodies.

Somehow, the course of her life had changed in the past two minutes. It was exciting. And nerve-racking. And won-derful, terrible, amazing, annoying, perfect and imperfect.

Daisy! The truth hit her, and hit hard. He'd warned her. If he moved in, she'd fall. Well, he'd moved in, and… *I'm falling for him.*

What was she going to do now?

18

"No shirt, no shoes—just take everything off."

THIS FEMALE WILL be the death of me.

As soon as the thought registered, denial clanged inside William's head. He wouldn't be dying. Not now. Not later. Not ever.

Instinct demanded he live, always. However, William had a second reason to survive, one just as compelling as the first.

When he'd first moved in with Hades, he'd learned spirits of the dead went up or down, without exception. The ones who went down became slaves of an underworld royal, no matter their station in life.

Usually, newcomers arrived via a reaper like Lucien. As a keeper of Death, Lucien sensed when someone died within the borders of his territory. He would flash to the body, free the spirit trapped within and escort it to its forever home.

Every day, Hell's kings, queens, princes and princesses sent out convoys of demons to collect any new arrivals. All were fair game. First come, first served. The royals kept some of the souls for themselves, and sold the rest. But, whether kept or sold, the dead always ended up getting a taste of their own medicine. Murderers were murdered again and again. Rapists were raped repeatedly. Beaters got beaten. Liars lost their tongues, and thieves lost limbs. For a thousand different reasons, escape wasn't possible.

If William died and ended up in Lucifer's territory...

Motions clipped, he returned Sunny and Dawn to the stable, along with the book and its case. Dawn darted under the bed, her safe place.

What he was going to do with the unicorn, he didn't know. He knew what he *should* do. Leave her in the stable and forget her until she'd broken the curse. Every day he wanted her more. Every day he *needed* her more. If he fell any harder, activating the curse...if she attempted to kill him...

But how could he abandon the woman who'd comforted a dying animal as it died? One covered in dirt, blood and filth. A mythical creature Sunny hadn't known, and yet she'd cried as if she'd lost her best friend.

Everything about her appealed to him. Her compassion and loyalty. Her honesty and integrity. Even her temper and her punishments. She amused and challenged him, arousing his mind as much as his body.

He cast his gaze throughout the stable, finding Sunny near the exit. She picked up the bag he'd dropped when he'd first flashed here and discovered her at the door, ready to bail.

Funny, but he used to portal to her, expending his magic. Lately, though, he'd opted to flash. He used no magic that way, but he reached her faster…because he was always in a hurry to return to her?

Something to ponder—later. As Sunny unpacked for him, a very girlfriendy task, new desires surged. Things he'd never expected to want. A loving partner. Companionship. Communion of souls. Unbreakable ties. Lifelong adoration and affection. Everything he'd once thought himself above. Everything he'd lacked but feared obtaining, so sure they'd be taken away from him.

He felt as if he were awakening from a dream. As if he finally, truly lived.

If I don't have this woman in my arms soon…

What about the curse?

Another subject to ponder later. Here, now, his mind remained on Sunny and all the things they could do to each other.

If—when—they had sex, would their emotional connection deepen?

Would he fall for her faster? Harder?

In the past, he'd used sex to feel better about himself. He saw the truth so clearly now. He'd merely wanted to be wanted. Understandable, considering the trauma he'd suffered as a child. But how different would sex be with a lifemate?

Must know!

Sunny set his video game system in front of the television, then strode to the closet, rolling her hips, making his shaft swell and ache with increasing ferocity.

Control! "Do you play?"

"Not yet, but I'll learn and kick your aster." She hung one of his shirts next to a dress. "I'm anticipating many man-pouts from you."

Though he heard her, he didn't compute her words. He

was enraptured by the sight of their clothes pressed together. Would their scents mingle?

Possessiveness strangled him, but urgency ruled him.
Their scents could mingle another way…

Must have her. "Your trust issues," he said, his voice
strained. "What did you worry about the last time I kissed
you? Besides my robot ways."

She hung a pair of his leathers. "That you'd try to harm
me or steal my horn, my source of life. Without it, I'll lose
my magic, my ability to shift and my best source of protection."

How many beings had made a play for that horn over the
centuries? "Since you refuse to shift, I can't *get* to yours.
Problem solved."

Shrug. Translation: *You're wrong, but I don't trust you
enough to offer the truth. Yet.*

"Work with me here, Sunny. Talk to me. You're going
to trust me fully eventually. Why not now? Think of it as
your couple-days anniversary gift to me."

Yearning softened her gaze. "All right. I'll tell you a
little story."

For some reason, his guts twisted. He had a feeling he'd
be furious by the time she finished.

"Our horns are conduits of power. Power is a drug," she
explained. "To demons especially."

"Go on."

"Once upon a time, unicorns were all sweetness and
light with no hint of a dark side. We lived to make the
world a better place, aiding strangers, granting wishes like
a freaking genie and sharing our riches with the poor. What
did we receive in return? Near extinction. Poachers laid
traps. A fair maiden in distress. A lost child. Once they
imprisoned us, they removed our horns to sell to demons,

leaving us helpless. Magic-less. *Then* Lucifer and his demons decided to cut out the middleman."

Her anguish tore through him with the speed of a bullet. And she wasn't done.

"Fast-forward a few hundred years after the slaughter of my village." She hung another pair of leathers, but not before he spied a gleam of tears in her eyes and nearly flashed away to murder Lucifer and present his head at Sunny's feet. "A demon possessed the guy I was seeing. I didn't know until he shoved blades in both my shoulders and my ankles, pinning me down. He would ask me to shift, again and again, and when I refused, he cut off one of my fingers or toes."

Red dotted his vision, rage shredding what remained of his control. "I'll kill him. All I need is a name." Actually, William wouldn't need one if he bargained with Hades for another ten-question session with the Sphere of Knowledge.

Sunny offered a small, soft smile. "He's already dead. I told him I'd shift and willingly give him my horn. Unicorns cannot lie, so he believed me."

"But you punished him with the horn instead." A statement, not a question.

"Oh, yes. I shifted and gave him my horn—straight through his neck."

"Good girl," he praised, so damn proud of her. But, his rage was far from appeased. He set his treasured book on the desk, then checked the display case. Locked. "What if we use magic to ensure I *can't* steal your horn?"

Shock pulsed from her. "You would do that?"

For her, he would do *many* things he'd never do for another. "Consider it my gift to you."

Excitement sparked off her skin. "How would the spell work?"

"Not a spell, per se, but a mystical pledge unbreakable in word or deed."

"I—wait. My paranoia is flaring." The excitement ebbed, her skin dulling. "This could be a long con. Vow now, attack later."

"My pledge will negate any kind of long con. You'll see." He crooked his finger at her. "Come here."

Sunny hesitated only a moment before trudging over.

"I'm going to make an incision in each of our palms to blend our blood." Best to explain every step of the process, lest she lash out. No one had a meaner right hook. "All right?"

A pause. Then, with her emerald gaze steady on him, she nodded and said, "All right. Let's do it."

19

"I'll be waiting at the corner of Climax and Bolt."

WITH HIS FREE HAND, William palmed a dagger. Sunny's trembles intensified, but she didn't dart off. *She's trusting me with more and more, and I'm about to cut her?*

He'd never hesitated to hurt someone, especially if their pain somehow aided him. Yet, the thought of Sunny experiencing the tiniest pang had him growling like a wild animal. She'd endured so much already. A shitty marriage, the loss of her people and centuries of solitary confinement.

Do you wish to sleep with her? More than anything. *Then. Start. Cutting.*

He did it. He made the cut, the incision as shallow as possible, but she hardly seemed to notice. As drops of crimson welled, he drew the blade over his own palm and linked their fingers, letting their blood mingle.

She shifted from one foot to the other. "How will I know the spell worked?"

"You'll know. You'll feel it. Just wait." Peering into her eyes, he said, "As long as you aren't trying to kill me, I vow I will not steal your horn. I won't hire someone to steal it for me, or command anyone else to do so. I won't scheme to obtain the horn at a later date. Do you accept my pledge?"

A dazed nod.

"Say it," he commanded.

She swallowed hard. "I accept your pledge."

Then. That moment. A bolt of power shot from him to her, and she gasped, stumbling back. Her jaw went slack. "You're right. I do, I *feel* it," she said, awed. "You truly won't—cannot—make a play for my horn."

Knowing he'd alleviated her fears... He wanted to bang his chest like a gorilla. How receptive would she be to his advances now? Would she like his kisses?

Every fiber of his being shouted, *Find out!*

Yes. He would brand her with his touch, his essence. Would explore the connection between us. Would take her hard and fast, then slow and sweet.

No, no. Not hard and fast. He might rouse her paranoia. He'd go slowly with her. So damn slow he'd agonize them both until they would die without an orgasm.

Arousal scorched him. How had he ever existed without this ferocious wanting?

Better question: How could he exist without it?

The urge to grab her, rip off her clothes and toss her on the bed, the floor—anywhere!—bombarded him.

No. Not yet. *Break the curse,* then *win the girl.*

He didn't know if he had the strength to resist the wanting and needing, but he would try. "I must take a shower," he managed to say in a somewhat normal tone, as if he wasn't a ravenous beast inside. "I'm still wearing burial grime."

"William," she whispered, trembling against him. "You said to let you know when I have a need."

That plaintive tone torched his already shredded control. "Do you want to be fucked, Sunny?"

Her breath caught. "I do."

"By me." Another statement. "Only me."

She nodded, anyway. "Only you."

"Today."

"Today," she said, her incredible scent enveloping him. "Now."

Waiting until she'd broken the curse ceased being an option. "I will take care of you, as promised, but first, I must shower." Alone. He had to calm before he touched her. "While you await me, why not indulge in your favorite hobby?" Bad idea. Bad! He pictured it and nearly came spontaneously.

Her brow furrowed. "You mean killing demons?"

"I mean fingering yourself. Do it, but don't come or we'll be checking that spanking off your list of fantasies." Nothing would make him shower faster. "Your next climax belongs to me."

Her eyelids turned heavy and her pupils enlarged, two circles of onyx ringed by emerald. "Spanking isn't on my list, but now I'm going to add it. Tell me. Would you prefer to keep your underwear on when I paddle you?"

Ha! Funny girl. "Lady's choice." Always.

Sunny wore a dazed, crazed expression he found irresistible. It was only fair. She made *him* dazed and crazed. Panting a little, she told him, "I think I'll study your book instead and wait for that hands-on demonstration of skill you promised me."

Minx. "Good call."

"Once I break your curse, you can flash me to Lucifer's palace. I'll take care of him *and* find Lilith for you."

The thought of Sunny going to battle Lucifer... No. Just no. Not gonna happen. He'd find another way to defeat his ex-brother. And if he didn't walk away now, he wouldn't be walking away at all.

Without making any promises, he kissed her forehead and strode to the bathroom, breathing deep, desperate for a hit of air without her maddening scent. No luck. His head spun. Her essence saturated every inch of the stable.

As he brushed his teeth, he noticed her toiletries intermixed with his, and his chest swelled with satisfaction. *She's safe and in my care.* The rest of the space boasted solid gold fixtures and a marble shower stall for six.

As a young prince, he'd gone through an orgy phase. Ah, the misadventures of youth.

He turned on the water and stripped. Droplets rained over the marble stall, a cloud of steam forming. Naked, he stepped under the waterfall. Hot water drenched him, washing away blood and dirt.

He wondered if he should climax here first. After he came, blood would rush back into his head, and his 69 IQ would receive a much-needed boost. He would calm, as hoped, and wouldn't rut on her, losing sight of her trust issues.

He might have stumbled with his unicorn in the beginning, but they'd since reached an understanding. She'd agreed to trust him. A trial run. He had to get this right. But, coming now would increase the odds of him reverting to his "robot" ways, an even worse development.

No getting off first, he decided. No taking the edge off. When you had a championship game, you didn't exhaust your best player during practice.

Eager to rejoin Sunny, William finished washing up. He anchored a towel around his waist. *Am I trembling like an untried youth?*

Accompanied by a steamy haze, he exited the bathroom. Water droplets dripped from the ends of his hair, running down the ridges of his chest.

He spotted Sunny right away and stopped, his heart punching his ribs. She hadn't done any studying, that much was clear. She'd taken his original suggestion. She lay on the bed, clad in scarlet silk, her pink tresses spread over a mound of pillows, the golden medallion around her neck.

As she glided her fingertips down her stomach, heading for her (non-granny) panties, she rolled her hips. Before she reached her destination, however, she snatched her hand back. "Freesia!"

Sexy little piece. He wiped his mouth and roved his greedy gaze over her. *Never seen a body so fine.* Those lush breasts were cupped by sheer material that played peekaboo with her hard-as-pearl nipples. Shimmery brown skin covered in a glorious tableau of rose tattoos glittered brightly. Three diamonds surrounded her navel.

There's no part of her I will not claim.

Slowly.

He moved forward, stopping at the foot of the bed. With a thick voice, he asked, "Why don't I finish that for you?"

"Mmm. Yes," she said in a gasp. "Finish me. I'm ready to try things with you. Wanton, wild things…"

Wanton. Wild. *Yes.* In battle, his blood had reminded him of fuel. Now? His blood was like a dark, potent wine. His heart raced, a freight train without brakes.

When she rolled her hands a second time and reached down, he snapped, "Keep your hand out of your panties, sundae. I don't try to do your job, so you shouldn't try to do mine."

"Agreed. But hurry! I've been waiting for you forever." She cupped her breasts, temptation incarnate. "I feel so good, but I want to feel *better*."

Hurry? Not this time.

He unleashed a stream of magic, and rose petals appeared on the bed, surrounding Sunny and perfuming the air.

She squealed with delight, causing his hard-as-nails shaft to throb.

As she watched, he dropped the towel and prowled closer. With a moan, she undulated her hips more forcefully. *Glorious female.*

If he wasn't careful, she would be his undoing.

Fisting the base of his erection and stroking up, down, he told her, "If I do anything that frightens you, tell me and I'll stop." *Don't make me stop...*

"William." A whispered plea. "Don't know if I'm ready for sex yet, but we can do other things, yes?"

"Oh, yes." Agonized by tumultuous desire, he placed one knee at the edge of the mattress, then the other. He shackled her ankles with his hands and tugged her down, down the comforter. Rose petals stuck to her dampened skin.

Straight out of an X-rated fairy tale, and she's mine. Mine forever. He gnashed his teeth. Correction: *mine for now.*

He planted her feet outside his thighs, keeping her legs spread. Her panties were soaked.

Breaths ragged, he said, "I know you haven't been the biggest fan of my kisses. Be a dear and endure for a bit, all right?"

"Y-yes," she promised. "I'll be a dear."

Silencing a ragged moan, he leaned over her and gently pressed their lips together. He suspected he'd have to ease her into it, but she opened eagerly. He rolled his tongue into her mouth, her taste registering. Sweeter than ever before. A roar of satisfaction sounded in his head.

So close to losing it. Must be careful. But inside, he burned. Any second, he expected to catch flame.

Sinking her nails into his back to hold him in place, she kissed him back. There was hesitation. No passive acceptance. A wild fervor had overtaken her, as if her predator's drive had disabled any lingering resistance.

Before, she hadn't known him so she hadn't been able to relax in his presence. Now? Relaxed? Her innate skill blew his mind.

Uncaring about anything other than her pleasure, he reached between their bodies to sweep a finger along the outer edge of her panties. Another gasp from her. Stronger tremors. She nipped at him, sucked, clawed and writhed.

"What are you doing to me?" she rasped. "What's happening?"

I could ask the same thing. He lifted his head, delighting as goose bumps spread over her limbs. Flashing a heated grin, he said, "Welcome to Pleasure 101, baby. Class is in session, and Professor Climax has a hands-on assignment prepared. Screamers earn extra credit."

"Too much talking. More kissing." A slurred demand, her voice huskier than usual. All the while, she continued rolling her hips, seeking contact.

If this was the result of earning a bit of her trust…

I want her full *trust. All of it.*

Back down he went, slanting his mouth over hers. He didn't let himself think, only feel. He held nothing back, letting his tongue dominate hers with hard strokes. It was a hot kiss. Dirty. Filthy, and he loved every second. Her little gasps and moans told him she loved it, too.

Then the kiss went nuclear.

They *devoured* each other, breathed for each other, but it wasn't enough. Kissing and touching would *never* be enough. Not with Sunny. He wouldn't be happy until he'd possessed her, body and soul.

Gentleness beyond him, William shoved his hand beneath her panties and plunged a finger into her slick, wet heat, dragging a moan from her. From himself. *Hotter than a forge.*

As he teased her clitoris with his thumb, her inner walls clenched around the digit he'd inserted, and she cried out, bowing her back to send him deeper.

"Sex! I want sex," she shouted. "Please."

No. Not this time. He wouldn't take her until she begged for sex *before* he touched her. "You've grown to care about me, haven't you, sundae? At least a little." *What are you doing?* He didn't *want* her to care about him, not yet. It would increase the likelihood of clinging and fits of jealousy—*his* clinging, *his* fits of jealousy. Yet, he couldn't stop himself from saying, "Admit it."

"I'll admit to nothing. Stop talking." She thrashed beneath him, locks of hair dancing over the pillow. "You're ruining my happy buzz."

"Am I, then?" He stopped moving, and her tight inner walls clenched around his finger again, as if to trap him inside. Sweat beaded on his brow and trickled down his temples. "If you want me to finger-fuck you properly, you'll tell me the truth. Say it. Say, 'I care about you, William.'" *Why are you pushing this? Why, why?*

"I care about…" With her nails embedded in his shoulders, she undulated against him. "Climaxing. Give me an orgasm, or watch me give one to myself."

Grinding his teeth with irritation, but unable to remain immobile, he increased the tempo of his thrusts, moving his finger in and out of her once again, mimicking sex. Her hot, drenched sheath contracted, and he hissed in a ragged breath. On his next inward glide, he wedged a second finger inside her. She was tight. Too tight. Strangling.

Perfect.

He wouldn't doubt if hundreds of years had passed since she'd last had sex.

"William!" She'd lost her inhibitions. She clawed at his back, arched her hips and chased his fingers with every outward glide. "Whatever you're doing, don't stop. Please, don't stop. Feels so good, baby."

Mmm, yes. So good. He needed more, wanted everything. *Can't get enough.* He licked a fiery path to her breasts and sucked on a beaded nipple. Her kiss-dampened areola darkened like his favorite sweet treat.

He inserted another finger, then another, her sizzling core stretching to accommodate the larger digits. He thrust them in, pulled them out. In, out. In, out.

"Tell Dr. Willy your most secret fantasies." His every panting breath scraped his chest raw, his voice gravelly.

"Should have…read my…diary." Lost in pleasure, she babbled, "My panties. Take them off. Please!"

"Not yet, sundae." The second he got them off, he'd be balls-deep inside her.

As she gyrated and tugged on his hair, a passion-fever flushed her glittery skin. Enchanted, he worked his way down. After hooking one of her legs over his shoulder to keep her open and vulnerable, he dabbled at her navel while teasing her clit, circling it with his thumb, slowly closing in...

Again, she thrashed against him. The sight of her. The sweetness. The heat and wetness. The sounds she made in the throes. *Want more.* Desire clawed at him, but only when she shouted incoherently, nearly out of her mind with pleasure, did he kiss his way down her belly, nuzzle her inner thigh and lick the outer edge of her panties, edging her closer and closer to an orgasm. So close, almost there...

Finally he nudged her panties aside to tongue her clitoris, tasting her feminine honey. His eyes rolled back. *Like a drug.*

With the next lick, she stiffened and came with a scream. "Yes! Yes!"

Her body had been made for sex. For him. Her rough cries thrilled him; her taste intoxicated him. *Still want more.*

He returned his fingers to her sheath and flicked his tongue against her clit. Shit! The orgasm had made her sweeter.

Want this every day. Every night.

"You made me come. You made me come and it was so much better than I hoped," she rasped, eyes gleaming with awe. "Do it again!"

Yes. William sucked on her clit, frenzied, fingering her harder, faster, quickly propelling her over the edge a second time. Her inner walls contracted with more force, he marveled. *I did this. Me.*

As she came down from her high, her shivers subsided and she sagged against the mattress, but the pulse at the base of her neck continued to thump. He wanted to roar with triumph. Finally, she stretched with languid satisfaction and heaved a heavy breath.

He watched it all, enthralled, his shaft throbbing. Beads of pre-come moistened the slit as he jolted to his knees.

"That was *amazing*," she breathed. "I want to spend the next thousand hours dissecting every sensation."

His every inhalation scraped his chest raw, his breaths like daggers. "Oh, we will discuss this." He would hear all the ways he'd pleased her. She would admit he'd claimed her—owned her. "But first..."

Sunny met his gaze, a slow smile lifting the corners of her mouth. "But first, it's your turn."

20

"Desire can be powerful, but fickle, especially after a man nuts up."

AMAZING WHAT A sense of safety can do.

Remove a possible horn amputation from the equation and boom, Sunny had no resistance to William. He'd given her the most sublime pleasure of her life, and she luxuriated, her body boneless, her mind at total peace.

Was this truly her life now? Beds scattered with rose petals. A once-fake boyfriend with the potential to become the real thing, who had a wicked tongue and an earth-shattering touch. Bliss. Connection, companionship, communion. Excitement.

Give this up? Never!

The fact that she'd orgasmed with another person, experiencing rapture like she'd never known, all without the relentless drive of mating season…it was huge! Now? *I'm addicted.*

The man had remade her. From unicorn-shifter to sex goddess. *Hadn't known what I'd been missing.*

But with pleasure came complications. Never had she felt more vulnerable. Never had she felt such tenderness for a man. Or anyone! Instinct demanded she walk—run—from William before she got hurt.

Understandable. From birth till this moment, she'd only ever been able to rely on herself. As their connection strengthened, and it would if they kept doing this, William would gain power over her. The power to build her up or tear her down. If ever he turned to another...

He won't! While he'd had his fingers buried inside her, he'd pushed her to admit she cared about him. Something completely out of character that made her think *he'd* come to care for *her*. Her heart raced at the possibility.

Had he? She gazed up at his beautiful face, not daring to hope. His flushed skin glistened with sweat, his lips red and puffy from their kisses. But his eyes...they were heavy lidded, his irises shockingly ferocious. In their depths, she saw staggering need, heat, hunger and aggression. *Obsession.*

Awe. As if she'd given him something no one else ever had. But what?

Never had a male looked at her in such a way—never had her life been so full of promise. *Maybe he* does *care for me.*

With a voice as shiver-inducing as his expression, he asked, "Did I put my sundae in a coma of bliss? Or are we role-playing Sleeping Beauty?"

Freesia! How could anyone be so deliciously playful and menacing at the same time?

And he wasn't even done. "Do you need another kiss right here?" He pressed the pad of his thumb against her sensitive clit, making her hips jerk.

Though she'd climaxed mere seconds ago—twice!—arousal surged anew, her body preparing for another sexual onslaught.

"Who says I'm Sleeping Beauty in this fantasy?" Using a combat move she'd learned when training to take down poachers, Sunny wrapped her legs around William's waist, hooked her ankles and cupped the back of his neck, then heaved his body under her own.

As he bounced on the mattress, rose petals clung to his skin and he laughed. But his amusement didn't last long, his hunger too great.

With a keening moan, she straddled him. Cool air kissed her aching nipples, delicious warmth pooling between her legs.

When he bent his knees, his body cradling hers, she rubbed her soaking wet panties over his shaft and traced a finger around both of his nipples. Small, brown and rock hard. Lightning forked over his skin, crackling just below the surface.

A true bounty of masculine delights lay beneath her, his massive shaft pulsing between them. Where to begin? What to do?

Why not live a fantasy and do something she'd always wanted to try?

"Settle in, get comfortable," she told him, nipping his chin. "I have *plans* for you."

He reached up to cup her jawline. "You give good plan, do you?"

"The best…probably. We'll find out together."

Muscles flexed in his abdomen. "You've never done this before?"

"Never trusted anyone enough." How would her inexperience with this act compare to the experts he usually bedded? Dread attempted a coup, but she cut it off at the knees.

Intrigue consumed his expression. Voice like gravel once again, he said, "Fair warning, beauty. This will be the equivalent of taking your driver's test in a Mack truck. But I want you to love it, so I'll pretend to be a gentleman for once in my life and do a courtesy pull-out." At a lower volume, he added, "Hopefully I survive."

What the hellebore! First, the new endearment got a five-star review. Second… "You'll take away my reward for a job well done?" She pouted.

He performed one of those patented "you just turned my world upside down" blinks, and she knew she'd delighted him. "You talked me into it." He interlocked his hands behind his head, all *you may service me, wench.* "I swear I'll give you every drop of your reward. Because I'm a giver."

He was the living embodiment of carnality. Aching for him, she kissed, licked and nipped her way down his torso, while her hands explored the many planes and ridges of his body. The farther south she traveled, the more he growled. One of his hands ventured into her hair, fisting the strands; the other gripped the headboard behind him.

When Sunny reached the object of her desire, she licked her lips. The man was hung. Mack truck? Try Mack plane.

While his ego didn't need a boost, she couldn't *not* praise the beast before her. "If ever you want to send me an unsolicited dickpic, I won't mind," she admitted, earning a chuckle. "And, yes, I can say dickpix. My magic filter considers it nonsense."

His chuckle morphed into a groan as she wrapped her fingers around the base of his erection. Hot as fire, hard as steel, soft as silk.

"You will tease me no longer," he told her quietly, fiercely. "Need this. Need *you.*"

He must *be coming to care for me.*

Sunny bent her head, breath puffing over his crown. As he issued a hoarse bellow, she sucked his length deep. So deep her gag reflex kicked in. Did she stop? No way! She did it again, and again. Because she couldn't fit the whole thing in her mouth, she had to use her hand, too, stroking and sucking, sucking and stroking, tasting the intoxicating evidence of his desire.

A string of dark curses left him. Then he snarled, "You want my pleasure to explode from me, don't you, beauty?"

"Not yet!" *Not ready for this to end.* She slowed her pace and eased her suction. Up, down. Up, down.

"Sundae." His harsh tone rendered her nickname an F-bomb. "Faster! Harder! I'll give you my come."

Uuuuuup. Dooooown. Never *want this to end.* Once again she slowed, easing her grip. Once again he cursed.

I did this. Me. Revved him up and made him crazed. Feminine power went straight to her head, making *her* crazed, until she felt like she hadn't had an orgasm mere minutes ago. She ached. She craved. With her free hand, she cupped his testicles; another, darker curse left him. This time, he released her hair, jolted upright and gripped one of her ankles.

"My beauty likes to tease? Very well." A few tugs, and he maneuvered her lower half alongside his upper half, then pushed her panties aside and slowly, languidly feasted on her needy core.

Sage! Freesia! Pleasure shot through her, an exquisite torment. He leisurely flicked his tongue against her clitoris, and she moaned. Her heart raced, and her blood burned.

Hoping he would increase his pace if she did the same, she sucked his erection faster and harder, just as he'd requested. Anything for another climax!

Faster.

Harder.

He did! He matched her pace. Pressure built, her nerve

endings buzzing, her skin stretching taut. When he slid one, two fingers inside her and scissored them—

Oh. Oh! Any moment, she would—

A third orgasm ripped through her, and Sunny screamed around William's shaft. As her inner walls clenched, he hurled over the edge as well, lifting his pelvis. His muscles tensed, his orgasm jetting down her throat, one hot lash after another.

She happily swallowed every drop.

Heart still racing, she sagged into the mattress, more trembly than before. More satisfied and vulnerable, too. Maybe...maybe this had been a mistake?

Thankfully, William had enough strength to pick her up and snuggle her into his side. They lay like that for several minutes, their breaths calming.

"You loved it," he said with a toothy grin.

Mistake or not, she couldn't resist this playful side of him. "I did. Learning to drive a Mack truck is *fun*." Shockingly enough, this part—being sated, holding on to each other, sharing breaths, *communing*—was even more so. Which made it more frightening the vulnerabilities.

For the first time, she'd truly trusted a man with her body and let go, experiencing every nuance of sensation. What if she trusted him with her future, as well?

Maybe, maybe not. This was new to both of them. His first relationship, and her first orgasm with another. Could they sustain this long-term?

Wanting to cling but knowing she'd shouldn't—for him, for her—Sunny climbed out of bed the moment she regained a modicum of strength. She had a job to do, after all. Now, more than ever, she wanted, needed, to break his curse. And she would. Nothing and no one would stop her.

21

"I don't hang around the bank after I make a deposit. Why hang around a woman afterward?"

WILLIAN STIFFENED AND BARKED, "Where the hell do you think you're going?"

"To the desk." Lest his masculine beauty draw her back to bed, Sunny kept her back to him as she bent down to pick up the clothes she'd dropped during his shower. "It's time to work on your book."

"No way. We're not done afterglowing." He flashed behind her and clasped her by the waist, then flashed her back to bed.

He manhandled her both gently and nongently, fitting her body against his as the medallion bounced between them.

She tried to don a stern expression but failed, a smile blooming. So, she tried for a stern tone. "What makes you think I'm interested in afterglowing?" Nope. Another failure.

I would commit a thousand crimes to afterglow with this male. She'd never gotten to do it before.

"For starters, I'm kind of a genius."

"Kind of?" She quirked a brow. "That's like me being almost pregnant."

He linked their fingers. Handholding—another first! With his free hand, he traced the medallion. "My superpower is looking at a woman, any woman, and knowing what she wants and needs."

"Let me guess. The answer is always a heaping helping of the Panty Melter." Sunny lightly pinched his nipple, ensuring she had his full attention. "Is that what *I* need right now? More of you?" *Or all of you.*

Whoa. All? As in everything…forever? She gulped. Would William ever give his all to a woman?

Before, she would have said no way, no way. Now? Maybe. Something significant had changed between them. There was an ease to their interactions now, a deeper intimacy and a hotter sizzle.

"My sundae already had what she wanted. A tongue-lashing." He ran her earlobe between his teeth. "It's my turn to—"

"No way! You had your turn, just like me."

"And I want information," he continued. "Why do you wear this medallion, but not the other?"

A topic guaranteed to ruin the mood. Any detail she provided could inadvertently reveal details she wasn't ready for him to know. "This one was given—" No, wrong word choice. "It came from my mother." Better. "The other did not."

He studied the medallion a little longer before moving on and cupping her breast. "What do you do for fun? Besides hunt and kill evil beings, I mean."

A breathy moan escaped. "I plan new ways to hunt and kill evil beings. Sometimes I'll have Sable at my side. She—" Sage! Well, the unicorn was out of the bag now. Might as well tell William the rest. "When Lucifer destroyed my village, there were six survivors. We split up, thinking we'd have an easier time blending with other species. If we need another unicorn for any reason, we send a magical SOS. Something I did before the conference. Sable responded and accompanied me. She was supposed to be in the hotel room, awaiting us. Either she spotted a poacher and ran, or she got nabbed. I'm telling myself she's just on the run."

He thought for a moment. "I think you're right. When my men killed the poachers and collectors, they set any captives free, but not before taking pictures. I went over every image and there wasn't a unicorn."

"Well, we still have the remaining five percent."

"Nope. They couldn't find half of five percent because the poachers and collectors were already dead. The remaining two and a half percent have since been beheaded. I'm texted updates."

Wait a sec. Every immortal who'd ever hunted her was now dead and gone? Just like that? She'd been on the run for centuries, and William had taken care of the problem in a matter of days?

Sunny marveled. This man… *Even more powerful than I realized.* "Did you release the other cryptanalysts?"

"I did. Early this morning, just as promised."

Her heart soared. "What else would you like to know, baby?" If they were going to stay together—*how long, how long?*—she needed to trust him with more than her body. "Oh, and in case you didn't know, this is a tit-for-tat situation. Whatever you ask me, I get to ask you."

"Fair enough." His warm breath fanned her hair, tickling her scalp. "Tell me everything. No detail is too small."

The fact that he wished to know everything about her was the cherry on top of her sundae. They'd started something true and meaningful, hadn't they?

"What do you know about unicorn society?" she asked.

"Not much." He walked his fingers along the ridges of her spine, sending ripples of white-hot pleasure along her nerve endings. "I know you do better with a pack."

"That's true." Oh, how she missed her pack. Although, lying in the comfort of William's arm, she felt as if she belonged for the first time in…ever. A heady feeling. One she never wanted to lose. "Herds are like cities—there are a lot of them. Packs are like neighborhoods within those cities. The more members, the stronger their magic. Kings are like presidents, and princes like governors. Every year, herds came together for the Festival of Exchange. Females who reached the age of consent were traded to prevent interherd breeding. I was the daughter of the king's best warlord, so on the day of my birth, I was betrothed to the three-year-old Prince Blaze. I was sixteen when we wed. I don't know why, but I expected Blaze to stop using our pack as his personal harem. He didn't."

The more she spoke, the tenser William became, and she didn't have to wonder why. He'd once used *the world* as his personal harem and helped wreck countless marriages. But he and Blaze had differences, too. William's temper was far more violent, yet his nature was so much kinder. He didn't lie. He *did* make her laugh, something Blaze had never done.

She kissed the spot just over his heart, then rested her cheek there. His body temperature jacked up, delicious heat enveloping her.

Lids growing heavy, she traced the tattoo on his pec. Two small swords that flanked a larger one. "What does this image mean?"

"It is Hades's seal," he explained, then gave her butt a little slap. "Go to sleep, sundae. You're halfway there already."

"No, I'm—" A big, fat yawn ended her denial. Fine! But she refused to sleep with someone nearby, even if that someone was William. Plus, she'd set zero traps. Mostly, she wasn't ready to put a plug on their conversation. "Tell me about Gillian. Yes, I know her name. No, I won't tell you who told me."

Once again, he stiffened. "I don't have to wonder who told you. I know. Pandora. But we're not done talking about you."

Seriously? "That's such a penis move," she grumbled, and he laughed.

"Penis move? Do you mean *dickpix*? No, sorry, I misspoke. Do you mean *dick*," he said, his eyes flashing with amusement.

"Yes," she hissed. Her cheeks burned, her humiliation spoiled by another jaw-breaking yawn. One way or another, she would learn something about him today. "I'm unable to say the D-word without tacking on another." Reverse alpha male had worked so beautifully before. Why not now? "If you'd like to postpone the conversation about your former ladylove, that's fine. I'll withhold sex until you change your mind." Tormenting him sexually…orgasm denial… *Sign me up!*

Where had this wanton side come from?

He must have liked it, because he smiled, his blue eyes twinkling. "You're *already* withholding sex, sugar tush."

"I'll withhold make-out sessions, then."

"Please. Now that you've had a taste of the good stuff, you're going to jump me three times a day. Minimum! So go ahead. Try to withhold make-out sessions. I dare you."

"You are so, so wrong about me jumping you." The number was probably closer to five. Still. "You asked for it, you get it. Consider my candy store closed."

In a singsong voice, he said, "Someone's forgetting mating season."

Well, daisy. "Answer my question about the girl, and I might—might!—open the candy store up on occasion. Like holidays. And every night before bed."

He exhaled a breath, and at first, she figured she'd pushed too hard and too fast, and he merely worked up strategies to bail. Instead, he surprised her by saying, "I only *thought* I loved Gillian romantically. If I had, I would have waited for her. But I feared the curse and continued to sleep around. That should have clued me in that I'd made a mistake, and we were destined to be friends, not lifemates. Alas. Later, when she wed another male, my pride was pricked rather than my heart. Another clue I missed. Then I kissed her and realized we had no spark."

When Sunny glided her fingertips along his sternum, she felt his heart leap, and she thrilled. "We definitely have a spark."

"No, sundae, we have an inferno."

We must. I'm melting... Then a thought hit, and she skipped several breaths. What if *she* were his lifemate? What if he fell in love with her?

Her heart leaped next. She wanted his love, despite the curse? Oh, sage. The curse. He hadn't let himself love Gillian because of it. He might not let himself love Sunny, either. Might not? Ha! If anyone had the ability to kill him, it was Sunny and her horn. He might fear the curse *more*.

Words began to spill out of her. "You can rest easy. I'm fifty percent—probably sixty…seventy-five…ninety percent sure your curse will never affect me."

His heart raced faster against her hand. "Explain."

"Some immortals are bulletproof. I'm curse-proof, because horns are siphons as much as conduits. Spells and curses don't stick."

Different emotions played over his features. Hope. Doubt. Excitement. Dread. "Can you siphon the curse from me?"

"I wish, but no. It's been a part of you so long, it's bonded to you. Removing it would kill you, the same way removing a demon kills the one possessed. You'd need some kind of spiritual patchwork afterward, and that's not my specialty."

He exuded hope and disappointment, one after the other. The first warmed her, but the second chased the heat away, leaving her chilled.

"Tell me about your childhood," she said, as determined to distract him as she was curious.

He tensed. "I don't remember my childhood."

Truly? "Not a single memory?"

"There *is* one." With a hand under her knee, he draped her leg over his own, clinging to *her*, as if he needed an anchor in order to continue. But that couldn't be right. Could it? "I see the memory in my dreams," he continued, his voice so broken it was almost unrecognizable. "A Sent One tells me and another boy that she loves us, but we should never have been birthed. A faceless man appears behind her and sinks a blade into her heart. Then the memory goes blank."

"Oh, William. I'm so sorry." What a terrible thing to tell a child. Or anyone! "For the record, I'm very glad you were born." To prove it, she kissed a corner of his mouth. Once, twice.

The darling man lifted his chin to give her better access, and she planted kisses on his brow, his temples, the tip of his nose.

"I shared the memory with Hades, and he told me to forget the woman, and the boy." The more he spoke, the more easily the words seemed to flow from him. "I was never to speak of it again, for all walls have ears, and if ever anyone discovered my connection to the boy, or if ever I met with him, a part of me would die."

Yet still he'd told her. *He doesn't just like me. He cares for me.* "Thank you for trusting me," she said, melting faster. "What happened to the rest of your memories, baby?"

Resentment frosted his eyes. "I believe someone erased it. I just don't know why."

"Uh, there are very few ways to erase an immortal's mind. Like limbs and appendages, memories can regenerate. Are there exceptions? Yes. But I'd guess your memories were hidden with magic rather than erased, and if that's the case, I *can* help you. Maybe. Probably. The problem is, I don't sense a curse in you." She recalled the barrier she'd encountered when she'd first touched the book. Fresh from a couple orgasms, her mind clear for the first time in forever, the answer crystalized. Excited, she told him, "I think the witch tacked on the magical qualifier."

He frowned. "Explain."

"The woman you love will kill you, but only after you fall in love with her, right? Well, Lilith ensured the curse couldn't be purged from you, only from the woman." She yawned again, her excitement no match for her strengthening fatigue.

Her eyelids grew heavier and heavier. Too heavy to hold up. "William," she said, sounding drugged. "I think I'm about to fall asleep…can't stop it. Do you know how long it's been since I—" The world went dark, and Sunny knew nothing more.

22

"Hate thy neighbors."

WILLIAM HELD A sleeping Sunny for hours, his body completely sated for the first time in…ever? A miracle, considering they hadn't even had sex. The unicorn truly was, well, a unicorn. One of a kind. *And mine.*

Moonlight seeped through the window to paint her slumber-softened features with gold. Had he ever seen a more exquisite sight? She had no tension, no fears.

He hardened, ready for another go—when *wasn't* he ready with her?—but he'd rather die than wake her.

He recalled the day they'd met, how tired she'd looked. Until now, he hadn't realized her trust issues had been keeping her up at night.

When had she last slept this deeply, dead to the world? The wonder in her tone as she'd drifted off… Had to be years, perhaps even centuries.

A pang threatened to rend him in two. What was he going to do with his unicorn?

For the first time, he had no thoughts about his next conquest. Why should he? With Sunny, he'd been present, utterly caught up as he'd watched her discover the pleasure to be had with a partner. Talk about a revelation!

The only downside? She'd never admitted she cared for him. The lack shouldn't matter. They were better off not caring for each other right now. But the lack fucking bothered him! She'd gotten to know him better, so she *should* care. It was only fair, since she'd made him care for her.

William scoured a hand down his face. He did. He cared for the lifemate he'd kinda sorta agreed to date. Even now, he clung to her, and he couldn't force himself to stop. Somehow, she'd wormed her way under his skin. Therefore, he needed to worm his way under *hers*. Because karma.

She released a puff of breath, and he caught himself smiling with contentment. Contentment. While cuddling. *Traveling a dangerous road.* If the curse activated, affecting Sunny, what would he do? What *could* he do? His stomach turned inside out at the thought. He wouldn't put her down, and he couldn't mute the feelings he already had.

Maybe if he locked her away until she'd fully decoded the book?

No, she'd hate him for it. As punishment, she would refuse to help him. At first, anyway. If decoding the book were the only key to her freedom, she would change her mind soon enough. But damn it, he didn't want to go that route. The guilt would ruin him. They'd have no future.

Look at me. Planning ahead to salvage a relationship.

He wanted more nights like this. Sunny coming undone as he tongued her. Talking after. Cuddling. Sharing breaths and memories.

Could she free his memories in addition to deciphering the book? Oh, to remember Axel and their parents...to know their lineage...to discover what they'd lost and why... William would have everything he'd ever wanted. Almost. He still had to find the tenth Hell crown.

HIS EARS TWITCHED as different noises seeped into the stable. If someone woke Sunny, that someone would die.

William flashed to the side of the bed, where he donned his leathers. After zipping up, he flashed outside. Two Sent Ones leaned against the stable wall, positioned between two of Sunny's spikes, giving each other a little sexual CPR.

"While I'm certainly enjoying the show," William said, soft but menacing, "your voices have the potential to wake my...girlfriend."

The two broke apart, peering at him with wide eyes.

William had never met the pair, had never worked with them and had no idea about their battle savvy, but that didn't stop him from snapping, "You wake her, you die. Spread the word."

He didn't wait for a response, just flashed into the stable. Once he'd stripped out of his leathers, removed his cell phone from his pocket and turned it to silent, he slipped under the covers, Sunny's body heat and sweet scent enveloping him. *Like a homecoming.*

He imagined keeping her...forever. Waking up to her radiant smile every morning. Getting called on his shit *always*. Teasing her from her bad moods. Floundering when she said illogical things. Arguing, bargaining. Bantering. Making her blush with innuendos. Caring enough to stick around and work through any problems. Making love every night, taking her body to new sexual heights.

Sounded like...paradise. A future he'd never dared to entertain. And still couldn't. Yet.

Once he'd defeated Lucifer and found the tenth crown, William would become a king of the underworld. A king required a queen.

Sunny...my queen.

The idea appealed greatly.

A unicorn-shifter was an unlikely mate for a king of the underworld, yes. One was dark, one was light. One was (somewhat) good, the other (somewhat) evil. But, oh, the fun they'd have.

His cell phone vibrated, breaking into his musings. Careful not to disturb Sunny, he checked the screen.

Daddy Dearest: My apologies for missing the predinner battle. Return tomorrow night. We'll chat about Axel. This time, bring the girl. I'd like to meet the woman Rathbone calls the new star of his spank bank.

First, Rathbone was an asshole. Second, William still dreaded introducing Sunny to his father. Hades had hated Gillian. *Too weak*, he'd said. *Not the one for you*, he'd added. What would he say about Sunny?

He texted back. We'll be there. Now, do us both a solid and gird your loins. I have an announcement to make.

Several minutes passed before a response arrived.

William checked his balls. Yep, he still had them. Time to nut up and make his father see the truth. He typed another text. Ready? I love you. I will always love you. Getting to know Axel won't change that.

There. Done. Now the wait—

Daddy Dearest: It will change. YOU will. This, I know beyond any doubt. Do not seek him out until we've spoken. Until then, think about what's more important. The father who raised you, or the brother who forgot you.

William popped his jaw. So no declaration of love from dear old dad. All right, then. Of course, to his knowledge, Hades had never said those three little words to *anyone*.

Though disappointed, he turned his sights to his next order of business, opening a group text with his sons. He typed, I have another secret task for you. There are five unicorn-shifters out in the wild. One is named Sable. Find her. Don't ask why, just do.

Black Attack: Why?

Red Abed: Whyyyyyy?

Green Machine: WHY, PAPA, WHY??????

Okay, his kids were assholes, too.

Green Machine: Aren't unicorn-shifters extinct?

William: They are not. Search as quickly as inhumanly possible. Any leads on Evelina or Lilith?

Black Attack: Lucy has men searching for Evelina, and I overheard one mention a possible sighting in Listeria. I'll be there within the hour. Nothing on Lilith.

Lucy—a hate-endearment for Lucifer. Listeria—a Hell realm named *before* the bacteria, known for its toxic atmosphere and criminal inhabitants.

Red Abed: I'm in the middle of an interrogation with the soldier Black overheard. If he knows anything more, I'll know something more. Soon.

Red included a video with his text. In it, a seven-foot-tall demon was strapped to a rack, sobbing. The fiend had ivory horns and a forked tail. Each of his limbs were limp, the joints pulled out of their sockets. Blood and sweat poured from gray scales. His eyes had been removed, leaving two bloody sockets.

William: Keep up the good work. By the way. Hades is having a family dinner tomorrow night, and I'd like you to be there.

Not wanting to make his father's mistake, he added, You're shits, but I love you. That done, he set the phone aside and—

His gaze lit on Sunny's diary. It was across the room, just sitting on the desk. His pulse quickened. She liked to write down her fantasies. A mistake—for her. He'd already decided to read every word. Why wait?

As sunlight replaced moonlight, illuminating the stable, William slipped from the bed and donned his leathers once again. Leaving Sunny's soft, warm, world-changing body proved more difficult this time. But he did it, the chance of reward great. He padded to the desk to flip through the pages. Every passage but one was written in code—

the passage written about him. The corners of his mouth quirked. *She* wants *me to read this.* What fresh torment did she have in store?

He scanned the words and discovered a list of fifteen sexual positions. Things he'd never heard of. The Brazilian cowboy. The topsy-turvy curvy-swervey. The snake-bake wrangler. Beside each position was a name. Lucien. Green. Rathbone. The men she wanted to practice with?

What the hell?

She goes too far! With the book in hand, William marched back to the bed. Along the way, he spied Dawn peeking out from under the bed. Shit. He needed to make provisions for her.

He paused long enough to create a doggy door, then walled off a section outside, adding grass. Inside, he conjured a food and water bowl, and a handful of chew toys.

Dawn darted over, one head drinking, the other head eating.

That done, he finished his trek to the bed and shook Sunny awake. "Sunday Lane, you tell me what this is or there will be blood!"

She blinked open her eyes and gifted him with a slow, sleepy smile. "Good morning to you, too, babe." The smile faded as her eyes cleared, and her jaw dropped. "It's morning. I slept. I slept an entire night."

Locks of pink hair tangled together as she stretched her glorious, lingerie-clad body. The sheet shifted, revealing most of her torso. Cool air drew her rosy nipples tight.

He tried to look away. He did. He stared instead, his shaft hardening. Shocker.

When she looked him over and licked her lips, he only grew harder.

"Answer me," he snapped.

Still stretching, she said, "Sure. If you ask nicely."

See! *Calling me on my shit already.* Deep breath in, out. "What are these sexual positions, and why did you write the names of other men? Let's start with Rathbone. If I'm morally compromised, he's morally corrupt. Did you know he has a harem stocked with a bevy of beauties? And I was there the day he staked his favorite concubine to a wall and made her watch as he secured her other lover to the dinner table, cut him open while he still lived and served his organs to demons."

"What are you—" Her gaze dipped to the diary. She snickered. "You were a jerk to me, refusing to take me to Hades's dinner, so I decided to punish you."

Diabolical temptress. Relieved, he set the diary aside. "In that case, I'll allow you to seduce me from my ire. *After* you show me your unicorn form."

"No and no. But I give you permission to seduce me."

He sat beside her, hip to hip, and slid a hand under her nape to lift her into an upright position. Those pink locks tumbled to her waist. Locks he fisted, trapping her face inches from his.

"We can continue to argue," he said, "or we can do what couples do in the morning and seduce *each other.* Lady's choice."

"How would you know what couples do in the morning? I'm your first and only girlfriend."

Good point. "Sunny," he said, keeping his tone gentle. *Can't let myself fall any faster. Must put some distance between us.* "I know we've teased each other about being a couple, but we aren't. Not yet." *It's her, or it's me. I choose...me?*

First, her eyes swam with hurt. Then they darkened and narrowed. "Did you not enjoy yourself last night?"

His heart clenched. "My roars to the rafters didn't clue you in?"

She didn't answer, just shook off his hold. He stifled a protest as she paced before him, still dressed only in her undergarments. "How convenient that you tell me we aren't a couple after you've given me a couple orgasms. Was that the plan? Addict me to your touch, then drop your bomb?"

He almost grinned. "You're addicted to my touch?"

She whipped around to glare at him. Then, inexplicably, she softened and crawled into his lap to rest her head on his shoulder. Voice whisper-quiet, she said, "I know we're not a couple, okay. Just as I know you care for me, whether you'll admit it or not. I just wonder if maybe we *should be* a couple. Unless I'm not enough to satisfy you? Do you still desire others?"

A muscle leaped underneath his eye as he wrapped his arms around her, locking her in place. "I desire no one else." *I might not desire another...ever.* And he wasn't panicked by the thought. "But I can't risk activating the curse."

"I let myself trust you enough to make out with you *before* you released me from captivity, and you can't trust me enough to risk the curse?" she asked, radiating hurt. "I'll be honest. Part of me understands. But part of me doesn't, because I'm certain the curse won't—can't affect me."

"No, you *think* you won't be affected by it. There's a difference." He traced his hand up and down her arm, luxuriating in her velvety skin. "Just decode the book as swiftly as possible, and we'll have this conversation again. Yes?"

As she flattened her palms on his chest, her nails sharpened into claws and cut into his flesh. He welcomed the sting, deserved it. Maybe even craved it. Hurting her like this hurt *him*.

"Maybe I don't want to have this conversation again,"

she said, snippy now. "I deserve a man who will move heaven and earth to be with me *regardless of the complications*, who won't look for a way out before we've even begun. Who thinks I'm enough. Apparently, that isn't you. So, at the end of our two weeks, I'll be moving on."

He tightened his hold on her. "Sunny—"

"I'm about to go through mating season, William. A time when my body *demands* sex. I'll need chains or a willing partner, but I refuse—refuse!—to chain myself in the underworld, making myself helpless while demons wait nearby." A familiar calculated gleam lit her eyes, filling him with dread and excitement. "I wonder if Rathbone is available."

Rage blazed through him, the urge to do murder returning in a flash. Damn her! And damn her good point. "I will take care of you this mating season."

"But only if I decode the book in time, right?"

He narrowed his eyes.

"No, thanks," she said, hiking a shoulder in a negligent shrug. "I still plan to do everything in my power to decode your book before mating season. But after mating season? My itinerary has changed. I'll be blowing this joint."

Every fiber of his being rebelled at the thought. He snapped, "Try to leave or be with someone else. See what happens."

She exhibited no reaction to his threat. "While I'm busy decoding your book, your kids will be out spying. What will *you* be doing?"

The way she stiffened, awaiting his answer... It mattered. She wanted him to name something specific, but what? "I'll be scheming, moving living pieces on the chessboard of war. I'll be antagonizing the enemy so he's more likely to make a mistake. Mostly, I'll be keeping a unicorn-shifter focused." The most difficult task of all.

Her shoulders rolled in. So, he hadn't given her the response she'd hoped for. Frustration mounted.

"In other words," she said, "you'll be having fun while the rest of us work." She wrenched from his hold and strode toward the bathroom. "Yeah, I'm definitely blowing the underworld sooner rather than later. Consider us officially broken up."

A denial screamed inside his head. He almost called her back. Almost dropped to his knees in thanks—emotional distance might just save their lives. In the end, he pressed his lips together, watching as she brushed her teeth and dressed in a tank top and jeans.

Without glancing in his direction—she'd dismissed him, as if he were unimportant—she sat at the desk, opened the book's display case and freed the book, ignoring him.

William ground his back teeth, a pain shooting through his jaw. "Just out of curiosity, what do—did—you wish I'd be doing while the rest of you work?"

"Something, anything that had to do with us, not war or curses. By the way, I get the dog in our divorce settlement."

They lapsed into silence. Hours passed, each one more torturous than the last. Eventually, he stood and paced while she continued to study. He cast constant glances her way, the woman both a pleasure and a torment to observe. When she concentrated fully, a crinkle developed between her brows. Adorable. When a passage vexed her, she chewed on her bottom lip. Sexy. When she forgot his presence, she hummed the loveliest song he'd ever heard. Soothing.

He'd handled things poorly with her—again. But how did he fix what he shouldn't want?

A strange noise caught his attention, and he frowned.

Sunny noticed it, too, her head lifting, ears twitching. "What *is* that?"

Dawn lifted her heads from the doggy buffet and howled.

"Put the book in the case." As soon as she'd complied, William unleashed a stream of magic to bespell and lock the case. Anyone who looked at it would see a creepy porcelain doll.

He stalked to the closet, donned a T-shirt that read Willy's Delicatessen, then grabbed a couple daggers and moved to the door, Dawn on his heels.

The noises grew louder. Had Lucifer sent another horde?

Daggers in hand, the medallion still burning a hole in his pocket, William braced and opened the door.

23

"I've only made one mistake in my long life—the time I thought I'd made a mistake."

SUNNY AND HER THREAT—promise—to leave must have wrecked William's brain. At first, he couldn't compute what he was seeing. Then the synapses in his brain started firing again, and he realized the army of Sent Ones had arrived at last. They were building makeshift abodes around the stable, Axel leading the charge.

Once he spotted his brother, a familiar pang of longing lanced him. Worse, a fist seemed to wrap around his heart and squeeze.

Despite Hades's request to postpone any conversations with his brother, he didn't have the strength to step back and close the door. Why should he? This was his chance to prove he could sustain a relationship with Hades *and* Axel. Then, at tonight's dinner, he could give the king a progress report.

He didn't need to glance over his shoulder to know Sunny was closing the distance. Though not even the slightest pitter-patter accompanied her footsteps, he retained a keen awareness of her every move.

Did all unicorns move so quietly, never really broadcasting their location?

Reaching his side, she crouched down to pet Dawn, the little hound ecstatic. As Sunny straightened, he inhaled her incredible scent, the beast behind his fly attempting to burst free.

Damn her! Mere hours ago, she'd sucked him dry. If he'd stayed true to character, he would've lost interest as soon as he'd come and focused his lusts on someone else. The next challenge. The newest amusement. Yet...

Not even close to being done with her. Can't even imagine it.

Could he do forever?

"Aw. How sweet. You got me a BBB."

He shouldn't ask. "What's a BBB?"

"Beefcake breakfast buffet." Sunny wiggled her brows and fanned her cheeks. "I'm starved, so I'm gonna need more than one beefcake. I'll take him. And him. Oh! And her."

Until that moment, he'd never had an urge to kiss and curse someone. "If you crave sausage, I've got a juicy link in my—"

"Don't you say it!" she cried, slapping a hand over his mouth. Scandalized amusement glittered in her gorgeous green eyes. "You're ruining my chance at making a good match! Our guests might get the wrong idea and think we're flirting."

"I was wrong. We *are* a couple. You insisted on a relationship, after all, and I agreed. No take backs. Meaning yes, you made my bed and now you can lie in it." She might be calculating, but he was wily. He could torment her with her own play. Latching on to her wrist, he brought her hand to his mouth and nipped the tip of her index finger.

Her plump lips parted on a gasp, the sound erotic to him.

He stared, Sunny a magnet for his gaze. Light bathed her, illuminating her glittery skin and the array of freckles that dotted her nose. A cool breeze blew a pink lock over her cheek—a cheek currently flushed with heat. When he ghosted his fingertips along her jawline, her breath hitched and her pulse quickened.

Her every reaction spurred an equal reaction in him. She flushed; so did he. Her breath hitched; so did his. Her pulse quickened; his did, too.

His awareness of her sharpened, his mind and body becoming a war zone. Bullets of desire flew in every direction. Blades of need sliced his calm to ribbons. Bombs of urgency exploded, shrapnel embedded in his every organ.

Want her again. Want her now. Not yanking her against him was the toughest thing he'd ever done. But now wasn't the right time. *Must resist. Will resist.*

But he inched closer, saying, "You want me more than you've ever wanted anything. Admit it."

She inched closer as well, as if trapped in the same war zone. "Maybe, maybe not. Definitely not as much as you want me."

Another inch, his heart beginning to pound. "You feel like you'll die without my kiss." *What are you doing? Stop!* He needed emotional distance right now. Not this, whatever this was.

With her next inhalation, their chests brushed. Friction sparked heat. Heat produced fire, the flames burning through his control at an alarming speed.

Screw emotional distance.

Voice as wanton as their last kiss, she whispered, "You would do *anything* to be with me."

"I wouldn't." *I might.* A fog of arousal enshrined William. If he didn't get this woman naked and in bed immediately, he would—

"Am I interrupting something?" Axel asked.

Sunny reared back, startled, as William slowly craned his head to address the intruder. Had the Sent One been anyone else, he would have paid dearly for such an interruption. The fact that William had lost track of his surroundings only deepened his irritation.

He arched a brow. "The intrusion couldn't wait?"

"And miss this killer glare?" Axel tsk-tsked. He wore a pure white robe, his golden wings shimmering in the light. "It's like you don't know me at all. Oh, wait..."

William pressed his tongue against the roof of his mouth, guilt seeping from an old heart wound. Clearly, Axel still harbored resentment. Forging a relationship with him wouldn't be easy.

His brother focused on Sunny, inclining his head in greeting. "We haven't been properly introduced. I'm Axel, your newest fantasy."

"Nice to meet you. I'm Sunny, your new obsession. I'm this guy's ex-girlfriend." She hiked a thumb in William's direction.

"We are together, and we're exclusive," William barked before the grinning Sent One had a chance to respond. *My unicorn. Mine!* Where was her paranoia with Axel? With Rathbone? "I'll give you the relationship you want," he told her, "and you'll give me space until the book is decoded."

"William. Babe," she began, as if she had the patience of a saint. She didn't. "You can't just decide—"

"I can, and I did. And why not?" he interjected, spreading his arms. "You did it first."

"Yes, and then I decided we were broken up." She turned to Axel, telling him, "I'm single, and I'm on the prowl for an honorable male interested in roughly two weeks of constant sex."

A cauldron of fury bubbled up, frothing inside William. My *unicorn*. My *codebreaker*. My *woman*. She would not be enjoying the company of another man, ever. *I am a prince of Hell, and I do not share!*

As the words echoed inside his head, he flinched. *I think I'm man-pouting?*

"We *were* broken up, yes," he managed to say calmly but fiercely, "but we just got back together."

Her features softened, his adamancy seeming to break through her resistance.

"I want to be back together," he told her. He'd find another way to resist her appeal.

She looked down. Heartbeat. Heartbeat. Heartbeat. Then she gazed at him with such admiration, such adoration, he could only reel. *Must see that expression every day for the rest of eternity.*

Had other women looked at him like that? Yes. A time or twenty. But he'd always remained unaffected, because they hadn't known him. He hadn't let them. With Sunny, he wanted to puff out his chest caveman-style. She knew him better, and she liked him, anyway.

Axel leaned against the door frame and crossed his arms, settling in. He winked at Sunny and said, "If ever you decide to ditch Little Willy, feel free to try and save me from my lecherous ways."

She winked right back.

Temper pricked again, William roared, "Enough!" Why

could he not predict this woman's reactions? Why did he *like* her unpredictability? It put him in a vulnerable position.

"Axel, this is Sunny. Sunny, Axel. My brother... I think." He slung an arm around his woman in a light, claim-staking hold, anchoring her against him. Then he arched a brow at Axel again. "What are we?"

Sunny reached up to sink her nails into his forearm, no doubt intending to push him away. She surprised him by melting against him, cradling his erection in the crack of her ass.

Need hammered at him, as if he'd never known a moment of satisfaction. Unbearable pressure...an unstoppable need for release only she could elicit.

Breathe. In, out. Good, good. He began to calm.

Oozing sympathy she'd never shown William, Sunny softly asked Axel, "Were your childhood memories buried like William's?"

He paused, eager to learn the answer.

The winged warrior offered a clipped nod, his good humor obliterated.

"Poor baby. When we fix William's head, we'll fix yours, too." She shrugged off William's hold to pat Axel's arm. "How about we take this conversation inside, neighbor? You can join me for a nice game of Clue. I'm trying to figure out who murdered Fun in the stable with a bad mood. Hint, I think his name starts with *W* and ends with *I-L-L-I-A-M*."

Grinning once more, Axel allowed her to maneuver him around William and Dawn, entering the stable. Heading for the kitchen, they bent their heads together, whispering and laughing.

William bit his cheek, tasting blood. *My woman and my brother should be whispering and laughing with me.*

He hung back as Sunny and Axel sat across from each other at the table. Sunny, for all her faults—too stubborn, too emotional, too suspicious and too damn beautiful for her own good—had a core of honor. She wouldn't start something with William, only to seduce his brother. Her flirting must have a different purpose.

Another way to torment me?

Damn it, why do I enjoy even that*?*

"Come on, girl," he said to Dawn, kicking the door shut. "Let's go speak with my brother before I murder him for hitting on my girlfriend." He used the word more easily now.

Halfway to the table, he heard Sunny tell Axel, "I'd be interested in hearing what you *do* remember about your childhood."

Again, William paused, his ears twitching as he awaited the answer.

"Perhaps I'll tell you," the Sent One responded, "once we've gotten to know each other better. Why don't you tell me all about your childhood instead?"

"Oh. Talk about me? Uh…" She shifted in her seat, suddenly agitated.

Well, well. Her trust issues had just flared, and William wanted to grin. *She trusts me, and me alone.*

On the move again, he told Axel, "I retained a single memory from childhood," taking over the conversation, saving Sunny from thinking up a better response. "The day a beautiful winged blonde got stabbed in front of us."

Axel gripped the edge of the table, his knuckles whitening. "That's my only memory, as well. We were babies. I mean, I know we were young boys, but we seemed so… innocent. I've always thought of us as newborns."

The comparison made sense to him. They *had* seemed

innocent. So new. So unsure and confused. "You don't know who she is?" William asked.

"I have questioned my brethren repeatedly, but only Clerici remembered her."

"Clerici?" Sunny asked, her brows furrowed.

"My leader, second to the Most High." Axel's tone evinced great respect. "He told me she isn't my birth mother, that she was part of a violent faction known as Wrathlings."

Wrathlings. William tensed. Long ago, a group of ten powerful immortals came together with a single goal: recruit an army of supernatural beings. They then used those beings to crossbreed predatory species, creating a supernatural army of creatures able to execute gods.

For years, William had hunted those ten, as well as their army of soldiers, all on Hades's behalf. He was one of the gods they'd targeted. William had done his job, and done it well. He'd slaughtered them, one by one, wiping Wrathlings from existence.

He'd never known his species of origin. Finally, he understood why. He must be one of the crossbreds. A fact he found disturbing. *Not a child born of love, but a product made for war.*

Had he killed his family when he'd killed the Wrathlings?

He cut off a roar of denial. No. No! Hades would not let him murder his relatives.

"This. Is. Freesia-ing. Unacceptable!" Hades's roar echoed off the walls, as if William had summoned him. "Freesia. Freesia!"

He'd arrived?

With a whimper, Dawn dove under the bed. Sunny vaulted to her feet, and Axel slowly rose to his. William maneuvered in front of his woman, shielding her. Of course, this put her and Axel at his back, something he didn't like. He hated having *anyone* at his back. But their safety mattered more than his discomfort.

"Watch your tone," he snapped, looking Hades over. The man looked awful, his black hair askew, his dark eyes rimmed red and glimmering with—no way. No way his father projected fear. His clothes were wrinkled—another first—his muscles tense. What the hell had happened to him?

One of the first lessons Hades had taught William? Your appearance was a weapon. With the proper clothes and a calm demeanor, you could instill terror in the heart of anyone.

For the king to come here in this condition… Something terrible must have happened. Or he'd just learned of Axel's arrival and had come running. Either way, fury bubbled up all over again.

Too raw to stop his next words, he snapped, "Tell me what you know about Wrathlings."

The color drained from Hades's face—yet another first. But what did it mean? His dark gaze darted between William and Axel before he blanked his expression of emotion, just like he'd taught his children. "They are extinct. What more is there to know?"

William remembered the day Hades had found "Scum." He'd said, *You have his eyes.*

Realization: Hades *had* known about William's ties to the group.

The fury spilled over, scalding William. Hades had known the truth, yet he'd ordered the executions, anyway. Never mind that he'd saved William from a life of prejudice and obscurity. *He should have told me the truth and given me a choice.*

"Let's backtrack a bit. Did a king of Hell just use *freesia* as a curse?" Axel laughed outright. "Roses! Lilies! Orchids!"

Hades stepped in his direction, all menace and hate. Once again, William acted as a shield, stepping in front of Axel. This infuriated his father, whose muscles bulged with aggression.

Sunny moved to William's side, took his hand and told Hades, "Hi, I'm Sunny. This is my home. You entered without permission and frightened my dog. Apologize before I—"

William placed a hand over her mouth, silencing her. Those who insulted or commanded Hades didn't usually live to see another sunrise. "Sunny, meet Hades. My father. Hades, meet Sunny. My woman."

The male stared at her, hard, taking in every detail until William snapped, "What are you doing here?"

Expression blanking again, Hades brushed a piece of invisible lint from his shoulder. "Did I or did I not tell you to stay away from the Sent One?"

"You did. And I told you I could love you both."

"Love?" Axel said, stumbling back.

"Look," Sunny said, unafraid of the monster she provoked. "Can this argument wait? Axel and I are about to be in the middle of finding out what kind of breakfast cereal we are."

The Sent One scratched his chin. "I'm leaning toward Trix."

She smiled a sugary smile at Hades. "I'm thinking you're a knockoff brand, like Kookies or Circus Balls. Or maybe you're a steaming pile of mashed oats with *zero* flavor."

"Anyone with sense knows I'm Franken Berry." Hades pointed to William. "Froot Loops." Sunny. "Lucky Charms." Axel. "Fiber One. Now leave."

"Nah. Don't think I will," Axel countered with a smirk. "I like it here."

Hades popped his jaw, unused to outright refusals. "You will leave of your own volition, or I will make you."

Another lesson taught by the king? Never make a threat unless you plan to follow through.

Hades always followed through.

William massaged the back of his neck. "There's no reason—"

"Go ahead," Axel said, spreading his arms. "Make me."

"Very well." A tornado of black smoke cloaked him in an instant and shot across the stable, collected Axel and tossed him outside, the doors slamming shut behind him.

"Stay here," William bellowed to Sunny. As an after-thought, he tacked on, "Please." Then he flashed outside, in the middle of hundreds of Sent Ones carting around lumber and tools. Several homes were already completed. Large huts with flat roofs for landings and takeoffs.

Where was—there. Hades was in humanoid form once again. He stood before Axel, Zacharel, Bjorn and two others. William caught the tail of what his father was saying and stilled.

"—will erect your homes in my territory, not his. Under-stand? Otherwise, you'll find yourself in a war against *me*."

To keep William and Axel apart, Hades had just threat-ened to go to war with an ally…while already at war with an enemy. What to do? From the beginning, William had trusted his father as much as someone like him could trust anyone other than himself. After everything the male had done for him, *grateful* didn't come close to describing what he felt. The very reason he'd allowed Hades to keep secrets so long, never really pushing for answers, despite a desperate need to know where he came from.

Now? Frustration pulled his strings. "Hades," he yelled.

All conversations ceased, silence creeping over the growing crowd. Every gaze found him, including Hades's. He and his father faced off, Axel momentarily forgotten.

Choosing to communicate telepathically, and keep the argument private, William groused, *They will stay here, surrounding the stable to better protect my codebreaker.*

The unflappable Hades suddenly looked utterly flapped. Again, the color fled his cheeks. —*You choose the Sent One over me?*—

For the first time, William thought his father exhibited something akin to panic. *I choose not to support the man who refuses to tell me why he's against my potential relationship with my brother.*

—*Because.*— Hades pressed his lips together, going quiet.

Because why? William insisted, refusing to let this go.

—*Because... I know what you do not. Why I kept you, but not the Sent One.*— Hades's dark eyes were stark. —*Long ago, my oracles presented me with a conundrum. If ever you and Axel were reunited in truth, you would work together to kill me and take my throne. How can I trust you now?*—

24

"Get in my way and get mowed down. It's science."

SUNNY FLOATED TO the bed to coax Dawn out of hiding. She needed a confidante, and who better than her darling fur-baby? They could bond over confessions and snuggles.

"The big, scary man is gone, sweetness. But even if he returns, you don't have to worry. Not now, not ever. I'm your protector, and I'll never let anything bad happen to you. That's a Sunny Lane gold-star promise. One I can keep. I'm kind of a superhero."

Once she had Dawn resting comfortably on a floor pillow, she spent a good ten minutes praising the dog for her bravery. As she stroked her belly, one of Dawn's heads nuzzled her while the other growled and bit her wrist hard enough to draw blood.

Sunny winced, the bite packing a powerful punch. No way she'd scold the little beauty for protecting herself, though. "We're going to be best pals. Like me, you have a dual nature, which can make life difficult. But as long as you do what you believe is best, you'll never have regrets."

The biting ceased but the growling persisted. No matter. Progress!

"Guess what?" she whispered. She cast her gaze around the barn, searching for any sign that someone hid nearby, listening. "William is falling for me, and not just because of his book. I mean, why *wouldn't* he fall for me? I'm, like, so supergood at sex now, he *insists* on an exclusive relationship, something he's never done with another. But just between us girls, I'm wondering if I should do as threatened and bail after I decode his book and kill his brother. I mean, William is a project. He's never had a full-time girlfriend. I'm worried he'll grow tired of me. Already he's waffled. He wanted me, then he pushed me away, then he wanted me again. And he's still holding me prisoner. I need to protect myself."

Although trusting him fully, holding nothing back, had begun to feel inevitable, which scared the crap out of her.

"Should I bail or shouldn't I?" she asked the hound. "If I stay, I'll need to make nice with his family. Not Lucifer, of course. Never Lucifer. But Axel and Hades."

Hades would be a tough nut to crack. He had a dark-as-night aura with pinpricks of light. It reminded her of a midnight sky, beautiful to look upon but lethal when you got too close without proper protection. He'd radiated menace and ruthless aggression.

Axel had an aura as blurry as William's, with splatters of red, indicative of rage and pain. Yet he'd looked at William with unmistakable longing. The same way William had looked at Axel.

Okay, so, if she was going to bail, she wouldn't do it

right away. She'd stay long enough to help the two recover their memories and built a proper brothership.

As Sunny continued to pet Dawn, the hound closed both sets of eyes and drifted off with a little puff of breath.

All right. Time to get back to work and decode that freaking book. Sunny stood and strode toward the desk but halfway there, a sudden, unexpected storm of arousal hit. Her nipples hardened, and her panties flooded with desire. A full-body shiver nearly rocked her off her feet, wrenching a moan from her.

When it past, she wanted to curl into a ball and cry. More storms would be coming now, only worse.

Focus now, while you can. Right. Upon Axel's arrival, William had secured the book's case with a (magical) lock. Had the silly man not realized she could siphon that magic away? Which she did. Voilà! Access to the book.

For one…two…three hours Sunny pored over every page and symbol without success. Why couldn't she break through the barrier, an extra layer of mystical protection, the equivalent of wrapping an enigma around a mystery? Or maybe a better description was a "magical encryption."

Every encryption had a key, even the magical ones. She just had to figure this one out.

She texted William: Bad news. I'm stuck at a roadblock. When you're done playing chase with your family, tell me why the witch cursed you. The info could unlock the code!

His reply came within seconds: She told me she loved me, and I laughed in her face.

Ouch. *Should have guessed.* The key must center around the witch's rage. It'd be a word, phrase, thought or emotion. Something simple, or the curse would never reach fruition. So…not a word or phrase. Probably not a thought, either. There were too many possibilities. As for the emotion…

Yeah. That one had real potential. *Think!* The witch wouldn't have wanted anyone who admired William to decode the book, only someone who'd enjoy seeing him suffer.

The answer crystalized, and she gasped. Had to be anger or hate. Since anger was far more susceptible to change and hatred more deeply rooted, she'd go with the latter. Which was easy for Sunny, considering her dual nature. She could both like and dislike someone at the same time; she just had to focus on one side of her nature. So, that was what she did. She flipped a switch in her heart, placing her vengeful side in the spotlight.

How she hated demons and the princes of darkness who led them. How William was Lucifer's brother. How William had locked her away. How William had broken up with her, demanded space—

There it was. Hatred. The emotion filled her up.

She focused on the book, and a shaft of warmth suddenly shot through her, the rest of the world fading away. *So dizzy.* As she released a heavy breath, the dizziness dwindled and—she gasped. Multiple symbols morphed into words.

Once upon a time...

She bounced up and down with excitement. She'd finally done it?

Problem: the words vanished from the page only a moment later, the symbols returning.

Her excitement dimmed. She refocused on the hate but...

No new passage opened up, but a thought whispered through her mind, as tempting as a shiny red apple. *I should kill William. Yesss. I should...so I will. I'll transform into a unicorn and sink my horn into his black, rotting heart.*

Fires of fury burned in her belly, her muscles tensing, readying for action. *He deserves this. And I deserve to be the one who ends him.*

Sunny released the book and reached for her medallion. She would hunt William down and—whoa! The whispers ceased, and the urges fled.

Ice-cold terror seeped into her bones. *Oh, hellebore!* According to William, the curse would activate as soon as he fell in love, spurring the object of his affection into killing him.

Had he just realized he had feelings for Sunny?

Maybe yes, maybe no. But she shouldn't—wouldn't— tell him about this development. She could already imagine the end result. *Once upon a time, a dark prince met a beautiful woman named Sunny, who made him crazed with desire. When he fell in love with her, the curse activated. She tried to murder him, so he did his best to put her down. The end.*

She would weather this alone. No, she would *master* this. She squared her shoulders and stiffened her spine, determined.

She'd told William the curse would hold no sway over her, and she'd meant it. Now she knew exactly what to guard against: insidious thoughts and desires that would sneak into her mind, amplified by a need to think horrible things about William in order to decipher the symbols... which meant she had to stop being so charming before he actually fell in love with her. And he would. If she decided to win his heart, he soooo would. She had so much love to give. Love he needed.

But first, she had to decode the book. And she had to do it while resisting William...who'd been right to want to wait, she realized now.

Maybe she wouldn't bail on him, after all.

Turning on the hate, Sunny spent another hour working on the book and managed to decode an entire paragraph.

As she jotted down the translation in her diary, exhaustion set in, segments blurring together. She needed to rest before she tackled another section. Which she would do, after she read over the handwritten page to check for typos, so she could text a photo to William. He'd be so happy.

Only two words into her read, the blood rushed from her head. Freesia! She hadn't written what she'd deciphered—a rehashing of everything William had told her about Lilith and Lleh. *Hell* spelled backward. She'd written "Kill William" over and over again.

No, no, no. Her mind was playing tricks on her; that was all. Queasy, and maybe a little magic-drunk, she rubbed her eyes and shook her head, then refocused.

The translation remained the same.

Sweat beaded on her palms. Had the curse already activated?

No. No way, she thought next. Despite what she'd written, she had no desire to end his life.

Her phone buzzed, a text coming in. Her heartbeat went from zero to sixty in a split second. Only William had the number.

She closed the book with a snap, locked it inside the case and tried not to tremble as she checked the cell's screen.

The Panty Melter: Any luck with the code?

Gulp. She replied, Yes. Your witch patterned the curse after a fairy tale. As the symbols are deciphered, they tell a story.

She typed what she remembered, leaving out what she'd written: Once upon a time, in the faraway Realm of Lleh, there lived a beautiful, powerful witch who fell in love with a handsome but conceited prince of Hell. Though she only wished to please him, he spurned her advances. In return, she decided to teach him a lesson he would never forget.

"I'm the only one who gets to teach William King a lesson," she muttered, jabbing her finger into the Send button.

The Panty Melter: How soon until you're finished?

Five words, zero emojis, yet his impatience and excitement pulsed through the phone.

Sunny: Translating that one paragraph wiped me out. I'm going to rest. I'll begin again in a few hours.

The sooner she finished, the sooner she and William could figure things out.

The Panty Melter: Don't wait up for me. Remember when I mentioned needing space? I'll be out all night.

Out all night? Bailing on her for the second time without offering an explanation? She leaped to her feet, the chair skidding away. Anger turned her core temperature to boiling, roasting her insides. Had he met someone? Did he plan to bed someone who'd caught his fancy?

If he didn't, Sunny would be even more furious with him! That would mean he'd made her worry—twice—for no reason.

She wouldn't ask him what he would be doing. Nope. If he cared about her, even the slightest bit, he would volunteer the information.

If you cared about him the slightest bit, you would trust him, even the slightest bit.

What a stupid thought!

Forget resting. This single girl was going to have herself a night on the town, one way or another. Because yes, she'd just broken up with William again.

Her index finger the hammer and her phone the nail, she jabbed at the keyboard, forming the words, No worries. I have plans.

The Panty Melter: What plans? With whom? You can't leave the stable and others can't enter.

Ignoring him, she checked the phone's address book. Sweet! He'd included other numbers, with notes.

Pandora—only if there's an emergency.

Baden—only if there's a really bad emergency.

Hades—only if one of us is dying.

There were a few other names, people she'd never met.

Gillian—only if you want to hear stories about my amazing amazingness.

Anya—only if you need help hiding a body or want to be framed for murder.

Zacharel—only if you're having too much fun and want it to stop.

Who was Anya? A former lover? Great! Fury turned up the heat again. Fuming, Sunny texted Pandora: Let's do a girls' night. Aka hunt and kill demons like true vigilantes.

She could enter the stable, no problem, and portal Sunny out.

Pandora's response came a few seconds later. I'm guessing Willy doesn't know what you're planning, because I haven't heard any man-pouting. But either way, I'm in! I know just the place.

Elated, Sunny typed, See you as soon as possible?

Pandora: Yep. I'll be there in five. Gird your loins, though. I won't be alone.

Ohhhh. Did she have a boyfriend? A girlfriend?

Sunny hid the case in the closet, then took the world's fastest shower and dressed in a black tank and a pair of camouflage pants with a thousand pockets she filled with an array of daggers she'd found in William's bag. *Mine now!*

Perfect timing. A portal opened near the bed. Wearing black clothes already splattered with bright red blood, Pandora stalked inside the stable.

She had a pink aura today. Meaning she rocked a good mood. On her heels was a gorgeous blonde with tanned skin and blue eyes, dressed in a skimpy halter top and a mini-miniskirt. Her aura possessed a rainbow of colors, and Sunny loved it. When this woman felt, she *truly felt*.

Dawn watched from her pillow, her two heads tilted in opposite directions. So cute!

"Sunny, this is Anya, a goddess of Anarchy," Pandora said. "She's engaged to a death-demon named Lucien, coruler of the Lords of the Underworld. She's also William's oldest and dearest friend."

"I am *the* goddess of Anarchy, thanks," Anya corrected, fluffing her hair. "And William's greatest inspiration. Before you ask, I do sign autographs...but only with other people's blood."

Really like this girl. Especially since she wasn't a former lover of William's. "How'd you and William meet?"

The goddess smiled with fond remembrance. "We had side-by-side cells in Tartarus."

Truly? "William spent time in an immortal prison?"

"Several years actually. He slept with the queen of Greeks. Her husband found out and sought vengeance." As Anya walked around the stable, inspecting things, she said, "What no one knew was that William *wanted* inside the prison. He had a list of prisoners to kill. Hades's hit list."

A man willing to be locked away for years, just to reach people his dad preferred dead…what dedication. What passion for a job well done. Sunny admired him a thousand times more.

"Would you stop talking so I can finish intros? Geez," Pandora said. "Anya, this is Sunny, the one I was telling you about. William's…" Frowning, she eyed Sunny. "What are you to William?"

"Captive employee of the month," Sunny groused, stiffening when Anya approached the closet. Demanding the woman stay away would only encourage her to peek inside. "He *insisted* we have an exclusive relationship. Later he texted to tell me he's staying out all night."

"Whoa, whoa, whoa." Anya hurried back to Sunny's side. "Did you say William agreed to be exclusive?"

"Yep. Clearly, he already regrets it. I mean, while I'd like to believe he's out there murdering his ex-brother, I suspect he had an emotional hard-on for me last night—" *after we climaxed our hearts out* "—so now he's running scared, determined to sever our connection." Talking to other women felt good. Right. Since William had already vetted these two, Sunny felt comfortable considering them prefriends.

The goddess nodded as she spoke. "Yeah, that sounds like our William. His emotional hard-ons usually end with a high body count."

Our William? No. Mine! Only mine.

Not mine, not really. Certainly not yet. "If he didn't need me to decode his book, he would have kicked me out. I'm sure of it."

Anya grimaced. "Man, I hate that stupid book. Do you know how many times I've tried to convince Willy-boy the witch wasn't stupid enough to give him a way out of the curse? She only wished to make things worse for him. Yet still he clings to hope."

Anya might be right. The book might just be a diary of Lilith's hate for William, nothing more. But Sunny had to admire his outlook. He had one possible lifeline, and he held on to it with all his might. Whether foolish or wise, only time would tell. Would Sunny stop decoding? No way. If there was a chance the witch had told the truth and given William a way out, Sunny wanted to know.

"You guys ready to go?" she asked.

"Always!" Anya tilted her head at Sunny and frowned. "For what we have planned, you're gonna need a weapon."

"No worries. I'm covered." She had William's daggers, yes, but they were backup. After unhooking the medallion from her neck, she fit her fingers over certain grooves, a black horn sprouting from the center, creating a spear.

One demon massacre coming up!

25

"A man always knows what he wants—something else."

IN THE MORTAL REALM, William raced down a shadowy alley, Axel at his side. He carried daggers coated with a paralytic, just as he used to do when slaying for Hades. Axel carried a pair of nondrugged daggers. If needed, the male could produce a sword of fire.

Dumpsters lined the walls of each building. A cool breeze carried hints of waste, urine and rotting food.

Hardly mattered. He was working with his brother to learn everything they could about the Wrathlings.

He wished his father had joined them, but after dropping his bombshell, Hades had flashed away. William had flashed, too, determined to learn everything Hades knew about his and Axel's past, but he'd ricocheted back. That's when realization had sunk in: his father had barred him entry.

He popped his jaw. He hated being at odds with the man. How was he supposed to kill him? *Why* was he supposed to kill him?

Whose eyes do I have, hmm?

Not knowing… William felt as if his chest had been ripped open, doused with acid and filled with rocks. Being forsaken by the man he loved above all others, a warrior he respected and adored, the king he had slaughtered entire armies to protect, the savior he'd revered, it hurt in ways he'd never thought possible. And why had he been forsaken? For a prophecy he'd never heard about, and an action he never planned to see through.

He tightened his hold on the daggers. At least he had a new lead on Wrathlings. After calling in multiple favors and contacting his spies outside of Hell, he'd learned of a vampire who'd supposedly left the Wrathlings before William started killing.

Now he and Axel chased the vampire through the back allies of New Orleans.

"Go up," William told Axel. "Fly overhead and cut him off."

With his next step, Axel flared those golden wings and leaped into the air. As soon as he landed, the vampire prepared to shift direction. William launched a dagger, nailing the bastard in the back of the knee.

A pained grunt sounded, and the male tripped and slowed, then limped, leaving a trail of blood. Then he froze, the paralytic kicking in.

William sauntered around him and stopped at Axel's side. The vampire gazed about wildly.

"You think to escape *us*?" Axel tsk-tsked. "I know my kind is supposed to slay demons and those who conspire with them, but I've never been good at following the rules.

You'll be next on my hit list if you fail to tell us what we want to know."

For a Sent One—for anyone—Axel had proven shockingly vengeful. Anyone who got in his way got mowed down.

A family trait, then.

"I am William of the Dark. This is Axel the Great and Terrible. Ah. I see you recognize our names. As Axel said, he will kill you if you try to keep secrets, but I'll turn my sights to your family."

The vampire whimpered.

"I'm going to free you from paralysis." Outside of Hell, William couldn't use magic for anything other than portals, so he'd have to give the vampire an actual antidote. He held up his hand, the ring on his finger glinting in the light. "Before I do, a warning. Strike at us, and he kills you. I kill your family. Run, and he kills you. I kill your family. Lie and… Are you starting to understand how this works? Blink once for yes. Blink twice if you're an idiot."

Blink. A single crimson tear rolled down his pale cheek.

"Good boy. But let's be sure you aren't tempted to strike or run, regardless of the consequences. Safety first, and all that." He nodded to Axel, who produced the sword of fire.

The vampire's eyes widened, projecting a message— *Please, no.*

Shockingly merciless, the Sent One went low, slicing through both of his ankles, amputating his feet. William caught the sobbing male before he fell and eased him to the ground. A fresh flood of crimson tears streaked his skin.

"There, there." William flipped the top off the ring, revealing a needle—one he pressed into the vampire's neck. "Now, tell us everything you know about Wrathlings."

The male flashed his fangs, suddenly able to move, pain

and fury pouring off him. "I know you murdered every last one of them!"

Maybe he had, maybe he hadn't. "If you want to earn the right to crawl away from this interrogation," William said with an evil smile, "you'll tell us the rest, without delay."

Withering, the vampire said, "You want to know about the babies."

He stiffened. Babies? "What babies?" William and Axel?

"Thousands of years ago, there were rumors," the vampire continued, his voice breaking. "Things I heard about but never witnessed. Only the higher-ups had access to the information."

"Tell us," Axel snapped, kicking a bloody stump.

The vampire screamed and gurgled blood. Between wheezing breaths, he said, "Experiments were done, certain species paired together to create immortal soldiers. Witches with vampires. Wolf-shifters with Harpies. Dragon-shifters with sirens. Sent Ones with demons. Fae with whatever else they managed to nab. When the children reached adulthood, they were then mated with each other. A witch-vampire paired with a wolf-Harpy. Those children grew up and were forced to mate with each other, too. A witch-vampire-wolf-Harpy with a dragon–siren–Sent One–demon."

William shared a look with Axel. They must have been part of the experiments, must be a mix of supernatural species. More than they'd realized. "What else?"

The vampire glanced between them, finally admitting, "My job was…to steal DNA from…specific beings. Gods and goddesses. They planned to create a new godlike species with all the strengths of other supernaturals and none of the weaknesses."

A shocking realization. If Wrathlings had worked with DNA, they might have artificially inseminated females, rather than having them get pregnant the old-fashioned way. *Anyone* could be in William and Axel's family line.

You have his eyes.

Whose eyes, damn it? Whose?

Axel squeezed his shoulder, a silent request for a private meeting, and William nodded before leading his brother a few feet away.

Axel whispered, "What if he told the truth? We might not ever learn who our parents are. They could be anyone."

"My thoughts exactly." He pinched the bridge of his nose. "We need to know if any Wrathling survived my murder spree. Maybe they kept records of their willing and unwilling donors. I'll go to Hades and find out what he knows." *If he'll see me.* His chest ached at the thought.

Had Hades known about the stolen DNA? *You have his eyes.* If he had, then he'd betrayed William in the worst possible way, using him to slaughter his own people.

Danger! About to blow!

No. Absolutely not. This, William not believe without hard proof. No way Hades was so cruel. Did the king have a cruel streak? Yes. But not with William. There had to be another explanation for his selective mutism.

"I'll get the vampire to a healer and question him further," Axel said, "then meet you back at the stable."

"No, not the stable." William wasn't ready to face Sunny. They'd been apart only a few hours, and he already missed her smile, her taste, her sass. Her everything. He needed to gain control of his desires first, and she made him feel like he was spinning out of control. Made him want what he couldn't have. "Let's meet at your cabin. We'll flash to Lucifer's palace and stake out his front yard." What would they see?

Axel nodded. "We can portal demons to your dungeon for a chat."

William grinned. "I like how your mind works, Sent One. I really do."

DARKNESS CREPT OVER the land, only to be pushed away by spontaneous bursts of fire. Atop a pile of dirt and ash over-looking Lucifer's territory, William lay on his stomach, shoulder to shoulder with Axel.

After Hades had refused to see William—again—he'd been a mess. He'd wanted Sunny, the very reason he'd stayed away from her. He'd visited the Lords instead to borrow their Cloak of Invisibility. Now he and Axel were invisible to all as they watched demons come and go.

This should have been an exciting and emotionally satis-fying night. He'd reunited with his brother, and his woman had begun to decode the book. For the first time, his future had *promise*. Yet, judging by their last chilly text exchange, said woman was now pissed off at him because he'd can-celed their plans.

Maybe he should have explained why, but… *I shouldn't have to explain anything to anyone!*

Like Hades doesn't have to explain anything to you?

Shit. His irritation with Sunny dissipated. He'd done her wrong, hadn't he? He'd insisted they were a couple. Of course he'd owed her an explanation.

"Hades's prediction," Axel said, breaking into his mus-ings.

"What about it?"

"Do you want to kill him and take his throne?"

Kill a man who'd provided shelter, prestige and training, who'd given him a purpose? "Not now, not ever. I cannot imagine a good enough reason to do such a terrible thing."

Unless Hades did, in fact, order him to slay his own family.

He gripped his dagger so tightly, the hilt cracked.

"Had you heard the prophecy before?" Axel asked.

"No. I'm sure Hades, being Hades, murdered everyone privy to the details, ensuring word would never spread."

A scream pierced the air, and he cast his gaze about, searching for the source. There. A demon tortured a human spirit.

On the outside, Lucifer's palace looked like a haven. Both tall and sprawling, with marble walls, towers and a steepled roof made of precious gems. All a deception. Demons of every size and shape occupied the surrounding area, most joining in to torture the human. Fires burned here and there, filling the air with dark smoke.

"Who raised you?" he asked Axel.

"A nice married couple who'd had trouble conceiving a child of their own," his brother replied. "Both were Messengers."

Messengers were often tasked with guiding a specific human down the right path, by whispering instructions into their ears. Humans couldn't hear spirits, but their hearts could receive a message from one; it was up to the human whether they followed any guidance or not.

"They were good to you?" Even nice people could do bad things.

"They were, yes, but I was too much for them. Too wild. Too rambunctious. Too everything." Axel puffed out a breath. "How about you? Hades treated you well?"

His fingers curled into the dirt beneath him. "He did. In every way but one. He commanded me to keep my distance from you. I didn't know why until today, when he explained the prophecy."

William stared down at his curled fingers, watching as claws grew from his nailbeds. *Ignore the pain in your chest.* "As for life in the underworld," he grated, "it's not a pleasant place for a child. You can stand in a crowd of thousands and feel alone. Everywhere you look, someone is being mutilated, and screams of agony are background noise."

Right on cue, a wind blew past, carrying a new scream.

"I wondered about you constantly," Axel admitted softly.

"Just as I wondered about *you*." Touchy-feely emotional crap wasn't normally William's jam, but he'd already missed so much with this male. Why not tell the truth? Even though they were related by blood, even though they were allies against Lucifer, they were also enemies. The respected one versus the dark one. Good versus evil. The demon assassin versus the demon prince.

Heartbeat…heartbeat.

"Your curse," Axel began. "Whoever you love romantically will try to kill you, yes?"

"Yes. The witch responsible gave me a coded book, promising I can break the curse if I decode it."

"You are certain she told you the truth?"

"The alternative leaves me without hope. So, yes." Logically, he knew the odds were not in his favor. But magic wasn't all-powerful. If something had a way into your life, it had a way out, as well. A door was a door. An entrance *and* an exit.

"The Sent Ones war with witches almost as violently as demons," Axel said. "I'll ask around, find out what other Sent Ones know about this kind of coded magic."

The offer surprised him. He doubted Axel would discover anything new, but he appreciated the effort.

"The female. Sunny," Axel said now.

Words barreled from him. "She is off-limits to you."
To everyone!

The Sent One snickered. "Defensive, are we? I'm not hoping to steal your woman away. Although I could, if I so desired. I just… I've been told you and I have a similar dating strategy. Get in, get out. And yet, you moved in with her. Why?"

Yes, Willy. Why? Every muscle clenched, he croaked, "She works for me. She's my codebreaker. I protect her from my enemies." *I crave her. And it's only getting worse.*

He'd decided to maintain his distance until she finished decoding the book. But…he was *still* falling for her, wasn't he? Still missing her the way he'd miss a limb.

"Tell me about the time before you met Hades," Axel said.

No part of William wished to share details about the cannibals. Relive the worst days…weeks…years of his life? No, thanks. But he craved a relationship with this man, and sharing significant events from his past might be the only way to bond.

Before he could respond, a commotion in front of the palace kicked up; they went quiet. William peered through a pair of binoculars, magic allowing him to see past a thick cloud of smoke emitted by the array of firepits.

Spotting the reason for the commotion, he belted out a dark obscenity. "I can't be seeing what I think I'm seeing."

Axel had a pair of mystically enhanced binoculars, too. He placed them at his eyes and snickered.

Sunny, Pandora and Anya had entered the yard at top speed, slashing and hacking through demons. Severed limbs plopped to the ground. Blood spurted.

"Your Sunny decided to show off for you?" Axel asked with a laugh.

"She doesn't know I'm here," he grated, keeping the binoculars trained on her. His heart raced. He'd known she enjoyed fighting demons, but he'd never seen her wage war.

Despite fear for her safety, his chest puffed with pride. The woman had skill, boundless grace and lethal precision. She was an angel of death, wielding a spear, toppling demons three by three. *Magnificent.* Of course, he hardened at the sight of her.

Not just hardened. Burned. For the first time in centuries, William felt truly demonic. Watching his female lay waste to the enemy, his every savage instinct clambered for attention.

Sunny's companions paused to cheer her on, and a glorious smile lit her face. Killing demons, having fun.

"What is she?" Axel asked, sounding awed.

What else? "My greatest torment."

26

"I want what I want when I want it. Give it to me."

MISSED THIS SO MUCH. Sunny used her spear to stab, jab and kabab every soldier in her path, leaving a trail of destruction in her wake. She laughed. Cleaning up Hell, one rapist, murderer and abuser at a time.

Since meeting William, she'd put her hobby on hold. And what had she gotten for her sacrifice? A domineering male who thought he could order her to stay put and stand down. A *foolish* male who held her captive.

A confusing male she'd wanted to kill only hours ago.

A POS male who let her worry about his whereabouts.

From now on, there would be no more tormenting him. No more bantering. No more make-out sessions.

Scalding demon blood poured down her arms and splattered her face, whisking her back to the present. A terrible odor saturated the air, a mix of sulfur, blood and char. There was no sun here, only blazing firepits and crackling torches.

Demons converged from all directions, accompanied by a cacophony of pain and anguish. Such lovely music. Her favorite battle soundtrack. *They get what they deserve.*

"I am judge. I am jury. I am executioner!" Pandora cried, brandishing two short swords.

"I am pretty, oh-so-pretty," Anya sang as she felled two demons, stabbing one in the eye and the other in the belly.

Both women fought with masterful skill. The more opponents they killed, the brighter their smiles.

Adrenaline imbued Sunny with extra strength and incredible speed, her stamina unmatched. If ever William saw her like this, he would be so impressed, and sorry he'd pushed her away.

How could he temporarily activate the curse, then treat Sunny like garbage? Unless he hadn't activated the curse at all. Maybe William hadn't been able to fall in love until a codebreaker came along and broke through the magical barrier?

She sucked in a breath. Had she inadvertently aided Lilith?

Was William out in the world, falling in love with some nameless, faceless woman right now?

Ridiculous! You didn't. He isn't. Now, no more thinking about him.

Claws raked her side, and she hissed. She'd let herself get distracted, and it had cost her, burning pain shooting down her legs. She nearly toppled, only an iron will keeping her upright.

Twirling the spear, she slammed the end into the offender's sternum, shattering the bone, then she faced her next challenger. Or tried to. Her body refused to obey.

Daisy! The demon must have injected her with some kind of toxin. Her internal thermostat jacked up. Sweat beaded on her brow and upper lip, and trickled between her shoulders. Her limbs trembled. She swayed. *Weakening?*

Had she gone soft in her captivity and lost her touch? She might need to retreat and regroup.

A whirlwind of motion, Anya decapitated the demon responsible for Sunny's injury. Pandora went low...lower... slicking her swords across his Achilles tendon.

Wheezing, dizzy, Sunny drew on a reservoir of strength and magic to force her body back into motion. She lifted the spear just in time, blocking a demon who hoped to use her neck as a snack pack.

The action brought a fresh wave of pain. *Ignore!* She had a mission—keep these bastards off her yard!—and she *would* complete it. Today.

This might be a hobby, but it was a beloved one. She gritted her teeth and jabbed a demon through the eye. Slice, straight across his neck. Rip, from navel to nose. Next!

A demon wrapped the end of his spiked tail around her calf and yanked, dragging her leg out from under her, breaking the bone in the process. Excruciating pain. Stars flashing before her eyes.

Other demons rushed over, surrounding her in seconds and quickly closing in... More claws raked her. Fangs and daggers, too. Hurting, Sunny rolled to her side. Though she poured blood into the char-laced ground at an alarming rate, she bucked and she kicked, doing as much harm to the demons as they did to her. The unicorn motto? Battle in public, hurt in private.

Vision darkening...

Pandora and Anya cut a swath through the growing crowd and made their way over. One claimed the spot at Sunny's left while the other claimed the spot at her right, the two working together to protect her from further attack. Forget being prefriends. The girls moved up the ranks. Genuine friends, baby!

For some reason, the demons began dropping and writhing before the girls delivered the next strike. What was—ahhh. In the distance, William descended from the midnight sky, ginormous wings of smoke gliding up and down, blowing dark tendrils across the battleground. Lightning flashed beneath the surface of his skin, forking over his eye sockets, his cheekbones, down his neck and arms. Shirtless, his muscle-cut strength and tattoos were on mouthwatering display. Rips in his black leathers revealed bone-deep gashes. Mud and other things caked his combat boots.

Eyes glittering with menace, expression raw and brutal, he was the incarnation of war, the epitome of sex and the king of violence, savagery and carnality. A single glance threatened to ruin her for life. No other man could ever compare.

Sunny lumbered to her feet, or tried to. *Come on, come on.* She drew on her magic… Yes! Success. But right away, dizziness attempted to knock her down again. She breathed through it, in and out, in and out, and remained on her feet.

The demons continued to collapse.

"We've got this, Willy. Go before—" The smoke rising from his wings reached Pandora, and she dropped, as well. Only, she didn't writhe in pain.

"William, don't you dare—" Anya dropped.

The wing-smoke must be laced with a drug. Would it affect Sunny the same way? Surely not.

Movement to her left. She turned her head. Axel glided across the battleground, gripping a sword of fire. Every time he came upon an unconscious demon, he swung, removing the head.

So…obviously William hadn't been out there man-whoring around, as she'd originally suspected. He'd intended to spend the night getting to know his brother. But why not just tell her? Why leave her in suspense? Unless he'd wanted her to worry, which sucked on a whole new level.

Or maybe he'd feared he was falling in love with her, and she would try to kill him, so he'd hoped to put a little emotional distance between them? That, she would totally understand. Hadn't she begun to do the same?

Heart fluttering, she met William's narrowed gaze, and daisy! Awareness buzzed along her nerve endings, making her want to touch...kiss...freesia.

As he stalked closer—unable to stay away?—he perused her from head to tail. Her heart fluttered with more force. "Bag and tag the demons still breathing," he called to Axel, never removing his gaze from Sunny. "We'll ask our questions." He took another step in her direction. "I hope your outing was fun, since you won't be leaving the stable ever again."

Ever? *He thinks to imprison me for the rest of eternity?*

She inhaled deeply. "You can take your captivity and shove—" Her world went dark, her knees buckling. She tumbled back to the ground. No, she tumbled straight into William's arms. He'd flashed to her, catching her before she ever crash-landed.

Just before she drifted off, a final thought drifted through her mind. *No need to ponder our relationship status; we're done.*

For a seemingly endless span, Sunny drifted in and out of consciousness. The first couple of times, she felt as if she were floating on a cloud of velvet-draped steel that smelled of William. Then she lay on a bed of clouds, a kaleidoscope of sounds filling her ears. Moans of pain. Rattling chains. Screams. Gurgling. *Whack, whack.* A pop, pop, pop. Grunts. *Pop, pop.* More moans.

She thought she heard William laugh. "Where do you want my blade to go next? Your genitals or your eye? No, you know what? Don't tell me. I'll surprise you."

"You'll do no such thing," Axel admonished. "It's my turn."

Sunny blinked open her eyes. Through a dim haze, she spotted William, pacing before a wall, where four bloody, mutilated demons were chained. And what a glorious sight he was. Her heart nearly leaped from her chest. With his face and arms splattered with black blood, he looked like a warrior on the cusp of his next battle. Truthful advertising. Spiked brass knuckles adorned his claw-tipped fingers.

He was shirtless, his leathers torn, muscles on display. *Too bad I'm done with him.* A stupid whimper brewed at the back of her stupid throat.

Axel crouched in front of one of the prisoners, his golden wings blocking the view. "I will give you one more chance to tell us what you've heard and seen inside Lucifer's palace, then I start cutting. Spoiler alert. I plan to start with your testicles. I promised myself this will be the year I finally hang demon balls like Christmas ornaments."

"Dibs on the left one," William said.

Brothers who torture together stay together.

Why had William brought her here? *Couldn't bear to part with me?* Or maybe he'd realized he could use her magic to ensure the prisoners told the truth. Not even demons could lie in her presence.

What a bluebell! She'd agreed to help him decode the book, and in return he'd agree to kill the poachers and collectors. No more, no less. Their deal had nothing to do with her lie detector ability. Now he owed her another boon. *And I know just what I want. Freedom!*

He would refuse, though, guaranteed. *So, so done. I*

*continue to aid him, and he can't trust me enough to set
me free?*

She might have to bring back the punishments.

Sunny frowned as she drifted off once again...

However long later, she blinked open her eyes, memories assailing her. Pandora and Anya. The battle. William. His threat. Passing out. Demon torture. Daisy!

She scanned her surroundings. William had returned her back to the stable and redecorated while she'd slept, adding more potted fruit trees and rosebushes to sweeten the air. He'd hung three life-size portraits. Wait. They weren't portraits. They were holograms.

In one, a naked William smiled and held a bottle of champagne in front of his penis. Like a GIF on a loop, he popped the cork and drank straight from the bottle before the image reset. In the next frame, a bikini-clad Sunny danced on a stripper pole. In the last one, she looked like a schoolteacher, her pink hair in a bun, glasses perched at the end of her nose. She wagged a finger at the viewer, as if she was in midscold for unseemly behavior.

With a chuckle, Sunny tried to sit up. Something yanked her back down. Confused, she looked left, then right, a scream brewing at the back of her throat. Rope bound her wrists and ankles to the bedposts.

Ropes for a little light bondage? *Sign me up—with anyone other than William.* Ropes for punishment? *Someone's gonna die!*

Her body ached, but she had no visible wounds, the gashes she'd received on the battlefield already healed. Considering she had damp hair and wore clean underclothes—a blue bra and a pair of matching panties—she had to assume William bathed her.

Wait. Were the panties…a thong? "William," she snarled. *Should have killed him when I had the chance.*

No! She couldn't let herself think that way. What you focused on, you magnified. What you thought about, you empowered. Adding fuel to the curse's fire was dumb.

So. Rephrase. *Should have punched him when I had the chance.*

She couldn't ask that he release her or even bargain for it. She had no leverage, and she would only weaken herself in his eyes, as well as her own. So, she'd have to fight or trick her way free.

"Yes, sundae?" He materialized at the end of the bed, as if he'd been there all along, waiting for her summons. He, too, had bathed, his hair as damp as hers. A white towel was wrapped around his waist. "I apologize for the images on the wall. Anya arrived with two portraits bright and early this morning. I burned those, so she came back with these."

"Why apologize? They're amazing. *She's* amazing. Unlike some people I know." The sight of his tattooed skin and immense muscle mass made mincemeat of her wits, her body automatically burning for his.

Maybe she wasn't done with him just yet.

Maybe she would use him for sex and ditch him at the first opportunity.

"I'd like to thank her with a basket of demon hearts," Sunny added. "Or do you think she'd prefer their severed heads?".

He did his surprised blink, a reaction she'd come to love. Considering his age, she'd bet few things surprised him.

"How are the others?" she asked, working to keep her tone pleasant. Daisy! A hint of breathlessness might have escaped.

"They're alive, thanks to me. After you passed out, a

backup demon horde arrived, and Axel lost a hand in the ensuing battle. Pandora and Anya got banged up when I tossed them through a portal."

A tsunami of guilt stormed through her. Had she resisted the urge to contact Pandora, both women and Axel would be safe and sound right now. "Where's Dawn?"

"On a walk with Pandora." Leaning against a bedpost, he crossed his arms over his chest. "Nothing to say about your current situation?"

Oh, she had plenty to say. And she would. With Dawn's absence, Sunny could commit all the violence she wished without frightening her sweet little hound. "I'll give you one chance to untie me."

"Don't worry, my sweet. I do plan to untie you...in time." He raked his gaze over her, a hard-on already tenting the towel. "First, you have crimes to answer for."

When he rubbed his palm along his length, she groaned, feeling as if their entire association was some kind of extended foreplay. Even when they argued, they lusted. "I have no idea what you mean. My crimes? Mine? No!" The more she spoke, the angrier she became. "We're talking about *your* crimes."

"To start, you ignored my last text," he continued. "Then you disobeyed a direct order, putting my sister, my friend and my codebreaker in danger and alerting Lucifer to your presence in Hell. No doubt he'll know what you are. He'll come for you, wanting you for his own."

"So? Let him come. I *want* to fight him. Now, for *your* crimes. To start," she said, mocking him, "you wanted space, I gave you space. But for some reason, you can't you extend me the same courtesy and leave me the hellebore alone."

A muscle jumped beneath his eye, and kept jumping. He remained silent.

"What's your goal here, William? Getting an apology out of me? Hearing me beg for mercy you don't have? Hearing me beg sexually?" Gaze glued on him, she pretended to writhe in pleasure. "Please, please, please put your fingers in…" Then she went still. "A wood chipper."

He didn't seem to note her words. His pupils flared, swallowing his irises. He scoured a hand over his face, taking an extra swipe at his mouth.

Such a sexy-hot action. In a snap, desire soaked her panties.

His nostrils flared. "You desire me, despite your bonds."

Sage! Wanting to punish him, she said, "Mating season draws nigh, remember? I want *everyone*." That had been true…in the past. Now she suspected no one else would do, that desire for William, and William alone, had turned her brain to mush.

"Everyone?" He traced his fingers over the upper edge of his towel. "Forget what Lucifer did to your pack. Do you know what he does to his female prisoners? Constant beatings and rapes. There's not an ounce of good in him. Would you welcome *him*?"

"Only so I could chop off his head! So let me at him, coach. Cut me loose and put me in the game! If you keep me locked up, I *will* grow to hate you. I might be halfway there already."

Fury pulsed from him, a spike against her skin. "You're going to defeat Lucifer? You, the woman who just got clawed and poisoned by demons. You were at death's door when I reached you, Sunny, and embarrassingly easy to knock out."

Her cheeks burned hotter with every word. Had she made mistakes out there? Yes. She'd expected the demons in Hell to be the same as the ones in the mortal world.

Wrong! They were stronger here, faster and more numerous. Something she should have considered. Instead, she'd rushed headlong into a situation, giving it no real thought. Next time, though, she'd have a plan A, B, C and D.

Hoping her next question would get a legit answer, she used a gentler tone. "If I'm so weak in your eyes, why did you tie me up?"

He slapped a claw-tipped hand against the poster, rattling the entire bed. "Because I require appeasement. Because I wanted you to know the seriousness of your situation. *Because I can.* Because you deserve it. You made me show a hand of cards I wasn't prepared to play. I went running to save you. Lucifer knows you're important to me."

I'm important! Bones going soft, she moaned and melted into the mattress. "How are you going to punish me?"

"How do you want to be punished?" Once again, he stroked his length above the towel.

Another moan escaped. What would he do next? What did she *want* him to do? She tried to reach out to him, desperate to touch him, but all she did was tug on her bonds and abrade her wrists. *Tied up, remember?*

"Sunny. I asked you a question."

Oh, yes. Did she want to be punished? Kind of? Despite everything, she was into this, into him. But. She'd let herself get sidetracked, when he had crimes to answer for, too. "I want to punish *you*. I'm tied up, held captive and used for my decoding skills. When you texted to tell me you wouldn't be coming home, you wanted me to think you were spending the night with another woman. Admit it."

His eyes flashed with incredulity. "You put yourself in danger because you were jealous? I would never inform you about a night with another woman through a text, duna."

"Would you skywrite it?" she snapped. He hadn't promised to never cheat; he'd only claimed he'd let her know before he did it. "Would you send me a certified letter? Use a megaphone?"

His anger flared up again. "You're blaming me for a crime I haven't committed. I've never cheated, and I will *never* cheat."

Maybe, maybe not, but her instincts shouted, *He's telling the truth.*

"Last night, I wasn't in my right mind," he admitted. "After Hades shoved Axel outside, he dropped a bombshell on me. He said that if I forge a relationship with Axel, I am, supposedly, destined to murder him and take his crown."

"Oh, William. I'm sorry." Such a devastating turn of events. "Is it part of the prophecy?"

"In a way. He mentioned an oracle." He rubbed the center of his chest, as if warding off a constant ache. "My first instinct was to get to you, confide in you and hear your thoughts."

But the need had scared him? Pulse leaping, she said, "Why didn't you?"

He lifted a brow. "You wish to hear I panicked? That I acted like a pussy?"

"Yes! Consider it foreplay," she blurted out, his crude language making her shiver. Knowing he was, in fact, falling for her both terrified and thrilled her, leaving no room for her anger. And okay, okay. Maybe she'd overreacted to his text. Not the captivity and rope, though. "Look. If it's a prophecy, there's still hope. Death doesn't always equate to physical death. Sometimes, death means a fresh start. Plus, there are always loopholes."

"Explain," he said, a habit of his.

"Prophecy—you can never speak the truth. Loophole—you tattoo the message on your body. Prophecy—no warrior has the strength to defeat a villain. Loophole—a scholar comes along and defeats the villain with her wits. We have only to find the loophole in *your* prophecy."

Hope glimmered in those electric blues. He took a step closer, his erection growing past the edge of the towel. A bead of pre-come wet the tip, making her mouth water for a taste. Her nipples drew taut, and her belly fluttered.

Still holding her gaze, toying with the towel, he rasped, "We had our first true argument as a couple. Now we will make up."

His desire fed hers, making her ache. Her blood heated, need for him a consuming blaze. She couldn't give in too easily, though, or he would realize he had power over her.

But I have power over him, too.

"Are you wet, sundae? Part your knees," he instructed. "Show me how much you want me."

She obeyed—slowly—and he sucked in a breath.

"Your panties are soaked." Lust turned his voice to smoke. "You need me. You need *this*." He ran his hand up and down his length with more force. "Tell me how badly you need it."

He expected her to say the words aloud, to admit she yearned for him. *Not until you admit it first.*

With a wanton moan, she arched her back, ensuring her breasts jiggled.

"Sunny," he all but snarled. "I gave you a command."

"And I say, make me," she breathed. "Or tell me how badly you need *me*."

He narrowed his eyes, a man possessed. "Why don't I show you instead?"

27

"Not sure what I like more. A woman's screams of pleasure…or an enemy's screams of agony."

BREATHLESS WANT AND world-changing need collided, setting off a chain reaction of sensation. William experienced all of the usuals to a shocking degree: heating blood, racing heart and throbbing erection. Plus a few extras: nerves on edge, a raw, hollow feeling in the center of his chest and an undeniable sense of urgency.

He could have lost Sunny today, unable to save her. He could have lost his decoder and lifemate in one fell swoop. Now he had her tied to his bed. Safe, sound and "super horny." Had he ever encountered a more alluring sight? Had he ever wanted a female so desperately?

Claim her. Don't just tie her to the bed; tie her to your side.

She's yours. Keep her.

What William felt for Sunny wasn't just explosive. It was

nuclear. Since meeting her, he'd slept with no one else—had wanted no one else. Perhaps he'd known deep down there would be no substitute for her. No one else smelled so luscious, tasted so sweet or fit him so perfectly.

That fit had never been so clear as he'd carried her back to the stable, fresh from battle; she'd molded herself to his chest, and he'd contemplated gluing her there forevermore.

Resist her sexually? No longer.

The fact that she'd made progress on the book…that counted, too. Big-time. Within a matter of days, the curse would be eradicated altogether. In the meantime, why shouldn't he be with the one he desired above all others? He could guard his heart, ensuring he didn't fall in love unless or until the proper time.

Voice like silk, he said, "How should I show you, sundae? Say it. Tell me what you need."

"Tricky, tricky. You made me think you'd take the first step, but you turned the tables on me. How do you *think* I want you to show me, baby?"

"I think you want something inside you," he rasped.

"Yes, please," she said, panting slightly. The ring in her forehead glowed softly, projecting rainbow sparks. *Mesmerizing.*

The next thing he knew, he'd moved to the side of the bed, his claws bared. His thoughts muddied. Those pale blue undergarments molded to her luscious curves, her rose tattoos a pleasure garden he planned to visit every damn day.

With a one-two slice, he severed the ropes that bound her wrists. Wait. Why had he done that?

"But first," she added, her voice firmer than before, "I'll show you why you don't need to worry about me on a battlefield." With no other warning, she launched a fist at his face.

The punch surprised him, ringing his bell. While he recovered, she freed her ankles. She kicked out her legs, slinging them around his waist and latching her ankles together. With a single yank, she tumbled him onto the bed—on top of her.

Delighted with her cunning, he laughed. Then she arched her hips. Her core rubbed against his erection, and his mind blanked.

Fragmented thoughts winked into focus. Soft breasts, hard nipples. Drugging heat. Intense pressure. Sizzling friction.

With the next roll of her hips, his towel came undone. His erection pressed against her panties, a cloth the only thing that blocked him from his ultimate destination.

I'm going to vacation there. Duration TBD.

She was smart; she used the remains of rope to pull herself into an upright position and straddle him. "See! I can handle myself." Triumph glowed in her eyes.

Pride stamped his every cell. Because of her skill, yes, and also her desire. "Can you handle *me*? I want…" He clasped her waist and fell back, rolling to pin her to the mattress. "To give you what you crave more than air."

Breathless, she replied, "No, you want to give *yourself* what you crave more than air."

He rocked against her. "You want me all to yourself. You would kill other women to be with me. You care for me. Admit it." He craved the words as much as her body.

She trembled against him, ribbons of silky pink draping the pillows. "You would cry if you lost me."

He thought he…might. "You think I'm special."

Beams of sunlight stroked her, and suddenly she appeared dusted in diamond powder. Her emerald eyes glinted with agonized bliss. When he rocked his hips faster, her lips parted on a broken gasp. The sexiest sound he'd ever heard.

"I do care. About you," she replied, her tone ragged. Her expression was gut-wrenchingly vulnerable. "I really do. There. Are you happy now?"

Yes! And no. He needed to remain emotionally distant, but her gentle admission cut through his defenses, soothing a wound that had festered for thousands of years. *Never should have been birthed? Wrong, Wrathling. This unicorn needed me to be born. I alone have the power to sate her desires.*

"I care about you, too, sundae." The admission slipped from him unbidden as he thrust against her.

She moaned, and he only wanted more. More of her moans. All of her loyalty. Her complete trust in him. Even her love.

How can I expect her trust when I do not offer mine? When I continue to hold her captive?

Moments passed as they stared at each other, his awareness of her deepening. He'd never been more cognizant of the difference in their sizes. The tall, muscled warlord and his seemingly fragile unicorn. And shit. Shit! She parted her legs wider, creating a cradle for his shaft, ensuring the tip pressed against her drenched core.

He rocked his hips again, the action necessary for his survival. Satisfaction beckoned, need for her ramping up, up, frothing inside him. *More. Now. All, everything.*

As she expelled ragged breaths, her heart raced in time to his. Passion-fever flushed her cheeks. "William," she said, moaning again.

"Sundae? Ready to come already?" So sensitive to his

every touch! "What happened to the girl who hates sex, hmm?"

"You killed her with pleasure. I—I don't want to play anymore. I just want." Torment in her tone, in her eyes. "Please."

Growls rumbled from him. *Take. What's. Yours.* Claim *what's yours.* Yes! William bent his head and snared her lips with his own, a fervor engulfing him. He ached. He throbbed harder than ever before—kissed harder, their tongues thrusting and rolling together.

With her, his pleasure heightened. Every sense engaged. Because he knew her, liked her and, yes, he cared for her. That care made him a conduit for a dizzying rush of madness. And he liked it.

With one hand, she combed her fingers through his hair, blunt-tipped nails scraping his scalp. With the other, she scored his back with more force. The slight sting sharpened his pleasure, until he thought he might spontaneously combust. *Worth it.*

He kneaded her breasts and pinched her nipples, little gasps escaping her, fraying his control bit by bit. When she pushed him to his back and rose above him once more, he offered no protests. She removed and tossed her bra, those beautiful breasts springing free. Wicked girl. Had he ever wanted like this?

"The panties have to go." He raked a claw along the center seam, the material falling apart. Contact. Feminine heat seared him.

Control fraying faster.

Beneath his shaft, a small tuft of pink curls that rested between the long lengths of her legs.

When he gyrated his length against her, flesh met flesh

and heat met heat. *Hot, liquid and world-shattering.* He hissed in a breath.

Back arched, she purposely rubbed her core against his erection. In a moment, pleasure became pain, and pain became pleasure.

She kissed down his neck, sucked on his pulse. Control? He had none. Not just frayed anymore, but completely obliterated.

"I want to fuck you," he snarled.

"Mmm, yes. Wait. No!" Panic flared in her eyes. She planted her hands on his pectorals. "Climax, yes. Sex, no. Not until I've decoded the book."

What had brought *that* on? He could push for an answer, ending this, or he could move on and find out after. "Very well." Was he disappointed? Beyond. Would he press her to offer more? Never. *No* meant *no*, period. "Kiss me."

Her hands flew down to cup his jaw. At the same time, he jackknifed to an upright position. They meshed their lips together. Once again, their tongues tangled, her breasts pressing against his chest, her nipples tormenting him every time they moved. Once again, he rocked, rocked, rocked his erection against her, the tip teasing her clitoris, driving him mad.

"The things you make me feel." Once, twice, she lashed her hips, no longer content to rub. No, she slammed against him with increasing force.

Not enough. Not nearly enough. He gripped the perfect globes of her perfect ass. Soft, yet firm. *Mine, all mine.* As he squeezed her, he jerked her forward and pistoned *his* hips.

"More," she commanded, and he happily obeyed.

Fire rushed through his veins, sweat beading over his skin; smoke enveloped his mind, a drug. He fisted a handful of her hair and lifted her face. Again their eyes met, the rest of the world ceasing to exist.

"William!" She beat her fists into his chest. "Stop."

"Stop what?" The kissing? Touching? Either way, he would rather die than stop, but in this, her word would always be law.

"Stop messing around and get to the good stuff."

The *good* stuff? He blinked rapidly, caught off guard. "Are you *complaining* about my technique? Again?" As he spoke, he played with her nipples, pinching and flicking them. "Or is my unicorn impatient for her pleasure?"

"Yes!" she said, thrashing beneath him. "You're going so slow. And you haven't even fingered me yet. Freesia-ing finish what you started! I'm ready."

She wanted hard and fast? *With pleasure.* William twisted, tossing her to her back. As she bounced on the mattress, he moved to stand at the side of the bed, grabbed her ankles and flipped her over. He manhandled her to her hands and knees, purposely rough, always watching her, ensuring her reactions never veered into fear or dismay. No, oh, no. His pleasure-hungry Sunny loved it, purring for more.

"Look at you," he said, marveling. Her breasts. Her ass... her feminine core. At this angle, he could see all his favorite parts. "Absolute, utter perfection."

With a waterfall of pink hair cascading over her back, she glanced over her shoulder and gifted him with the softest, sweetest smile. Things inside him beginning to crack. Resistance, reluctance. Civility, perhaps. His heart nearly stopped, the need to pleasure, protect and be with Sunny overtaking him completely, perhaps even rewriting his DNA.

The male who'd sought satiation and merriment in the

arms of countless others, desperate to feel wanted, burned to ash. From those ashes arose a male with new purpose. *I will have Sunny and no other!*

She was passion, temptation, carnality and lust. She was seduction incarnate. And she was *his.* "Do you trust me, sundae?"

"I…do." She sounded surprised. "You won't hurt me."

"That's right. You will *never* have reason to fear me. In this, I'll never take what you do not offer, or push for more than you're willing to give. If I do something you don't like, tell me, and I'll stop immediately. Your consent, your enjoyment, mean everything. Do you understand?"

"Yes," she said, a tremor in her voice. "Please, William. More."

Her passion-glazed gaze heated as she watched him climb back onto the bed. He remained on his knees, his legs between hers, and flattened a hand in the center of her back. With a little push, he made her lean down, positioning her magnificent ass higher in the air. Her lovely face rested against a pillow.

Seeing her like this… His body felt like it was strung tighter than a bow. In, out. He extended an arm between her legs, saying, "Give me your hand."

Without hesitation, she reached back. Holding on to her wrist, he guided one of her fingers inside her drenched sheath. When he felt it was sufficiently wet, he replaced the digit with another. He repeated the process until all five fingers were coated in her honey. Her moans came continuously, caressing his ears.

His tremors worsened as he positioned his erection against her pink, pouty lips. The heat! Though he wanted only to sink inside her, he resisted, calling on every bit of power, magic and resolve. The moment he felt he had a modicum of control, he began to move, mimicking the motions of sex, rubbing his shaft against her swollen little clitoris.

As she gasped his name, he told her, "Fingers on my cock, sundae."

Again she obeyed without hesitation. He continued to move, rocking back and forth. Back and forth. Right into her palm. She squeezed him, magnifying his pleasure a thousandfold.

"So big," she praised. "So hard."

He rotated, changing the angle of his thrusts. The tip of his shaft hit her where she needed him most, and she cried out. Again. And again. With a hand resting on her lower back, he glided his thumb to the crack of her ass. She moaned louder. Faster. On his next inward glide, he pressed that thumb *into* her ass.

She jolted, shocked. Then she melted into his touch, bucking into his hold. "William! Wicked man...more!"

One day, every part of her would crave every part of him. He would make sure of it.

He quickened his pace, hitting her clit at a clipped pace while fingering her deeper. Her little hole clenched around his thumb, eliciting an answering clench low in his gut. The need to climax worsened. *Don't come. Not yet. Will last for her.*

Too good, too good.

He bit his tongue, tasted blood. Just beyond the bed was a full-length mirror he'd brought in before Sunny had awoken, planning to watch her as he worshipped at the altar of her body. Her luscious breasts swayed as her hand worked his length.

Faster, harder. Soon, they were both uttering unintelligible words. He pumped his shaft faster; she gripped his erection harder. Again and again, the plump head slammed against her clit. When she began to rock, chasing his length, he switched directions. Slam, slam.

"So close…need…now…give—yes!" she screamed, coming and coming hard. A flood of that honey drenched his shaft. Her inner walls spasmed around his thumb.

Tightening her grip on him, she reached back with her other hand and tugged on his balls. William still wasn't ready to come—he wanted to last forever, wanted more of this, more of *her*—but he couldn't stop the climax as it jetted from him.

He threw back his head, roared to the rafters.

28

"Be mine. Just kidding. Be gone."

SUNNY SNUGGLED AGAINST WILLIAM, her heart galloping in time to his, her breathing uneven. His warmth and scent cocooned her, ensuring a low level of pleasure still hummed inside her. But that pleasure was growing more tainted by the second. Any moment now, she expected him to sever contact, say something awful and leave, regretting how vulnerable he'd been with her, even though they hadn't technically had sex.

Not that it mattered. Their connection had strengthened, and the intensity of their attraction had deepened. She'd felt it happening, and knew he had, too. If he'd been panicked by the thought of commitment before, he might be ready to race to the hills now. In fact, he hadn't spoken a word since they'd collapsed on the mattress, utterly spent.

As one minute bled into another, he simply toyed with her hair and traced the ridges of her spine, as if content to be near her. But Sunny began to resent the silence. If William was going to act like a pouty man-baby about his growing feelings for her, she needed to know, so *she* could run for the hills. Because, little by little, despite everything... *I'm falling for him.*

What they'd done had blown her freaking mind. She didn't just want more sex. She wanted fidelity. Trust. A family. Eternity.

She wanted everything he had to give. For real. What did he want?

Since he hadn't bailed, she decided to test the waters. If she started with fun questions, maybe she could get him to open up. "If you could describe your life with a movie title, what would it be?"

He answered quickly, as if he'd known the whole of his life. "I'd be a double feature. *A Series of Unfortunate Events* followed by *I Am Legend.*"

"Liar! You'd be *Get Hard* followed by *Sausage Party.* I mean, do you know how many times I've had to hear about your link?"

He grinned. "You'd be *Willy Wonka and the Chocolate Factory.* Big Willy is going to eat...you...up."

She snort-laughed. Deciding to push a little harder, now that she had him talking, she asked, "So, how'd things go with your dad?"

Between one blink and the next, misery pulsed from him. "Hades believes I plan to kill him, so he's barred me from his home. He won't even speak to me."

Different parts of her constricted. "I'm sorry, baby." She wouldn't offer a platitude about time healing all wounds. Some wounds festered. Some scarred. While she hadn't caused his broken heart, she desperately wanted to help mend it. "A rejection is never fun, but one day, it might be a blessing. With their actions, people show us who they are. If your father can cut you from his life, he doesn't deserve you."

He pulled her even closer and kissed her brow, but said nothing else.

"How did you come to be part of Hades's family?" she asked. "I mean, I know you mentioned he and Lucifer rescued you from a hellish realm, but I hear supernatural adoptions are complicated."

A pause, rife with strain. Would he deflect now, regretful about his previous admission? Would he leave?

He surprised her yet again; he explained, "After the woman I believed to be my mother was killed, I awoke in a Hell realm. Not just hellish. I was enslaved by—" Gaze wild, he said, "Cannibals and rapists. They called me Scum. I'm not sure how much time passed before Hades showed up with Lucifer. They killed the entire clan and asked me to go with them, to live with them and act as Hades's hand of vengeance. I did. Sometime later, I wore a pair of bands that melted into my flesh, bonding me to the king."

"Oh, William. The things you must have suffered in the Hell realm. I'm so sorry." The fact that she'd once called him scum… Guilt and shame seared her. No wonder he'd flinched when she'd done it.

"Everyone suffers at some point," he said, his voice gruffer.

"Does other people's misery make your past any less awful? No." Hurting for him, she traced a heart over his, well, heart. "You and Lucifer were so close. What made him want to sacrifice you? For that matter, what caused the rift between Hades and Lucifer?"

"Lucifer had staged a coup. He planned to sacrifice me to acquire my strength, and use that strength to de-

feat Hades." Again the muscle beneath his eye leaped. "He
failed with me, but still ambushed Hades."

Poor William. Lucifer had destroyed his family, just as the
bluebell had destroyed hers. Only, William had to suffer the
betrayal of a loved one on top of everything else, and he'd
had to do it *after* the witch had cursed him. Now he lived
with the knowledge that his own father, the man he loved
best, had lied to him, keeping him away from Axel for selfish reasons. Yeah, Sunny had listened to their conversation.
William had endured one blow after the other. No wonder
he'd never wanted to be part of a committed relationship.

"I'm so sorry for your pain," she repeated. "I'm sorry
for every century you didn't get to spend with Axel. Hey!
Speaking of, I figure you must have Sent One DNA, since
you were designed by Wrathling. Although, now that I think
about it, Sent One DNA tends to take over. If you were part
Sent One, you'd have wings like Axel. Feathered wings, I
mean, not smoky ones. Or maybe not? What do I know?
Anyway. Even though I've always fought for Team Good,
I never thought I'd date a possible Sent One."

She'd hoped to tease him into a good mood, but he stiffened. "What kind of men did you date before me?"

"You want the truth, the whole truth, and nothing but the
truth? I picked weaker males with honest, nonviolent auras
who wouldn't succeed if they made a play for my horn."

He gave his patented eyebrow lift. "Do I want to know
about *my* aura?"

"It's blurry," she told him. "I can't read it, and I don't
know why."

"Perhaps because I'm more than a hybrid, my DNA possibly spliced from multiple species." He shrugged, then
changed the subject. "Why do you refuse to reveal your unicorn form, even though I've vowed never to steal your horn?"

Since he'd opened up to her, she decided to bestow the same honor upon him. "Shifting is incredibly personal. Like stripping to reveal my naked body. In that form, I'm more powerful, yes, but I'm more vulnerable, too. Which is why we usually only shift during a battle, *if* we know we can kill everyone who sees us. To see the horn even once is to understand how it works, something we've kept secret for a reason. It would put me at a major disadvantage."

"The explanation doesn't apply. We are together."

"For now," she quipped. They'd made no permanent arrangement.

"Together a few days and already preparing for our split?" He pursed his lips. "You trust me to pleasure your body. Why not this?"

Do it. Tell him. "Because you're a flight risk. Because, with my dual personality, I'm weird, and there's no denying it. What if you get tired of dealing with me? What if someone else catches your fancy? What if I fail to decode your book? What if you leave me locked up and I have to fight you to leave?"

Putting her on her back, her disheveled prince of darkness loomed over her, wicked, wanton and, for some reason, livid. "We'll drop the unicorn thing—for now. Why did you insist on forgoing sex until the book is decoded? You weren't worried about it before."

Because she was falling for him so quickly. Too quickly. Because he might be falling for her. Because the curse had proven stronger than she'd expected. But telling the truth would be a huge mistake. However, a lie would be unforgivable.

His phone buzzed, saving her from having to think up a proper response. Voice firm and unbending, he said, "We aren't done with this conversation."

"Sure thing, babe. I'll pencil in a rehash on the thirty-second day of the month."

He looked to be fighting a grin. "Keep it up, and I'll stuff something in that smart mouth of yours." Adjusting their positions, he leaned over to grab the cell from the nightstand.

Sunny caught a glimpse of the screen.

Black Attack: You'll be pleased to know I did it. I bagged and tagged Evelina. She's currently resting uncomfortably in my dungeon. Also, we've made no progress with Lilith or that Sable chick. There are zero rumors about them, and no scent to follow.

Radiating extreme excitement as well as disappointment, William sat up and texted back, Keep searching for Sable. Do not give up until you've found a trace. For now, forget Lilith. I'll come by later tonight to speak with Evelina, and I'll have a female with me.

He will? And he'd chosen to send his boys after her aquaint—oh, who was she kidding?—*friend* rather than his witch. Sunny swallowed a dreamy sigh, glitter bombs detonating in her heart.

The fact that there was no trace of Sable was actually a good sign. If someone had her, they would have left a trail, but on her own, Sable knew how to hide to avoid detection.

Black Attack: A woman will be with you, huh? Awww. Am I getting a new mommy?

William: You're getting a spanking.

"What about your dinner with Hades?" Sunny asked softly.

"Don't think he has any desire to spend time with me." Stiff again—no, stiffer—William squared his shoulders, as if bracing for a blow. "I think he's done with me." His voice shook, only slightly, but enough to notice.

She hugged him tight. "William. Babe. He might think he's done with you, but you're the Panty Melter. Is anyone ever really done with you? He'll come around. Besides, if you want to stop his maybe/maybe-not prophecy, there's a simple solution. Don't kill him."

He opened his mouth. Snapped it closed. Opened, closed. She smirked. Finally, he sagged atop the mattress and puffed out a breath, repeating, "Smart-ass."

"But a smart smart-ass," she said. "Who's Evelina?"

"The half sister of the witch who cursed me, and Lucifer's wife. She ran away the week after the wedding, and has remained in hiding ever since. I plan to use her against Lucifer. And don't even think about attempting to convince me not to use an innocent. I have no plans to harm her."

"First, I would never attempt such a thing. I would succeed. Second, using an innocent is something Lucifer would do. Sure you want to go that route? Lastly, just because you have no plans to harm her, doesn't mean she'll walk away unscathed. Accidents happen."

His nostrils flared, a dark oath barreling from him.

Sunny laughed. "I kid, I kid. Just wanted to prove I would, in fact, succeed. I'm a solid sixty percent on board with using her, but only if we have safeguards in place." Would he heed her advice, or dismiss it?

Several other texts popped up, and he made no move to hide the screen to prevent her from reading. So, read she did.

Green Machine: LET ME DROP EVELINA OFF IN YOUR DUNGEON!

Red Abed: He's just mad because the little wildcat spat in his face.

"Black Attack, Green Machine and Red Abed," Sunny muttered. *Why aren't I Sunny Bunny?* "Tell me about their mother." The last time she'd asked, he'd flushed and changed the subject.

Now he flushed. "Unlike other magic wielders," he said, shocking her, "I don't burn through what I absorb. I store it, until I take one drop too much. Then the magic bonds with whatever emotions lives in my heart and spills from me in streams of smoke, somehow creating adult immortals."

"So you're both father and mother. That's incredible, and usually something only a god can do. I don't get why you're embarrassed by it."

He did his surprised blinking thing, and she couldn't help but add, "FYI, I have no plans to crack uterus jokes, or ask if you're on your period and need a fresh tampon… for now."

"How kind of you." A corner of his mouth twitched, as if he fought a new smile. "I birthed four horsemen of the apocalypse."

"Then you most certainly do have a god in your line. Maybe Ares."

Blink, blink.

She kissed his stubble-rough cheek, disentangled from him and stood to shaky legs. "I better figure out what I'm going to wear to meet your kids." She padded to the closet, where she dressed in clean undergarments, one of William's T-shirts and a pair of shorts. Then she glided to the desk and settled in. "I'll decode until you're ready to go." *Just be careful.* If the whispers started up or a single urge sparked, she'd stop immediately.

He tensed up, but said nothing else. Her brow furrowed. Why tense? He wanted the curse gone, right?

As he strode to the closet and selected a plain T-shirt and jeans, she opened the book and forced herself to concentrate on the symbols. Since she'd already broken through the witch's magical barrier and (kind of) rested up, she had no trouble deciphering another sentence.

The lesson begins with a curse, and ends with a funeral.

She wrote it down. Desperate to learn more about the pathway to that funeral, she traced her fingertip over the symbols. Come on, come on. But…nothing.

A burning pain shot through her head, heralding the whispers. *Kill him. Kill him now. Now!*

No. No way. But maybe? Sunny fingered the medallion that hung at her neck. How easy it would be to stand, close the distance, pretend she wished to kiss him and stab him instead.

"You learned something new," William said, moving to her side. "Tell me."

As she inhaled his masculine musk, the whispers stopped and the urges faded. Horrified, she released a shuddering breath. Would she have done it? Would she have stabbed him? She thought she…might.

Guilt and fear returned with a vengeance. She might need to rethink her strategy. Trembling, she pointed to a line of symbols, never really touching the page. "They say, 'The lesson begins with a curse, and ends with a funeral.'"

He ran his tongue over his teeth. "Basically, Lilith coded a hate diary?"

"Maybe, maybe not. Once she's done disparaging your good name, she might give step-by-step instructions to break the curse." But how likely was that?

A swooshing sound rose up, the stable shaking. More Sent Ones arriving? She leaned to gaze out the window. Since the Sent Ones moved in, the landscape had undergone a vast change, from sparse and sooty, to a wonderland teeming with cabins, trees and flowers. Warriors marched here and there, on patrol.

The fact that her wicked lover might be part Sent One still shocked her. Of course, he might also—or instead—be a dragon-shifter. They produced wings of smoke. Maybe he had Fae in him, too. Why else would he be impervious to her magic? And the way he seduced…just like the nymphs. The way he spoke, like the sirens. The way he moved, as graceful as the vampires.

A hodgepodge of species had been a specialty of the Wrathlings, who'd hailed from different worlds and realms. Did William have some other creature(s) in his DNA, as well? The more she knew, the better she could help him.

Pandora returned with Dawn, and the hound bounded over to Sunny, excited to see her. *We're bonding!* She petted the little darling behind both sets of ears without getting bitten more than twice. What progress!

"Come here, girl," William called, and Dawn darted over, leaped onto the bed to curl into his side.

Traitor! "Thank you," Sunny said to Pandora, who remained in the door.

Tossing the dog's leash on the desk, Pandora said, "She almost yanked my arms out of my sockets, so you're paying for a masseuse."

"We could put another girls' night on the books," she

said, deciding to test the limits of her freedom. Had she made progress with William or not?

"I'm in! Gotta complete a few assignments for Hades first, but I'll be texting soon." Pandora left.

William made no comments, protests or sounds of disapproval. Maybe he'd opted to let Sunny come and go at will?

Beaming, determination to be with him renewed, she picked up the book to study as she paced. One way or another, she would decode this book for William and resist the curse.

How much time passed, she wasn't sure; she lost track, a familiar wave of dizziness and heat sweeping through her again and again, stronger than before. Strong enough to topple her. Instead of trying to catch herself, preventing an injury, she hugged the book close, protecting it. So, when she hit the ground, she *really* hit, air gusting from her lungs.

William flashed to her. He set the book aside and eased her into a sitting position. She pushed *him* aside, desperate to see the pages. More symbols morphed into words!

"The rest of the sentence!" A good one, too. *"'The lesson begins with a curse, and ends with a funeral...unless he performs one small task.'"*

Eagerness palpable, William said, "Keep going. Please."

Please. Had he ever pleaded with her before? That he did now, over this, something he wanted most in the world... *Can't let him down. But not sure I can resist those dark urges.*

"Are you hurt, sundae?" Concern laced his voice.

"I need...need...to be alone." Yes. The solution. "Okay?"

He flinched, though it was barely perceptible. Had she not been watching intently, she would have missed it. Guilt flared. In her efforts to save him from harm, she'd hurt him.

"Very well," he said, his tone now devoid of emotion. "I'll visit someone who enjoys my company."

She snagged his wrist to hold him in place, and he let her. Eyes watchful, he moved closer to her. Hoping she'd pleased him, she moved closer to him, too. They stared at each other, their breaths growing uneven.

So she was getting turned-on only minutes after she'd planned to murder him? So what? Look at him. His body, sculpted with all those muscles. His tattoos, lickable. And the way he watched her right back, his eyes heating again, as if he'd just found his next meal.

"You want me close," he said, his eyes shimmering. "You want me gone. Tell me, Sunny. Why would I want more of this?"

Ouch. "I knew my dual personality would get to you." No need to mention the curse.

He didn't contradict her, which hurt way worse. "Did learning more about my past ruin me in your eyes? The things done to me. The things I did. Yes, I slept with married women in the past, nullifying their commitments. An action I regret. At the time, I considered the husbands fools for binding their futures to someone, anyone, and they deserved what they got. Over the past few years, I've encountered genuine examples of loving relationships. For the first time, I see possibilities."

Possibilities...with me? "I'm sorry," she whispered. "I'm sorry I made you think your past disgusted me. It doesn't." His life had shaped him. She liked who he'd become. A man, a warrior, who fought for what he believed in, with a heart more fragile than she'd ever realized.

His gaze dropped, lingering on her lips. Her gaze lingered on his, too, those beautiful, soft lips capable of making her mindless with bliss. She shivered, her arousal deepening.

Lightly pinching her chin between his fingers, he forced her gaze to lift. Something he must love to do. "You're not sorry you asked me to leave?"

Can't tell him the full truth. He'd only panic. But again, she couldn't lie. So, she shook her head and went with, "I was in a bad mood and feared I'd hurt you." Truth. Kind of.

"Don't worry about hurting me. Worry about pleasuring me." He licked his lips, as if he could already taste her. "I'm hungry. Ready to feast."

Resist. Take a moment to calm. "All right, but I'll require a meal of my own." The invitation left her lips unbidden.

"I will gladly—" He released her suddenly, as if she'd burned him, and stood.

Okay, what had she done wrong?

Tone sharp enough to cut glass, he said, "Someone's coming."

Really? How'd he know? She listened, but detected no odd noises. "Who?"

A knock sounded at the door and she jolted. "William?" Axel called.

Dawn remained on the bed; at the sound of the Sent One's voice, her heads jerked up. She bared both sets of teeth. A vicious growl echoed through the stable.

Sunny scrambled to unsteady legs, raced to the desk and returned the book to its case. Confused by the hound's reaction, she strode over, hoping to comfort the little darling.

"Enter," William called. "I've disabled the magical blocks."

Hinges squeaked, the door opening. Axel stalked inside—
Sunny did a double take. Whoa. Before, his aura had

been as blurry as William's. Now? It was solid black, with no hint of light.

The kind of aura demons possessed.

Unless Axel's personality had undergone a drastic change in the past day, their guest was someone *pretending* to be Axel.

A shape-shifter.

Like Rathbone.

Or... Sunny stiffened. The Great Deceiver. Lucifer.

29

"All the world is a stage. Immortals play the predators, humans play the prey. Go ahead, break a leg."

IN A HANDFUL of seconds, William ran the emotional gamut. Worry for Sunny's well-being. Fury over her dismissal. Determination to make her want to show him her unicorn form. Confusion about her moratorium on sex. Hatred for Lilith. Happy to see his brother. Pissed off that he couldn't finish his argument with Sunny and have hours of makeup fellatio.

How did not having sex with her feel so much better than having sex with someone, anyone, else? How could he crave more from her, more *of* her, never less?

He was desperate to keep her *and* cut ties, a sentiment that magnified every time he glanced in her direction. She was the first woman, the first person, to make mincemeat of his iron control, and there'd never been a less inopportune time. *So much at stake.*

"Hello, William," Axel said.

"Welcome," William replied.

"Thank you." As Axel stepped into the stable, Dawn barked louder and louder. "I came to tell you Lucifer attacked a group of Sent Ones. I fear this was the first of many strikes. We must prepare."

Sunny jumped to her feet, her breasts bobbing beneath her shirt. The color had drained from her cheeks, his concern returning in a flash. Was she sick?

She met William's gaze and whisper-bellowed, "Your penis is cute."

His penis—William stiffened. She'd just uttered her safe word, which must mean Axel's aura didn't belong to Axel, but Lucifer. But she had to be wrong. William had taken magical precautions to prevent something like this.

On the flip side, Dawn hadn't barked the last time Axel visited.

If William made an aggressive move and his little sundae had gotten this wrong, he might shatter the already fragile bond he'd managed to establish with Axel. But if she was right, and he did nothing, Lucifer could kill them both.

Lifting his chin, he eyed the other male. Axel looked the same as before, zero differences. He'd have to find the truth another way.

Protect Sunny at all costs. Safeguard the book, and the medallion.

The order surprised him. All costs? Even his own life?

No time to analyze or rationalize. If their guest *was* Lucifer, he'd either come to steal the book, enact a fact-finding mission—get in, learn William's plans, get out—or to ambush and kill. Or maybe even try to drive a wedge between William and the real Axel? Lucifer fed off misery, like an emotional incubus.

"I'm glad you came, Axel." Excellent. His casual tone shouldn't set off any alarm bells.

The maybe/maybe-not Sent One watched as Sunny leashed the still-barking Dawn and led her to the bathroom, where she sealed the two-headed monstress inside, just in case a fight broke out.

"Axel," he snapped, testing the other man's reaction. "You know the rules. No looking at the girl."

An amused blue gaze slide to William. "You're right. My apologies. She's a beautiful woman, and you're a lucky man." His voice was an exact match for Axel's. Only, William had never given a "no look" order. "I'd like to discuss next steps, and how we'll protect ourselves against Lucifer's second attack, but I'm happy to come back later, if you need a moment to finish the discussion about your penis."

He bit his tongue, tasting blood. How many times had he looked at an enemy with amusement, certain he had victory in the bag? Countless. Should he attack? And what had happened to the real Axel?

Shit! Knowing Lucifer, Axel still lived, but only as collateral. He might be imprisoned, a blade poised at his throat. His life in exchange for Lucifer's safe passage, just as Hades had taught them. Always have a contingency plan. Or, Axel might be out there, oblivious to Lucifer's schemes.

"Yes. Please stay." Offering a sugary sweet smile, Sunny sidled up to William, rested her head on his shoulder and tucked her hand into his, secretly passing him a dagger. *Good girl.* "I might have a way to kill Lucifer. Maybe I should get your take first?"

His chest puffed with pride. Smart girl, tempting the male with false information, without telling a single lie.

"Do tell." A flash of glee crossed fake Axel's face. "I'm *certain* I can help."

She looked to William, as if seeking permission to proceed. But he knew his unicorn, knew she wanted a sign that he would cooperate with whatever plan she'd cooked up.

As he peered into those gorgeous eyes, something swelled inside his chest. Time and time again this fierce female had proven herself capable of anything, but her safety came first. "You have plans with Pandora, remember? You go, and I'll fill him in." With his gaze, he told her, *Do not cross me on this, woman.*

With *her* gaze, she replied, *Silly Willy. You've already been crossed.* "Did I forget to tell you Pandora and I delayed our plans?" She patted his cheek, smiled another sugary sweet smile and motioned to the kitchen. "Let's talk at the table, shall we?"

Damn her. At least she'd chosen the perfect spot. William had a semiautomatic mystically hidden beneath the tabletop.

He escorted his unicorn there, never giving Lucifer his back, or revealing the blade concealed against his forearm. When he offered Sunny the corner chair, she shook her head and motioned for *him* to sit.

Rather than argue, he bit his tongue and eased down. "So gallant," he muttered.

She remained behind him, her hands resting on his shoulders.

Lucifer chuckled and eased into the seat across from William. "How domesticated you've become."

A dig meant to infuriate him? Too bad. He *liked* his arrangement with Sunny. But he didn't want the bastard to know what she'd come to mean to him.

He wagged his brows and flashed a lascivious grin. "You don't know what you're missing. My stable mistress might be a lowly witch with little magic—" to explain anything mystical she might do "—but she makes up for her *many* shortcomings with tons of head. Isn't that right, snookums?"

She shocked the shit out of him; she leaned down to kiss his cheek. "So right, boo boo bear. It's all in the fingers. Massage a man's scalp with enough pressure, and he'll be putty in your hands."

Smart-ass. Do not smile.

"Now, this head-massage-loving nymphomaniac is going to make hot cocoa. Who wants some?" She skipped to the kitchenette to prepare drinks. With poison? William had no idea what she planned, and the mystery intrigued him.

Morning light streamed through the window, illuminating "Axel," revealing hard, harsh eyes that did *not* belong to his brother. Sunny was right; he knew it beyond any doubt now.

Somehow, William found the strength to evaluate his options and *not* strike. If Lucifer had Axel...

Should he bargain? No way. He couldn't trust Lucifer to keep his word. Battle? No. What if Sunny got caught in the crosshairs? Magic? Lucifer had his own, and it was stronger than William's. The only option left? Trickery.

"Go ahead and tell us your plan, sugar tush," he told Sunny. "The suspense is killing us."

"Okay. Check it." She puttered around, gathering the proper ingredients. "We all know Lucifer is a piece of garbage, right? Like, a real steaming pile of poo."

Had the male stiffened ever so slightly, a hint of malevolence flashing in his irises? Jubilant, William said, "Yes. Garbage." With one hand, he clasped the semiautomatic under the table. With the other, he readied the knife. "We all know. Everyone knows."

Lucifer's next smile sparkled a little less. "Everyone

knows," he parroted. "Oh. Before I forget. Lucifer told you the witch, Lilith, still lives. I've heard a rumor that he plans to use her against you somehow."

Ah. Here it was, the attempt to send William into a frenzy of panic. "I'm not worried," he said, and Lucifer narrowed his eyes. "My codebreaker solved the mystery of the book. The curse is broken already."

Brittle smile. "How exciting."

Lucifer's shock was headier than ambrosia.

No footsteps sounded as Sunny returned to the table, two cups of cocoa in hand. She placed one in front of William, then moved around the table, headed for Lucifer.

William stifled a denial, head, his muscles knotting with sudden, intense strain. He didn't want his woman near the fucking devil.

The other male noticed his upset, and *he* realized the truth—William knew his true identity. No more waiting, then. Time to strike.

William hammered at the gun's trigger. *Boom, boom, boom!*

Lucifer had been in the process of standing, the bullets nailing his thigh. He grunted, but didn't collapse.

A smiling Sunny tossed the steaming chocolate in Lucifer's face. As he roared with pain and rage, she revealed the blade hidden against her arm and stabbed him in the throat. Once, twice, thrice, her motions fast as lightning. No hesitation, just pure aggression.

As a spray arced over the table from Lucifer's jugular, she spun behind him and stabbed his brain stem. Lucifer gasped for breath and finally collapsed. She skidded to the floor and hacked at his neck to remove his head.

When she finished, she laughed happily and held up the bloody blade like a gold medal. "I did it! I won!"

William watched, held immobile by shock and awe. She truly had—familiar male laughter rang out. Though Lucifer's headless body remained on the floor, a second, very alive Lucifer stepped out of thin air, coming up behind Sunny to place a knife at her throat.

No, no, this can't be happening. Panic crashed over William in icy waves, blood rushing from his head. A loud ring tolled in his ears. He'd thought Lucifer had shape-shifted into Axel, but he'd actually created an illusion of Axel and an illusion of invisibility over himself. No doubt he'd entered the home behind his illusion.

William should have known better; he should have expected this.

Just get to Sunny! Nearing a frantic state, he leaped up. His breaths came hard and fast. He used the table as a step stool, dropping down in front of Sunny. Her eyes were wide, her skin once again devoid of color. The stable grew deadly quiet, Dawn no longer barking. Why?

"That's close enough." Lucifer released a gleeful laugh. "I must say, you gave a good effort, brother. Just not good enough."

Red dotted his vision, fury melding with a surge of protectiveness. *Get to Sunny, damn it. He thinks to take her from me. No one takes her from me!*

Careful. Must stay calm. Must stall. William grated, "The same could be said for your disguise, asshole."

"Ah, yes. You did figure out my ruse faster than I assumed. What gave me away?"

"Axel isn't a piece of shit."

The laughter stopped. Lucifer grated, "Be a lamb and bring me your book, brother, nice and slow, or I kill your woman, nice and quick. And don't bother trying to convince me your curse is broken. I recognize a lie when I hear one."

Give up his book? His only hope for a life worth living? A future with Sunny. No! But would he have a future with Sunny if she died? No, again. Shit! What other options did he have?

"Ticktock," Lucifer said. "Make a decision before I make it for you."

"William," Sunny whispered. Her voice trembled, tears welling in her eyes, wetting her lashes. "I'm so sorry."

She cries? It wasn't fear he saw in her irises, he realized, but disappointment. *She cries because she thinks she disappointed me.* A savage roar left William, shaking the stable.

The little darling. He'd never been prouder of her.

"Now, now, brother," Lucifer said, smug. "She's only a mistress, yes? When she's dead, you can get a new one."

"You will not harm her!" he bellowed.

"Oh, but I will. Gladly. You slaughtered a contingent of my demons. For that, you will lose your most treasured possession. The book, and perhaps the woman." Lucifer pushed the tip of the blade deeper, a drop of shimmery blood trickling down the vulnerable column of her throat. "I'll be applying more pressure every minute. Within two, I'll reach her carotid." He lowered his head to run her earlobe between his teeth, smiling when she jerked her head to the side. "I know why you keep her here."

His stomach flipped. *Reveal nothing.* "Do tell."

"*She* is your decoder, and a unicorn. So, I can kill her, then take her horn, or take the horn and leave her alive. The choice is yours, and time is running out."

The panic redoubled, choking him. Yet it was nearly overshadowed by his need to lash out, to kill, to bathe in this man's blood. Sunny, without her magic…

When she'd told him about other unicorns who'd lost their horns, her mournful tone had suggested they were better off dead. Now true fear etched her features, the mere possibility nearly breaking her.

Sweat beaded on William's brow. His heart hammered, racing faster. Growls reverberated low in his chest—so much for revealing nothing—he grated, "If you do it, if you harm her—"

"You'll make me pay?" Lucifer finished, faking a pout. "Not that. Anything but that." He pushed the knife deeper. "Funny how you went from telling me I wouldn't harm her to practically begging me to refrain. Tsk-tsk. So weak. And nearly too late. The clock will soon run out." He grinned, smug. "Only one more minute to go."

"William," she repeated, the tremors in her voice so much worse. "It's okay. I'll shift for him and give him the horn."

So she could stab Lucifer, putting herself at even greater risk? No again. "You won't." *Think.* He would—

Suddenly, glass shattered, a snarling Dawn busting through the window, her body flying through the air, colliding with Sunny and Lucifer. One of the hellhound's heads chomped on Lucifer's wrist, ripping his hand away from the unicorn. The other head chomped at the bastard's face.

Sunny dropped, and so did Lucifer's knife. Without pausing to catch her breath or take stock, she grabbed the weapon's hilt and jabbed the blade into the back of his knee. Finally, he toppled.

"Look out!" William shouted, grabbing Sunny to fling her away from the danger zone. As she skidded across the floor, he reached for Dawn.

Too late.

Lucifer's body burst into Hell flames—a natural de-

fense mechanism. Those flames wouldn't harm William.
Because of his connection to Hades, he remained immune.
But those flames *would* consume everyone and everything
in their path, including Dawn, who whimpered as her fur
scorched and flesh blistered.

Lucifer rolled back, escaping William's slashing blade.
The blaze quickly spread over the floorboards, smoke thick-
ening the air. Then he vanished.

He had a choice. Pursue Lucifer, or save his girls?

No contest. Moving as fast as inhumanly possible, he
gathered Sunny, who grabbed Dawn while sobbing, "My
poor plant-babies." Next he flashed them outside, set them
on the grass, then flashed back into the stable, grabbing
the book and a potted plant. He flashed back to his girls.

"My diary!" Sunny shouted.

Damn it! He flashed back to the stable. As soon as he
had the diary in hand, he flashed back, regathered his girls
and his belongings, then flashed to his bedroom.

30

"What's yours is mine, and what's mine is mine."

SUNNY TOSSED AND turned all night, unable to sleep. As usual. Just not for the usual reasons. She'd lost her home and all of her clothes. William had jeopardized his own safety to ensure her well-being and save Dawn, because Sunny had been bested by a stupid illusion.

Why hadn't she seen the truth?

William had deposited her and Dawn in his bedroom, cleaned and patched their wounds, then taken off, saying only, "Our trip to see the boys and their prisoner has been postponed. I will hunt Lucifer. You will doctor Dawn, and check my book for damage."

He had yet to return, but she wasn't upset about his overnight abandonment. Not this time. How could she be? The man had saved her, Dawn, a plant *and* her diary. And when Lucifer had held a knife at her throat, William had radiated such rage and determination.

He's got it bad for me, and only me!

She grinned as she walked to the desk, intending to study his book. Halfway there, her phone buzzed. Hopeful, she checked the screen and found a text from William.

The Panty Melter: Be ready in one hour. We have received permission to flash into Hades's palace. We have a meeting with the kings of Hell. There's a dress and undergarments in the closet. Wear the first. Consider leaving the rest behind.

She shivered and texted back: Two dates in two days??? (Go ahead and cross "the giving and accepting of space" off your list of skills, baby.)

Studying would have to wait. Sunny showered and donned the lingerie William had left for her. The bra and granny panty set with all the colors of a rainbow were too pretty to leave behind. Plus, no thong! The dress looked like something a sexy Little Bo Peep would wear. A pink fit-and-flare to match her hair, with white lace on the shoulders, a bow between her breasts and ruffles that ended above her knees. The shoes resembled ballet slippers, with pink ribbons interwoven up her calves.

She curled her hair, pinned back the sides and applied a light layer of makeup to complete the look. The end result? Adorable. But she looked twenty years old—if that—and so weak she'd be snapped in half by a halfway decent wind. No doubt William's intention. She'd begun to understand how his mind worked. The man considered everything a weapon. The weaker she appeared, the more the kings would underestimate her.

Their mistake! Sunny found a piece of plain paper and a

clear glass from the minibar. A glass she filled with water to the halfway mark. She made a pallet on the floor, directly beneath the window, where sunshine streamed inside the room, golden and cheery. She laid the paper on the floor, in the middle of the brightest beam, then set the glass of water on the bottom edge. Just like that, a rainbow appeared on the paper.

A trick she'd learned as a child, the refraction of light providing a much-needed boost of energy.

Next, she made a pallet on the floor, near the rainbow, and carried William's book there. *I will resist any urges to harm my man.*

I will.

Could she resist, though? She'd have to. She couldn't *not* study the book and doom William. Things were just getting good between them.

Better to be free than trapped, as she knew firsthand. So, she must, must, must keep plowing ahead.

Very well. As she settled into place, she had a perfect view of William's bedroom. Or inner sanctum. A spacious master suite with more of Anya's portraits hanging on the walls, mirrors on the ceiling, a video arcade in the corner, a freaking waterbed and a vending machine of booze. Gold star! She loved it all, even the bookshelves lined with more of the skulls in his collection, with little plaques to describe the former owners.

The stepfather. Repeatedly raped his young stepdaughter. Pissed himself during his vivisection.

Soon, they would add Lucifer's skull to the mix.

Focus. But, the more she studied the book, the more dizziness plagued her, screwing with her vision. On the plus side, symbols changed to words faster than usual. This time, she didn't try to make sense out of what she was reading;

she simply wrote down every word, hoping that would keep
the whispers at bay.

Kill him.

No, no, no! Sweat beaded on her brow as she fought,
fought so hard. But the urge to obey proved treacherous.

The door opened and closed with a loud snick, startling her. William strode into the bedroom, wearing a black
T-shirt and leathers. *As gorgeous as ever.*

Energy poured off him, seeming to crackle in the air,
and she began to calm. He took one look at her and did a
double take. "Your hair."

Kill him. KILL HIM. Now!

Nope. Not calm. Sunny tensed. *Must fight this!* Yes,
yes. She plugged her claws into the floorboard, anchoring herself down, and breathed deeply. At some point, the
dizziness did ease, along with the urge to kill him. The
whispers did quiet.

Then his words registered, and she frowned. "What's
wrong with my hair?"

"It changed again." Satisfaction oozed from him as he
closed the distance and knelt beside her. He looked over
her setup and nodded, impressed. "A makeshift rainbow."

"I wanted to be strong for our meeting with Hades."

"You look like..." He pinched a lock of her hair between
his fingers, and she saw the strands were a pretty silver-
white. Next rainbow, she bet the tresses turned black. Her
favorite. "Sex. I like it."

His million-dollars-an-hour lips lifted in a slow, devastating smile. A savage punch of lust nailed her, her limbs
trembling, her heart racing. In seconds, her panties got
soaked.

"Wh-what color are my eyes?" she asked.

"Purple." Ghosting his knuckles along her jawline, he said, "You are well, sundae?"

"I am." She leaned into his touch before motioning to her diary. "You're about to be super happy. I decoded so much more of your book and wrote the passages in mine."

He picked up the diary, perused the pages and paled. Horror radiated from him.

But, but...why horror? "I know the new paragraphs are ramblings about how foolish you were to dismiss Lilith, but progress is progress, right?" she rushed out.

"You don't know what you wrote, do you?" he asked gently. He picked up his book next, straightened and walked to his dresser, where he locked both tomes in a drawer. What didn't he want her to see? "Ready to go, sugar tush? Or would you rather have an orgasm or two before we leave?"

She glanced at the locked dresser drawer and decided to break in as soon as they returned, then settled her gaze on the bed. Her stomach fluttered. Unfortunately, she suspected a couple of orgasms would only make her horniness worse. Kind of like an appetizer. She needed the full meal, but she couldn't shake the fear that the desire to kill him would strengthen exponentially after sex, because their feelings for each other would strengthen.

"Never mind," he said before she could decide on an answer. "We'll go."

Wait. What? She opened her mouth to ask, but he was frowning, no, scowling, his attention riveted on the bed, too. A shadow passed through his electric blues. He said, "We leave now."

Okay. What had just happened? What was she missing? "Am I going as eye candy or guard duty?"

"Eye candy slash moral support slash lie detector. If anyone tells a falsehood, you are to use your favorite safe word—*penis*. And, sugar tush? I need you to trust me a little more, trust that I will not put you in danger and release me from my promise not to mention the medallion."

Ugh. Shockingly enough, she did trust him, so she nodded. In return, he gifted her with a blindingly bright smile, the perfect reward for her sacrifice.

AFTER TEXTING HIS self-appointed decorator, Anya, to request a replacement bed, William linked his fingers with Sunny's and flashed to Hades's throne room. He'd had too many women in the old bed, and the thought of making love to his lifemate there—

Making love? Who are you?

He popped his jaw. *I'll make like to her, not love. Not yet.* Was there potential for love? Yes. Okay? Yes. Were his feelings for her greater than his fear of the curse? Absolutely. As proven by his actions these past few days.

What he felt for her... He wasn't sure how he'd ever believed someone else belonged with him. The more he learned about Sunny, the better she fit him. They had common interests. They both enjoyed winning, hating Lucifer and dishing punishments.

With Sunny, William had discovered a new appreciation: receiving those punishments. If she didn't care, she wouldn't try to improve his behavior. The woman kept him guessing, too. He never knew what she'd do or say. The fact that she came alive for him alone roused his every possessive instinct. Her changing appearance intrigued him. He had his variety, but kept the woman he carved above all others.

He could not give her up.

A pang lanced him. As if he'd needed more proof that Sunny was his lifemate, he'd just discovered the curse had begun to affect her. In her diary, she'd written *Kill William* and *William must die* again and again. Yet, she'd no clue she'd done it.

Even now, horror vibrated in his bones. He'd once thought he would lock her away if ever she reached this point, but he couldn't bring himself to do it. She hated captivity, and rightly so. He would not subject her to days... weeks...months of fear and pain. Which meant the curse was far more insidious than he'd ever realized. The more he cared for Sunny, the more her well-being mattered. At this rate, he might end up *helping* her end his life, just so she thrived.

His self-preservation instincts protested. He wouldn't help anyone end his life, and he wouldn't let his feelings for Sunny affect his decisions. He *must* proceed full steam ahead, regardless of their feelings. Only then could they have a future together.

A future... Yes. He wanted a future with her.

He wanted forever.

Therefore, he would take action to ensure he got it.

They stopped outside Hades's throne room, all alone. No guards stood before the closed doors. Interesting.

No better time.

He turned to Sunny. Realizing he'd taken her hand automatically, he brought her knuckles to his lips and kissed them. "From this moment on, you are free. If you wish to leave me, I will understand. However, I'd like you to stay with me. In my bedroom." A smart move? Probably not, considering the curse affected her. But he'd rather be with a willing Sunny and roll the dice.

Her brand-spanking-new purple eyes shimmered with astonishment. "Are you asking me to move in with you?"

"I am." He nodded for emphasis.

"I… You… You're setting me free? Truly? I can leave right now, and you won't stop me?"

Pang. "Truly. So say yes, you'll move in with me," he all but pleaded, more strained by the second. If she said no… She couldn't say no.

She merely gaped at him. "We're really doing this here? Now?"

"We are." He wanted the matter settled ASAP. "Say yes," he repeated.

"But…are you sure you want this? It's a big step. An *official* step."

Still not a yes. Heart racing, he backed her into the double doors. "Not a big step. We're already living together. If you fear I'll be untrue, you can rest easy. I will not stray, I vow it. I will be by your side, protecting you at all costs."

She searched his face for several prolonged seconds, the suspense killing him. He nearly yanked her against him, just so he could bury his nose in her hair and draw in her incredible scent. Anything to feel closer to her.

Then she said, "Yes. No. I don't know! The curse…"

So his worry had rubbed off on her. But that, he could combat. "Big risk, big reward, sundae. Take a chance on me. On us."

She chewed on her bottom lip, thoughtful. Finally, finally, finally she nodded. "All right. Yes. I will stay with you. And I will protect you at all costs, too."

Something akin to joy snuck up on him. He wanted everything she had to give. Right here, right now. If not for the meeting…

He planted a swift kiss on her lips—*can't resist her*—and stepped back. "We'll talk more when we return home. You ready to speak with my father?"

Confident nod. "Let's do it."

With his free hand, he gripped the hilt of a bone dagger. Then, he kicked open the doors. Side by side, he and Sunny strode inside the throne room.

"Oh, my... Wow." She gawked, whispering, "Is this heaven? Because this feels like the beefcake edition of heaven."

William popped his jaw. Even when he'd been on a date, he'd never hesitated to admire another woman. As Sunny gaped at the nine kings, each male perched upon Hades's dais, she mimed wiping away drool.

I deserve this, I really do. Oh, to go back and kick his own ass.

"Don't worry, Ever Randy," she said, squeezing his hand. "I'll be going home with you. Sure, I might picture Rathbone's face, but—"

He growled, and she laughed. Tease!

Hades sat upon a throne of skulls, an adorable black cat perched in his lap. He stroked her fur Dr. Evil–style, maintaining an emotionless expression—something he did with everyone *but* William. Until now.

His joy drained away, as if a plug had been pulled. Hades wanted nothing to do with him. Had written him off, same as he'd done to Lucifer. A fate William had never thought he'd have to endure.

A part of him would die because of Axel? *You nailed it, Hades, but* you *are at fault, not a prophecy.*

Sunny lifted their joined hands and nuzzled the back of his against her cheek. A gesture of comfort, support and love.

Did the most exquisite female in the worlds love him? The thought excited him more than sex ever had. A true shock.

Suddenly he had the strength he needed to focus on the other kings, ignoring Hades.

There was Rathbone, of course, the greatest shape-shifter ever born. Achilles the First, who inspired terror in everyone he met. Everyone but William and apparently Sunny. Nero, who refused to use a title. Baron the Widow Maker, who collected women like other males collected baseball cards and was once William's hero. Gabriel the Maddened One, whose sanity came and went. Long ago, he'd trained William in the art of sword making. Falon the Forgotten, who had the ability to possess anyone, at any time. And did, often. He'd possessed William several times, as a joke. Lastly, Hunter the Scourge and Bastian the Un-invited, brothers whose mere presence caused certain living things to die slowly.

He'd always admired these males. Like Hades, they wielded extreme power.

He cast his gaze throughout the rest of the room. It boasted golden walls, a diamond floor and stained-glass windows. Another deception on Hades's part. The lack of "evil" decorations tended to put people at ease. A grave mistake, usually their last.

"Who's the girl?" Baron asked, his deep voice echoing.

"Hello to you. Hi, Rathbone." Sunny waved so sweetly she made William think of an innocent Little Bo Peep surrounded by big, bad wolves.

When he'd first seen his warrioress in such a dainty outfit, with her sexpot silver-white hair mussed, her purple eyes bright, he'd hardened painfully, as if he'd overdosed on a shit-ton of Viagra.

He was still hard as steel.

"I'm Sunny Lane. I—"

"Belong to me. She's mine," William interjected. Claiming her puffed his chest with pride. "A slight to her is a slight to me."

"And he's mine, in case anyone was wondering. Oh! Look at the pretty kitty!" Wrenching from his hold, she bounded toward Hades without a care.

Each of the kings braced, resting a hand on a weapon. William flashed in front of her, acting as her shield. She crashed into his back and would have ricocheted backward if he hadn't wound an arm around her waist, holding her steady.

Her breasts smashed into a spot beneath his shoulder blades, so wonderfully soft.

"She merely wishes to pet the cat." His voice, though husky with desire, deepened with authority as he added, "Let her."

Sunny didn't wait for permission. She stepped around William and crouched down to pet the cat. "Hello, pretty baby. What's your name? Since people are dumb and suspicious of black cats, I bet it's something ferocious like Venom or Killer." With a wide, toothy grin, she claimed the animal. Again, without permission. "Why don't I call you Love Bug?"

Hades issued no protests.

As she nuzzled that dark-as-night fur, William drew her backward. Where was her usual paranoia? Evil surrounded her. Unless…the answer hit him, air hitching in his lungs, joy filling him anew.

She feels safe with me. She expected him to take care of any threats or problems, as promised. *I will, beauty. Gladly.*

The moment the cat sniffed William, she leaped into his arms.

"Not this again," Sunny muttered.

The kings watched her with different levels of amusement, annoying William greatly. *She amuses me. Me, and no other.*

Ready to jump-start the meeting, he announced, "I have a golden medallion with strange carvings. Lucifer tried to obtain it, and failed. Whatever it is, it teems with dark magic."

Now his audience went still and quiet. He had their full attention.

"How?" Hades demanded, deigning to speak at long last.

One word. One question. A voice dripping with disdain. Once again, William's joy drained away. He loved Hades. He would always love Hades. Yet, the gulf between them seemed to grow every time they interacted. If not for Sunny, he might have broken down.

"Doesn't matter how I got it," he said, unwilling to reveal Sunny's part in its acquisition. "Do you know what it does?"

"Doesn't matter," Hades echoed. "You will give it to me."

Any other time, William would have obeyed. With the tension between them, with Sunny's attachment to the item, he grated, "No. I'll be holding on to it."

The other kings snarled with fury. So. They'd turned on him, too. Wonderful. *Ignore the hurt. Focus on your own fury.*

Hades donned his customary blank mask.

"You disobey a direct order?" Achilles asked.

Falon stroked two fingers over his dark, stubbled jaw. "That is what I heard."

"Then your ears are working." William displayed a manic smile. *Try to take it, I dare you.* "It's mine, and I keep what's mine."

Sunny cooed to the cat, unconcerned by the thrum of violence in the air.

Drumming his fingers on the arms of the throne, Hades stated, "I called this meeting to inform you of Lucifer's actions. In the past two days, he has used his deceptions to steal someone from each of us, and vowed to kill a captive every time we strike at him."

William tensed all over again. The bastard never kept his word, which meant he'd be killing the captives regardless.

Had he come to the stable to abduct Sunny?

"Who did he take from you?" William asked his father.

A pause. Finally Hades snapped, "Who, and what. The mirror."

His precious. The magic mirror that contained the Goddess of Many Futures. If she told Lucifer their battle plans *before* they struck… Shit. Shit!

Sunny faced the kings, incredulous. "Are you kings or pansies? Take your people back already. Problem. Solution."

William found a sudden urge to laugh, but tried for a stern expression. Sunny…interacting with others, especially powerful men…there was no better entertainment. And no better female. "You're not making any friends, sundae."

"So?"

He lov—liked her attitude. Liked her more every time she opened her mouth. Or moved. Or breathed. And damn it! He was *still* hard, aching to sink inside her at long last. *Must have her. Soon.*

Soon isn't soon enough.

Today.

He wasn't sure how much longer he could go without coming inside her, branding her with his essence.

Nero bowed up, as if preparing for battle. "You will mind your tongue, girl, or you will lose it."

Blood like lava, William took a step forward. On command, smoky wings burst from his back. "Speak to her like that again, and our alliance ends."

"Enough!" Hades shouted as he pushed to his feet. "Do we have any other orders of business?"

"Yes." William breathed deep. "I have Evelina. Lucifer doesn't know—yet. I'll let him know any harm to your loved ones assures her death."

Evelina's defection had been a major blow to Lucifer's pride. If she died, he would be unable to achieve vengeance. Knowing Lucifer, he would do *anything* for vengeance.

The kings nodded, their satisfaction obvious. All but Hades; his expression had blanked once again.

"I want that medallion, William," Hades intoned. "Give it to me."

Another command. "If I don't?" he asked softly.

Silence reigned, aggression charging the air.

"If you don't...we go to war," Hades said simply.

He could not be serious. Had his father, the man who'd loved and raised him, truly threatened his life?

Incredulous, William looked to Sunny.

"Your penis is cute," she said, earning snickers from the kings. Again, from everyone but Hades.

Translation: Hades had told the truth. He *would* war with William. Over a medallion.

His incredulity turned to hurt. Hurt turned to anger. After everything they'd been through, this was how their relationship would end?

He met his father's gaze, hoping Hades would back down. Instead, his father—ex-father?—lifted his chin, the picture of stubbornness.

Yes. This was how their relationship ended.

The anger deepened, seeping into William's bones. His soul. He would not drop to his knees and beg for forgiveness, as part of him wanted to do. He would not cry or lament. Not here, and not now. Later...

"You may show yourself out." Hades stood, turned on his heel and stalked from the room, calling, "Naomi. Come."

The fur-baby leaped from William's arms to chase after her skin-dad. Halfway there, she morphed into the biggest panther he'd ever seen.

"You are making the prophecy self-fulling," he called. "Do you realize that?"

Silence.

For a moment, William stood rooted in place, angrier by the second. Until Sunny threaded her fingers through his, reminding him of her acceptance and desire for him.

Lifemates made your life better. *Will not allow anyone to take her from me. Ever.*

"Let's blow this joint and go home, baby," she beseeched for his ears alone.

Home. Yes. Business had concluded. He nodded to the kings. "Ladies." Then he flashed away with Sunny.

31

"The big, bad wolf huffed and puffed and blew her panties down."

SOMETHING INSIDE WILLIAM had changed. Sunny had noticed it when they'd reached Hades's palace, but she'd *really* noticed it when they'd appeared in his bedroom. He was tenser, his eyes frenzied. Even his aura had changed, embers blazing inside the blur. Embers of rage and hurt.

Hades had been so cruel to him. It had taken every ounce of her self-control not to shift into her unicorn form and stab the king in his black heart.

Right now, William paced through the room—their bedroom—every stomping step breaking another piece of her heart.

"I suspect it feels like a death in the family, and it sucks. But you are not at fault here, baby," she told him, easing onto the edge of the bed. "Hades's actions speaks of his character, not yours."

He scoured a hand over his face. "Stay here. I'm taking Dawn for a walk." He flashed to the hellhound, then flashed away, the two disappearing from view.

He never acknowledged her words, but Sunny didn't take his abandonment as a rejection. She understood loss, and the need to be alone with your thoughts. She also knew William and knew he needed touch the way others needed air; it made him feel alive, accepted, important and wanted. Everything he'd missed as a boy. It was why he'd slept with so many women.

So, when he returned, Sunny knew just what to do. Sex! No more waiting. Around William, her level of arousal remained on constant simmer, every sensation enhanced.

Just the thought of being with him drew her nipples taut and soaked her panties. The fact that William had asked her to move in… She wondered, *Am I the one he's been searching for? Am I his lifemate?*

The possibility made her heart leap. *Do I* want *to be his lifemate?*

She thought she…did. But before she contemplated the ins and outs of their relationship, she should check the page he'd locked in the drawer. He could return at any moment.

Heart thudding, she raced to the dresser and pried open the top drawer, liberating his book and tearing a page—*the* page—out of her diary. He'd probably expected her to forget about it. Not a chance.

As she scanned the words, the blood rushed from her head. Everything rushed from her head but a cloud of horror. *He must die. Die. Diiiiiie. Dieeeeeeee. Die die die. Diediediedie. William must die. William must be killed. Kill him. Kill him dead.*

The passage rambled on, but she could stomach no more

and returned it to the drawer. No wonder he'd paled when he'd looked it over.

Why hadn't he kicked Sunny to the curb that very instant?

Why had he asked her to move in with him?

Unless he merely wished to guard her?

No. She discarded the notion. The man wanted her. That, she knew beyond a shadow of a doubt. The way he looked at her, as if he'd never beheld something so fine... *Oh, yes. He wants me.*

Okay. Forget the note—for now. She would decode the book as fast as inhumanly possible. In fact, she would study until she'd decoded every symbol. Tomorrow, she would study the book until she'd decoded every symbol. No stopping until the deed was done, the curse broken. Tonight, she was just a girl, and William was just a boy. They would christen their move-in.

Sunny returned the book to the drawer as well, then hurried to the bed, where she removed her dress. In her undergarments, she crawled atop the covers and lay down. Hey! The bed was different. This one had a soft mattress, four posters carved with dragons and a wispy white canopy draping the sides. But...but why would he exchange the bed during their absence?

She remembered his strange behavior before the meeting, how he'd wanted to make out only to abruptly change his mind. Because he'd wanted a new bed?

And who had started a fire in the hearth? The flames had warmed the air to her favorite temperature: toasty.

William returned a few minutes later, minus Dawn. Must have left her with Pandora. His hands were fisted, his shallow breaths coming fast. A rise of his fury, or arousal?

"Hello, William," she rasped. "I have a present for you."

His gaze zoomed to her and narrowed, as if the predator had just selected his prey. "I went on a walk to clear my
head, but every step away from you made the chaos worse."

"And now?"

"Even. Worse." Motions clipped, he gripped the back
collar of his shirt and tugged the material overhead. Voice
as rough as gravel, he said, "Throughout my life, I've been
tortured in every way imaginable, but I find nothing as
torturous as this. Seeing you, and not being inside you."

It's happening. We're really going to do this. Tremors
shook her. All she could do? Nod.

He watched, his gaze heating. "I want to fuck you, sundae. Hard."

His voice was even rougher. A caress to her senses,
as always, but a caress from a calloused hand. Delicious.
"Y-yes. Be with me." *Please.*

He stalked to the foot of the bed, graceful but menacing.
Heat radiated from his massive body, engulfing her in invisible flames. His lusty scent acted as kindling.

His immense size made her feel fragile, but powerful,
too. He was big and strong, yet he trembled same as her,
as if the sight of her unmanned him.

What would he do next? A question she thought she
would wonder every day they were together.

He toyed with the fly of his leathers, and she watched,
mesmerized, her breaths coming faster, sharper. Flutters
ignited in her belly. "William," she rasped, maneuvering
to an upright position. "Kiss me. Touch me."

"Soon," he promised. "First, show me how much you
desire me." A command from a conqueror.

She tore at her bra. Her panties. Naked, she reclined on
the mattress, her knees up but closed.

His gaze heated. *Burning.* He looked at her as if she

were the only other person alive. As if the world had been torched and she was his only lifeline.

As if he would die for her—or kill to be inside her.

"Show me," he demanded.

Slowly she parted her thighs...

The sound he made? A guttural groan of pure need. He swiped a hand over his mouth, an action she'd come to adore, the muscles in his biceps and abdomen contracting. "So pink and pretty—so damn beautiful—created just for me."

Dazed, she parroted, "Just for you." *How did I ever consider this male unskilled?* She lowered her gaze to his erection and licked her lips. "Is *that* just for me?"

"*That* has a name," he teased unexpectedly, stroking up and down, up and down.

"Princess Sparkles?" she teased back. "Big Willy?"

"Master. Say, *I want only to please you, Master.*"

He didn't think she'd do it. So, she did it. With one little tweak. Staring at his shaft, she rasped, "I want only to please you, baby. Come closer."

The teasing ended abruptly, ravenous hunger darkening his features.

"Your turn," she purred. "Say, *I live only for your pleasure, Mistress.*"

The corners of his mouth twitched again. "I live only for *our* pleasure, sundae."

Mmm. She liked the sound of that.

"Touch yourself," he commanded now. "Show me how you—the best lover you've ever had—likes to be sated."

Eager to obey, she dragged a hand down her stomach and slid a finger deep into her wetness. Pleasure. Bliss. With a groan, she undulated, rocking her hips.

His yearning was palpable. A mating call, like calling

to like. He kicked off his boots and disarmed, dropping his weapons to the floor. Metal clinked as the pile grew. And grew. That done, he slid his zipper down, his erection popping free. Moisture already wet the slit.

She fingered herself faster. He panted; she panted, too, their ragged breaths providing an erotic soundtrack.

He pushed the pants down and off, and she ate up his body with her eyes. His tattooed chest and mouthwatering eight-pack acted as the appetizer, but the goodie trail that led to the new center of her world provided an entire meal.

The most beautiful man in the worlds is mine.

Yes, countless others had enjoyed him. So what? *They were merely practice for me.* And, to be honest, she kind of felt sorry for them. Their first taste of undiluted bliss had been their last.

"Is this what you want? What you need?" He stroked his length, up, down, his ferocity and excitement fueling her own.

"Yes! Give it to me." Empty, aching, she arched her back, sending her fingers ever deeper. Her whimper of rapture blended with his grunt of praise.

The foot of the bed dipped as William climbed onto the mattress. He prowled up her body, his wild eyes heavy-lidded. Every time his hands brushed against a different part of her, the corded muscles in his abdomen flexed.

He is perfection.

When he had a fist pressed beside each of her temples, he wedged his hips between her thighs, pushing her legs farther apart. He rested his erection atop her small triangle of silvery-white curls, shuddered with pleasure.

Nothing between us but searing heat.

He clasped her wrist and brought her fingers—the ones

wet with her arousal—to his mouth. He laved one after the other, driving her wild. Never had she ached so fervently.

Voice a drug, he snarled, "How do you *taste* like rainbows?"

Don't know. Don't know anything but need. "Kiss me," she pleaded, moaning.

Leaning down, down, he slanted his mouth over hers. His tongue thrust inside. *Masterful.* She might taste like rainbows, but he tasted like a dark, rich wine. *Intoxicating.*

They exchanged breaths and rubbed against each other, every movement pressing his erection against her clitoris. Pressure mounted, inhibitions crumbling.

Groaning, he lifted his head. "Look at my sundae." Arousal stripped away his humanity, revealing a true prince of darkness. "You love what I do to your body."

The satisfaction in his tone launched her into a frenzy. She thrashed and strained. She tried to say, "I want more." But she moaned incoherent words. Shameless and wanton, she rolled her hips, chasing the tip of his length.

Always he edged the other direction at the last second, preventing penetration.

With one hand, he shackled her arms over her head. With the other, he kneaded her breasts and pinched her nipples. Lightning flashed over his skin, emitting sultry, heady heat.

"Can't get enough." He dipped his head... His lips closed around her nipple and sucked, hard. Harder. As he alternated between sucking and pinching, sucking and pinching, a glorious madness overtook her.

Want him.

Will have him.

Never had she been so aroused, so fevered. When he traced his fingers down her stomach and slowly inserted a finger into her core, she ground against his hand. So good!

"More," she demanded. "Another finger. Put it in. Please!"

"How my sundae loves her pleasures." With his next inward plunge, he worked a second finger inside, wringing a breathless cry from her. The stretch…*ecstasy*.

A stray thought whispered: *Must give as much as you take.*

She slowed. In all their time together, she'd never asked him about *his* secret fantasies. A travesty. Sunny wanted him to know this bliss. What had he always wanted to do with a woman, but never had?

Think, think. Could she think? The deeper he worked those fingers, the faster he scissored them, his knuckles caressing her inner walls, hitting all the right spots. Pleasure became agony, agony became pleasure.

Lick his tattoos. Tongue his nipples. Suck his testicles.

Yes, yes. But once again, he thrust the two digits in deep, deeper, and she lost her mind, crying out. *Come first, then think and lick, and flick and suck.*

"A third finger," she pleaded. "Give it to me."

"Not ready." He pushed the words through gritted teeth. "You're too tight, sundae."

"Complaining?"

"Tormented. Want to give you something bigger."

Like the wily unicorn she was, she wound her legs around his waist and locked her ankles—trapping his fingers inside her and his erection against her inner thigh. He was so hot she felt forever branded.

He heaved a breath. Sweat trickled from his brow, and tension branched from his eyes. He was seduction incarnate, a warrior without equal. *And mine.* But she wasn't as wily as she'd thought. By trapping his fingers, she'd ensured they couldn't move. *Need friction!*

She dropped her legs.

He released her wrists and cupped her nape. Crazed, she combed her fingers through his hair, embedded her nails in his scalp and drew his mouth back to hers.

Their mouths crashed together, their tongues rolling and thrusting. Finally! He wedged in a third finger, and oh, the stretch. The burn. He thrust them, and withdrew. Thrust, withdrew, changing his pace with every stroke, ensuring she could never anticipate his next move.

She could only writhe and beg and score his back. Still pressure built. So close, so close. She needed—

That.

He rubbed his thumb against her throbbing clit and sent her hurling over the edge, screaming his name.

32

"I'm good at three things. Sex, killing and sex. Yeah,
I'm so good at sex I had to mention it twice."

WILLIAM WAS LOST in the throes. Watching Sunny come, her
face radiant with pleasure…feeling her inner walls clench
around his fingers… She'd come alive, all the colors of the
rainbow glowing in her eyes, her hair switching from white
to blue to pink to black again and again.

Was there a more glorious sight? *I am undone.*

He'd been with inhibited and uninhibited lovers, greedy
ones, selfish, giving, those with and without fetishes, those
cold or hot, sadists and masochists, those seeking to win
him or hurt him. But he'd never been with a woman who
made him desperate to possess her body and soul.

Before her inner walls ceased clenching on his fingers
and she sagged into the mattress utterly sated, he removed
his wet fingers.

As she unleashed a stream of unicorn curses, he spread her

wetness over her lips, around her nipples. Her breasts fit his hands, as if they'd been made for him alone. *All* of her fit him.

Two puzzle pieces, locked together.

When he placed the tip of his erection at her entrance, her curses turned into pleas.

For a moment, he felt as though he was forgetting something. As soon as the thought formed, however, it vanished, pleasure his only concern.

"Do it!" she cried. "Please."

"Am I...hurting you?" he gritted out.

"No, no, don't stop." she commanded.

Heaving every breath now, he slid in an inch...two, but she was tight, so damn tight. More sweat beaded on his brow. His muscles bulged with tension. Not slamming inside her required every ounce of his strength.

After licking her lips, he pushed in another inch. Wet heat seared him. His bulging muscles began to tremble, extreme effort required to maintain a slow and steady pace. *Will not fucking hurt her.*

She moaned his name. In one swift move, she sank her nails into his ass and lifted her hips, *forcing* him to thrust to the hilt. Finally, he was fully seated inside her.

He'd thought, hoped, the pressure would ease.

The pressure grew worse.

"That brought a little more pain than I expected," she offered, breathless.

Guilt surged. *Reached a point of no return.* He was losing the ability to think or see past the pleasure. He wanted more, and he would have it. "Tell me when...you are ready...for me to move," he said, between breaths.

She licked her lips and nodded, then gave her hips an experimental rock. He bit his tongue to stop a roar, a sexual haze falling over his line of sight.

Another rock, this one stronger. Then another and another. Her eyelids turned heavy, her lips parting on a gasp. At the same time, he reached between their bodies to thrum her little bundle of nerves until she continually rocked up, mimicking the shallowest of strokes.

I won't last.

I will, damn it. Her pleasure came first, now and always, but staggering arousal had ignited his most ingrained aggression, and it was taking a toll. The need to hammer into her, to brand and to claim besieged him. *Control!* He would be the best lover she'd ever had—better than Sunny herself— even if it killed him.

William withdrew to the tip, still teasing her swollen clit.

When a flush darkened her cheeks, she cried, "I'm ready, I'm ready!"

Yes! With a roar, he surged back in, shaking the bed. Little moans escaped her as she curled her body around his, so he did it again. And again. Again. He hammered into her.

"Harder!" she commanded. "Faster!"

No. *No?* Slower. He wanted to savor this. But when he hooked an arm beneath her knee, forcing her legs to open wider, his control frayed. With his other hand, he gripped the headboard, his bicep flexing.

Once again, he slammed to the hilt, the pleasure nigh blinding him.

He bent his head, taking her lips in a wild, wicked kiss. *My angel...my seductress...my everything?* They sucked on each other's tongues, nipped at each other's lips. Their teeth clinked, not usually something he enjoyed. With her, with the ferocity of their lovemaking, he saw it as a sign of their passion, and only wanted more. She tasted of heaven, her lush body his portal there.

He wanted to be *her* portal to heaven. Wanted her to crave this, and William, every day for the rest of her life.

"Don't stop, don't stop, never stop," she panted.

Last, damn it! "So good, love. So good. You please me...in every way." He plunged in, pulled out, the friction scrambling his thoughts. Mindless, he unleashed. Pounding. Pounding.

She arched beneath him, sending him deeper, deeper still. A scream left her, her inner walls clenching on his length, bathing it in hot feminine honey.

Can't withstand the pressure. Too much. With a final thrust, William threw back his head and roared, coming in a rush, emptying himself inside his woman.

The little unicorn wrung a savage climax from him. The most savage of his life.

When the spasms abated, he collapsed atop her, but rolled to the side, keeping her within his arms. As she curled into him, he kissed her forehead, the tip of her nose and the pulse that raced at the base of her neck.

Contentment overwhelmed him, an odd and wondrous sensation. A smile teased the corners of his mouth, and he said, "Now you're only the second-best lover you've ever had."

"Arrogant bluebell," Sunny muttered, smiling inside.

William barked out a laugh, a genuine laugh, and she realized the ones she'd heard in the hotel bar had been fake. All she could do? Snuggle into his side and peer at him with awe. *So beautiful.* Amusement softened his features and turned his baby blues into stars.

He petted her hair, saying, "Can you deny it, sundae?"

While inside her, he'd called her "love," an endearment she missed and yearned to hear again. *Did* he love her?

A staggering need arose. *I want him to love me. I want to make him a member of my pack.*

Tracing a fingertip around his nipple, she answered his question at last. "No. I can't."

He smiled at her, eyes sparkling, a reward for her honesty. "I've never lain with a lover and discussed my life, have never wanted to…until now. I'm desperate to learn more about you."

Desperate. Yes. "I want to learn about you, too."

"Tit for tat?"

"Agreed."

"Ladies first. Start with how much I pleasured you."

Oh oh oh, what was this? Did someone need reassurance? How adorable! "Pleasured…put in a coma of bliss…"

His chest puffed with well-deserved pride. "The same is true of me. Never knew such pleasure existed."

All right. She'd needed reassurance, too. His words went straight to her head.

A thought occurred to her. "Where's Dawn?"

"Baden and Katarina are introducing her and the rest of the hellhounds to the wilds of Hell, their natural habitat." His cell phone buzzed. He checked the screen and frowned. "I have multiple messages from each of the kings. They're making offers for the medallion."

"Like what?"

"A palace. Other artifacts. Slaves. Souls."

Guilt scorched her. She had yet to tell William what the medallion was, exactly, and what else it could do. To tell now or not to tell?

Tell. Definitely. No pondering necessary. They were an official couple now, and he deserved to know. Did it have the potential to blow up in her face? Yes. He could use it to increase his strength, his magic. To subdue her. But. She did trust him. More than she'd trusted anyone in eons. But…

She would be confirming one of his biggest fears. He

would learn how easily she could kill him. It would ruin this precious moment. And what if she lost him because of it? Her stomach churned.

Tomorrow, she decided. She'd tell him tomorrow, and also discuss the terrible things she'd written under the curse's influence. Today, nothing would interrupt their escape from reality.

"I think you should tell them no," she said.

"Planned on it." He kissed her forehead, only to tense. "Shit! We never talked about birth control. We are so close to mating season, and I just came inside you."

We, not *you*. Proof they were a couple. To her surprise, he didn't seem upset so much as surprised. "I've never forgotten before."

Oh, wow. Contraception hadn't been a blip in her mind. But then, that was one of the mystical ramifications of mating season. "Magic *makes* unicorns and their lovers forget contraception, which is why I've always preferred to chain myself somewhere secret. But you don't need to worry about going without one today. I can't get pregnant outside of mating season, and even then it isn't guaranteed." Not ready for a baby—yet—she added, "Let's hang reminders throughout the house and all over our bed." *Wear a rubber.* Just in case.

Dragging a hand down the ridges of her spine, he said, "I'll have the signs up as soon as I can walk. Guaranteed, we'll be doing this again very soon. When it comes to Sunny Lane, I am insatiable."

Goose bumps spread from her nape to her toes. "I'll give you an hour, no, half an hour, no, fifteen minutes, no, five minutes to rebuild your strength, then I'm having you again, signs or no signs."

He gifted her with a tender smile, gently hooking a lock

of hair behind her ear. "What do you wish to do with your life, sundae? Break codes?"

Good question. "For so long, my only goals were survival and killing Lucifer. Plus, people who have life plans are super annoying because they've managed to do something I haven't. I'd like to have everything figured out, too, you know? Although, now that I think about it, maybe I'll join the mercenary game and slaughter demons for a paycheck. Oh! Maybe I'll put together a ragtag team of bad as—butt superheroes, and we'll clean up the mean streets of Hell."

"Uh-oh. My Sunny said a naughty word."

She humphed. "I can say the names of worlds and realms, as if, but only when I'm referencing said worlds and realms."

"Good to know." He winked at her. "If you go with option B, you'll need a superhero name. No need to rack your brain for one, though. You'll be My Little Horny."

Ha! "Then you'll have to go by the Lone Rider." As he chuckled, she moved her hands all over him, learning him. "While we were otherwise occupied, I realized I don't know *your* secret fantasies. Or your life plan."

"Fantasies—sleeping with a unicorn-shifter curled against me, and awaking to find she's still there. Life plan—becoming a king of the underworld. I *will* be a king. I have only to find Lucifer's former crown."

First, her heart swelled with more lo—like. Then her mind wallowed in confusion. "Why must you find his crown? Why aren't you a king already?"

A long stream of air seeped from him. "Long ago, I moved out of Hell. I didn't like the male I was becoming here—too dark, no hint of light—and thought I could be a better man topside. I was wrong. I still warred, still killed, still abandoned the women I slept with."

"What made you return?"

"The war with Lucifer. I want him dead, and I will do anything to get it done. Also, the longer I've been here, the more I've realized *I* choose whether I'm light or dark, not my location. I'm no longer a young male in his early hundreds. I'm older, stronger and wiser. As for the crown," he said. "Long ago, eleven crowns were forged in the heavens, each representing a different power. Lucifer stole ten of them."

"Of course he did."

"The eleventh crown is rumored to enslave the other kings, but no one has found it yet."

"Maybe *I* can help." No, no maybe about it. She could, and she would. Sunny longed to show William how grateful she was to have him in her life, and to know pleasure and satisfaction for the first time.

Maybe she could present the crown to him—while in her unicorn form.

She scoured her mind for any reason to continue denying him. He would have eternal access to her horn, able to call it forth and remove it while she slept. He hadn't actually copped to being in love with her, and he might not be there yet.

But...none of that mattered to her. She wanted to show him. And she would. *After* she'd dropped the bomb about the medallion.

With a sigh, she reached up and back to flatten her hand on the headboard and push, changing positions, but a splinter pricked the pad of her finger. "Ow!" She yanked her hand to her chest.

William swooped in fast, latching on to her wrist to look over her hand. After gently, tenderly plucking the splinter free, he punched the headboard and growled, "That will teach you to harm my woman."

She chuckled. Silly, adorable male.

"Better?" he asked.

A wealth of incoming footsteps made her ears twitch. William must have heard them, too. He stiffened.

"Expecting visitors?" she asked.

"No."

Suddenly, the door burst open, a contingent of Sent Ones storming into the bedroom. Eleven in total. Three were Elite, and the rest were Warriors. They carried swords of fire.

Since the Sent Ones were her neighbors, she'd taken pains to learn their names. A furious Bjorn led the charge, shouting, "William! Today you pay for your crimes."

Holding the sheet to her chest, Sunny jolted to an upright position. How dare they interrupt her afterglow? William jolted upright, too, his eyes stark with fury.

"There's a gun in my nightstand," he informed her. "If anyone looks at you, give them a Sunny Lane special."

A bullet to the face?

He surged to his feet. Gloriously naked, he bent to grab two of his discarded daggers. His beautiful lightning flashed, his smoke wings forming. Only, the smoke must have lost its potency. Or maybe he produced more than one kind, depending on the situation? Maybe she'd grown immune to it? Whatever the reason, she remained unaffected. But so did the Sent Ones.

"You have three seconds to exit my bedroom," William snarled. "Or you will suffer."

33

"Welcome to Big Willy's little house of horrors."

IF WILLIAM DIDN'T get his way, he *would* commit murder. So he was naked. So what. He'd give the Sent Ones a thrill before he removed their heads. And he *would* remove their heads if they stayed. They hadn't just invaded his home, his sanctuary. They'd dared bring violence to Sunny's door, perhaps undoing her sense of safety. But the worst of their crimes? They'd ruined snuggle-fucking-time.

For that, they would die screaming. "Three. Two."

The Sent Ones remained in place.

"Very well. You suffer."

"Don't taint your growing bond with Axel by killing his friends," Sunny called. "Just spank them a little."

She didn't sound frightened; she sounded excited.

Very well. For her, and for Axel, he would only injure the bastards, then dump their unconscious bodies at camp.

"Which crimes are you referencing?" he asked Bjorn.

"As if you do not know."

The Sent One Warriors surrounded William, their wings blocking him from the Elite.

"Stay back. William is mine." Bjorn unleashed a war cry.

Instead of retreating, the Warriors attacked.

They dared disobey the orders of their leader. For that, William would spank them extra hard. He kept his arms in a constant state of motion, slashing, slashing. Each blade slicked into one of the challengers' eyes. But the male healed quickly and continued getting up. The male shouted, agonized, but still he fought, blindly swinging his fiery sword with shocking accuracy, as if he'd trained for this. Perhaps he had.

"Tell me what you think I did," William demanded of Bjorn.

"Do not pretend ignorance," the Elite bellowed.

William caught a glimpse of him. The male had decided to hang back while the Warriors received their punishment. How obliging.

Bjorn's rainbow eyes glittered. For a moment, William wondered if the Sent One had ties to unicorns. Then he recalled Bjorn's title: Last True Dread. No, Bjorn came from one of the most violent species in history, the Dreads. They'd had colorful eyes, too.

Getting his head in the game, William cut down another Warrior—who began to rebound—and performed a mental rundown of the facts. *Eight Warriors. Six males, two fe-males. The Elite hung back. One blinded, able to heal any moment. No sign of Axel. If anyone makes a move toward Sunny, they* will *die, consequences be damned.*

Flaming swords came at him from every direction. He struck and ducked, his skin blistering. William could withstand normal, natural fire without injury and pain, but he could not withstand the purification, or cleansing fires of the heavens. The heat invaded his blood, his bones, his marrow. He felt as if he burned to ash from the inside out.

Careful to avoid direct contact, William drove his opponents away from the bed, toward a specific portrait across the room. The one of him—naked, of course—holding a keyboard in front of his junk.

What his uninvited guests didn't know? The keyboard was imbued with magic. *I planned for every kind of invasion, setting traps accordingly.* These rats had no idea they'd entered a viper's den—*the* viper—and they had no idea of the evil he could unleash. But they would.

When he reached another discarded dagger, he swooped down to grab it. As he straightened, he hurled the blade at the painting, the tip embedding in the *S* key. Instantly, spikes popped up from the floor.

Grunts and groans. Shock and pain. The Sent Ones wavered on their bleeding feet, trying to avoid more of the spikes. When that failed, they used their wings to hover.

The massive size of their wings coupled with the limited space hobbled his opponents. Or so he'd expected. In reality, the battle escalated, the Sent Ones swarming him from the air.

One of the Warriors glanced at Sunny. Enraged, William maneuvered behind him and slicked a dagger across his throat. *Heal from* that. Gurgling blood, Slit Throat released his sword of fire. It vanished as he fell. With a heavy thud, he crashed to the floor.

Not a fatal blow, but a painful one. One down, seven to go.

Defending against blow after blow, he worked his way back to the bed, where he picked up yet another discarded dagger. With one toss, he hit the *W* key. A secret panel opened on a bedpost, two short swords at the ready.

On the offensive, William gripped the swords' hilts and jumped back into the fray. As quickly as he moved, the others struggled to track his movements, allowing him to stab one after another as they searched for him. Streams of crimson streaked the floor, the walls.

What must Sunny think of him? Was she disgusted by his ferocity? She must be. He kept hurting beings known for their compassion and kindness...to anyone other than demons, vampires and witches.

Bjorn spun in midair and flared his wings as far as they could go, clearly ready to take over. Bone hooks protruded from the golden feathers. "You...will...pay."

One hook sliced through William's cheek. Another cut his shoulder, sending him flying back. A wall stopped him, knocking the air from his lungs. A moment of dizziness. He blinked rapidly, attempting to clear his line of sight.

Sensing the approach of a female, he turned to the side—just in time to watch Sunny lift and aim a gun. She winked at William as she squeezed the trigger. *Boom!* The scent of gunpowder saturated the air, the bullet nailing the female in the heart.

Safe to say she's not disgusted by me. William barely had the strength to look away as he fought off another Sent One.

He wanted back inside that body.

Focus. Two others struck at him simultaneously. He went low, raking his claws across their torsos, injecting his Hell venom. This time, they would *stay* down.

Their soft screams of agony enraged two other Sent Ones, who'd recovered and now swung their flaming swords faster.

They received a dose of venom, too. They also stayed down.

William dematerialized, flashing behind his next challenger, pushing the male into a Sent One already swinging her sword. An arm plopped to the floor, minus its body.

Slash. Jab, jab. Kick.

"Go, William!" Sunny called, still excited. "You've got this, baby!"

Empowered by her cheers, he threw an elbow and focused on the Elite. "Tell me what you think I did," he bellowed, "or I stop playing nice."

"*You* tell me where she is!" Bjorn's words lashed like a cat-o'-nine-tails. He lunged at William.

Slash, parry. "She who?"

Slash, slash. "As if you do not know!"

"I don't." William gave his wings a hard flap, jumped up and kicked out, nailing an approaching Warrior in the nose. Cartilage snapped, and blood spurted. William didn't lower, not right away, but twisted to hurl a dagger between the man's eyes.

As the victim dropped, William opened a portal directly behind him. The male fell through…and reappeared directly in front of William. He grabbed the bastard by the hair, holding him in place.

The last Warrior, a female, had already swung her sword in William's direction and couldn't stop her momentum. The sharp metal slicked through her brethren's abdomen, his intestines spilling out.

This was the second time he'd led her to hurt her brethren. Horror contorted her features, and she paled.

He tossed the body at her, throwing her across the room. She slammed into the wall and slid to the rug. To keep her down, he tossed his remaining dagger, pinning her in place.

Eight down, only the Elite to go.

"That's what you get!" Sunny shouted at the body.

He met Bjorn's gaze and slowly lowered to his feet. As

they circled each other, he said, "I'm guessing the 'her' in question is Fox the Executioner."

Bjorn swung the sword, once, twice, then parried as William made a counterstrike. "We saw you stab and take her."

"Not me. I haven't stabbed a woman…today. Or I hadn't."

They plowed into furniture, overturning side tables and chairs. Vases shattered, shards flying. The Sent One had skill. He fought like a demon, going for the eyes, throat and groin. The kind of fighting William respected.

The other male grated, "Do you think to convince me Axel is to blame?"

"No doubt it was Lucifer. He must have shape-shifted to look like me," William grated right back. "The same way he shape-shifted into Axel to attack me."

"You lie!"

"Often. But think, you fool. All Sent Ones have the ability to taste lies. What do you taste right now?"

Bjorn's eyes widened, and his motions slowed. Finally, he lowered his sword, the flames dying. He cast his gaze over the carnage and withered. When he landed on Sunny, he withered further. She perched at the edge of the bed, dressed in William's T-shirt, glaring murder at the Sent One.

William yanked on his leathers, his motions so forceful he nearly ripped the material. "Tell me everything," he snapped.

The Sent One hung his head. "I'd done it. I'd captured her. Fox was my prisoner." Pain coated his words. Was that…lust glowing in his eyes? The Sent One wanted the one who'd killed ten of his brethren? *Good luck with that.* "She ran from me, and you—Lucifer caught her, stabbed her in the gut and vanished with her."

Nothing good ever happened in Lucifer's company. Fox would not escape unscathed.

"Apologize to Sunny and vow not to kill Fox," William said, "and I'll consider helping you get her back."

He expected protests from the Sent One. Immortals had their pride, after all, but Bjorn immediately pivoted to Sunny.

"I apologize for frightening you, for damaging your bedroom and threatening your man."

She narrowed her eyes. "How dare you! I was *never* frightened."

William fought to maintain a stern expression.

Bjorn pivoted back to him and said, "I cannot vow I won't kill Fox. The order for her death came from Clerici himself. But I will vow not to kill her without first coming to speak with you. Agreed?"

A halfway decent compromise, considering the severity of Fox's crimes. Besides, William suspected the male would convince his king to let the female live. That lust...

Yeah. Bjorn had it bad for his prisoner.

"Very well. Agreed." Axel should be pleased. *The things I do for family.*

"Tell me where Lucifer keeps—" Bjorn canted his head to the side, then rushed to the window to peer outside. William followed and saw a bloody, wounded Fox crawling into camp, cursing anyone who attempted to aid her. "Never mind." Without another word, the Sent One rushed from the bedroom.

"You're just going to leave the bodies in here?" Sunny shouted after him.

Another set of footsteps sounded. William flashed to Sunny, assuming Bjorn had decided to come back and finish what they'd started. But it was Axel who stalked into the room to scan the sea of unconscious, bleeding Sent Ones. Flames of rage danced in his baby blues.

"They had it coming," William snapped, already on the defensive.

"I know," was the reply, shocking him. "Had I known what they planned, I would have stopped them. I only just returned from a meeting in the heavens. When I heard what was happening," Axel said, his tone hardening with every word, "I came running. Thank you for the vote of confidence, though."

Wonderful. He'd just tainted his relationship with his brother with suspicion and anger. William popped his jaw. What would go wrong next?

34

"Take a date home to meet the family? Sure. Let me grow a dad belly while I'm at it."

"BOYS," SUNNY ANNOUNCED, approaching William's side. "Your relationship is new. There are going to be kinks as you learn to trust each other. Forgive each other for this misunderstanding and move on. And by *move on*, I mean *clean my room*."

William did his blink, blink.

Funny thing. Axel did it, too. How adorable they were together.

The two nodded, some of the tension draining. William even leaned over to kiss her brow.

"When we finish," he said, "I'll take you both to see my boys and meet Evelina."

Sunny watched William the entire time he and Axel worked, panting. She loved how his biceps bulged every time he tossed an unconscious Sent One through a portal back to camp. Mostly, she loved the way he glanced at her, as if to reassure himself that she hadn't looked away.

As he'd once done for her hotel room, he used magic to dissipate the blood. Then Axel left to change into a clean robe, and William accompanied him, casting her a final look over his broad shoulder, one as warm and vulnerable as it was lusty.

With a shiver, she prepared to meet his children. Hair in a loose bun, she hurried through a shower, brushed her teeth and applied lotion, then donned a pair of panties she thought William would love, and a super sexy pink dress that molded to her curves. Strappy white flats completed the look. Heels were so not her thing. She just wished she had jewelry.

Unicorns loved sparkly things. Something she'd lost interest in while she'd been on the run. Now? *Gimme.*

She grinned. How drastically her life had changed. From sneaking into one run-down motel after another, alone, always alone, to orgasms, mythical battles, magical decodings and secret meetings.

When William and Axel returned, they were both showered and wearing clean garments.

Spotting her, William stopped abruptly. Lust, wonder and pride blazed in his electric blues.

"You like?" she asked, breathless. She spun slowly.

"Axel, you need to leave." William took a step toward her. "We're experiencing an unexpected...weather delay. Yes, that sounds believable. We'll leave in an hour, once this particular storm has passed. Meet us in—"

"Oh, no. We leave *now*." Even though she would do bad, bad things to slide into bed with William, she shook her head. No way she would put off this meeting. "There's been a change in forecast. That big storm has been down-graded to a light drizzle."

Laughing, Axel punched his brother in the arm. "Do you have a *light drizzle* in your pants, Ever Randy?"

Seeing them together and at ease made her heart swell with happiness.

Expression wry, William adjusted his hard shaft and closed the distance. He wound an arm around her waist, asking, "Ready?"

She arched a brow. "No portal?"

"No need. Inside Hell, I can flash anyone I can touch."

"Down here, I have the ability to flash, as well." Axel approached William's other side. "But I've never seen the territory owned by your children. I'll need to hitch a ride."

Flashing wasn't a skill Sent Ones usually possessed. How many traits did these brothers share, and what were their differences?

Sunny *had to* help them regain their memories, sooner rather than later. If she made the pair part of her pack, her magic would increase, tripling the odds of success. Would William want to be part of a pack, though? A kind of merging of minds? She'd have twenty-four-hour access to his thoughts.

He kissed her temple. "Away we go."

Suddenly, the foundation beneath their feet vanished. The bedroom vanished, too. A second later, a new location materialized around them. An elaborate parlor room with crystal chandeliers, papered walls and velvet settees. Three gorgeous males who looked to be in their late twenties occupied different seats, each one reclining and smoking a cigar.

The pungent smoke tickled her throat, and she coughed. As soon as her eyes adjusted to the haze, she studied William's boys more intently, and oh, wow, they were seriously battle-hardened, radiating savage brutality. The smoke obscured their auras, preventing her from gaining the upper hand, learning more about them than they were able to learn about her.

The lack was both a kindness and a cruelty. Information was power, and she desperately needed power right now. But a jumble of thoughts was already blowing through her mind like a parade of tumbleweeds.

A meeting had never been so important. She wanted, needed, to make a good impression, but she had no idea how to proceed. Her personality type tended to annoy or charm, rarely anything in between. What if she couldn't win these boys over? Already they were glaring at her.

Or maybe someone behind her?

She turned. Nope. Her. She was the target of those death glares. What had they been told about her? While she hadn't given two sages about the kings' opinions, she gave *all* the sages about these boys'. Family mattered.

What if they told their dad to ditch her?

She gulped, panic unfurling.

The boys snuffed out their smokes and stood. They were so tall, so muscled and now even more furious. Why, why, why?

Unaware of her turmoil—shouldn't a boyfriend sense this kind of thing?—William released her and walked over to embrace each of his children. What a beautiful, heart-wrenching sight.

Feeling as alone as ever, no, more so since she'd now tasted of companionship, she wrapped her arms around her middle. The males had what she'd tried not to let herself crave since the destruction of her village—love and support. They were a true family, their affection obvious.

Will I ever be a part of this? Here, now, nothing had ever been so important to her. And seriously, how was she supposed to act? Smile and wave? Show no emotion?

Her stomach turned over, a thought occurring to her. For their relationship, William brought an entire family to the table. Not just his sons, but his siblings and his plethora of friends. Maybe, one day, his father. Sunny brought baggage and a missing unicorn-shifter.

Unbalanced.

"Sunny, Axel, these are my sons, Red, Black and Green," William said, ever the proud papa. "They are horsemen of the apocalypse, but also shadow warriors. Boys, this is Axel, my brother, and Sunny, my woman." He offered the descriptions without hesitation or rancor.

"I—I can guess who is who," she said, her voice reedy. The smoke had thinned, revealing their auras. The gorgeous bald man with a jade aura... "You're Green. Nice to see you again."

Green gave a clipped nod. "I'm known as the bringer of death."

"That's, uh, great?" She shifted to point at the equally gorgeous blond with a dark-as-jet aura. "You're Black."

Black nodded, as well. "The bringer of famine."

She shifted in the other direction, pointing to the—yep—gorgeous black-haired one with a scarlet aura. "You're Red."

He did the clipped nod, too, but more aggressively. "I am the bringer of war."

That said, the three dismissed her, facing Axel.

"I need your autograph." Black hiked his finger at William, saying, "This one keeps a scrapbook of your victories."

Axel blinked with surprise, and glanced to William for confirmation.

He inclined his head, his cheeks flushed, and Axel's surprise redoubled.

Sunny barely refrained from blurting out, "I have victories, too!"

Grinning, Green patted his brother on the back, telling Axel, "We might be your biggest fans."

Red lit a new cigar, taking a puff before telling the Sent One, "Admired your work at the Third Battle of Lleh."

"*Greatly* admired," Black said for emphasis, then claimed the cigar for himself. "You took down more witches and warlocks than anyone else in history."

"I'd heard what they did to William," Axel responded, "all those centuries ago."

William blinked with surprise.

Desperate to be part of the conversation, Sunny asked, "What are shadow warriors?" Showing interest in their lives was an excellent start. Surely.

William said, "When I birthed them—"

"With your magic vagina," Green piped up, earning snickers from the others.

William flipped off his boys before continuing. "I believed my magic somehow contained the essence of the horsemen of the apocalypse. Prophecies claim every set of horsemen will one day battle it out, the winning foursome compelled to ride across earth, spurring the end of the world. After what we learned about the Wrathlings, I think someone in my familial line was—is—a horseman."

That tracked. "I'm kind of shocked that there's more than one set." But then, she'd bet Hell business stayed Hell business, secrets kept throughout the ages.

"The many different sets come from different species, at different times, in various ways, but they are always birthed in sets of four." His voice hardened, like a sword dipped in fire, hammered, then finished in ice. Thinking about the loss of his daughter? "A multitude of oracles have claimed I can reincarnate White."

Oh, yes. The daughter. "What's the catch?" Sunny asked.

"I can only do it after my sons have died, or I'll create a new set of four."

The boys bowed their heads, taking a moment to mourn the loss of their sister. When they looked up, they glared at Sunny again.

Perhaps they were attempting to intimidate her? Maybe scare her away so she would never harm William?

Normally, she'd glare right back, hurling an insult or two for good measure. With a mantra of "be nice" screaming inside her head, she pasted on another smile. "Why can't White be reincarnated the old-fashioned way, *without* the boys dying?" Sunny…pregnant with William's child…

She shivered with one part shock, one part longing. She'd thought she wasn't ready but…maybe?

How would William feel about the idea?

And what about Lucifer? As long as he lived, her children would be in danger.

Okay, time to change the subject. "Where's Evelina?"

"The dungeon," Green groused.

"Show Axel the way down," William instructed. "Sunny and I will be along shortly."

Uh, what the what? Why the delay?

The moment their companions exited the parlor, William spun her, pressing his chest against her back, and coiled his strong arms around her. He nibbled on her earlobe, his shaft hardening against her bottom. "Tell me what's wrong so I can fix it."

How did he know something was wrong? What were her tells? "If the underworld kings hated me, so what? They aren't important to you. But your boys are, and they already dislike me, and I don't know why. They don't even know me yet."

"*You* are extremely important to me. And they don't dislike you. They merely worry you'll succumb to the curse and harm me."

Oh…daisy. They *should* worry. "Maybe I shouldn't be important to you," she said, sniffling. A freaking sniffle, like a freaking pansy. "We haven't discussed the passage I decoded."

He sighed, his breath fanning her nape. "Let's discuss it, then. Tell me what happens when you work on the book."

Being tucked up against him made her next words easier *and* more difficult. "A dark and dangerous force comes over me, whispering thoughts in my ear. *Kill him. William must die.* Maybe because you fall for me faster when I'm working, so the magic gets stronger? And I'm sorry I didn't tell you. I just… I feared how you'd react. The good news is the urge goes away as soon as I walk away from the book."

She wrung her fingers, awaiting his response. He hadn't stiffened or—*wait*. She had one thing to add. "I'll never give in to the urges, I swear! And I'm close to finishing, I know it."

Tightening his hold, he said, "If I had a single qualm about your intentions, you'd be in the magically patched-up stable. But I trust you, just as you trust me, remember? Plus, you're the strongest person I know. If anyone can overcome a compulsion, it's you."

She whimpered with relief. "Thank you for the vote of confidence, but, um, maybe you should stop falling for me. For now, anyway. At least until the book is decoded."

His husky chuckle teased her ears. "I'll agree not to fall

for you anymore…if you'll agree to stop being so freesia-ing magnificent."

"I can't promise that," she said so seriously, so forlornly, he chuckled again.

He sobered quickly, grating, "Is the falling mutual?"

"Yes, you fool," she said, sinking deeper into his embrace.

In response, he nuzzled his cheek against hers.

Mmm. "How did your boys act when they met your other women?" she asked, curious.

"You are the first."

Really? Her heart leaped. "What about your friends? Have they met your sons?"

"A few of the Lords have, but I never made introductions. They stumbled upon each other."

Hold up. "Not even Anya and Pandora have met your horsemen?"

"Correct." He flattened his hands on her stomach and drew them up slowly. "I can tell my unicorn likes this news." Up a little more.

"Of course I do!" *I'm special to him.*

Up…

Would he… Yes! He cupped her breasts, sending a delicious cascade of heat through her.

Panting, she turned to face him. While she would have given anything to stay in this position, she kissed his lips quickly and said, "Let's go meet Evelina. The sooner we start, the sooner we'll finish, and the sooner you can take me home and get me out of this dress."

35

"Don't beat yourself up. That's my job."

WILLIAM LEANED AGAINST a wall and crossed his arms over his chest. Green remained at his side. An underground catacomb stretched out before them, the air dank, musty and surprisingly cold considering their locale: the center of Hell. Dried blood stained the brimstone walls, and water dripped from a cluster of "screaming crystals"—prisms that trapped sounds of agony and misery inside; those sounds seeped out at different intervals, the volume cranked to full blast.

He watched, captivated, as Sunny did her thing—take over.

"You two. Out of my way." She pushed past Red and Black to stand beside Axel at the door of Evelina's cell, where the prisoner slept fitfully on a cot. "Why hasn't she awoken? Why are her hands tied?"

"The little wildcat hurt herself trying to flee, so we drugged her," Red explained, a little snippy for William's liking. "And she's bound so that she can't wield magic or shape-shift."

Sunny went ramrod straight. Uh-oh. *Here comes trouble.*

"She isn't evil," Sunny snapped. "I'm staring at her aura right now, and she's furious, wounded, terrified and sad, but she's not evil. So you won't drug her again. Understand? Say the words back to me."

Her defense of the witch reminded him of her kindness to the children who'd admired her hair, her sweetness with the dying hellhound and her instant love for Dawn.

The perfect queen. My *queen.*

"You cannot command warlords like us," Black snapped back, "when you lack the strength to enforce it."

A slow, confident smile bloomed, a wild gleam in those purple eyes, only fueling William's hard-on. "Try me."

Until now, he hadn't realized he had a type, or that his type would be a pendulum of emotion, but he liked what he liked. He enjoyed soothing her temper. Thrilled when she donned her invisible captain's hat, assuming control of a situation. Her fear that his boys wouldn't like her? *Adorable.*

He'd never seen her so vulnerable, had never realized how desperately she craved a family of her own. He'd known she missed other unicorns, had known she was lonely, but he hadn't computed the depths of that loneliness. As deep as his own had once been—before Sunny.

Both Red and Black peered over their shoulders, giving William an "is she for real?" look.

He played helpless, hiking his shoulders. "Consider Sunny your stepmother. Do what she says."

Oh, she liked that as much as his earlier confession, her chin lifting.

The boys glared at him before muttering in unison, "We won't drug her again."

A smile teased William's mouth.

"You are falling for her," Green remarked quietly.

"Falling hard, yes." Why deny it? "She is...valued." Dare he say cherished?

"And yet, she has the power to kill you."

More so than his boys realized. "She does, but she won't." As quickly as he was falling for Sunny, she was falling for him, the truth gleaming in her eyes every time she glanced at him. Or melted in his arms.

"Your woman's idea about White," Green said. "You think there's a chance Sunny could...?"

"I do," William replied more softly. The second the topic had come up, he'd imagined her pregnant with his babe—and he'd liked it. Wild possessiveness had surged through him, demanding he make imagination a reality. He thought he'd sensed longing in her, too.

With the start of mating season mere days away, they could do it. Maybe. Yet...

He knew it would be better to wait. He craved more time with Sunny, just the two of them. *Look at me, planning for the future, rather than living day by day.* But the war still raged, the curse still loomed, Lucifer still lived and William had yet to find the tenth Hell crown. So far, he had no leads.

So many obstacles against them.

A commotion drew his gaze back to Evelina's cell. The royal witch had awakened. Bellowing in a language William didn't know, she struggled to rise from the cot with her arms tied behind her back. When she succeeded, she darted to the back of the cell, pressing her back against the wall. Clumps of dirt were stuck to her hair, obscuring the color of the strands. Mud had dried on her skin, so thick she must have fallen into a sea of the stuff just before being carted away. Her irises were lovely, green rimmed with silver, her pupils as big as saucers. She wore a tattered gown as muddy as the rest of her.

"Where did you find her?" William asked Green.

"An immortal brothel."

Why would she stay or work in a brothel, if she hoped to hide? At her wedding, a witch cast a spell over Evelina—at Lucifer's insistence. If ever she slept with another male, or orgasmed, Lucifer would know. He would also know where she was, and who she was with.

"Let me in the cell," Sunny commanded.

Again, his boys looked to him for permission. Curious about what his unicorn planned to do, William nodded, straightened and closed the distance. He would enter at her side. If Evelina made a move against her, Evelina would pay dearly.

Though no one touched the lock, Red opened the door with a wave of his hand. Sunny stepped forward, but William flashed in front, entering first.

Evelina met his gaze and cringed, inching into a corner.

Peering at her, needing her to see the seriousness of his expression, he said, "Harm the girl, give her even the barest scratch, and I'll gift you to Lucifer within the hour. Nod to show you understand."

Tremors racked the witch-shifter's small body, but still, she nodded. She looked to Sunny, the horsemen, Axel, then back to William, only to zoom back to Axel and visually trace his wings. Her eyes widened before she bellowed a string of unintelligible words, seeming to take the Sent One to task.

"Anyone know the language?" William asked.

A chorus of "no" belted out at different volumes.

Sunny took another step forward, slow and steady. Still,

Evelina yelped and scrambled along the wall, moving farther away. When Sunny took a second step, the girl bared her claws and hissed.

Shoulders sagging, Sunny looked to William. Tears pooled in her eyes, the sight of them nearly sending him into an unstoppable rage. "Why is she afraid of me? I only want to help her."

"Sometimes the only way to help someone is to walk away." He tugged her against him, holding her close. He told his boys, "Ensure news of Evelina's capture spreads to Lucifer *without* harming her."

"Or touching her," Sunny added with a sniffle.

He fought a smile. Such a soft, gooey center beneath her hard, chocolatey shell.

"I will ensure Lucifer knows." Axel's unbending tone echoed through the chamber. "He might not believe others, but he'll believe a Sent One."

His brother wasn't wrong. Lies burned to death before ever escaping a Sent One's mouth.

"And," Axel added, "I will take the girl with me. I can keep her in a place Lucifer and his demons cannot reach."

No doubt that place belonged in the heavens. "She's part witch," William informed him. Sent Ones considered witches as evil as demons. "A magic wielder, like me."

Axel arched a brow. "I've never known who or what I was. Not really. As if I would judge another for being what *they* are."

Like this man more and more.

His boys issued immediate refusals, but William silenced them with a glance. What to do? While Evelina would be safer in the heavens, the Sent Ones might not give her back when the time came.

"What do you think?" William asked Sunny.

Red frowned, Green scowled and Black spat a curse. This was a first. He'd never sought advice from anyone other than Hades. *Ignore the pang.*

"I think…" She curled her fingers around the collar of his shirt. "Yes. Let Axel take her where she'll be safest. But first, demand concessions."

He flashed a smile. "I love the way your mind works."

At the word *love*, her breath caught.

Oh, shit. He'd just used the dreaded L-word, and he'd… He…

Meant it. And he could not take back the words.

Or the emotion.

He loved the way her illogical mind worked. How she helped those in need. Her courage, her strength. Her sense of humor, and her loyalty. Her dark side. Her soft side. Loved her goofy, loved her serious. He loved the way she demanded his best. The way she responded to his every touch. Never had she cowered from him. Never would she. Every single day, she gave him a new memory to cherish.

He just loved her, period. The emotion flooded him in torrents, nearly drowning him. *No denying it a moment longer.* She'd been made for him, and he'd been made for her. They were a pack. A family.

The future Hell king, and his treasured queen.

His heart slammed against his ribs, fear surfacing. Damn it! This was bad. So very bad. Surely the curse had just activated.

Why hadn't she raged and attempted to remove his head, the only sure way to end him?

She petted his chest, as if she sensed his turmoil.

He needed to stop loving her. *It's her, or it's me.*

It's…her. It will always be her. Stop loving her? Too late. The code had to be broken. Soon! And if she tried to kill him in the meantime? What would he do? If he fought back, he risked harming her. A total nonstarter. What did that leave?

Axel smiled a cold smile. "What kind of concessions? I don't slaughter anyone who tries to stop me?"

Spoken like a true...whatever our last name should be. Hiding his turbulent emotions behind a carefree expression, he said, "I want Evelina brought back when I demand it, and I want Fox spared for her crimes against your people. She may remain Bjorn's prisoner, but she must not be killed." She'd murdered ten Sent Ones, yes, but only because her demon had overtaken her. Did she deserve punishment? Yes. And she'll get it. But death? No.

Several beats of silence. Then, "Agreed," Axel grated.

"Then so it shall be." Leaving the Sent One with Evelina, William took Sunny's hand and flashed her home... back to the book, for better or worse.

36

"To meet me is to crave me."

ONE MINUTE BLED into another as William prowled through the bedroom, adhering Wear a Condom notes everywhere. Sunny watched, concerned about his stiff movements and unwillingness to glance her way. Something was wrong.

They'd returned over an hour ago. He'd handed her the book, then started on the reminders. He'd been working at warp speed ever since, muttering about the effing curse. Of course, he'd used the actual F-word.

"We need to talk," she finally said.

"Not in the mood for chitchat."

Instinct screamed, *Get this settled.* "So? I said *need*, not *want*, and *need* wins. Now that we're official, it's your duty to ensure I have everything I need."

He flashed her a scowl, still not meeting her eyes. "Then talk."

Seriously, what was his problem? Before they'd entered

the dungeon, he'd been kind and sweet. But maybe his boys' dislike *had* rubbed off on him, despite his claims to the contrary?

A rising tide of nausea took her by surprise. "If you're super worried, just chain me in the dungeon next to Evelina until the end of mating season."

"No." He adhered a note to the dresser with more force than necessary. "I will take care of you."

"I'm still decoding your book, William, and there are still moments I want to kill you. Plus, what if the notes make no difference and you forget to wear a condom? Now isn't the time for a baby, not even a chance for one."

"Because you don't want me smuggling an ally into your womb?"

"Not until Lucifer is dead." But...would the desire to kill William cease if he had an ally on the inside?

He said nothing more, and Sunny took his silence as an affirmation. *Chained, it is.* Disappointing but necessary.

As he bent over, putting a note on the floor, her belly fluttered, a raspy moan escaping her. Was he hoping to take her there?

He froze, and her heart raced faster. Slowly, he straightened and faced her. The moment he spied her expression, he hardened, tenting his pants. Her body responded, heating, aching...preparing for invasion.

Arousal, stronger than ever before. Familiar sensations bombarded her. Her nipples beaded. Her blood heated another thousand degrees. The most delicious aches plagued her...until they became the most painful. Her panties dampened, and her core clenched, desperate for him. Her skin tingled, seeking his touch.

The urge to mate consumed her.

It felt as if their conversation had flipped a switch labeled

Forever Turned-On. As if every drop of arousal she'd ever experienced had returned and doubled...tripled in strength.

She didn't have to wonder what this was.

Mating season had started early.

"William," she said, panting. Was that plaintive tone truly hers? "It's happening...mating season." *Too soon.* Now all of his efforts were for naught. The condom reminders would only work outside of the actual mating. If he remembered, she wouldn't be able to come, making sex a form of torture for her. "You need to leave. Please. No. Stay. No! Leave. But first, the chains! Hurry!"

Blink. He vanished. Blink. He materialized at the foot of the bed. Heat pulsed from him, caressing her. "I'm not going anywhere, sundae."

"But you're worried, and I understand, I do. But I won't be able to come without *your* come. Without it, you'll just make everything worse." She lowered her gaze to his erection and licked her lips, her inner walls contracting. *Pin him down. Sink my nails in his chest. Impale myself on his massive shaft.* She'd ride him and come so hard she'd see stars.

"You are my female. My woman," he said. Snarled, really. "What you need, I provide. If it's my seed, then so be it."

"No!" She thrashed her head in denial.

"I'm going to worry regardless. Fear has me in a chokehold. What if we're forced to part because of the curse? What if you attack me? There's no way in hell I'll harm you either way, but pregnant..." He shuddered. "You'll succeed, which means you'll be left alone with a child to raise. You'll both be a target for Lucifer, and *that* is what I do not want."

He only wanted to protect her. He might even love her, despite everything stacked against them. But...

She loved him, no question. Because there, in that moment, Sunny surrendered her heart to William of the Dark, the Ever Randy, son of Hades, prince of Hell. He'd put her first, put her needs above his own, and any remaining resistance had shattered.

I love this man. He's mine, and I'm his. They would be together forever. A family. A pack. *Her* pack. Her everything.

"Baby," she said, using her best schoolteacher voice. "I want this with you. I do. Vow to lock me in the dungeon after mating season and stay away until the curse is broken, and we can be together this way. Right here, right now."

His expression softened, oh, so tender, before dark desire took over. Nothing would stop this man from having her. If Bjorn or anyone else dared to barge into the room, she had no doubt William would tear them to shreds. No male had ever looked more menacing. Or aroused.

"I will destroy worlds to keep you safe," he snarled.

Oh, yes. He does. He loves me.

So why don't I want to kill him?

"Take me, then. Hard." This was the last time she'd see him before she broke the curse. Why not make as many memories as possible?

Without hesitation, he gripped the collar of his shirt and tugged it overhead. Mmm, how she loved when he removed his shirt like that. His muscle-cut torso made her stupid, as usual. And she hadn't gotten over his pecs, that eight-pack or the goodie trail. But today's winner? The head of his erection, stretching past his leathers, fighting to break the zipper.

He stroked his length, watching her watch him. "This is what you crave?"

More shivers. If sex had a voice, it was William's. Husky, low and deep, an auditory caress that reached every atom of her being.

"More than anything," she rasped. Already her control burned away… "Give it to me."

With a wicked smile, he snagged her ankle and yanked her to the far edge of the mattress. She squeal-laughed as he ripped her dress down the middle, the sheer garment basically disintegrating, leaving her clad in her panties. The ones she'd worn just for him. Her granny panties.

He noticed and immediately flipped his gaze up to hers. The look he gave her…hot, amused and tender… "You are a treasure, sundae." He hooked his fingers inside the panties and slid the material down her legs.

Cool air kissed her overheated skin. Moaning, she undulated her hips, seeking contact. Little growls left him. He set her feet on the bed, right where he wanted them, keeping her knees parted, and her butt halfway off the edge.

"Stay just like this." He released her and kicked off his boots, then pulled down his zipper and let his leathers drop. His erection bounced free. He was naked, and he was magnificent. "Tell me this is mine, sundae," he commanded, cupping her sex.

"It's yours." She reached out to wrap her fingers around the base of his shaft.

"Uh-uh-uh." He plucked her hand free and said, "I'm going to outlast my unicorn." After kissing her palm, he sucked two of her fingers into his mouth. At the same time, he slid one of *his* fingers deep inside her. When he circled her little bundle of nerves with his thumb, she cried out and lifted her hips. "You, lost in the throes…this portal to paradise soaking my hand… It's the most beautiful sight in all the worlds."

He was the most beautiful sight in all the worlds. Leaning over, he pulled his finger free of her. She groaned in protest, until he planted his fists beside her hips and rested his shaft atop her mons. The contact—

She sucked in a breath, a hot, needy haze descending over her. So good! Heat to heat. Hard steel to damp silk. Still leaning…grinding his erection into her clitoris…he bent his head to suck a nipple into his mouth. Rapture shot through her, glorious in its intensity.

After so many centuries of chaining herself in difficult-to-reach places during mating season, miserable and agonized, she would now experience it with William…the man she loved with every fiber of her being.

Frantic, a little crazed, she looped her arms around him and raked her nails over his back. Not exactly what she'd imagined, but better. He sucked on her other nipple, one after the other, sending new tides of rapture to her core, then he licked and nibbled his way up her sternum, his brows drawn. A sign of pain? He continued to ascend. As he placed the most tender kiss at each corner of her mouth, ravenous hunger filled his baby blues.

He needs me as much as I need him.

He licked the seam of her lips. When she opened, he thrust his tongue past her teeth, rolling it with hers. A reverent kiss. But, as usual with them, it quickly burned out of control.

Around them, the air charged with electricity. Pressure built, and desperation sharpened. *Need friction so bad.* She writhed, bowed her back and rubbed her clit against his shaft. She was panting. So was he. The sensual haze thickened, blocking out all other thoughts. The ache…the heat… the sheer need…they were too much. *But I need more.*

"William, please. No more waiting. I'm going to die if I don't come. Please!"

"You need your man?" He remained unhurried, even

as sweat trickled down his temples…as tension pulled the skin around his eyes taut.

"Yes!"

"Who is your man, Sunny? Say it."

"You. William."

Expression fierce, jaw clenched, he growled, "You care for me."

Why deny it? "I do. I care."

Sublime satisfaction blazed in his eyes. He maneuvered her to her stomach, then lifted her hips until he had her on all fours. But he didn't enter her right away. No, oh, no. Her male trailed his fingers up the ridge of her spine before wrapping a blindfold over her eyes…

37

"People always show you who they are, it just takes time. And sometimes a dagger."

WILLIAM HAD NEVER known such frenzied, clawing need. Arousal infused his cells, turning his blood into lava. He burned. He ached. He craved this woman more than breath. She was the only person he knew willing to endure her worst fear—solitary confinement—for an extended and unspecified length of time, just to keep him safe.

No wonder he loved her.

Will take this slow. Savor. They'd had sex before, yes, but they would be making love now. He would make this the best night she'd ever had, something to remember for the rest of their lives. A shared memory; the best kind.

To keep Sunny grounded in the moment and discourage her fears, he'd blindfolded her. *You will anticipate my every move, beauty...*

When next he touched her, gliding his fingers *down*

her spine, she cried out with bliss. He kissed the indention above her ass before kneading and nipping a cheek. She panted her breaths, goose bumps spreading over her limbs.

"Could keep you like this forever," he said, utterly entranced by her.

She rocked her hips, unable or unwilling to stay still. Had there ever been a more sensual sight?

"Do you trust me, sundae?"

She rasped, "You know I do."

Running his hands from the backs of her knees, up her inner thighs, he drew moans and groans from her. As he plunged a single finger into her core, those moans and groans increased in volume.

Now *he* sucked in a breath. "So hot, so wet. So tight."

"Sooooo ready," she said, chasing his finger as he withdrew it.

"Ready, yes, but not ready enough." He placed one knee on the edge of the mattress, then the other, looming behind her. On the next inward thrust, he inserted a second finger, stretching her.

Crying out, she arched her back and fisted the sheets. Trembling, she said, "More."

His absolute favorite word, uttered by those rosebud lips. Gritting his teeth against the powerful avalanche of lust gaining new ground, snatching up more and more of his control, he scissored those fingers and worked them in and out, mimicking sex.

Passion-fever spread over her skin, giving it a rosy undertone. The transformation entranced him and wrapped him in a blanket of heat.

"William," she said, breathless. She reached between them to gently squeeze his testicles.

Control, damn it! "Someone likes to play dirty." He barely managed to push the words out of his mouth.

As he removed his fingers a final time, she babbled denials.

Eventually, he cut her off. "Don't worry, love. I've got something bigger for you." He just needed to do something first… What, what? Casting his gaze through the room in an effort to remember, he noticed little notes posted everywhere. Oh, yes. The condom. The condom he couldn't wear if he wanted Sunny to come.

He absolutely wanted Sunny to come.

With the tip of his shaft resting at her entrance, he clasped her hips and drew her backward slowly, impaling her on his cock. His breaths came faster, and far more shallow. Hers, too.

Being gloved by all that wet heat… He fought the urge to come. *Must last.*

He bit his tongue, tasting blood, as her body accepted the final inch. Tremors rocked her against him. He clasped her on both sides and drew her upright, putting her back flush against his chest. Her desire still wet his fingers—fingers he grazed over her lips, so he could lick away her feminine honey when next they kissed. A new addiction.

With one hand, he cupped and kneaded her breasts while pinching her tight little nipples. With the other, he strummed her swollen bundle of nerves. All the while, her inner walls clenched around his length, wrenching curses from him.

William kept his lower body still, ratcheting up her pleasure as he ran her earlobe between his teeth. Any minute she would—

Sunny arched her back. Yes! Movement! Her breasts pressed against his palms, stealing his thoughts. Wild and wanton, she turned her head toward him, seeking his lips.

Desperate for her, he captured her clitoris between two fingers and squeezed her hip, urging her up. His shaft inched out of her, nearly popping free...until he thrust forward once again, filling her.

Her ragged cry echoed from the walls. A starting bell of some sort.

William—utterly—unleashed.

He pounded inside her, again and again, the bed shaking. Her next cry tapered into a breathless moan. "Yes, yes!"

In, out. In, out. In. On the next retreat, he didn't shove back in. Yet. Instead, he flipped her around, so that they faced each other. Only when she wrapped her legs around him, and he claimed her lips in another earth-shattering kiss, did William thrust home once again. Thrust, thrust.

When he required greater friction than their current position allowed, he tossed her to her back. Thrust, thrust. Then *she* flipped *him*, straddling his waist as she rose above. He thrust harder... Harder. Faster.

"So close, love. I'm going to give you every drop. You ready?"

"Ready! Please, William. Please."

Never had he burned or ached like this. Never had he felt so sated *before* a climax. With his woman's plea for more ringing in his ears, her breasts bouncing above him, her sex gloving his shaft with liquid fire...

No stopping it. Finally he let go, hot jet after hot jet lashing from him.

Sunny threw back her head and screamed, her entire body convulsing. When she collapsed atop him, he rolled her to her side, removed her blindfold, and held her close. *Will never let her go.*

They hadn't just had sex or made love. They'd *communed*, two souls made one. Exactly what the Lords had often spoken about when they'd explained the difference between sex with a stranger and sex with a mate. Until now, William hadn't truly understood the difference. His satisfaction hadn't come from his climax, but his partner's.

If anyone tries to take her from me, I will do murder. I will have this every day for the rest of my life.

"We'll get to rest a few minutes, then the urges will start up again," Sunny told him between panting breaths. "If you can't keep up—"

"Can't keep up?" he bellowed.

A giggle escaped her, soon becoming a laugh. The sound enchanted him. The sight of her, too. Amusement lit up her entire face, making his heart race. As much as he wanted more sex and more afterglows, he wanted more of her merriment most of all.

A smile a day keeps my homicidal tendencies at bay.

"Let me rephrase," she said.

He arched a brow, all *let's hear this.*

"If, at any point, you have to leave, not because your stamina sucks and you need a break, but because…reasons, I'll understand. I'll ridicule you for eternity, but I'll understand. Just be ready to be attacked the second you get home."

"I might have to leave to speak with Hades," he replied, hurt crackling in his tone. "But there's nothing I'd rather do than take care of my woman during a…difficult time. And, yes, giving you orgasm after orgasm is going to be difficult for me. A real hardship. When mating season is over, you're going to owe me so big."

Another giggle. "So big," she echoed. "As a reward, I might do a fashion show for you, and model my favorite granny panties."

"Maybe? No. You *will*," he said with mock ferocity. "The offer's been made and accepted. No take backs."

"Oh, I can—" She gasped, her blunt-tipped nails curling into his chest, holding her prey in place. "William, it's starting again."

"First of all, my name goes on your roster for permanent mating season duty. Second, you just lie back and let your man do all the work." He drew her bottom lip between his teeth. "You're about to discover my stamina is unmatched."

HE NEVER ACTUALLY vowed to lock me away, only to give me what he thought I needed.

After two weeks of sex, sex and more sex, Sunny awoke with a clear head for the first time in eons. Her fourteen-day deadline to decode the book had passed times two, yet William didn't seem to mind. He seemed happ—

The realization about him smacked her upside the head, and she jolted upright, her mind whirling.

During mating season, her man had perfectly divided his time between satisfying her and war. What she'd needed, her baby had provided. She'd luxuriated in a tide of bliss, losing count of the number of times she'd licked his tattoos, sucked him dry or rode him to climax.

But now mating season had reached its conclusion. Yay! Boo! No, no. Definitely yay. William slept like the dead beside her, and a soft smile spread over her face. Poor darling. She and the war had exhausted him.

As she stretched her sore, sated body, morning sunlight deluged the bedroom. More thoughts filled her head, things mating seasons had made her forget. No forgetting now. William's curse. It had to be dealt with and fast. Only then could they truly start their lives together.

Sunny extracted her limbs from William's as carefully

as possible and lumbered to unsteady legs. Dude. She kind of felt like she'd survived a nine-car pileup. Once she had the book in her possession, she gathered her diary and a pen, then returned to the bed to prop herself up on pillows. Satisfaction hummed inside her as William slept on.

All right. Let's do this. She opened the book to the page she'd last decoded and traced her fingertips over the symbols. In a snap, her blood heated. She frowned. Mating season hadn't ended?

Still heating...

Sweat sheened her skin, yet the air seemed to cool by a hundred degrees, her limbs quickly freezing. Her teeth chattered.

Steaming hot and ice-cold at the same time? Madness!

Kill William.

She gasped. *Not this. Not so soon.* She'd only just begun.

So close to the end. Can't give up now. Keep your eye on the prize and forge ahead. Break the curse, and the madness ends.

She focused on the symbols. *Kill him!* Heating. Freezing. Her heart thudded, reminding her of a gavel after a judge delivered a life sentence. *Kill, kill, kill.*

No. Never. Unless...she *needed* to kill him? Born to kill the princes of hell—wasn't that her fate? Her only purpose in life? *Yessss.*

No! Fight this! Must decode.

Must kill.

Wait! She should chain herself to the bed. Then she could study, and she wouldn't have to worry about harming William. The man kept shackles in his closet, for goodness sake. Fate.

Sunny stood a second time, tiptoed to the closet and dug out the chains. On her way back to bed, dizziness nearly toppled her. *Breathe. Just breathe.* Somehow, she managed to stay upright—quietly—and reach her side of the bed.

She tried to secure one end of the chain to a bedpost, but her arm refused to obey her mental commands. She merely jabbed the chain at the poster, as if she were stabbing it.

What the hellebore? She tried again. Jab. Something warm and wet sprayed over her hands, the chain slipping from her grip and thumping on the floor. But…she saw nothing out of place. Her hands appeared clean and dry.

A hard hand reached out from the poster to wrap around her wrist, holding her captive. A hand. From the poster? Confused, nearing panic, she struggled to get free. The hold proved too strong.

"Sunny!"

William's voice, sharp with fear. She blinked rapidly, a new terrifying reality taking shape. William held her. He was covered in blood, and so was she. A bloody dagger lay on the floor, not a pair of chains.

Sunny gasped. She'd mistaken a dagger for a link of chains? Had she hallucinated and picked up a dagger? But why? And…and…she'd stabbed William? Oh, freesia, she had. It was his precious lifeblood that wet their hands.

Horror punched her, knocking the air from her lungs. Wheezing, she stumbled back. Or she would have, if he hadn't tightened his grip. "I thought… I thought I was standing at my side of the bed, not yours. I thought I held chains, not a dagger. I thought…" He had two wounds in his chest. Because of her. Because she'd stabbed him. Twice!

Hot tears streamed down her cheeks. Any bravado she'd managed to cultivate about her resistance to the curse utterly disintegrated.

"William, I'm so sorry. I didn't realize… I didn't know…

I wanted to protect you. I... I..." She crumpled into herself, her knees buckling.

Despite his injuries, he flashed behind her, catching her before she hit the ground. He flashed her atop the bed, his back propped against the headboard, her cheek resting against his shoulder. More of his blood wet her skin as he wrapped a strong arm around her, but she didn't care. Anything to luxuriate in his embrace. With his other hand, he petted her hair.

"I'm so sorry," she repeated.

"Shh, shh. It's okay. I've got you, love. A little light stabbing is foreplay. No big deal."

He was comforting *her*, after she'd stabbed him. What if she had killed him...

Another sob shook her. She had to make this right. "I want to show you my unicorn form."

He kissed her temple, then astounded her by saying, "Not like this. You'll show me because you want me to see you, not because you feel guilty for giving me some internal body bling."

More understanding from him, when she deserved castigation. He wasn't going to protect himself against her, was he? He thought, like she had, that he could contain and control the situation. A mistake. One she would rectify.

If he wouldn't take measures to protect himself from her, she would have to take measures to protect him. She would...leave.

Another sob bubbled up, but she tamped this one down. She'd leave for a little while, only a little while, holing up the way she used to do during mating season. Finally, she would finish decoding the book. Then, and only then, could Sunny return and be with William always and forever.

My love, my life.

38

"War is like chess—I always win."

WILLIAM'S WORST FEARS had come true. He'd fallen in love, and the object of his affection had made a solid attempt on his life, without even realizing what she was doing.

For two weeks, he'd made love to Sunny at all hours of the day and night. While she'd slept, he'd fought and interrogated demons, and hunted leads for the tenth crown, all while avoiding Axel. He'd hoped to clear his head before next meeting with his brother, but his thoughts had only grown more chaotic.

How his life had changed in the weeks since meeting Sunny. He had a lifemate. The curse had activated. He had a future without Hades. A soon-to-be king of Hell was related to an Elite 7—would Axel be punished for their connection? What if another Sent One accused William of a crime, as Bjorn had done? Axel would be caught in the crossfire, forced to choose.

Should William cut all ties?

And what about Sunny, his potential queen and murderess? Did he maintain the status quo with her, letting her continue to study the code while guarding himself against future attacks?

Deep down, he had a sinking suspicion the attacks would only worsen. That, one day, the trance or whatever overcame her would be permanent. Or did he do what he'd once considered a nonstarter and burn the book to *prevent* Sunny from studying it? Every time she cracked open the pages, she worsened.

He frowned, a thought occurring to him. *Why* did she only worsen when she studied? Did his feelings for her strengthen during those times, adding fuel to the curse's fire, as she suspected? Or did the book itself dictate the curse, rather than William's feelings? And if so, what did it mean for them?

As she slept against his healing chest, her warm breath fanned his skin. He combed his fingers through her hair. Silvery moonlight bathed her in intervals, flashing bright to illuminate her ethereal beauty, before fading, then flashing again.

Losing focus. Right. The curse. During mating season, the curse hadn't influenced Sunny in the least. Then she'd woken up, studied a passage and, boom, she'd stabbed him.

How would she react when she woke? Would she try again, or be herself?

Though he hated to leave her, William tucked her under the covers, showered, dressed in his customary attire, then grabbed his cell, intending to contact Axel. The time to talk again had come.

He frowned when he discovered new texts.

Green Machine: Lucifer knows we have Evelina.

Red Abed: To say he's pissed would be an understate-ment. But. He's PISSED.

Black Attack: Be on guard today. Twice this morning Lucy tried to sneak into our home, disguised as one of us.

Damn it! This was exactly what William didn't need right now. Inhaling for calm, he cast a final glance at Sunny—sleeping fitfully without his nearness, injecting apprehension straight into his veins—placed a magical barrier around the bedroom, ensuring no one could enter without her permission, then flashed to the door of Axel's country estate in the heavens. A mansion made from gorgeous woods, gold and precious gems. Smooth diamond sheets provided a flat roof.

He knocked a little too forcefully. A crack spread through the center of the door. He'd never been here before, but he'd secretly researched Axel after realizing he might be the little boy from his memory. Pictures hadn't done justice to this area of the heavens. A clear, baby blue sky with no sun. Light came from their leader, the Most High. Birds of every color soared through the lavender-scented air. In the yard, trees teemed with golden apples, figs and pears.

The door swung open, Axel appearing, his dark hair rumpled, his eyes sleepy and hooded, shirtless, his leathers unbuttoned, only partially zipped. He sported claw marks on his throat, and bruises on his pecs. His wings had a couple fist-size bald spots, as if someone had ripped out handfuls of feathers.

"Rough night?" William asked. "Or a really, really good one?"

Axel pivoted to allow him inside. "The little hellcat didn't want to bathe. I made her. As soon as she realized I had no plans to harm her, she settled down…somewhat."

Striding into the foyer, he said, "We can return her to—"

"No!" Axel barked. Then he scoured a hand down his face. More gently, he repeated, "No. She's safest here, so here she'll stay."

The poor bastard was attracted to the girl, even though his fellow Sent Ones despised witches. If Evelina reciprocated the attraction, the two would have a difficult road ahead. If they were fated…

Worth every hardship.

"Lucifer knows about her," Axel said, his jaw clenched. "He donned your face and tried to sneak into my cloud. I scented out his deception, and whisked Evelina here. Now he's out for blood."

"He's always out for blood. But how do you know I'm not Lucifer, trying again?"

"Eyes express emotion he cannot hide." Axel walked to a wet bar beyond the foyer, the only piece of furniture in a space large enough to accommodate his wings. "Something to drink?"

Determined to maintain a clear head, he declined. "Have you learned anything new about coded curses?"

"I have not, I'm sorry. Has something else occurred?"

Words spilled from him. "I did the stupidest, most brilliant thing and fell in love with Sunny. I expected her to attack the moment I realized it. She didn't. She only attacked when she started working on the book. Is it possible *the book* is cursed?"

"Possible, yes. Likely, no." Axel poured himself a shot

of whiskey. "A curse is a living organism, a parasite that requires a host. It feeds off thoughts, emotions, words, finally becoming a self-fulfilled prophecy."

Pacing, he said, "Let's say I'm not actually cursed. Let's say the book isn't cursed, either." No one had ever *sensed* a curse, only magic. "What would entrance Sunny and lead her to kill me?"

Axel fell into step beside him, keeping pace. "I don't know, but if it only happens with the book…"

"Then the book is at fault, despite being curse-free."

"Something about it must poison her mind against you."

Poison… He recalled the vial of poison the Goddess of Many Futures had revealed to Hades, as well as the vial of poison Sunny had drawn. Could *the book* be poisonous? But how? The pages coated with some kind of chemical? No. Would he have noticed it?

What about the ink?

He sucked in a breath. The fucking ink. Sunny liked to feel the symbols. Had she been poisoned every time she'd made contact?

Had he cursed *himself* every time he'd requested her aid?

His hands fisted. Oh, how Lilith must have loved the idea of *that*. He stopped abruptly, his stomach twisting. She hadn't cursed him. She'd cursed the ink, giving him the means to destroy himself. And he had.

Worse than a fool. A gull, easily deceived.

Fury burned through him, only to fade as waters of hope rained over him. No book, no murder attempts. He could torch the pages and have Sunny. But… If he was wrong, he would destroy his only means of obtaining freedom.

He imagined Lilith laughing as he met and discarded woman after woman, afraid to fall in love. Imagined her gleefully bragging about her genius and his idiocy, smug as she told her friends all about his efforts to save himself, only to make things worse for his present, and his future.

"I must go," he said. "I'm going to try to speak with Hades one last time and find out what he—" William pressed his lips together, waiting.

Axel had ceased moving, his head canted to the side, his expression dark but frozen. No doubt other Sent Ones were speaking to him telepathically.

William would give him one minute more, but no longer. Then he would leave. *Get to Hades, then Sunny.* One way or another, the issue with his book would be resolved *today*.

Within thirty seconds, the Sent One snapped out of it. "Hordes of demons have invaded the camp of Sent Ones, and my men require my aid. I cannot flash while I'm in the heavens. I need you to take me back to Hell."

Demons invading his turf… William wasted no time, cupping his brother's shoulder and flashing him to the campground. But…there were no Sent Ones present. No demons, either. The place had been deserted.

A sense of foreboding prickled his flesh. "Go," William said. "Find your brethren. I must get Sunny to safety." If the horde had invaded his home… William cursed.

They embraced.

"Be well, William."

"And you, brother." Though he wished to linger—Sunny had taught him the beauty of a good cling—William stepped back and flashed to his bedroom. "Sunny?"

He rushed to the bed—not there. His heart raced. He stomped into the bathroom. No sign of her there, either.

He wouldn't panic. Not yet. He sprinted about, searching for any clues. There! A sheet of paper rested on her pillow. Trembling, he lifted it. His guts clenched. Tearstains marred the paper, and they were still damp.

He read, *I've left, and I've taken your book. Please don't try to find me. I promise I'll return once your curse is broken. Tell Dawn I love and miss her, okay? But maybe don't tell her I'll miss you more.* :)

No, no, no. *Now* he panicked. She'd gone, and she'd taken the book.

But she hadn't been gone long.

Must find her! He called her cell, only to hear it ring. The device rested on the nightstand. *Think!* To escape him so quickly, she must have been flashed. Who would she ask to flash her, though? And how would she communicate—

The cell phone. She'd left it so he couldn't track her, but probably hadn't thought to erase her messages. Not if she'd been in a hurry.

He cued up her texts and found an exchange with Hades.

Sunny: I need to speak with you. It's important. How soon can you pick me up?

Hades: Check your door.

Claws sprouted from William's nails. The exchange transpired sixteen minutes ago. If she went with his father... *There's still hope.*

Frantic but determined, William texted Axel an update, arranging a meet-up, then hurriedly strapped weapons all over his body. On his way, he remembered the medallion he'd stashed away, intending to study. He had yet to practice with it, and usually refused to wield an untried weapon. But Sunny had said the medallion could paralyze an opponent for seconds at a time. Those seconds could be lifesaving. And hadn't he felt fated to use the medallion?

Very well. He would make an exception. He followed Sunny's lead, hanging the medallion from a chain and securing it around his neck.

As soon as it slid beneath his shirt, touching his skin, its magic swept through him, plumping his muscles with aggression and strength as if he were some kind of Berserker. *Should have done this sooner.*

Now to get his woman back, kill his ex-brother and find his crown.

SUNNY'S HEART RACED faster than a speeding bullet. She'd been wide-awake when William had left their bedroom. Seconds later, she'd jumped to her feet and rushed around to gather everything she might need.

Since he'd programmed Hades's number into her cell phone, she'd contacted the king to ask for a one-on-one conference. She'd wanted to contact Pandora or Anya, but she'd feared they would tell William her plans. Besides, this way, she could help repair his relationship with his dad before she went into hiding.

Only minutes later, there'd been a hard rap at the door. She'd opened up to find Hades. He'd patted her down, discarded her weapons and flashed her to his home. Well, all but one weapon. The medallion still hung around her neck. That, he hadn't noticed, thanks to her magic.

As soon as he'd learned the reason for her request, however, he'd deposited her in William's old bedroom and told her, "I don't have time for such matters. Lucifer has attacked the Sent Ones. *If* you remain in this room without causing trouble, we'll talk after I've put out a few fires."

That conversation had occurred roughly ten minutes ago. She'd spent half the time investigating William's things. A closet filled with novelty T-shirts about Big Willy. Mason jars filled with clear liquid and organs. Romance novels, books about war, codebreaking and game theory filled the only bookcase.

Her ears twitched, telltale noises drifting from somewhere below. *Battle* noises. Her brow furrowed. What was going on down there?

She opened the bedroom door, cringing at the slightest squeak. Thankfully, no one shouted protests or commands as she tiptoed into the hall. She ignored the riches and treasures around her, keeping her attention on the armed soldiers once posted along the walls, now leaping into action, rushing down the staircase.

She followed, the scent of brimstone and sulfur permeating the air. Still no protests. The closer she came to the throne room, the louder those battle noises became and the faster her heart galloped. Swords whooshed and clanged. Bones popped. Blood gurgled.

Screams and wails blended with gleeful laughter. No matter which way she looked, demons fought soldiers.

Sage! This was a full-on invasion.

Some of the demons had multiple horns and forked tails. Others had bloodstained fangs and ultrasharp claws. All had hard scales and a thirst for blood.

Demons. Must. Die.

Muscles tensing for battle—*not yet, not yet*—she pressed her back against the wall and slipped into the shadows, sneaking about.

More demons congregated at the doors of the throne room. Bodies and body parts littered the floor, pools of blood in every direction.

Finally a demon noticed her and launched her way, only to be blocked by other demons and soldiers already engaged in combat. Heart thudding, she yanked her medallion free and dropped to the floor. After she smeared blood on her face and chest, she played dead. One minute passed, then two, the demon reaching her at last.

He spun, searching for her. When he spotted her, seemingly dead, he howled and lashed out, kicking her in the stomach. She didn't let herself huff a breath or react in any way. Not stabbing him in retaliation required willpower she hadn't known she possessed. But the moment she engaged, she would lose her advantage. An advantage she needed to save for the rescue of Hades. William would want her to save his father at all cost.

Finally, the fiend moved on. Adrenaline dulled a twinge of pain as Sunny inched closer to the entrance of the throne room. She paused to let a group of combatants fight their way past her, then inched closer again.

"You will cease this madness, Lucifer!" Hades roared, his voice seeping past the doors.

Lucifer was here? Excitement melded with malice. *He dies by my horn* today!

The bastard's gleeful laughter echoed from the walls. "I will not cease until you know what it's like to lose everything. Even now, my armies are gathering your allies. They'll be brought here, where they'll watch you and your precious William die."

Kill William? Like hellebore! She reached the entrance and peered through the crack in the door. Oh…daisy. More dead bodies. In the far corner, a contingent of Sent Ones punched their own temples and tore out hanks of their hair.

A blonde woman in a tattered brown robe stood before the winged Warriors. She was pale, emaciated and dirty, but she kept her arms extended, her hands aimed at the winged warriors. Must be a witch, tormenting the males with her magic.

Countless demons. A powerful witch. A hated prince of darkness. How was Sunny supposed to subdue them all? She needed William, her knight in shining armor. Her pack-mate. The one person she shouldn't be around.

As Hades bellowed a curse, the wrongness of her last thoughts hit her with the force of a baseball bat. What was she going to do, cower until he got here? Was she a coward or a unicorn? A fragile flower or a demon slayer? A loser or a superhero? She did not need a man to save the day. She didn't need *anyone*. She could—and would—do this herself!

Once again, Sunny peeked through the crack between the door and its frame. Demon hordes formed a circle around Hades and Lucifer, who still fought. The king's army had been neutralized, the soldiers lying on the ground, either motionless or writhing in pain.

Black smoke wafted from Hades as he spun and thrust two short swords at Lucifer, who blocked and slammed a massive ebony wing into Hades. As the king stumbled back, the prince did it again, spinning to hit Hades with a wing. This time, the membranous appendage swept the king off his feet.

Sunny fit her fingers around the grooves in the medallion, the horn growing from the center. Time for the unicorn to step in.

39

"All hail the king!"

WILLIAM MET UP with Axel at the edge of the Sent One camp-ground, as planned.

"I was able to locate an injured Sent One," Axel told him, a vein throbbing in the center of his forehead. "The demons hit hard, then flashed everyone away. The witness escaped, but not before he heard mention of Hades's palace."

He stiffened. They'd flashed to Sunny's current loca-tion. Demons...attacking his mate... "We flash to Hades's throne room *now*." Words he group texted to his every ally.

As if he and Axel had been partners for centuries, they turned in unison, standing back to back, their swords at the ready.

Hell vanished, total chaos coming into view. Lucifer and Hades fought in the overcrowded throne room, two torna-dos continually slamming together, moving so fast even William had trouble tracking them. Dead and dying soldiers carpeted the floor. The odor of old pennies, urine and waste, bowels emptying upon death tainted every breath.

He'd entered a literal shit storm.

Where was Sunny? He cast his gaze about…and found the missing Sent Ones, who appeared agonized by an invisible force.

Gillian and Puck appeared beside them, took stock and launched into the fray.

William's boys appeared next. Then Pandora. Then a handful of Lords and Ladies, including Anya and Keeley. Even more Hell kings.

For a moment, William stood paralyzed by an outpouring of gratitude that they'd dropped everything to come. Awed by the fearsome sight they presented. Humbled that they loved him enough to put their lives at risk to save someone *he* loved.

As his friends got busy killing demons, William caught sight of a familiar face and sucked in a breath. Lilith. She *had* survived.

He hadn't seen her in so long. Now she stood near the Sent Ones, her arms raised. She looked as haunted and defeated as her half sister. Clearly, Lucifer had put her through hell.

William waited for satisfaction to come…but it remained at bay.

The medallion heated against his chest, even more magic seeping into his skin, into his blood, his brain…not dark magic, though, as he'd originally suspected, but *pure* magic. His muscles plumped another couple of inches, and his bones refortified, stronger than steel. His cells fizzed.

Different colored lights began to glow from everyone. Auras, he realized. *This is what Sunny sees?*

But how could the medallion affect him this way?

Ponder later, fight now. He launched into motion, removing the head of a demon who approached.

Other demons noticed him and Axel, and attacked en masse; claws swiped at him, fangs chomped and tails whipped. Determined to find Sunny, he swung at the next demon to approach and yelled to Axel, "I must find Sunny."

"I'll guard your back. You lead. I'll follow."

Now satisfaction filled him. Brandishing his swords, removing limb after limb, he surged forward. Axel remained close, guarding his back as promised. They left a trail of dead demons in their wake. Problem: their efforts made no difference. The moment one demon toppled, two others took its place. The fiends just kept coming, soon surrounding them.

We might...lose?

No! The key to winning a battle—be adaptable. "New plan," he grated, stomping on a tail to halt a demon's retreat, then lopping off his head. "We'll free the Sent Ones from the witch's magic. They can fly overhead and search for Sunny."

As they backtracked, the medallion heated against William's chest. He was surprised his shirt wasn't smoking. Why—

Even though his fingers were not fitted around the medallion's grooves, a sharp, bony protrusion grew, slicing through his shirt.

He dropped a sword to rip the medallion free of the chain.

A loud, booming war-neigh sounded, echoing off the walls. Demons went still. Actually, everyone went still, all eyes zooming to the doorway. A massive warhorse—no, a war-unicorn—came blazing into the room.

Sunny.

William's jaw dropped. *She. Is. Magnificent.* Feral, neon red eyes. Large, sharp teeth. Her scarred flesh bore every color of the rainbow. A ridged black horn the exact dimensions of their spears protruded from the center of her forehead, a glowing, golden ring around it. The exact size of the medallion.

He comprehended three startling facts all at once. The medallions were amputated unicorn horns. *Her* horn had activated his medallion, drawing the spear—horn—forth. And to see a horn on a living unicorn was to want—need—it for your very own, its magic like a potent wine, inspiring instant, unwavering obsession.

No wonder Sunny had insisted on hiding her unicorn form.

She galloped through the throne room, plowing into demons. With her horn, she ripped through scales, armor and bone, black blood dribbling down her face. After she impaled two demons, she shook her head, sending the pair flying, and mule-kicked the fiends behind her.

This was not a woman who needed saving. Others needed saving *from her*, and he couldn't be prouder.

None of his enemies had managed to topple him, but love for Sunny might do the trick.

Everyone else felt as he did—obsessed. No one could look away from the horn, everyone frozen by the sight. Even Hades and Lucifer went still, peering at her as if mesmerized.

Sunny focused on the witch. Shouting with pain, Lilith beat her fists against her temples. At the same time, William's spear heated, vibrating with a strange, new magic.

No. Not new, and not strange. *Lilith's.* His horn worked with Sunny's, siphoning the witch's magic. And Lucifer's illusions apparently. The Sent Ones stopped pulling their hair, and the number of demons decreased by seventy percent, at least, every illusion vanishing.

A corner of his mouth curved up. The smoke around Hades and Lucifer dissipated, revealing two bloody warriors with an array of gashes. Hades was panting and pale, obviously weakened. Lucifer was…no longer beautifully flawless. He'd changed in ways William had never imagined, his eyes sunken and bloodshot. His cheeks had hollowed, his skin sallow. His hair had thinned, and his shoulders had stooped. William's smile widened. *Deserved.*

The two predators circled each other. The remaining demons attempted to surround them, creating a wall, but William's allies slaughtered each and every one. *They* created a wall.

Frothing with rage, ready to end this, William pushed his way past the crowd and sneered, "My turn to play. Or are you a coward, ready to flash away?" *Could* the bastard flash, or had the ability been siphoned from him?

Lucifer twirled a dagger between his fingers. "Why don't we air our dirty laundry instead?"

"You shut your mouth," Hades snapped, pointing a finger at him.

Lucifer grinned, smug, and eyed William. "Did you know Hades is the one you and your precious Axel were created by Wrathlings to kill? They took the most powerful traits of the most powerful gods and creatures to create you both, making only slight differences in your DNA. You're almost the same person. As if the world needed two of you." He laughed, bitter. "When Hades learned about you, he gave chase and killed the Sent One determined to hide you. But you and Axel escaped. So he hunted you and found you with the cannibals, intending to kill you. Only, he decided to raise you as his own instead, using your skills to aid his cause. I suppose at some point, he grew to love you. He feared you would learn the truth if ever you reunited with your brother, so he schemed, lied and gambled to keep the two of you apart."

Lies! Had to be. But as Lucifer had spoken, Hades had paled. And... William hissed. Searing heat rushed up his arm, invading his head. The horn he held... It was still connected to Sunny...a lie detector and a siphon. *His* magic drained.

Magical walls tumbled down in his mind, childhood memories flooding him. Suddenly, he was a little boy, locked in a room with young Axel, being observed by multiple Wrathlings.

Young Axel took his hand and whispered, "We'll find a way out, brother. We will."

The image faded, a new one already taking shape. He and Axel were a bit older and bleeding on a floor, surrounded by a multitude of Wrathlings punching and kicking them.

"Fight back," one shouted. "Do you think the gods will go easy on you?"

Again, his mind blanked. Again, a new scene formed. Young William struggled against the ties holding him to a table as a man in a white robe said, "Let's see how quickly you regenerate, shall we?" and ran a dagger down his abdomen. He howled with agony, blood pouring from him.

"Axel," he screamed. From the distance, Axel screamed back.

Blank. More images. William, sitting on the floor of his cell, his knees drawn up to his chest as he rocked back and forth, plagued by unshakable loneliness.

Why did no one but Axel love him? Why did no one but Axel want him?

The door to his cell opened, and the woman he'd assumed was his mother rushed inside. She dropped to her knees before him, placing her cold, clammy hands against his temples, forcing his gaze to meet hers. "Hades learned of your creation. He's here, and he's going to slay you. I'm going to hide your memories, yes? If you do not know who you are, he won't know who you are. Then I'll whisk you and your brother to safety. Yes?" she repeated.

Present-day William stood rooted in place, everything he'd ever believed about his life crumbling like those magical walls. Parts of him burned; the rest of him iced. As he blinked into focus, rage and anguish cast a red haze over his line of sight. He inhaled sharply, exhaled heavily, his hands fisted. All that pain. All that loneliness. All the love he'd poured into Hades. And for what? Betrayal at every turn.

He couldn't bring himself to look at Hades.

"Aw, did the truth break your wittle brain?" Lucifer taunted.

With ruthless precision, William shoved the memories deep into his mind. Later, he would withdraw them for further study.

He peered at Lucifer—and grinned again. "Long ago, Lilith predicted one brother would slay the other. *I'm* supposed *to win our war.* Why else would fate gift me with a unicorn? A horn of my own? The fucking *genetics* to get the job done?"

Lucifer went pallid.

The crowd parted briefly, Sunny entering the circle. She galloped between Hades and Lucifer, who looked ready to vomit. She stopped abruptly—and mule-kicked Hades, sending him stumbling back, out of the way, leaving an open path for William.

That's my girl.

William and Lucifer circled each other. Despite the

male's abysmal condition, he wasn't out for the count, still shockingly strong and fast.

"If you want a piece of me, brother," Lucifer spat at William, "come and get it."

"He's mine," William shouted to one and all. "I'm the only one who touches him. The rest of you can watch."

"Yeah, baby!" Anya called.

"Make it hurt!" Keeley shouted.

"Bust his balls!" Gillian cried.

William struck, swinging the spear; Lucifer blocked with a sword. *Whoosh. Bam. Bam. Bam.* Again and again, their weapons slammed together, impact sending powerful vibrations up his arms.

Grunting, Lucifer faked a left, then went right, stabbing William in the side. Blood gushed from the wound, pain overtaking him. Did he slow? No! He spun, going low, sweeping Lucifer's feet out from under him. As the male floundered, toppling, William repositioned and slammed the horn into the bastard's chest. Bull's-eye. Right in the heart.

Upon impact, Lucifer froze, paralyzed, but he recovered quickly, rolling to a stand. Enraged, he attacked again. *Bam, bam, bam. Whoosh. Bambam.* When one struck, the other blocked, but at a much slower pace than before.

Lucifer jabbed a dagger at William's face. He reared back, just not in time. The blade sliced a shallow cut in his forehead, blood trickling into his eyes, momentarily blurring his vision.

Finish this! When Lucifer attempted another jab and slash, William parried and caught the blade. Even as metal sliced his palm and terrible pain radiated up his arm, he yanked the weapon free of his brother's grip, leaving the male with a single dagger.

Lucifer stumbled back, clearly stunned by the development. One of his eyes was swollen, his nose was broken and his lip split. A front tooth had been knocked out.

Knowing the piece of shit would attempt a retreat, William shouted, "Axel!"

"On it!" The Sent One rallied his comrades, who tightened the circle around them.

Sunny trotted around the inner edge, huffing and puffing. Hades—

Still not looking his way.

William and Lucifer prowled around each other once more. "I'm going to enjoy killing you," he spat.

Lucifer hissed, past any sort of bravado, and threw himself at William. They crashed together, another brutal dance ensuing. They stabbed, ripped and punched. Though dizzy, William managed to fit his hands around the male's neck, his claws cutting past skin and muscle, hot blood dripping. He tossed Lucifer to the ground, amused when he skidded to the edge of the circle.

Anya kicked him in the temple, and Keeley stomped on his windpipe. Gillian punted his testicles. Gasping for breath, Lucifer jacked upright and lumbered to his feet.

Too easy? Maybe. But William slammed one end of his spear into the floor and used it to vault and swing forward. His boots slammed into Lucifer's chest, knocking him down a second time. William followed, a red haze falling over his eyes. He pinned Lucifer's shoulders with his knees. *Hurt him! Make him beg for death.*

With one hand, he whaled. With the other, he twirled the spear, preparing to deliver a death blow. Snarls collected deep in his chest.

His brother bucked while doing something odd with his hands. No, not something odd. He'd unsheathed the blades strapped to his knees, hidden under his leathers. Now he stuck William in the side and back once, twice, thrice.

William hissed in pain. No wonder the bastard had let himself get pinned. Too easy indeed.

Suddenly acid attacked his every cell, weakness invading muscle and bone. Poisoned? Lucifer bucked him off easily and rose, standing over him. The shit bared his too-sharp teeth in a semblance of a smile as William tried and failed to stand. Then the bastard stomped on his face.

More pain shooting through his jaw. Bones shattered. Stars winked through his vision, and nausea ravaged his stomach. Maybe, just maybe, the kick loosened a few screws in his brain. In that moment, he knew what to do. Always Lucifer used trickery to win his battles. Today, William would, too.

Gleeful but hiding it... Maybe... He waited until Lucifer delivered a second kick. William caught his ankle and flipped him onto his back, even knowing his ex-brother would pop back to his feet. Cockroaches always came back.

Look at me, Lucy. Too dizzy to stand. Blinded by blood. All pretense. From his spot on the floor, he swung the spear—and missed. Okay, maybe he wasn't pretending. He *was* dizzy, and he *was* partially blinded, but he *wasn't* out for the count.

Grinning, Lucifer edged closer, expertly sidestepping the spear. He drew back his elbow, preparing to throw a dagger; testing the truth of William's condition before he launched a death blow?

Whoosh.

William had to fight not to brace as the blade arced through him, sinking into his heart. A direct hit. The pain... more poison. Every beat of his heart sent a new cascade of acid through his veins.

As his world grew dark, his friends shouted encouragements. They sounded miles away, but their energy helped purge the weakness. Another plan formed. William rolled into a ball, as if to protect his vital organs. An action meant to mask another.

He readied the spear. *Just need Lucy to come closer...*

Cocky as he was, Lucifer took the bait. Twirling his sword, he did it: he closed the distance. As he raised the weapon, preparing to swing, William rotated to his back, met his ex-brother's gaze and grinned.

The bastard paled, because he knew. It was too late.

Lucifer screamed as William shoved the spear up, up through his groin and torso, the tip coming out through his throat.

Panting, sweating from exertion, William maintained a tight hold on the base of the spear. He felt no joy—yet. Lucifer couldn't escape and wouldn't want to try, any movement increasing his pain a thousandfold, but still he lived. No death, no celebration. Only sadness?

He frowned. Sadness? Because he mourned what could have been? An unbreakable bond. Friendship. Trust. Exactly what he would have with Axel; he was determined.

"Do not render a death blow," Hades bellowed at William. "Somehow, he's made himself deathless, like a Phoenix. If you slay him, he'll only reanimate stronger. I know this beyond any doubt, because I've killed him a dozen times."

More secrets Hades had kept. William *seethed*.

"We'll leave the piece of shit on the spear, locked in the dungeon, then surround him with mystical blocks. Just until we figure out a more permanent solution."

And Lilith? What would he do about her?

His gaze roamed over the throne room, but he found

no sign of her. Had she run off during the fight? Probably, but so what? William had no desire to go after her. The woman had tormented him for centuries, yes, but she'd also ensured he met Sunny. For that alone, he would forgive her every crime.

"Take a bow!" Anya called.

"I did it!" Keeley shouted. "I won for us!"

Gripping the end of the spear, he lifted Lucifer above his head and executed a perfect bow. The crowd cheered wildly as blood trickled from the corners of Lucifer's mouth.

"The Sent Ones thank you, William," Axel said, his brethren bowing their heads in a show of respect.

"I'm so proud of you!" A grinning Gillian jumped up and clapped.

Like the Sent Ones, the kings of Hell bowed their heads.

Sunny, the one he cared about most, watched him, her red eyes unsure.

Unsure? Why? He handed the spear to Axel and flashed over to nuzzle her snout and pet her hair. The more he petted her, the more she glowed. Fur and hooves disappeared. She began to shrink, and soon his perfect ray of sunshine stood before him, a golden ring remaining on her forehead, brighter than before. That glow wouldn't go away, would it? From now on, he would be able to draw forth the horn with or without her approval.

Wait. She was naked. "Turn around or die!" he shouted at the others.

Of course, no one obeyed. Rathbone tossed him an extralarge T-shirt. A shirt saturated with the king's scent. William gritted his teeth.

After he'd maneuvered Sunny's arms through the appropriate slots, he drew her close. She melted against him, their bodies seeming to fuse together.

He kissed the glowing ring and told her, "I love you, Sunny. I love you so damn much. If you leave me again... never leave me again."

"I love you, too. And I never wanted to leave. I only wanted to protect you." She rubbed two fingers around the light. "You see it now. You'll always see it, so you'll always know where to cut, if ever you wish to remove my horn."

He kissed the bright ring again, the rest of the world fading from his awareness. "Darling, I've seen the faint outline from the beginning. It's one of the reasons I guessed what you were."

"You did? Truly?"

"Truly."

Her eyes widened. "Then the Wrathlings must have used Fae or unicorn as one of your DNA components. Or both!"

"If I'm part unicorn, I guess that makes me your new king." He might not ever know what all he was made of, but he didn't care anymore. He was what he was—Sunny's man, Axel's brother. Hades's son?

"Actually, that makes me your queen, a much more exalted position," she said with a toothy grin. "But I wonder if you're the king of other species, too, making me their queen, too, of course. We've got to find out! More kingdoms, more places for our animals to live. Congrats! We're having a menagerie! And sage! I wish you'd told me you saw an outline of the horn. I might have shown you my unicorn self sooner."

Please. He knew his unicorn. "You would have run for the hills, love."

She shrugged. "Yeah. Probably."

They shared a happy smile, until her amusement fled. Pupils enlarged, she stepped away from him, severing contact. Roses bloomed in her cheeks.

"What's wrong, sundae?" he asked, confused and concerned. Everyone else stared at him in the same way. And why the hell was the upper part of his scalp burning...burning, hotter and hotter?

"Fetch a mirror," Sunny commanded anyone and everyone.

Someone obeyed. Footsteps. Silence. Everyone continued to stare at him, and he scowled. More footsteps. Sunny shoved a handheld mirror in his direction, and he clasped the handle. In the glass, his reflection revealed...

What the hell? He saw a crown. A crown had appeared atop his head, made of brimstone and bone. All around it, different-size spikes stuck out, creating a buck-like horn effect.

To his shock, Hades was the first to bow. The others quickly followed suit. Actually, everyone but Sunny followed suit. She remained at his side, her head high.

"How?" he demanded of Hades.

Hades's voice filled his head. —*The legends you've heard about needing to find a crown are false. In actuality, the kings of Hell choose who rules at their sides. The moment we are in accord, a coronation occurs. If you wish to reject this honor, you have only to destroy the crown.*—

So, Lucifer's crown had not been hidden but destroyed. *Mind reeling. Anger and hurt rising.* The hidden crown was another childhood lie on Hades's part, and the death blow to their relationship. "You and I are finished. Done." Bitterness coated his words. *Ignore the sadness in the undertone.* "I want nothing more to do with you. Yet you want me, your fated killer, ruling at your side?" Now the bitterness escaped on a laugh, an-n-nd, yes, there was still an undertone of sadness. Damn it!

Hades raised his chin, eyes narrowing, upper and lower

lashes fusing. He demonstrated no guilt, no remorse of any kind. "I did what I thought was necessary to survive. I didn't know I would grow to love you."

Fury shoved his next words out of his mouth at warp speed. "If you loved me, you would never have kept me from Axel. You would have saved Axel, too."

"I did save Axel. I gave him to the Sent Ones. And I kept the two of you apart, not just to survive, but to keep you in my life." His chin dipped ever so slightly, as if...as if... No. As if he did feel guilty. But Hades never entertained guilt. Not for any reason. "I did not wish to give you up."

"And yet you did give me up," William snapped. "Since Axel's arrival in Hell, you have avoided me."

"Yes. I gave you time with him, without interference."

"And your reaction over the medallion?"

Hades closed his eyes and inhaled deeply. "I knew you could use it against me. I would have given it back once we'd reached an understanding. I admit I handled things... poorly."

As much of an apology as he'd ever given.

William gazed around the room, seeing the people he loved and protected. His pack. Could he hate his father for a life well lived? No. In the end, he announced, "I will not choose between you and Axel. If you insist I do, that is *your* choice, and your loss. Eject yourself from my life or not. I'll carry on regardless, as I've proven."

Hades peered at him, silent, for a long while. Ultimately, he offered a brusque nod.

Something inside William loosened, almost like a net splitting open to release a great weight. "I'm going home with my unicorn to celebrate our victory."

"And my coronation."

"And our upcoming marriage."

"Marriage?" With a squeal of happiness she jumped up and wrapped her legs around his waist. "You want to marry me?" Her smile quickly faded. "What about the curse? The book—"

"The book was poisoning you, love. Every time you studied the symbols, you were hit with another dose of mystical poison, warping your mind against me. Without the book, you'll only want to kill me when I'm withholding orgasms, just to hear you scream. Also, the word *want* is an understatement. I *demand* marriage. I'm a king, so I can do that now. But first, you get a spanking for leaving me."

She laughed, the sound warming him. "Sure, but you get a spanking for being injured."

"Deal." He faced the crowd, catching smile after smile. "Everyone is invited to my home for the first annual Ball and Chain Celebration in an hour…no, three days…no, a week…no, two weeks. The spanking takes time." Without another word, he flashed Sunny to their bedroom and tossed her on the bed.

As she bounced, her grin returned, those purple eyes sparkling brighter than ever. "Since I'm going to honor you with my hand in marriage and become your queen, you have to meet my list of demands. I expect a throne the same size as yours, and none of that ridiculous *the queen gets a smaller one* business. And I believe there should be a national pajama day. And—"

"Love, what you want, you get. Always. But National Pajama Day only happens if I get to pick your pj's."

"Are you saying my pj's will be skin?"

"Oh, good." He positioned his body above hers and rubbed the tips of their noses together. "You understood."

She wound her arms around his neck, saying, "I understand that you're stuck with me forever."

"Forever isn't long enough." He kissed her then, letting himself get lost in all that was Sunny Lane, the love of his life. And what a life it would be, with her at his side.

Epilogue

First Annual Ball and Chain Celebration

SUNNY PERCHED UPON William's lap while he lounged in his new throne. Yes, her throne had been built next to his…a little bigger than the king's. While his throne was made of what looked to be interlocking unicorn horns, hers was made of diamond sheets that reflected flecks of colored light. At their feet was a dog bed/throne for Dawn, who rested comfortably.

They watched their friends party in their new palace. Along with the crown, William had been gifted with the territory formerly owned by Lucifer. Sunny and her man had been working tirelessly to clean the place up. She'd even dubbed the land a safe zone for anyone seeking asylum from demons.

Life was good. William had burned his book, and they'd cheered as the pages turned to ash.

"You made this possible, love," William said. "Is there anything you can't do?"

"Yes. Lose." As he laughed, she added, "Or find Sable."

"She's out there. My boys finally had a sighting. We'll find her, I swear it."

When William made a promise to Sunny, he kept it. So, she wouldn't worry about her friend. "You know, we did this together, baby. I'm so thankful for our new pack."

"As I am." William stood, lifting Sunny. He set her on her feet, and led her to the dance floor he'd had installed.

He'd also had windows installed, so she'd always see the great outdoors. And he'd used magic to ensure rosebushes grew along the walls all year round.

As Sunny snuggled up to her man, she moved her gaze over their guests. Anya danced dirty with Lucien, and Puck danced extremely dirty with Gillian.

Sunny loved Gillian. The girl had sass.

Gideon and Scarlet stood off to the side, chatting with Amun and Haidee. Both females were heavily pregnant. Earlier Sunny had heard mention of a "mucus plug" and she'd wanted to cut off her ears.

Maddox and Ashlyn ushered their twins, Urban and Ever, along the buffet table, which boasted a nice selection of meats, cheeses and flower petals.

Reyes and Danika, Aeron and Olivia, Galen and Legion played darts with a poster of Lucifer acting as the bull's-eye.

Paris and Sienna talked and laughed with Koldo and Nicola—well, with Nicola. Koldo maintained the same expression as always: homicidal.

Hades and Pandora walked a circle around the room, their heads bent together.

Father and son had been working to rebuild their relationship. As for Hades's sort-of prophecy, Sunny figured she'd been right, that death hadn't meant actual death but a new beginning.

With Lucifer impaled on the horn and locked in the dungeon, they were *all* getting a new beginning. And soon, they'd know how to kill him for good.

Sunny already had ideas. Somewhere out there was something known as the Morning Star. Oh, the things it could do.

She'd mentioned it to William and he'd told her the Lords of the Underworld had been searching for the Morning Star for a while. With the information she had, she suspected they'd find the Morning Star in no time.

Laughter drew her gaze to Strider and Kaia. They played on the gauntlet William had rigged. *A real-life video game*, he'd said. Sabin, Gwen, Bianka and Lysander played, too. Strider was winning, because Kaia kept taking out his competition.

Sunny grinned. William had the best friends. And now so did she!

Torin and Keeley were petting three new hellhounds brought by Baden and Katarina.

As soft music continued to float through the ballroom, Reyes and Danika, Kane and a pregnant Josephina, Zacharel and Annabelle, and Cameo and Lazarus all moved onto the dance floor. Then Bjorn and Fox did the same, so, of course, Thane and Elin did, too. Their buddy Xerxes watched from the sidelines.

William's children—no, *their* children, since she was their stepmom and all—played poker and smoked cigars.

The trio had been out searching for Lilith, so William could apologize and thank her. No joke.

The only one missing from the celebration was Viola, the keeper of Narcissism. She'd been missing on and off for a while. William had expressed concern about where she was and what trouble she was causing, so Sunny had sent out her other unicorn pals to look. Her people were free again!

What an incredible life Sunny now lived. She traced her fingertip over the sun tattoo he'd inked into his chest in her honor—a sun for his Sunny.

To show her appreciation, she'd implemented No Shirt Mondays. And Tuesdays. And Wednesdays, Thursdays, Fridays and Saturdays.

"I saw you and Gillian talking earlier," William remarked. "I'm glad you two are getting along."

"She's wonderful." Gillian might be Sunny's favorite visitor. There was no one more passionate than Gillian, who fought to help women and children stuck in abusive situations. "We're planning ways to torture you, if ever you need something more than a spanking. Oh! Did you know she's pregnant?"

"I did not, but I'm happy for her. And I'm pretty sure we'll spawn our first brat next mating season."

She smiled. "You think Axel is crushing on Evelina?" She watched as the Sent One moved off to the side to check his phone. He had a camera on the girl at all times.

"For sure. He hasn't killed her as ordered, and not because he fears my wrath. Thankfully, now that Bjorn is dating Fox, no one should care who Axel ends up with."

"Well, if anyone has a problem with it, they *should* fear your wrath. Everyone should. Well, except me." All of the underworld knew if you messed with Sunny, you'd have to deal with William's wrath…after you dealt with *Sunny's* wrath. "You're going to make an amazing king."

"I know," he said, and she grinned. More and more of his memories were returning.

When the song ended, they returned to the throne.

Hades approached and eased into the diamond one. "I

found my magic mirror in Lucifer's bedroom. The goddess has gone quiet, and won't show me images. I think Lucifer did something to her, magically speaking, and I'd like you to siphon it, as you did for Axel."

With William's help, she'd aided Axel's memory recovery. "Happy to," she replied. "Once you've properly apologized to my fiancé."

William grinned.

Hades compressed his lips into a thin line, but also nodded. Peering at William, he said, "I'm not the same male I was when you were a child. You helped change me. You were so damaged back then. You needed things I knew nothing about—kindness and understanding. We learned together. As you grew older, I feared I would lose you if ever Axel became part of your life. I feared you would remember the purpose of your creation, and you would try to do what you were programmed to do, and I'd have to do what I do best. Put a potential assassin down."

"As if you could," William said with a snort.

Now Hades's lips twitched at the corners. "You aren't wrong. You've become a strong man. A powerful king. I'm proud of you, and I'm sorry for my part in your pain." He patted William's hand and stood, then rejoined the party.

"Better?" she asked William.

"Much," he said, squeezing her hip. "I still love him."

"Well, he's part of your pack. *Our* pack." She rested her head on his broad shoulder, utterly content. Never in all her wildest dreams had she envisioned a life like this. So full, so exciting. So promising. "His actions, despicable as they were, played a part in bringing us together, and I'll always be grateful for that."

"I had the same thought about Lilith. How can I be upset, when you brighten my life, chasing away the darkness?"

She beamed at him. "We're going to have an amazing future, baby."

"The best."

They shared a look, and that was all it took to rev her engine. "How would you feel about leaving—"

He flashed her to their bed.

"—the party?" she finished with a laugh. Then he kissed her, and she forgot the rest of the world. There was only William and this moment, a lifetime of happiness ahead.

* * * * *

Read on for a sneak peek at
New York Times *bestselling author Gena Showalter's*
next thrilling all-new novel, The Warlord.

Prologue

THEY ARE ANCIENT WARRIORS, evil to the core, and loyal only to one another. Known as the Astra Planeta, the Warlords of the Skies, Wandering Stars—the beginning of the end—they travel from world to world, wiping out their enemies. Drawn to war, they finish even the smallest skirmishes with pain and bloodshed. To see one is to know you'll soon greet your death.

With no moral compass, the Astra Planeta kill without mercy, steal without qualm, and destroy without guilt, all to receive a mystical blessing—five hundred years of victories, without a single loss.

If they fail to obtain this blessing, they automatically receive a curse. Five hundred years of utter defeat.

The time has come for the next bestowing, each Astra Planeta forced to complete a different task. To start, their leader, Alaroc Phaethon, Emperor of the Expanse, Roc of Ages, Giant of the Deep, the Blazing One, must wed an immortal female. A tiresome chore, to be sure, but not the full extent of his duty. Thirty days after the vows are spoken, he must sacrifice his bride on an altar of his own making. If she dies a virgin, even better; he and his brothers-by-circumstance will receive a second blessing.

Roc has performed this sacred ritual twenty times before, and he has never wavered in his duty. Murder an innocent female? Shrug. Because, if one Astra Planeta fails to complete his task, all fail.

Roc will cross any line to succeed.

There has never been a woman alluring enough to tempt him from his task. No warrioress powerful enough to overcome his incredible strength. No enchantress desirable enough to make him burn beyond reason.

Until now.

Don't miss the next all-new hardcover novel,
The Warlord *by* New York Times *bestselling author*
Gena Showalter!

Copyright © 2020 by Gena Showalter

Dear Reader,

The first time William the Ever Randy stepped onto the pages of my novel, he took over. He became a number one draft pick for my readers. Good thing, because I fell in love with this powerful, irreverent playboy prince, too. He has zero fears, a warped sense of humor and the strength to take whatever he wants. Throughout the series, this mysterious man has kept a boatload of secrets from us. He's infuriated us and driven us wild with lust. (Or just me?) I could not wait to tell his story. What does his coded book say? Where does he come from? How did he bond with Hades? The time has come to finally find out...

Love,
Gena Showalter

A searing Lords of the Underworld tale by
New York Times bestselling author

GENA SHOWALTER

**featuring a beastly prince and the wife he will
wage war to keep.**

"Gena Showalter never fails to dazzle."
—Jeaniene Frost, *New York Times* bestselling author

Order your copy today!

HQNBooks.com

PHGSTDW1019Max